ELLERY QUEEN'S
MEMORABLE
CHARACTERS

Stories collected from issues
of *Ellery Queen's Mystery Magazine*
edited by Ellery Queen

**Edited by Eleanor Sullivan
and Karen A. Prince**

THE DIAL PRESS

Davis Publications, Inc.
380 Lexington Avenue
New York, New York 10017

FIRST PRINTING

COPYRIGHT NOTICES AND ACKNOWLEDGMENTS

Grateful acknowledgment is hereby made for permission to include the following:

A Day of Encounters by Anthony Gilbert; © 1971 by Anthony Gilbert; reprinted by permission of Curtis Brown Associates, Ltd.

A Time To Remember by James Reach; © 1970 by James Reach; reprinted by permission of Ann Elmo Agency, Inc.

One Clear Sweet Clue by William Bankier; © 1969 by William Bankier; reprinted by permission of Curtis Brown, Ltd.

The Theft of Nothing at All by Edward D. Hoch; © 1977 by Edward D. Hoch; reprinted by permission of the author.

The Day of the Bullet by Stanley Ellin; © 1959 by Stanley Ellin; reprinted by permission of Curtis Brown, Ltd.

The Perfect Model by Margery Sharp; © 1956 by Mercury Publications, Inc., renewed 1984 by Davis Publications, Inc.; reprinted by permission of Blanche C. Gregory, Inc.

The Man Who Liked Noise by Ernest Savage; © 1977 by Ernest Savage; reprinted by permission of the author.

Time Out of Mind by Peter Godfrey; copyright 1948 by Publicitas, renewed; reprinted by permission of Richard Curtis Associates, Inc.

The Other Shoe by Charlotte Armstrong; © 1962 by Davis Publications, Inc.; reprinted by permission of Brandt & Brandt Literary Agents, Inc.

Report on a Broken Bridge by Dennis O'Neil; © 1971 by Dennis O'Neil; reprinted by permission of the author.

Spring Fever by Dorothy Salisbury Davis; copyright © 1952 by Dorothy Salisbury Davis, renewed; reprinted by permission of McIntosh & Otis, Inc.

A Hell of a Story by H. R. F. Keating; © 1982 by H. R. F. Keating; reprinted by permission of the author.

Traveling Light by W. R. Burnett; copyright 1935 by the Crowell Collier Publishing Company, renewed; reprinted by permission of Scott Meredith Literary Agency.

The Sisterhood by Gwendoline Butler; © 1968 by Gwendoline Butler; reprinted by permission of the author and John Farquharson, Ltd.

4

"Q"

CONTENTS

INTRODUCTION

This year marks the 175th anniversary of the birth of Edgar Allan Poe and the 135th anniversary of his death. Poe, of course, created the detective story with "The Murders in the Rue Morgue" and his detective, C. Auguste Dupin—poor but of "illustrious parentage," romantic and eccentric, the first of many memorable characters, detectives and others, who have inhabited the mystery scene ever since.

In introducing Dorothy Salisbury Davis's story, "Spring Fever," in the November 1952 issue of *Ellery Queen's Mystery Magazine,* Ellery Queen said: "We have a conviction that you won't ever completely forget Sarah Shepherd and Frank Joyce." Ellery Queen also once said of his own books about detective Ellery Queen: "Any book you haven't read is a new book to you. Each new generation is finding Ellery all over again."

It was with this in mind that this new Ellery Queen anthology was assembled—the choice of stories featuring some of the magazine's most unforgettable characters over the years *(Reader's Digest* has its unforgettable characters and so does *EQMM!)* and the opportunity to introduce them (not only Sarah Shepherd and Frank Joyce but also Ellery Queen and a good many others you are unlikely to forget), perhaps for the first time, to a whole new generation of readers. With thankful homage to Edgar Allan Poe, who started it all.

The Editors

Anthony Gilbert

A Day of Encounters

I noticed the woman the minute she came into the pay clinic—St. Barnabas' Eye Clinic where I go every six weeks about a little trouble I have. I'm Martita Browne and you've probably seen my books all over the place. Eggheads despise them, but I consider myself a benefactress. Even in the Affluent Society lots of women lead pretty dreary lives. So my books are like a magic mirror that reflects them as they see themselves, not as they appear to husbands or families—beautiful, loyal, courageous, even though they may scream at the sight of a mouse, and above all irresistible to men; and, naturally, only to be had at the cost of a wedding ring. Services like that are worth paying for, and, to do my readers justice, they pay at the rate of substantial royalties to me every year.

This newcomer—I realized at once I'd never seen her before, you get to know the regulars—didn't resemble my heroines in any way. For one thing, she was past forty, not good-looking, though she had a lively face that was somehow demure, too, which wasn't without attraction. But though her clothes were good—her crocodile bag alone had set someone back about sixty pounds, her scarf was pure heavy silk, and her shoes handmade—she lacked something, a kind of vitality perhaps. There was a man with her, presumably her husband, a fair, quiet sort of fellow, but not living on the bread-line—far from it. An expensive house in the suburbs, I thought, with central heating, a double garage, storm windows, at least one trip abroad every year, and not a package tour at that.

I usually sit in a sort of alcove that holds only three or four chairs, and hardly anyone else ever chooses them. The patients have an idea that if they sit in the middle of the room they'll be seen sooner, but of course it doesn't help; it's all poppycock—you're seen when the doctor's ready for you and not before. I'd brought the proofs of my new book with me—*Not Wooed But Won*—and I thought I might get quite a lot of work done while I waited. I could see it was going to be a busy clinic this afternoon.

I was a bit surprised when the newcomer came to sit beside me. "Is it always as crowded as this?" she asked. "Willy said he'd be back in an hour and he does hate waiting." Then before I could reply she saw the proofs on my lap—I hadn't begun, so the title page was on top. "Are you Martita Browne?" she asked. "Did you write that?"

I knew what was coming, of course. She'd always longed to write, but there'd never been time; her life story would make a wonderful plot, and since she'd never use it—and of course I'd disguise the names. If I've heard that once, I've heard it a hundred times. I was wondering how I could suggest that none of my readers would be interested in a woman in her forties when she gushed on, "People say that sometimes your heroes are too good to be true, but of course that's nonsense. I know because—well, you might say I married one of them. You might have taken Victor for your model."

"I thought you said his name was Willy," I murmured.

"Victor was my first husband. Willy's as different as chalk from cheese. Victor had everything—good looks, a marvelous figure, tall, dark, alluring—it wasn't surprising all the women were after him. I'm sure they must all have gasped when they heard it was me he was going to marry. I wasn't even young—twenty-eight—you'd never have a heroine of twenty-eight, would you, Miss Browne?"

Well, she knew I wouldn't. My readers never see themselves as more than twenty-five at the very most.

"I wasn't in the least like one of your heroines," the voice babbled on. "My father—he was a minister with a great sense of fun—everyone said so—used to call me Miss Brains-Before-Beauty. Count your blessings, he'd say. Brains are often a better investment. And I put mine out to usury like that man in the Bible, whose ten talents turned into twenty talents. I never really thought I'd get married."

"But there was Victor?" I remarked.

"Yes. He came into this office where I was working—actually, it was my own business—and it was like the sun coming in. He was a bit younger than me, but he said he preferred mature women. Girls never had any conversation except hairdos and what he called 'parish pump' subjects."

"What was his job?" I asked. It was quite automatic. I couldn't have even a minor character in a story without knowing his background, and obviously Victor wasn't going to be minor.

"Oh!" For the first time she sounded evasive. "He was a sales representative—went round to the big industrial houses."

"A success?" I bored on. You might say it was none of my business, but the woman had thrust herself on me and I had a right to some return. Anyway, you can never be sure where you'll find plot and character ideas.

"You'd have thought with those looks and that charm he couldn't fail, though he always warned me it was cutthroat competition, and I suppose he wasn't ruthless enough. Still, at first everything went all right, and then he started going 'on the road.' You know what that means? The firms—and they weren't always the same firms—sent him to the outlying districts. He made a joke of it. Someone's got to carry news to the heathen, he'd say, but—oh, Miss Browne, it was like playing Shaftesbury Avenue and then finding yourself sent out with a second-class repertory company. Luckily I wasn't called Miss Brains-Before-Beauty for nothing. I'd sold my business when I got married, so I had a nice little nest egg put by, and believe me, it came in very useful."

Candidly, I didn't think this was getting me anywhere. A plain woman had been married for her money—that's what it amounted to. But of course there had to be a third party, otherwise there was no story at all. And even I couldn't believe *she* would turn up with a lover.

"So what happened?" I encouraged.

Her reply startled me. "Oh, he died."

"Victor died?"

"Yes. It was a bit sudden."

I had a fresh idea. "Sudden enough to attract the attention of the police?"

She took off her handsome gloves and folded them carefully on her knee. Her rings would have paid my rent for a year.

"Anyone could tell you *are* a writer. You know all the answers."

But did I? There'd been an odd note in her voice when she said, "Oh, he died." Not grief, not relief either, but a sort of lack of confidence, as if she couldn't be certain. But that was nonsense. You either know your husband's dead or you don't. Or perhaps she knew he wasn't, and he was blackmailing her. It seemed pretty obvious she'd struck it rich in her second marriage. I was so deep in calculations that I missed the next few sentences, but what I did hear nearly blew me out of my chair.

"You couldn't call it murder, could you?" the voice pleaded. "I've waited eight years to hear someone say that, only there was never anyone to tell. I don't even have a sister."

And wouldn't tell her if you had, I thought grimly. Not if you've got the sense you were born with.

I realized now, of course, that she had no doubts about dear Victor's death—a posh funeral and wreaths three foot deep, most likely. No, it was the way of it that worried her. But—murder? I hadn't time to think straight.

"What did the police make of it?" I asked. "I mean, who mentioned murder?"

"There were only three alternatives—accident, suicide, or murder—and no one could believe it was an accident."

"Why should it be a suicide?"

"Well, there was this girl—Elizabeth Sinclair."

Inwardly I heaved a sigh of relief. So we'd got to the heart of the story at last—the third side of the triangle, without which there's no story at all.

"People used to ask me sometimes—aren't you afraid of someone trying to steal your handsome husband now that he's away from home so much? But I wasn't. Oh, there might be incidents, but a sensible wife shuts her eyes to them. He was away three or four days on end sometimes. Frankly, I didn't see how he could afford to leave me. It's a cruel thing to say about a dead man, Miss Browne, but—well, charm's like anything else: it gets tarnished, and thirty-six is different from twenty-four, which was his age when we married. It appeared he'd met this girl—she was barely twenty-one—and it had been love at first sight for both of them."

"I thought you said he couldn't afford to keep a wife. Or did Elizabeth have money?"

"She was the only daughter of a very rich man—the only child—and she'd get everything."

"Unless Daddy married again." I took for granted he was a widower.

Her mouth hardened. "You didn't know Victor. He'd have insisted on a prenuptial settlement—and he'd have got it. I don't say Daddy would have approved, but Elizabeth was the kind no man can resist. Now, *there* was a heroine for you, Miss Browne. Dark and slender and—glowing. You remember Shelley's moon-maiden, with white fire laden? She made me think of that. I only saw her the once, you know."

"You mean he brought her?" Victor was proving himself less and less like one of my heroes.

"She brought herself. 'I thought if I came in person, perhaps you'd understand,' she said. 'Oh, how can you want to hold onto him when you know it's me he loves? Why won't you divorce him, Mrs. Hughes? You've had twelve years—'

"And, of course, Victor could live another thirty. But not with this girl, I decided. If I'd been tempted to yield before, I was iron-hard now.

" 'Surely she made you see—' That was Victor talking, when he came home.

" 'So it was your idea?' I said. 'I might have guessed it. You must be mad if you think I'd make it possible for you to ruin that girl's life,' I said warmly. 'She's made for better than secondhand goods.'

" 'I won't give her up,' Victor said.

" 'There's no law to stop your setting up house,' I agreed. 'But would Daddy like that?' He raged, but he didn't move me. 'You'll only marry her over my dead body,' I said. Have you ever noticed, Miss Browne, how often clichés come home to roost?"

"But it was Victor's dead body," I pointed out.

"Yes."

"And there was talk of murder."

"It's what the police would have liked to believe," she said bitterly. "I suppose you can hardly blame them. You don't get promotion by arresting motorists for illegal parking."

"You want to be careful," I advised her sharply. "You never know who may be sitting next to you in a place like this. There's an ex-Superintendent Humbolt who comes here sometimes." He was one of the few useful contacts I'd made at the clinic; he'd helped me out of knotty problems once or twice when my heroines had been more featherbrained than usual. I knew what he'd say about Victor. Never trust charm, it's the most powerful weapon in the devil's armory. I've heard him say that more than once. "But why should anyone think it was murder?"

She went off at a bit of a tangent. "If you saw someone who'd cheated you sitting on a balcony, say, and a chimney pot started to topple, and you knew it would hit him and you didn't yell out, would that make you a murderer?"

It wasn't the sort of problem I've ever been called on to solve. Murder's taboo in my kind of tale. "Accessory before the fact?" I hazarded.

"Ah, but whose accessory? You can't be accessory to a force of nature—but what else caused the chimney pot to fall?"

"A good question," I agreed. I wondered what the pious would say. An act of God? Not very complimentary to God, of course. Not that I supposed a chimney pot had actually played any part in this story. And of course it turned out to be just an analogy.

But talk about clichés! The truth was almost as incredible—the truth as she told it, that is.

It seems that it was Victor's custom to make their after-dinner coffee.

"And you let him do it, even after you'd refused him a divorce?" My most addlepated heroine would have had more sense than that.

"If he'd meant to—to do away with me—he'd never have chosen anything so obvious."

"Sometimes the most obvious thing is also the most subtle."

"Anyway, that night—it was a few days after our conversation about Elizabeth and I thought he was accepting the situation—he'd just brought in the coffeepot and tray when the phone rang. I went to answer it, expecting it to be for me. But it was for Victor. When I came in he'd just poured out the coffee. 'Well, that was quick,' he said. 'Or was it a wrong number?' 'It's for you,' I told him.

" 'Chaps do choose the most inconvenient times,' he grumbled, looking at his coffee. 'He might have waited another five minutes.'

" 'It'll take five minutes to cool—or are you afraid I might lace it with arsenic while you're out of the room?' I said.

"He stared. 'That's a nice thing for a wife to say to her husband.' He jammed the cup down. 'Don't let yours grow cold. I poured it out'—and he went off, shutting the door behind him. It's funny, Miss Browne, how trifles can hold your attention. I hadn't thought anything about his pouring out both cups till he called my attention to it, and it made me wonder. You see, he knows—knew—I love everything piping hot, and if it had been Leila Hope on the phone—the call I'd expected—well, it's always ten minutes before she hangs up.

"I'd picked up my cup, but now I put it down and crept over and opened the door. The telephone was in an alcove in the hall, so that I could hear without being seen. Victor was laughing and joking, then suddenly his voice changed. 'I'm very anxious about her,' he said. 'She gets these moods, you can't reason with her, and she's inclined to be morbid. I can neither laugh nor argue her out of it.'

"I shut the door and came back to my chair. So that was his game, I thought. I was to be represented as being eccentric, so that anything might be expected of me. Automatically I picked up the coffee, and then the notion came to me. I'm not a writer, Miss Browne, though I'm quite a reader. And being alone so much I'd had time to think. And I wondered why he'd been so anxious that I drink my coffee hot. It wasn't like him to worry about things like that. And then his saying I was morbid."

I interrupted rather brutally. "So you decided he'd poisoned the coffee and then gone off to the telephone. But how did he know it was going to ring then?"

"He could have arranged it, knowing I'd probably answer. Oh, I didn't think he intended murder. He knew the surviving partner would be the first suspect, and there was no one but ourselves in the house. But don't you see, that meant he could tell any story he liked! I thought he'd put in enough of whatever it was to make it necessary to call a doctor, who'd say it was attempted suicide, and then later, if, for instance, I fell under a subway train or something—I don't drive a car—everyone would remember the first time."

"Why didn't you pour the coffee out of the window?" I suggested sensibly.

"I didn't think of that, only of upsetting the table, and that would have meant breaking the cups; but then I'm not clumsy, so I'd have aroused his suspicions at once. Besides, I didn't see why he shouldn't be—what's the phrase?"

"Hoist on his own petard?"

"That's it. Biter bit. So—oh, Miss Browne, I switched the cups. I thought it would serve a dual purpose—make him uncomfortable and let him see I knew what he was up to. I thought of it as a self-protective measure."

"And when he came back?"

"I'd finished my cup, and he drank his—well, mine really. Then we each had a refill, and soon after he said he was tired and how about bed? Happy dreams, he said. Those were the last words I ever heard from him. When I went in next morning with a cup of tea—we had separate rooms by then, since I'd found out about Elizabeth—oh, it was clear he wasn't going to be interested in tea any longer.

"The doctor said he must have been dead for quite some time; and he couldn't give a death certificate, he'd have to inform the coroner. That's when the horror suddenly became real. You're very clever, Miss Browne, not to have crimes in your books. People who like violence can get it in the newspapers. The police were in and out of that house like—like mites in a cheese."

"What was it he'd taken?"

"One of the barbiturates. I don't understand about medicine—I'm never ill, neither of us ever was. I hardly take an aspirin six times a year. Of course, they searched everything, almost took the paper off the walls, but they couldn't find even an empty vial. And seeing that I practically never went to a doctor they couldn't have traced the stuff to me, however much they'd wanted to."

"Where did they think he got it from?"

"No one knows, but he did travel for a firm of pharmaceutical chemists at one time. He could easily have got it that way, though I've heard you *can* get hold of drugs even without a doctor's prescription. But that was only the beginning. Accident was ruled out—which left suicide or murder. Everyone said he wouldn't have committed suicide, and I didn't think he would myself."

She paused, but I wasn't letting her stop there. It's not often an hour-and-a-half wait in a clinic can bring you a plum like this. "So it *had* to be murder?"

"Only it couldn't be. What advantage did I gain from his death, I asked them? I didn't inherit a penny—in fact, after the funeral I had to pay a large tailor's bill—he was very dandified about his clothes. If I'd wanted to be rid of him I had only to walk out. I had my own means, you know."

"You didn't think of telling them the simple truth?"

Her eyes stared at me, as round as pennies. "Well, naturally I thought of it; and naturally I held my tongue. There was no proof and if I let them know I had a suspicion—well, there was only my word for it that *I* hadn't doped the coffee. They wouldn't have got a conviction, I know that, but the mud would have stuck to me for life. Anyway, the verdict was death from barbiturate poisoning, with insufficent evidence to show how it had been administered.

"But that was bad enough. I was conscious of very odd looks wherever I went, and people in shops suddenly and mysteriously didn't have the things I wanted. A little later I changed back from Ruth Hughes to Ruth White—they're neither of them conspicuous names, are they?—and I came south. In London they might never have heard of Victor Hughes and quite likely they hadn't. Anyway, it's like that hymn you learn at school. 'They fly forgotten as a dream—' "

"And in London you met Willy?"

"Well, that was three years ago. I still had my capital and I went into partnership with a woman who ran an agency. I supplied the competence and she supplied the charm, which seemed to me quite a fair division of labor. When I met Willy—he was so different from Victor they might hardly have belonged to the same species."

"And yet they say that when people marry again, they always choose the same type," I reminded her.

"I suppose there has to be an exception to every rule. Victor had been so popular, but Willy seemed so—so neglected. He'd been a widower for years, had a bookshop and was the studious type. The shop had great potentialities, but, oh, Miss Browne, the confusion in it, everything so hugger-mugger it would take a week to find anything a customer wanted. Willy lived—very uncomfortably—in two rooms above the shop. The first time I invited him back to my apartment for a meal he said, 'This is what I call a home. I've seen nothing like it since Edna died fifteen years ago.'

"He was so vague—if he'd been in Victor's shoes the police wouldn't have found any trouble at all in believing he'd taken the stuff himself thinking it was saccharine. I had a sense of responsibility towards him. That was the start. Of course, it was never like Victor, but I was forty-five by then, an age when your ardor has cooled off. And then, when once you've been married—even if it hadn't worked out too well—well, it seems unnatural to be living alone.

"Anyway, we got married. I kept up my interest in the business—Willy had the shop, you see, and it wasn't as though we were likely to have a family—and weekends we worked among the books. I tell you, Miss Browne, you wouldn't recognize the place now. It's got quite a reputation. We can tell customers right away if we've got what they want in stock, and if not, where we can get it and how long they must wait. A few months ago we put in a manager, a very capable fellow of about forty-five—sometimes I say to Willy I don't know how we'd get on without Mr. Brett. It means Willy isn't tied down so much, he can go to book sales, have a bit of private life. Mr. Brett's a bachelor—it doesn't seem to matter to him how long hours he works."

I only had time for one more question before her name was called. "Did you tell Willy about Victor?"

She looked astounded, as though her eyes would drop out of her head.

"Of course not! All that happened to Mrs. Victor Hughes, and to me at least she's as dead as her husband. Nothing whatever to do with Willy."

Then her name was called and she jumped up with the eagerness of all new patients. I saw that she'd left her umbrella leaning against the chair, but I supposed she'd come back for it. I got down to my proofs at last; a while later I heard a creak as some heavy body descended alongside mine.

A voice said, "Well, Miss Browne, still at it, I see?"

I looked up and there was my old friend, ex-Superintendent Humbolt, though he doesn't insist on his former title any more. Pulling rank, he calls it.

"This is a day of encounters," I said. "I haven't seen you for a long time."

"Come for my semiannual checkup," he told me. "Fact is, my sight's not what it used to be. There's one disease none of the doctors can cure, and that's *Anno Domini*. And a good thing for the race it can't. We'd all be living in trees like chimps—there wouldn't be anywhere else to live."

"Oh, come on," I jollied him. "You're not that old. I was wondering if you could give me some advice."

"I knew it," he said mournfully. "All you ever want of me is a chance to pick my brains."

"It's a point arising from a story," I explained, carefully not saying it was one of mine. "If you'd been married to a man who tried to murder you, and later on you decided to marry again, would you tell Husband Number Two about Number One?"

"I'd never put the notion of murder in any husband's mind," he replied promptly.

"That solves my problem," I told him, and then he shook out his newspaper and I got to work.

A bit later a rather diffident voice said, "I was looking for my wife, and I believe this is her umbrella." And I looked up to see the rather vague-looking man who'd come with the "late" Mrs. Victor Hughes.

"It's quite a relief," he told me. "I thought I'd lost her."

An odd sound, like a bear chuckling to itself in a sardonic sort of way, came from behind the open newspaper.

"You want to be careful you don't make a habit of it, Willy." The newspaper was lowered. Ex-Superintendent Humbolt might appear to be grinning but his voice was the voice of Jehovah. "This 'ud be the third, wouldn't it? It never pays to overdo things. People get such strange ideas. Funny, you know."

"I don't call that very funny," said Willy. "I'm surprised at you, Mr. Humbolt."

"Your wife's seeing one of the doctors," I intervened quickly. "I don't suppose she'll be long."

"Don't want to get caught up in the rush hour on the underground," Humbolt went on, and Willy said, "I've got the car. We live out at Sheepshot now, and Ruth doesn't drive. Still, it's a nice house and a big garden. My wife enjoys gardening."

"Nothing wrong with gardening so long as you don't dig too deep." I had never thought that Humbolt could be so malicious. And then *she* came hurrying back, saying, "Oh, Willy, did I keep you long? I had to wait, and the doctor thinks I should come again in six weeks."

"It'll be Harley Street for you next time, my dear," said Willy.

"You must meet Miss Browne, Martita Browne, the famous writer. You know." She didn't pay any attention to Humbolt. After all, she'd never set eyes on him before.

"Why did you say that about losing wives?" I demanded as soon as the couple was out of earshot. I simply had to know. If an angel had summoned me with a trumpet at that moment, I wouldn't have heard.

"The object of the police is to try and prevent crime," Humbolt said in his deceptively quiet way. "Poor Willy! He's lost a couple of wives already. Such a careless fellow—or could I be wrong? I mean, no doctors, no deathbeds. Number One was drowned in the South of France. They'd only been married two years. Something went wrong, the boat overturned, he kept swimming round and diving for her; they saw him from the shore, but he couldn't find her. She was under the boat, and they said she must have hit her head on something that knocked her out.

"Then about three years later he married again. It was the Costa Brava this time, and he was miles away, sunbathing. She'd taken the car—she brought that and some other very nice bits of goods you'd not turn your nose up at, Miss Browne, to the marriage—and had gone to visit friends. When she didn't come back he got anxious, phoned the friends' house, but she'd never arrived. Then he called the authorities, but you know how it is in Spain. *Mañana!*" He looked at me questioningly.

"I understand," I assured him. "Never do today what you can put off till tomorrow."

"She'd been dead for hours when they found her, under the wreck of the car. One of the Spanish police said, 'What a waste! Such a beautiful motor!' Nothing about the lady, but I daresay when they found her she wasn't so beautiful."

"What did they think had happened?"

"No one could tell for sure, the car being in the state it

was—something gone wrong with the steering, perhaps. Only—she had been proud of that car, had had it completely overhauled only the week before, when they'd left England. Still, there were no witnesses and a car can't talk. The advantage of coming to a sticky end in a warm foreign climate is you can't hang about waiting for relatives—"

"You mean, she was buried in Spain?"

"Both wives were buried abroad. Good sense really. The authorities make a lot of hoo-ha about shipping a corpse home—much less trouble and, of course, much more economical to have it buried on the spot. Wonder if the new Mrs. Willy likes to travel."

"I don't think she said. Just that she'd met him by way of business. Gone to his shop to buy a book, I suppose." That surprised me. She looked the sort who would expect to get her reading from the Public Library.

Humbolt shook his head. "They met at her place of business, not his."

"She said she ran some sort of agency with another woman."

"That's right. Marriage bureau. Fact, Miss Browne. They'll tell you there's one born every minute, and you don't have to be a policeman to know it's true. Convenient for chaps like Willy: you get all the statistics about the lady—age, looks—they have to supply a photograph and not one taken twenty years ago at that—financial position—the agency does all your homework for you. It's my belief if a chimp walked into one of those places they'd match him up with a woman chimp."

He thought a moment, then went on, "I suppose it occurred to Willy he could hardly do better than to marry the boss. To my way of thinking he's no matinee idol, but somehow he gets the women. That quality called charm, I suppose. She kept on with her interest in the agency, and he had the shop—got a very good name now, I understand, quite a little gold mine."

"I thought you were retired," I remarked maliciously.

"Once a copper always a copper. I'll retire when they start ringing the churchbell for me. Still, as you say, no skin off my nose."

"It proves one thing," I said. "Women do always go for the same type. Willy may not look remotely like Victor, but they're chips from the same block."

I saw I'd really got his attention now. "Who's Victor?"

"Victor Hughes—her first husband."

"First time I heard she had one before she married Willy. Sure she's not pulling your leg?"

"After he died—"

"How was that?"

"You could call it a sort of accident."

"With or without wifely assistance?" The Day of Judgment will hold no shocks for that man.

"Let's say that she took a chance and it came off." I told him in detail about her switching the cups. "And if you don't believe me," I said, "there's bound to be a record. I'm not sure where it happened, but somewhere up north."

He shook his head. "Not me, Miss Browne. You've just reminded me, I'm retired and if there wasn't a trial—or was there?"

"There wasn't enough evidence to charge her. They never seemed to think of the fourth alternative—that he might have been the one with the murderous impulse."

"You bet they thought of it, but the police can't go on feminine intuition, not the way ladies do. No witnesses, no proof she'd ever handled a barbiturate in her life, and, like she said, no motive. Anyway, it wasn't my manor and the Chief Constable wouldn't thank me for raking up an old case. I've no fresh evidence. You might say it's a good thing she knows how to take care of herself, seeing who she's married to now."

"But you can't leave it at that," I exclaimed. "She could be in danger this very minute."

Humbolt has one of those India-rubber faces that can change under your eyes. Now he looked like a bloodhound—sad, a bit bloodshot, long drooping jowls. "You don't have to worry about her, Miss Browne, now that Willy knows we've met her. Even he 'ud be hard put to it to explain a third tragedy. Of course, if I was to drop dead, or you—but you take it from me, there'll be no need to search the newspapers for her name this side of Christmas."

Only the ex-Superintendent was wrong. About four months later I picked up my *Morning Argus*—the posh papers are no good to writers like me—and there he was on the front page:*Well Known Bookseller Falls to His Death*. It was in France—that was true to type, I thought—they'd been staying in one of these big old-fashioned hotels with a balcony and steps leading to a courtyard, a fountain, flowers, that sort of thing.

There was a gate in the trellis you could unbolt if you wanted to go down. The widow said they'd been talking and she went back into the bedroom for a cigarette, and the next minute she heard a scream and a sort of muffled crash and the trellis gate was swinging. It was two stories to the courtyard and Willy never recovered consciousness.

Everyone in the hotel was shocked—such an affectionate couple! Only they changed their tune when some busybody dug up the story of his previous wives. Then they started to talk about the mills of God grinding slowly, Providence seeing to it that he'd fallen into the pit he'd dug—meaning he'd opened the gate intending to give her a fatal shove, and then forgotten he'd opened it.

Her story was they'd been in the courtyard earlier, looking at the fish in the fountain, and he must have forgotten to bolt the gate after them. No, there was no family tomb, and burial on the spot, she was sure, was what he'd have preferred.

A few weeks ago I happened to be passing the bookshop. It was just about closing time, and Ruth came out with a tall dressy sort of fellow—forty-five or forty-six, I'd say.

When she saw me Ruth said, "Fancy meeting you again! Do you still go to that eye clinic? Do you remember me telling you about Mr. Brett? You did read about Willy, I expect? Wasn't it terrible? But he was always so absentminded. I don't know what I'd have done without Malcolm."

It was easy to see who Malcolm was—easy, too, to realize she probably wasn't going to have to do without him.

I haven't seen Mr. Humbolt since—perhaps he doesn't come to the clinic any more. Of course, I'm only a writer of romantic tales, not works of logic or mystical speculation; but I do sometimes wonder, if there really is a Hereafter, what Victor and Willy are thinking now.

James Reach

A Time To Remember

I had arrived early at my office in the Grand Central area and started to work on a difficult brief for a new and desirable client of my one-man law firm; but I hadn't been at it long when the interoffice buzzer sounded. I frowned in annoyance as I picked up the phone; I had told Miss Cooney, secretary to myself and the other attorney with whom I share the office suite, that I didn't want to be interrupted by anything short of a major emergency.

"Sorry to disturb you," said Miss Cooney, "but there's a Mr. Banning here and he insists on seeing you."

"Banning?" The name didn't mean a thing to me. "Do I know him?"

"No, you don't, Mr. Foster, but he says it's extremely urgent and—" Miss Cooney's voice faded in volume but rose in indignation quotient as she apparently held the phone away from herself and called out, "Sir, you can't do that! *Sir*—"

But "sir" could and did do that. The door to my office was thrown open, disclosing a tall, crew-cut, conservatively dressed man in his early thirties. Miss Cooney hovered worriedly in the background, but I told her to return to her desk. I would deal briskly with the intruder and get rid of him.

"Sorry I had to barge in," he said, approaching my desk. "You're Mr. Foster—Leonard Timmins Foster?"

"I am," I said tartly, "and I'm very busy this morning. I suggest you ask my secretary to make an appointment for some day next week—"

He had extracted a leather folder from an inside pocket, and now he flicked it open and thrust it at me. It bore an official-looking seal and enclosed a document affirming that the bearer was one John Joseph Banning, in the employ of one of those colossal supergovernmental agencies concerned with intelligence, counterespionage, and the like. The identifying photo was an unmistakable likeness of the man who confronted me across my desk.

Feeling what I supposed was a natural trepidation about the import of his visit, I asked, "What can I do for you, Mr. Banning?"

"I'd like you to come with me, sir."

"Come with you?" Apparently my foreboding was well founded. "Where?"

Banning shook his head. "I'm not at liberty to disclose that now."

"But—" Resentment flared in me. "See here, Banning. This brief I'm working on is vitally important, means a great deal to me. Can't this—whatever it is—be put off till some other time?"

"No, sir; afraid it must be now. You can of course refuse my—ah—request. In which case we'd have to take certain measures. In your best interests, Mr. Foster, I wouldn't advise that."

I wasn't convinced that he really had my best interests at heart, but I was not disposed to put the question to a test. I sighed in resignation and asked, "How long will I be gone?"

"Possibly until tonight; tomorrow afternoon, at the latest."

As I reached for the phone Banning's strong hand clamped down on mine, holding the receiver in its cradle. "No phone calls, please," he said.

"But, damn it," I protested, "I've got to let my wife know that I may not be home for dinner—"

"That," he said, "has already been taken care of."

Downstairs, Banning led me to a black, chauffeur-driven limousine waiting in a no-parking zone. We were whisked to Central Park, and there, in the Sheep Meadow, a helicopter was warmed up and ready to take off. In minutes we were deposited at LaGuardia Airport, where we boarded a twin-engined jet. The plane was unmarked, but the pilot, I noted, wore the uniform and insignia of an Air Force major.

We were airborne, by my watch, for one hour and seven minutes, and in all that time neither Banning nor I uttered a single word. I was conjecturing, with increasing worry, on the significance of this enforced trip; while for his part, Banning perused, with complete absorption, the pages of a current newsweekly.

It was not until we had circled a huge complex of single-story red-brick buildings superimposed on rolling green farmland and had come to earth on an adjacent landing strip that I ventured my first question.

"Where are we now?" I asked.

Banning considered before deciding, apparently, it was safe to answer. "Maryland."

So at least I knew which state I was in.

A jeep driven by an Air Force sergeant delivered us to the largest of the red-brick buildings, which sprawled over at least an acre of the Maryland countryside. Banning ushered me through a seemingly endless maze of corridors before we stopped at an unmarked door.

"Will you wait in here, please?" he asked.

"Wait for what?" I demanded. "See here, it's high time you let me in on the meaning of this ridiculous rigamarole."

"You'll know very soon now, Mr. Foster." With a firm hand on my elbow Banning propelled me into the room, then closed the door behind him.

I was alone in what appeared to be a small conference chamber; it was furnished with a long polished mahogany table and side chairs upholstered in black leather. The room was windowless; in the baseboards and near the ceiling were heating and air-conditioning vents, and Currier and Ives prints adorned the walls. I could not guess where the eavesdropping device had been installed, but I was certain that one was somewhere in the room. I tried the door through which I had entered—the only one in the room—and found that it was now locked.

My watch ticked the minutes away with agonizing slowness. Half an hour went by before the door was finally opened and a man walked in.

He was stocky, powerful-looking, graying, possibly five years older than my forty-seven and two or three inches shorter than my five foot eleven. And he looked vaguely familiar to me.

He stopped just inside the doorway and scrutinized me carefully before he spoke. "You are—? I know you—?" I detected a Slavic accent in his speech, more an intonation, really. "I think—yes. You are—wait, wait, I will remember— Yes! You are dear, kind friend Lenny!"

He bounded across the room and enveloped me in a bone-crunching embrace. Then he held me at arm's length, smiling fondly and searching my eyes for the recognition that was not there. "You do not remember yet, but I do not tell you. Soon—soon it will come to you."

He touched a hand to his right ear, fingering a jagged scar where a sizable chunk of earlobe was missing.

"Mikail!" I exclaimed.

"Aha!"

"Mikail—Mike—Zigorin!"

"Correct, correct, my friend!" he roared exuberantly. "A miracle, Lenny, is it not, that we shall meet again like this so many years after?"

"Yes," I agreed, "a miracle."

Again we embraced, and the memories came flooding back to me . . .

Berlin, spring of 1945.

I was a young lieutenant in the communications section of Airborne Army headquarters. Our unit, together with elements of an armored division and several service batallions, had been selected as the first American occupying troops in Berlin. The Russians, of course, had preceded us into the city.

It was an awesome and depressing experience. No one who was not there in those first few postwar weeks can possibly visualize the fearful bleakness of the dusty rubble, the almost total devastation of what had once been a great world capital. The stench of death, of rotting carcasses, lay heavy upon the atmosphere. And men were still dying violently: the city had not yet been completely pacified; occasional snipers' bullets would pick off soldiers in the streets, and the victims would invariably be Russians, never Americans. The enemies from the East were the feared and hated ones; and the Berliners, in their first tentative contacts with us, confided their hope that we would throw the Russians out and take over the occupation by ourselves.

They were a scraggly lot, those Berliners. Gaunt and hungry-looking, they had been on near-starvation rations during the last months of the war. Now they brought out their hoarded treasures—diamonds, jewelry, musical instruments, small pieces of furniture—to barter with us for a few packs of American cigarettes, a pound of butter or a can of coffee from our mess-hall kitchens.

The Russians were on a different kind of buying spree. They were battle-hardened veterans, tough and cocky and often high on vodka, but friendly enough toward us in those early days. They had just been paid off, many of them for the first time in months or even years, and they swarmed the streets with fistfuls of occupation marks, buying up anything and everything the GIs had to offer. They were especially avid for wristwatches and would readily pay four, five, or six hundred dollars for a thirty-dollar stateside time-piece. A not uncommon sight was a Russian soldier with the sleeves of his uniform jacket rolled up, proudly displaying both arms covered with strap watches from wrist to forearm.

The center of this three-way black market activity was the broad, once beautiful, once tree-shaded avenue known as Unter den Linden, near its terminus at the Brandenburg Gate. Hotels, important government buildings, private mansions, had formerly lined both sides of the handsome thoroughfare; now many of them had been leveled, most of the rest of them had been gutted, and not one of them had been left completely intact.

One sun-drenched afternoon I was walking along Unter den Linden toward the Gate, where a headquarters jeep was to pick me up, when I was stopped by a Russian officer going in the other direction. He seemed young for the colonel's stars he wore. His hand was outstretched and he was smiling jovially.

"Comrade Lieutenant," he said, shaking my hand energetically, "me Russky, you Amerikaner, but we friends, correct?"

"That's right," I said warmly. "I hope we can be friends."

"Good, good!" He nodded, beaming. Then suddenly he grasped my elbow, examined my gleaming chrome government-issue wrist-watch, and clucked admiringly. "Bew-tee-ful! I buy, no?"

"Afraid not—"

"We friends. Any price you want, I pay."

"But you don't understand. It's not my property, so I couldn't—"

I broke off. I knew, suddenly, that something was about to happen. I didn't know (and still don't) what had alerted me to the danger—perhaps the momentary glint of sun on steel—but I couldn't take the time to reason it out. I threw myself at the surprised colonel and we tumbled to the sidewalk together just as a shot rang out from the street-floor window of the hollow shell of a building near which we had been standing.

From the closeness of the pinging sound of the bullet I guessed we'd have a near miss, but I didn't realize just how near until I saw the colonel put a hand to his ear, then stare wonderingly at his blood-smeared fingers.

That was my introduction to Mikail Zigorin.

After the sniper had been dragged out of the ruined building by the Russians and hustled away to be stood up against a wall and shot (if he was lucky), and after a medic had patched up the colonel's ear, he was touchingly, volubly grateful. He extracted from a pocket a huge wad of occupation marks that must have been the equivalent of five thousand American dollars, and thrust it at me; it was all I could do to keep him from stuffing it into a pocket of my Eisenhower jacket. He vowed undying friendship and total obligation to me: if at any time, now or in the future, I should ask anything of him, he would topple mountains, divert rivers to get it for me.

During the next weeks Zigorin sought me out constantly, and we got to know each other well. He was a buoyant, good-humored man with a booming laugh and an irrepressible eagerness to please. He showed me off proudly to his colleagues as the great Amerikaner hero who had saved his life. He plied me with vodka, with caviar and other delicacies from his mess kitchen. He took me to the beer-halls and rathskellers that the Berliners were just beginning to reopen with the permission of the occupation authorities, and insisted on picking up every tab.

About a month after the sniper incident Zigorin appeared one evening at my billet in the Zehlendorf section of Berlin, where American headquarters were located. There was a doleful expression on his face, and his voice was thick with emotion, as he announced that he had come to say goodbye; he had been recalled to Moscow and would have to leave early the next day.

It was not without a pang of regret that I heard the news: I had grown fond of the man and I realized now that his departure would leave a void in my life. I am not the demonstrative kind, and instead of speaking I could only grasp his hand to convey how I felt about his going.

We exchanged home addresses (his in a Moscow suburb, mine in lower Westchester), and promised to keep in touch. "Lenny," he said, "my dear, good friend, someday—somewhere—we shall meet again. This, my friend, I know."

"I hope so, Mike," I said, reflecting privately on the unlikeliness of it. "Perhaps we will."

He threw his arms around me in a parting embrace; then he was gone.

We did keep in touch, with increasing infrequency, for the next—oh, five or six years. Much of our correspondence touched on the startling and rapid changes taking place in Berlin. I wrote him of my progress (or rather, lack of it) as a struggling young lawyer. For his part, he never mentioned anything about his work, although I gathered that he continued to pursue his career as an army officer.

Inevitably, communications between us petered out. In later years I'd read occasionally, in news reports from the Kremlin, about a Marshal Zigorin, who had attained a position of some importance in the Soviet power hierachy, and I'd wonder if he could possibly be my old friend Mike; but then I'd shrug the question off as no real concern of mine but a reminder, merely, of something that had happened long ago and far away . . .

Now, in the top-secret conference room, we exchanged greetings and reminiscences of the old Berlin days. Then Mikail asked, "You do well as a lawyer, my friend?"

"Pretty well—now," I replied. "And you, Mike—how've you been doing?"

He shrugged, and his face clouded over momentarily. Then, instead of answering my question, he reached into a pocket, got out a wallet, and extracted from it a dog-eared snapshot. "Look, Lenny," he said. "Something you will perhaps remember. Long ago you sent it to me."

I took it from him. It showed a family group photographed by a neighbor, consisting of my blonde wife, myself, and our twin sons. They had been infants in the snapshot; now they were seniors at Princeton, complete with beards and Beatle-type haircuts.

I smiled over it and started to say, "I don't believe I kept a copy of this—"

"Then it is yours," Mikail interrupted. "Keep it, keep it."

"But—you've been carrying it around in your wallet all these years?"

"Correct. To remind me always of my dear friend Lenny and my debt to him that never I shall be able to repay."

"Well—" I turned aside to conceal my embarrassment at his effusiveness. "If you're sure you want me to have it—" Carefully I placed the snap in my own wallet.

Something was puzzling me, and I mentioned it now. "Mike, how was this meeting arranged?"

He shrugged. "I do not know how—I am only glad that it was."

"When you entered this room, you didn't know you were going to find me in here?"

"Not that I would find *you*. Mr. Banning says that there is someone he desires I shall meet and talk with."

"Strange," I mused. "I wonder why the elaborate staging of this scene, why all the secrecy—"

"I know, Lenny," Mikail said with a rueful smile. "I know why the secrecy. It has been—how shall I say?—a testing."

"Testing of what?"

Before he could answer that question the door was opened and Banning walked in.

"Will you come with me, Mr. Foster?" he said. "Mr. Zigorin, please remain in this room."

I followed Banning through more stretches of corridor until we came to another unmarked door; he opened it and stepped aside for me to enter. We were in a small anteroom presided over by a second lieutenant in army uniform, a holstered sidearm attached to his web belt. Banning nodded to him; the lieutenant pressed one of a panel of buttons on his desk and a buzzer sounded, releasing the lock on the door to an inner office.

The rugged, seamed face of the man sitting behind the uncluttered desk would have been easy to recognize by any reasonably observant member of my generation. Although he was in mufti he wore his invisible four stars in the set of his shoulders, the pugnacious thrust of his chin, the aura of authority, ingrained by years of top command. General Ben "Hatchet" Hyatt had led a tank corps in World War II, had been a member of the Combined Chiefs of Staff later, then had abruptly disappeared from public view about five years ago. Since then his name had rarely been mentioned in the news columns, and now I understood why.

The general waved me into a chair beside his desk, and Banning turned and left the office, closing the door behind him.

"Now, Mr. Foster," Hyatt began, "the reason you have been brought here—and I apologize for having to do it the way we did—was for the purpose of identifying the man you have been with, the man who calls himself Mikail Zigorin—"

"*Identifying* him?" I said incredulously. "Then why couldn't I have been told, briefed about it beforehand?"

"If you had been expecting to meet Zigorin, and a man walked into the room and told you he was Zigorin, you might have accepted him without question. No, Mr. Foster, I wanted that meeting to be a surprise—for both of you."

"It was for me, all right."

"Well? Can you identify him?"

"Why—yes, I think so."

"You're not sure?"

I thought about that for a moment. "It's been so long," I said, "but—yes, I'm reasonably sure. —You were able to hear us in that room?"

Hyatt nodded, not bothering to deny it. "He recognized you first, or said he did, and only then you seemed to recognize him—"

"Because of that missing piece of earlobe. Could that have been faked?"

"Easily."

"But he remembered so much of what happened in Berlin—and later our correspondence—why, he even had that snapshot of my family I sent him twenty years ago."

"None of that is conclusive, Mr. Foster—persuasive, perhaps, but certainly not conclusive."

I stared at him. "Do you mean to say, General—" he smiled briefly, acknowledging my recognition of him "—that you suspect the man of being an impostor?"

"We have to consider the possibility very seriously."

"Why?"

Hyatt sighed. "I'd hoped we might avoid having to go into that, but—very well. However, let me remind you that you are still a reserve officer in the Army of the United States. As such, you are ordered not to reveal, under any circumstances, any of what you are about to hear. Understood?"

"Understood."

"First, what we know as facts: for the past ten years or so Marshal Zigorin had been the director of the Soviets' external intelligence operations. About three months ago he suddenly dropped out of sight. There were several conflicting rumors, although the Russians tried to keep the whole thing hushed up: he had suffered a nervous breakdown, he had been liquidated, he had defected—nothing our intelligence people could pin down. Last week the man you just met contacted us. He claimed to be Zigorin, said he wanted to come over to our side.

"Naturally we listened to his story, and what he told us was damnably disturbing. If he's really Zigorin and his information is reliable, then we've been completely off base about some of our important defense postures and would now be required to make rapid and radical adjustments at the cost to us of hundreds of millions, perhaps billions. —Do you begin to see, Mr. Foster, why your identification of the man is so crucial?"

I considered the question thoughtfully. "But aren't there others besides myself, General, who could positively identify him?"

"No one we know of. None of our people ever had more than brief glimpses of him. He never granted interviews, never in the last ten years appeared officially in public. We do have pictures of him in our files. They match up pretty well with this fellow we have here, down to that damaged earlobe. But that's not good enough."

"And how," I asked, "did you find out about me and my connection with Mikail Zigorin?"

"He told us, made quite a point of it. You were, so to speak, one of his credentials."

"Then isn't the fact that he was willing to meet me, and as he put it, be tested by me—that he had enough information about what happened in Berlin to risk such a test—isn't that presumptive proof of his identity?"

Hyatt shook his head. "Assuming the man is an impostor, it would have been no trick at all to get that information from the real Zigorin."

"Assuming he's an impostor, what happened to the real Zigorin?"

"We'll never know for sure; but triggered by the occupation of Czechoslovakia or some other policy decision he opposed, he may have tried to defect and been caught at it. That would have given the Russians a ready-made opportunity to hand us a ringer and foul up the works for us.

"So I'm afraid, Mr. Foster," he went on, "that you're our only hope. *Think*, man! There must be something—some circumstance, some little incident that's eluded you up to now—that can make it certain one way or the other."

I got up to pace, straining at the bonds of my memory. I wished fervently that I had not suddenly been saddled with this monstrous responsibility, but since I had—I stopped in my tracks. A circumstance *had* occurred to me.

"Maybe, General," I said. "Just maybe."

Back in the conference room, luncheon trays were served to us. Over soup and sandwiches we continued to reminisce about the old Berlin days. Now, as we poured coffee and lighted cigarettes, I asked, "By the way, Mike, what ever happened to Uschi?"

"Uschi?" He looked at me inquiringly.

"Don't you remember the pretty young blonde we met one evening in the beergarden on Koenigstrasse?"

"The beergarden on Koenig—of course, of course, Lenny! How could I have forgotten? Uschi."

"We saw a lot of her after that evening. She loved to dance and we found her great company." (She was the first and only German with whom I'd ever established any kind of personal rapport.)

"As you say, my friend." He nodded vigorously.

We smoked in silence for a few moments. Then, as if a sudden recollection had burst upon me, I exclaimed, "Mike!"

"Yes?"

"You saw her again—afterwards."

"Uschi? I saw her again?"

"You wrote me about it—maybe three or four years later. She had married and was living in East Germany. Her husband was a government official, they had come to Moscow for some sort of conference, and she looked you up. Don't you remember, Mike?"

He seemed to be searching his memory; then he clapped a hand to his forehead. "*Da!* Yes, yes, now I remember—"

"She was happy, you wrote me. They were raising a family; two little girls, I think you said."

"Two girls, correct."

"And you never saw her again after that?"

"No, Lenny. After that one time in Moscow, not." He looked at me with a wry little smile that was half an apology and half an entreaty. "It has been so many years, my friend, so many busy years. One cannot remember everything."

"No," I agreed, "one cannot remember everything."

The lieutenant buzzed me into Hyatt's inner sanctum. The general turned his piercing gaze on me and his chin jutted out challengingly. "Well, Foster?"

"You can forget it, General," I said. "If that man is Mikail Zigorin, I'm Napoleon Bonaparte."

He let that sink in, then: "Positive? You'd be willing to take an oath on it?"

I held up my right hand. "On my honor as a reserve officer in the Army of the United States."

He sighed, an enormous sigh. "How were you able to smoke him out?" he asked.

"Why—" I glanced at my watch. So much had happened since I had arrived, innocent and unsuspecting, at my office that morning that it seemed inconceivable it was only a little after two o'clock. "I'll answer that question in a minute, sir. But is there any reason I can't be home in Scarsdale in time for dinner?"

"Mmm. That can probably be managed."

"Then may I call my wife and tell her so? I'm sure she's been concerned about me since your people phoned to tell her that I might be away overnight."

Hyatt considered my request for a moment, then he pressed an intercom button and instructed the lieutenant to have the call put through. In a minute the phone rang and the general motioned for me to pick it up.

"Hello," I said.

"Lenny, that is you? You are all right?"

"Fine. And I'll be home for dinner."

"I do not understand, darling. What has been happening?"

"Oh—nothing much, really; little misunderstanding. I'll tell you about it when I see you. Okay?"

"Okay. 'Bye, Lenny."

"'Bye, Uschi."

William Bankier

One Clear Sweet Clue

I want to tell you about Otto Grant, the best trumpet player ever to come out of Philadelphia. Can I support that? No, but I heard him at his best and I don't expect to hear anybody better.

He was a very black man, tall with shoulders like a good heavyweight. The trumpet he played almost disappeared in those big hands of his and when he stood up in the spotlight for a solo you saw those two big black fists with a couple of fingers like cigars moving on top of the horn which he seemed to be molding in his hands as though it was a soft handful of gold. And from the bottom of the tubing he had a little pair of toy leather boxing gloves hanging, the kind of thing you see suspended from the rearview mirror in a taxi.

Everybody else in the band wore a suit, but Otto never did. Otto always wore slacks and an expensive cashmere sweater. In the winter he wore a white shirt under it with the collar open, and in summer, like on the July night when this ugly thing happened, he wore nothing under it. So he stood up there, this giant of a man, with the cashmere buttoned just at the bottom and the sweat glistening on his ebony chest, and the little boxing gloves swaying from that golden horn while he blew the whole room back against the walls.

Listen, you ever hear Roy Eldridge play "After You've Gone"? Well, Otto was like that, only cleaner and a lot more powerful.

But don't come into Le Big Bang club looking for Otto Grant; he doesn't play there any more. Oh, you'll probably find Eloise Carpentier's blonde head weaving about the bar unless they've busted her again. And you'll find Tancred Falardeau—he's the fat man playing the piano and drinking Cinzano. For free. He owns the place, too.

Who am I? Well, I'm the guy in the mirror there, the one losing his hair but not his smile. My name's John Keeley. I write advertising copy all day, so I can afford to sit here nights and play tenor barstool.

That's exactly what I was trying to do the night it happened. But at first I had trouble getting in. I drove up about 9:30 in my old MG with the top down and angle-parked in Tancred's private zone out front. It was empty, so he must have come down by cab that night. There was a lineup of a dozen or so couples leaning on the old painted brick front—McGill guys and kids from U. de M. in their ice-cream jackets and girls in miniskirts supporting Montreal's claim to more good leg per yard of downtown pavement than any other city in North America. There were also a few hippies down from the Lincoln Avenue district with their beads and beards and sackcloth looking like a bunch of slaves who had stolen the sandals off their Roman guards.

There was obviously no room inside. But with the windows open I could enjoy the music along with the comfort of my bucket seat. Not to mention a cool breath of air drifting up from the St. Lawrence. I was sitting easy, watching the night insects two-stepping on my windshield when Tony d'Amico came by, tried to buck the line, and was thrown for a loss against my fender.

"Eh," I said, "be my guest."

"Johnny," he called, flashing a couple of rows of those white teeth he keeps like a keyboard in that polished mahogany Steinway of a face. Tony d'Amico is forty-five year old with a wife and about 400 kids at home. I saw his wife once leading part of the pack through Morgan's in search of shoes. She was carrying the ten-pound bonus that went with each baby, and the kids trailed after her with closed-up faces like a lot of little worried old people. Tony, meanwhile, looks about nineteen. And acts it.

"Thanks, my friend. No room inside, eh?"

"Oh, there's plenty of room. But all these people and I have just discovered that with both front windows open, the whole building acts like a big speaker and if you stand in the right place you get stereo."

Tony searched my eyes a moment, then grabbed both my shoulders and shook hard. "Ah, you advertising guys!"

"How's the instrument repair business?" I said.

"Good. I'm reconditioning all the instruments for the Black Watch band now."

"I've got an idea for you, a new musical instrument you can develop."

This time Tony was already grinning. "Yeah, yeah?" he said, licking his lips.

"Well, everybody has electric guitars, right? So you're going to come out with the first gas guitar. Gas is cheaper than electricity—everybody knows that."

"Sure, and when the cat is on the road, staying in one of those beat-up rooms, he can heat the room with his guitar and also cook his meals on it."

"The way I see it, only one problem," I went along.

The black eyebrows went way up in anticipation.

"When it's outdoors, what's to keep the wind from blowing out the pilot light?"

We were choking and hitting one another when Eloise Carpentier floated past. This girl must weigh a hundred and twenty pounds—hell, I can *see* almost that much uncovered—and yet she moves without touching anything or anybody. A hummingbird. She hovers. No friction anywhere. And she smiles with just one side of her mouth like she knows what *you're* thinking, old friend.

Rumor had it she and Otto were kind of close the last week or so and now she saw me and moved close to the car, but not touching, and said, "You see Otto out here, Johnny?"

"No, but I heard him playing before. He must be on the stand."

"I was in earlier but he wasn't there. He was late. If you see him tell him I gotta see him right away."

"Sure, Eloise."

There was no problem with the lineup when Eloise went inside. They melted and flowed around her and she was gone.

"That dolly wants just one thing from Otto," Tony said. "He better stay clean."

"What one thing is that?"

"Well, you know how she is."

"No, how is she?"

"The big H. That's why she hangs around musicians all the time—she figures they can help her feed her habit. Lucky she has money."

I had never heard that about Eloise. Well, maybe it explained her distance from me at least. If she was an addict, then I was not her man and she must have sensed it. But the information was unsettling and suddenly I didn't want to kid around with Tony d'Amico any more. So I eased myself out of the cockpit and stepped over the car door.

"Guess I'll crash in the back way. Want to come?"

"This is so nice, I'd like to sit here. Do you mind?"

"Help yourself . . ."

The alleyway was dim and cool compared to Notre Dame Street. I picked my way among the garbage cans and the crates and squeezed past a fat limousine parked near the back door of the club. There were two people standing close to the dead end of the alley. I recognized the slight black-skinned one. He was a busboy on Tancred's staff. The other man looked familiar.

"Hey, Mr. Keeley," the boy said, and it was the voice of a nonswimmer in deep water.

"What's up, Peter?"

"Just go inside, mister," the other one growled. "This doesn't concern you."

I recognized the older man now, from years ago on the Main. He was a little thicker through the middle but his teeth were still bad and he still wore a couple of day's growth of whiskers under the narrow-brimmed straw hat.

"How's the dirty-picture business?" I asked casually.

"Just go inside, and no sweat."

"Come on, Pete," I said, "I want to talk to you."

The hood put one hand on the young man's arm. "He owes me dough."

"It's protection," the boy said. "I only make sixty bucks a week. I can't afford to be shook down."

The back door of the club opened then and a cocktail waitress pointed out the scene to Otto Grant, who eased past her into the alley.

"Keep out of this, Grant," the older man warned. "We leave you musicians alone, so don't interfere."

"He's gonna thump me, Otto."

"No, he isn't. Inside, Pete." The boy ducked under Otto's arm and scuttled through the door.

"That's a mistake, Grant," the man said, but that was all he could get out before Otto took two handfuls of jacket and shirt and lifted him clear off the ground and slammed him hard against the brick wall. Cloth tore and buttons rattled on the pavement. Then Otto dropped him.

"Get out of here," Otto said, "or I'll turn you around and smooth your face off on that brick."

The hood slipped into his car and started the engine. Before he drove away, his contorted face appeared at the window. "This isn't over, black boy."

When the alley was quiet again, I said to Otto, "That's trouble for sure."

"If he wants to make trouble for me he'll have to get in line. I got all kinds of enemies."

Protection racketeers are one kind of enemy, but I would never have nominated Air Corps personnel from the Plattsburgh air base as another kind.

It started around 11:30 when Otto came off the stand at the end of a set. The boys in uniform wanted to buy him a drink but Otto was on his way to the bar to sit with Eloise. This raised the volume of the voices from the military table, and one that was well coated with the molasses of the deep South got on Otto's back particularly. I didn't see the first punch but I did see the tall black figure in cashmere wading into the uniforms and there was blood and screaming and smashed furniture and splintered glass.

Tancred played "Stars and Stripes Forever," but that didn't help much. In fact, things calmed down only when the cops arrived a few minutes later. When she saw the badges, Eloise disappeared into the Ladies' Room—which reminded me of Tony d'Amico's comment earlier. Tancred refused to press charges against the Air Corps lads but asked them to stay away. So the atmosphere cleared and young Pete swept up the debris and everybody sat down again, exhilarated and happy not to have missed the brawl.

I went backstage to find Otto sitting on a Coke case with a wet handkerchief held against his mouth. Tancred was walking back and forth, still nervous.

"You see this guy, Johnny?" Tancred said. "He's a hazard. Now he can't even play."

Otto turned the cloth and I saw the bruised lip. No trumpet for a while. "What set it off?"

"I put my kinky woolly head too close to the girl with the smooth blonde hair. In Alabama that means war."

Tancred poured several Chiclets from the package directly into his mouth, chewing them into the quid. As he wadded it into his cheek he looked like a fat Nelly Fox at the mound for a conference. "Okay, we have customers to entertain. Go home, Otto, and look after that mouth. Put meat on it, or call the doctor. Have you got the key?"

Otto shook his head. He was looking tired.

"Take mine." Tancred pulled a key from a jingling ring and tossed it to Otto and the trumpeter left.

I hung around till one and then I cut out and broke the law by driving home with my limbs sluggish with beer. I parked the car on Crescent Street outside my appartment building, just begging for the law to hit me. Then I pursued my antisocial course by neglecting to brush my teeth, undressed raggedly, leaving my clothes where they fell, and dropped into bed heavily.

The telephone rang. I turned on the light and picked up the receiver, noting the time was 4:50.

"Hello?"

"Johnny, this is Tancred. Otto is dead."

"What?"

"I'm down at the club. The cops found him in the alley."

"Dead? What happened?"

"He was beat around the head. Can you come down?"

By the time I got to the club they were taking Otto away. If you could call that long still shape on the stretcher Otto. I wanted to see him, for some reason, and one of the attendants drew back the sheet. The broad black face was composed; he appeared to be asleep. I saw the bruised lip from the fight earlier, and another mark above one eye.

Tancred must have read my mind because his voice, soft just behind me, said, "It's the back of his head. There must have been quite a lot of blood, but there's not much in the alley. So he was killed somewhere else."

"Were you the one who found him?"

"No, a cop on the beat. Routine check. I was still inside but I was in my office upstairs in the front. I didn't hear anything."

The sun was rising and the alley was bright. The police ambulance left and a bus hissed its brakes on Notre Dame Street. Tancred took me inside and introduced me to a plainclothesman, Detective Sergeant Charland.

"Were you with the man last night?" Charland asked.

"Yes, I talked to him a couple of times."

"You saw the fight?"

"With the Air Corps guys? You think they did it?"

"They had reason," Tancred said.

"We're checking it out. Anything you can tell us we don't know?"

I remembered the confrontation with the protection hood in the alley. "Yes, I think I have a better lead." I told Charland about the scuffle and suggested he talk to young Pete.

"We know those guys. Okay, that's all for now. Neither of you go away for a while, eh, without letting me know. I may want to see you again."

Tancred offered me a drink after the police left but I didn't feel like it. I said I'd drive him home and he accepted. Neither of us spoke as my MG roared up Bleury Street and onto Park Avenue, past Fletcher's Field and the Cross on the Mountain glimmering pale against the lightened sky. I turned into Outremont, negotiating the empty streets swiftly, passing dozens of fine homes set back on the high terraces away from Côte Ste. Catherine Road, stopping finally before the one that was the Falardeau family home.

Tancred was the only one left since the death of his parents in an air crash, not counting an older sister who lived in Miami and whose name never crept into Tancred's conversation. There had been plenty of room for Otto Grant to live here and now the population of the great old house had diminished again to one.

"Come in, will you, Johnny? Just for a few minutes?"

He didn't have to draw up a list of reasons why he didn't want to open the heavy oak door and step into the cool marble and mahogany vestibule alone. I kept in step. In the dining room Tancred found glasses and a bottle of brandy, and this time, without asking, he poured generous splashes into a couple of balloon glasses, handed one to me, and raised his to his lips.

"Wherever the hell he is," he said.

I drank to that and then followed my host down steps and around a narrow corner into a large room heavily draped at both ends. Acoustic tiles were set into the ceiling and several comfortable chairs were arranged to face a bare wall that held a built-in record player and amplifiers with speakers in all the corners.

The floor in front of the chairs was bare parquet and this is what surprised Tancred. He stopped and looked at the shiny floor and then he said, "What happened to the rug?"

My attention was diverted to the cabinet of records backed against the wine-colored drapes. A door hung open, several records were scattered on the floor, and at least one was broken. I touched Tancred's arm with my glass and inclined my head.

"Good God," he said, walking to the records and sorting through them. "These are my old Django Reinhart seventy-eights—collector's items. What's been going on here?"

"Anything missing?"

"I can't tell until I check. But what happened?"

Sergeant Charland came up with a lab man and a couple of constables right after we called him. They went over the room and found some scuff marks at one edge of the parquet floor, an area not covered by the missing rug, and, a few minutes later, some dried blood and bits of hair on a sharp edge of the record-player cabinet.

"It happened here all right," Charland said. "We'll check out the hair sample and the blood but it will turn out to be Grant's, I'm sure." More questions followed, concerning Tancred's relationship with Otto. Then, just before he left, the Sergeant produced a large fat manila envelope and spilled its contents onto the seat of a chair. "These are the personal effects we found on the body. Would you look through them and try to see if anything is missing, something you knew he carried?"

Tancred spotted it first. "Where's his mouthpiece?"

"His what?"

"The mouthpiece of his trumpet. It was a very special one that Otto designed himself and had custom-made. Whenever he wasn't playing he packed up his horn in its case, but he always carried the mouthpiece in his pocket."

A check of Otto's bedroom dresser failed to show up the mouthpiece. "Anyway, everything else was in his pockets. It's missing all right."

"Well, that's something to go on," Charland said.

But the police didn't go very far. In the months that followed, Tancred and I checked back with them to see if anything had developed; but there was no break in the case. The story was long gone from the newspapers—in fact, two more recent nightclub killings erased the memory of Otto Grant. All Charland could tell us was that the Air Corps boys were proved innocent and so was the young hood from the protection racket. It wound up a case of "person or persons unknown."

Tancred found a new trumpet player, adequate but no Otto, and autumn followed summer, and then came the long Montreal winter with the street outside full of snow and the fireplace blazing to the right of the bandstand and waiters hustling jugs of mulled wine to the jazz fans. It was so cozy inside we were almost sorry to see spring arrive. Then it was July again, almost a year since Otto had been killed.

And that was when the fantastic thing happened: Otto Grant came back to point the finger at his killer. If you believe in signs, you have to believe he spoke to us from the grave in the language he used better than anybody.

It was a warm Sunday evening. The club was closed and Tancred and I were strolling the downtown streets. We left the Peel and Ste. Catherine intersection with its lights and pretty girls and walked south into Dominion Square, attracted by the sounds of a band playing in the bandshell in the lower park. They sounded quite good, with that exciting quality a band takes on when it plays outdoors.

We hurried along the walkways past the display cases containing the annual exhibition of local artists. There was room on one of the back benches, so Tancred and I slipped in and made ourselves comfortable. The band finished the "Washington Post" march and the conductor acknowledged the applause and announced the next number—"Carnival of Venice."

Then it happened.

The trumpet soloist had no sooner begun his first straight melody chorus before the famous variations when Tancred said, "That's Otto!"

It wasn't, of course. The soloist was a short red-haired man, but there was something familiar about the clarity of his tone. Tancred's ear is much better than mine and he could hardly contain himself. "That's Otto's mouthpiece! I'll lay odds!"

The concert was long, but we hung right in till "Oh, Canada." Then, as the benches cleared and the musicians bent over their instrument cases, we approached the bandstand. The red-haired trumpet player was a cheerful little man.

"The mouthpiece? Yeah, I've had it for a few months. It's got great tone, eh?"

"And power. Where did you get it?"

"I had my horn reconditioned and the guy offered it to me for ten bucks."

"The guy who reconditioned your instrument? Who was that?"

"Tony d'Amico."

We didn't call on Tony that night because it was Sunday and he would be home with his family and our business, which was a year old, could wait another day.

Next morning I picked up Tancred in the MG at ten o'clock and we drove down to Vitre Street where Tony had his shop. There were no customers in the front of the store. We went behind the counter and into the back room and found Tony with a small blowtorch doing some work on the tubing of a big brass Sousaphone. We sat on a bench till Tony finished his work and then he joined us.

Tancred got right to the point. "How come you had Otto Grant's mouthpiece?"

There was the big white grin but the dark eyes in the mahogany face were wide and alert.

"I don't have anything of Otto's."

"Not now. But you sold Otto's mouthpiece to a trumpet player in the Fanfare de Pompiers. We spoke to him last night."

A lot of air went out of Tony and he sat down slowly. Nobody said anything. Back in the shop a repairman was tapping the bell of a trombone. Then Tony said quietly, "It fell out of his pocket. When I was rolling him up in the carpet."

"God help us, Tony," I said, "how did it happen?"

He got up and began walking back and forth, five paces this way and five paces between us and the worktable. "I didn't expect anybody to come in on me—I knew you'd be at the club till after two. It was those records of yours, Tancred. I'd heard them when I was at your place a couple of times, those old Vocalion sides and all the early Dickie Wells stuff and Chu Berry. It was a crazy thing for me to do, but I was going to steal a couple of them.

"I was getting the ones I wanted when all of a sudden there was Otto in the room. Even then I guess I would have been all right if I'd just kept cool and said you gave me permission to come in and listen. But I felt so small, really, and I didn't want you ever to know, so I tried to make a move for the door. Then Otto came at me. I guess he wouldn't have if he knew me but I don't think he recognized me, there was only a dim light on.

"Anyway, I got in a lucky punch on him—he could have handled me otherwise, easy. And he slipped and hit his head on the sharp edge of the cabinet—hit it real hard. When he didn't move for a while, I checked and found he was dead. I didn't want him found in your place—it seemed to me if he was found behind the club they'd link him up with the pushers or the racketeers down there."

"And that's what happened to my rug."

"Yes, I rolled him up and the mouthpiece fell on the floor, so I just slipped it in my pocket. Then I drove him downtown and waited till things got quiet. Around two-thirty I took him down the alley and left him. Your rug is in my garage back home, behind a lot of junk."

"And the mouthpiece. Did you need the lousy ten bucks?"

"I just didn't want it around. I figured nobody would ever spot it, so I sold it to that band player."

Tancred said, "You might just as well have sold him Otto's right arm."

We agreed to let Tony speak to his wife at home before we took him to the police. The three of us squeezed into my MG and we drove out to Ville d'Anjou where Tony lives.

As we came up Tony's street, with Tony kind of perched up high on the back of my car because it's really only a two-seater, some of his kids spotted us and came running. There must have been six of them to start with and one had a drum and some had kazoos. And this ragged little band began stepping along beside the car playing "When the Saints Go Marching In." When we reached the d'Amico home and turned into the long driveway, several more of his kids joined the orchestra, some playing, some singing, one clacking maracas, and one waving his T-shirt in front like a flag.

And that's the way the triumphant procession approached the house, with Tony trapped up there like a conquering hero and his wife out on the porch now, smiling and waving and with a big question mark on her face.

The whole thing outside, along with what happened when we went into the house, is a scene I'd like to erase from my mind forever. But I haven't been able to forget it yet and I guess I never will. Or big Otto either.

Edward D. Hoch

The Theft of Nothing at All

"*Nothing?*" Nick Velvet repeated incredulously.

"Nothing at all," the fat man said, smiling at Nick's reaction.

"Let's get this straight. You'll pay me my usual fee of twenty thousand dollars to simply sit at home and steal nothing at all on next Thursday?"

"Exactly." The fat man, who said his name was Thomas Trotter, lit a cigar. "And if you're successful at it, I may want to hire you again for the following Thursday at the same fee."

"How could I not be successful?"

The fat man smiled again. Nick decided that he liked to smile. Perhaps he'd read somewhere that fat people are supposed to be jolly. "I think we understand each other, Mr. Velvet." He stood up to leave, taking a thick envelope from his inside pocket. "Here is one-half of the money now, in hundred-dollar bills. The rest will be paid on Friday, if you are successful in stealing nothing."

"I'll be successful," Nick assured him.

For the rest of the week, until Thursday, Nick puzzled over it. Thomas Trotter had come to him in the usual way, referred by someone in New York for whom Nick had once performed a service. And he couldn't believe that Trotter didn't want something for his money.

Something. But what?

"It's so good to have you home this week, Nicky," Gloria told him on Thursday evening. "Usually you're chasing off somewhere for the government and we never get to have much time together."

"Next week I'll be getting the boat out of drydock," he decided. "It should be warm enough on the Sound by then."

She glanced at the clock and headed for the television set. "You don't mind if I watch, do you, Nicky?"

"What? One of those crazy cop shows?"

"No, no. Not this early in the evening. It's the state lottery drawing."

Nick grunted and went out to the kitchen for a beer. He was

vaguely aware that the state had begun televising the lottery drawings at 7:30 on Thursday evenings. Done up with blinking lights
and screaming winners just like a network game show, it had proved
to be the most popular Thursday night TV show in the state.

He went back with his beer and settled into a chair opposite the
television, watching with mild interest. Gloria had got out her lottery tickets, waiting for the moment when this week's winners would
be chosen. This was done by a complicated method involving a previously run horse race, coupled with the choosing and opening of a
sealed tin can to reveal two of the digits.

When the grinning announcer finally called out the complete number, Gloria moaned. "Oh, Nicky, I was so close!"

"Better luck next week."

"The weekly winners all get a crack at the million-dollar jackpot
drawing in three weeks."

"Hmmm." He picked up the evening paper.

"You're not even watching, Nicky!"

"Sure I am."

By the end of the evening when he went to bed, $20,000 richer,
he'd pretty much decided that Thomas Trotter was nothing more
than an eccentric millionaire.

He'd also decided to take the money again if it was offered for
another Thursday of non-stealing.

"Well," Trotter said, slipping into the booth opposite Nick the
following afternoon, "you did very well."

"I did nothing." If he'd been a detective, Nick might have been
curious as to why a man who said his name was Thomas Trotter
wore gold cuff links initialed *RR*.

"Just what I wanted you to do." Trotter signaled the waiter and
ordered a glass of wine. Nick ordered a beer. "Would you like to do
the same thing next Thursday?"

"For another twenty thousand?"

"Naturally."

It was Nick's turn to smile. "Sure!"

The fat man nodded and took an envelope from his pocket. "This
is the balance on yesterday's assignment." Then a second envelope.
"And this is your advance for next Thursday."

"Fine! You keep coming back as long as you want to!"

But by Monday, Nick was beginning to grow irritable. Gloria
commented on it after dinner. "Nicky, what's the matter with you

lately? You used to enjoy having time off to be around the house. Now everything seems to get on your nerves. And you haven't said any more about taking out the boat."

"I'm all right," he insisted.

But Thomas Trotter was bothering him. Another Thursday was coming—another theftless Thursday—and Trotter's weekly twenty grand was getting to him.

What in hell would he do if Trotter offered him the deal for a third week?

On Tuesday evening a call came. "Mr. Velvet?" a woman's voice asked.

"Speaking."

"I understand you steal things," she said bluntly.

"I don't discuss my business on the telephone. Perhaps we could meet somewhere."

"Could it be tonight? I'd want to hire you for this week."

"This week?" He thought of Thomas Trotter. "It wouldn't be Thursday, would it?"

"How'd you know?"

"I had a hunch." He gave her directions to a cocktail lounge in a nearby shopping center and arranged to meet her there in an hour.

"Going out, Nicky?" Gloria asked.

"For a while. Maybe it'll improve my mood."

The woman's name was Rona Felix and she was waiting for him alone in a booth near the back of the lounge. The place was very much like the one where he'd met Thomas Trotter, and Nick wondered if maybe some chain supplied suburban cocktail lounges with high-backed booths especially for couples carrying on illicit affairs.

Rona Felix probably wouldn't have been interested in that. Though she was still in her thirties she had the sour look of a woman whom life had passed by. The way she wore her hair, the lack of makeup, the frumpy coat that covered her shoulders—all spread the message that she was a woman who'd stopped caring about her looks.

"It's good to meet you, Mr. Velvet. I've heard a great deal about your exploits."

"Who from?"

"People you've helped. I understand you'll steal anything valueless for a fee of twenty thousand dollars."

"That's correct."

"Could you steal something for me this Thursday?"

"Never on Thursday," he said with a grin.

"What?"

"I'm otherwise occupied this Thursday."

"Oh." She seemed crestfallen. "I was counting on you."

Nick had once been kidnaped by a man to keep him from taking an assignment. He was beginning to wonder if the fat man had been up to the same sort of trick. "Could I ask you a question? Do you know someone named Thomas Trotter?"

"Trotter? I don't believe so."

"All right. Could you tell me what the job involves? Perhaps I could do it tomorrow. Or Friday."

She shook her head. "They only bring it out of the vault on Thursdays. It has to be a Thursday."

"I couldn't steal anything valuable enough to be kept in a vault."

"Could you steal a hundred tin cans?"

"I suppose so. It would depend on what's inside them."

"Just numbered plastic balls. The manufacturing cost is only a few dollars and their value to anyone would be absolutely zero."

"And yet they're kept locked in a vault every day but Thursday?"

"That's correct."

Nick thought about it. "You needn't tell me any more now, since I can't do it this Thursday in any event. But how about a week from Thursday?"

"All right," she agreed after a moment's hesitation.

"Meet me here next Monday night and you can fill me in on the details."

"Fine."

He smiled at her. "Now since you're a prospective client, let me buy you a drink."

"No, thank you. I have to be going."

"Very well. Till next Monday."

Nick went home and found Gloria ironing shirts. "That didn't take long, Nicky."

"I was just arranging for a future assignment." He glanced at the TV set, where a cop was chasing someone down a darkened alley. "Say, I noticed they have a studio audience for that lottery drawing on Thursday nights. If we can get tickets let's take a drive up there and see it."

"You mean it, Nicky? This Thursday?"

"Sure. I'll see about it."

He was beginning to think he should know more about such things.

The weekly drawing of the state lottery was telecast from an elaborate set in the studio of Channel 17 in the state capital. There were about 200 seats for the studio audience, and Nick had to rely on an old political friendship to obtain tickets on such short notice. But as he settled into his tenth-row seat next to Gloria, he saw at once that the journey had not been a vain one.

A short-skirted girl who served as the assistant to the master of ceremonies appeared from the wings, wheeling a cart on which rested 100 vacuum-sealed metal cans. As the show began the M.C. ran quickly through the standard procedure, explaining it to the few new viewers who might have tuned in. The winning number consisted of six digits, the last four of which were determined by a previously run horse race. For the first two digits a member of the studio audience was called on stage to choose one of the 100 sealed cans. The can was opened and a plastic ball bearing a two-digit number from 00 to 99 was extracted.

There it was.

Rona Felix was offering him $20,000 to steal those 100 cans. He was certain of it. And he was just as certain that Thomas Trotter was paying him $20,000 *not* to steal them.

The week's winning number proved to be 450098, and after it was determined, interest shifted to the six finalists from the previous drawing. These were holders of tickets which had five of the six digits correct, and they took part in a game-show type of competition for instant cash prizes.

"Didn't you enjoy it, Nicky?" Gloria asked on the way out.

"The whole thing seemed awfully complicated."

"They have to make it that way so there'll be no cheating," she explained.

"I suppose so."

The master of ceremonies, a toothy young man named Cappy Sloan, was standing at the door saying goodbye to the departing audience. This was his chance to build a show-business career on a lucky job with the state lottery, and he was making the most of it.

"Pardon me," Nick said. "Could I ask you something?"

Cappy Sloan shot him a smile. "Sure, as long as it's not next week's winning number. That I don't know!"

"I do some free-lance articles for our local newspaper downstate, and I was wondering if I might come in sometime and see how things are run backstage. Maybe next Monday or Tuesday I could get some pictures of the equipment—"

"It would have to be Thursday," Cappy informed him. "After the show all the equipment is locked in a special vault here at the studio. We can't have anyone tampering with it, you know. It doesn't come out again till next Thursday, a few hours before showtime."

"Could I call you about it next week?"

"Sure, sure! The state loves the publicity."

They went on their way and Gloria asked, "What was all that about, Nicky? You don't write articles."

"I might take it up," he said with a smile.

The next day was Friday, and Nick kept his appointment with Thomas Trotter. The fat man was waiting in his usual booth, looking uncomfortable. "You're ten minutes late," he told Nick.

"Friday night traffic. Had a good week?"

"Until yesterday."

"What happened yesterday?"

"You were at the state capital, at the lottery telecast."

"Well, yes. We've been watching it on television and thought it might be fun to get tickets."

Trotter looked distasteful. "Was it fun?"

"Sure. You know, a night out. I didn't see you there."

"You were quite visible when the camera panned the audience." He took an envelope from his pocket. "But since you kept your agreement to steal nothing, here's the balance of your money."

"Thanks."

"The offer stands for another week."

"I may have an assignment for next Thursday."

"Cancel it."

"I can't offend a client," Nick said. "Their money is as good as yours."

Thomas Trotter leaned back. "All right, thirty thousand to steal nothing next Thursday. How's that?"

"I only charge thirty thousand for especially dangerous assignments."

"This could be especially dangerous for you if you cross me."

"All right," Nick said with a sigh. "Thirty thousand to steal nothing next Thursday. It's a deal." Whatever Trotter was up to, it was costing him a total of $70,000 to have Nick do nothing.

"And stay away from the state lottery."

"Now wait a minute—that's not part of the agreement."

Trotter waved aside his objection. "All right, so long as I have your word you will steal nothing."

"You have it."

"I have only ten thousand with me. The other twenty will be paid next Friday. Same time, same place."

Nick stood up. "Mr. Trotter, it's a pleasure doing business with you."

On Monday he met Rona Felix as planned. It was a warm spring day and she wore a colorful print dress that made her seem a bit more feminine.

"Well?" she asked him. "Will you do it?"

"Steal one hundred tin cans next Thursday? I'm sorry, but I can't."

She was openly disappointed. "But I thought—"

"Miss Felix, I asked you last week if you knew a man named Thomas Trotter and you said no. Now I must ask you another question. Who knew you were planning to contact me?"

"Why . . . no one."

"Think carefully. Two weeks ago, a full week before you actually contacted me, I was approached by Trotter. Frankly, he's paying me a great deal of money in an obvious attempt to frustrate your plans."

"He is? Why would he do that?"

"I should tell you that I know the assignment involves the state-lottery drawing in some way," Nick said.

This seemed to startle her. "How could you—? Oh, I suppose you watch it on television. All right, it does concern the lottery. And for that reason the theft must be accomplished this Thursday. It's the last week before the grand drawing for the million dollars."

"So you're paying me twenty thousand to make a million."

"Not exactly." Hesitating a moment, she finally asked, "Why should I tell you any of this if you can't help me?"

"I may have some suggestions. And it's not costing you anything to talk."

"All right. If you're familiar with the lottery, you know that the first two digits of the winning number are chosen by opening one of a hundred vacuum-sealed aluminum cans, each containing a numbered plastic ball. The lottery commission has two sets of numbered balls, and the canning is done under guard by a local firm. One of the sets is always in the vault, and when it's removed on Thursday for the show it's immediately replaced with the other set for use the following Thursday. The canner picks up the entire used set each Thursday night for repackaging, though only one of the hundred cans has been opened."

"And you want me to steal the set of cans when it comes out of the vault. Why? What will it gain you?"

"I didn't know you asked so many questions."

Nick smiled. "If you want my help, I have to ask questions."

"Oh, very well! If the cans are stolen just before showtime, they'll be forced to use the set just delivered for the following week. And that's the set I want them to use."

"It's gimmicked."

She nodded. "The final drawing is foolproof, and I can't be sure of winning the million. But each of the weekly winners gets a minimum of $100,000, and that's good enough for me."

"What about the horse race determining the final four digits?"

"That part has been attended to. It needn't concern you. The set of aluminum cans is my problem."

"You wanted to hire me for last week originally. If you'd gimmicked a set of cans at that time, wouldn't they be coming up for use this week?"

She shook her head. "It's not as simple as that. I don't know the number I need until I buy my lottery tickets for the week. Look, I'll give you an example. Suppose I know the horse race numbers are going to be 3456. I have to find a ticket to buy that ends in those numbers. It's not as impossible as it sounds in this state, because the numbered tickets are supplied to dealers in consecutive sheets and most places will let you look through the sheets to pick a lucky number. After trying a dozen or so places I'm likely to find a 3456.

"But for the first two digits I have to settle for whatever I get—say 123456. The sealed-up set of balls are already locked in the vault, immune from any sort of tampering. My only hope is to gimmick the new set of cans containing next week's numbered balls and then force the lottery to use that set a week early. That's where you come in. See?"

"My God!" Nick said with real awe. "How'd you ever dream up this thing?"

"My boyfriend at the canning company helped."

Nick's first impression had been wrong. If she'd stopped caring about her looks, it was only because she already had a steady man. "But the person who chooses the can is picked at random, or else he's a guest dignitary. With all the cans unlabeled and identical, how can you possibly gimmick it?"

"The guard they send over with the cans every week is a joke. He sits and drinks coffee."

"Still—"

"And it's easy to substitute a box of a hundred cans for the box he's been watching. All I need is the two-digit number to give my friend a few days before Thursday, so he can prepare the gimmicked set of cans."

"Okay. Suppose you want to open a can and find a ball numbered 12. How do you gimmick it when the can's going to be chosen at random by an unknown person?"

"That should be obvious, Mr. Velvet. In the gimmicked set all hundred cans contain balls with the same number."

"And you think you can get away with this?"

"I'm sure I can. I've been watching the operation for a full year. They never open more than one can. There's no reason to."

"I have to admire your plan," Nick admitted. "I wish I could help."

"But you must! It all depends on you! Someone else might be caught stealing the cans, or might fail to even reach them with the guards and everything. It has to be you!"

Nick thought about it. He thought about the fat man's $50,000, with twenty more to come. And he thought about this bright young woman's fantastic scheme.

There just might be a way . . .

"I'll see what I can do," he told her at last.

"This Thursday?"

"This Thursday."

To steal or not to steal.

Nick pondered the question all the next day, going over assorted plans and possibilities. He still didn't know where Trotter fitted into the picture, and that could be a danger.

On Wednesday afternoon Gloria found him in the kitchen, rummaging through a drawer. "What are you looking for, Nicky?"

"Just something I need. I was hoping we had one the right size, but I guess I'll have to go out and buy one."

She didn't question him further. After a dozen years of living with him she was used to his odd behavior.

On Thursday, Nick drove to the state capital and parked in the lot behind the Channel 17 studio. When the guard at the door stopped him he said he was there to see the lottery M.C., Cappy Sloan. After a five minute wait Sloan appeared. "Do I know you?" he asked Nick.

"You've probably forgotten. Last Thursday evening, after the telecast, you said I could come over this week and do a story on the lottery."

"Oh, yeah, I remember. Well, we're setting up for tonight. You can come in and watch if you promise not to get in the way."

Nick followed him down a long corridor and onto the large sound stage where the weekly sets and props for the state lottery were being assembled. "A lot of work here," Nick commented.

"Sure is! And especially this week. The Governor himself is coming tonight to lend his support. He'll choose the can containing the first two digits of the winning number."

"Really? I picked a good week to come."

"Yeah," Sloan agreed. "Say, what'd you tell me your name was?"

"Nicholas. Joe Nicholas."

"Well, Joe, back here is the studio's vault. The state had them build it special to store all this lottery paraphernalia between shows. And these are the hundred cans with their numbered balls."

Nick took note of the guard hovering nearby.

"After each show the cans are picked up by a local company that replaces the opened can and returns them all to us next Thursday. They just delivered 'em and we've put them in the vault for next week's show."

"Next week is the million-dollar drawing, right?"

"Sure is!" Cappy Sloan confirmed. "This week's winner is certain of a hundred thousand, but they'll also have a crack at that million-dollar jackpot."

Nick casually lit a cigarette. It tasted strange to him, since he hadn't smoked in years. "I'd like to see the board where you hang the winning number. I've got a little camera here and maybe I can snap a picture of you standing next to it."

Cappy Sloan grinned. "Sure, right over here."

As they passed a large wastebasket full of paper and debris from some previous show, Nick carefully flipped away his cigarette. He spent some time posing Sloan for the picture, and he wasn't at all surprised when he heard a stagehand bellow, "Fire!"

"Damn! That wastebasket's blazing!" Cappy Sloan ran to join the others in fighting the fire.

Nick made certain no eyes were on him and then pushed the cart containing the hundred tin cans behind a convenient curtain. He went at his task, working fast, knowing he'd have only a few minutes at the most. Though the smell of smoke was heavy in the air, the fire was quickly extinguished and he heard Cappy Sloan calling for him.

"Hey, Nicholas! Where'd you go?"

Nick kept working. One more minute . . .

"Nicholas!" Sloan called out.

"Right here," Nick replied. "Just looking around." He finished his task and stepped quickly around the curtain.

"Don't go wandering off," Sloan warned. "The guards don't like it."

"This is a fascinating setup," Nick said, leading Sloan away from the cart. "Where's the light board that flashes when one of the finalists wins?"

"That's over here."

They spent the next twenty minutes looking over the backstage setup. It was risky, Nick knew, because any minute someone might happen to glance at the cart. But he had to arrange for a proper exit.

"Cappy," a voice boomed from the control room, "the Governor's on his way."

"So soon? It's two hours till showtime."

"He's dining with the station executives. They want you there too."

"Damn! All right, I'll be there." He turned to Nick. "That completes the tour. Duty calls. But I'll arrange for a ticket so you can see the show."

"I'd appreciate that."

Cappy Sloan grabbed a tie and jacket he had tossed over the back of a chair and started to put them on. He was heading for the aisle, still knotting his tie, when a girl on stage shouted, "Cappy! What happened to those cans?"

He stopped and turned around. "What do you mean, what happened to them, Phyllis? What does it look like happened to them?"

"It looks like somebody opened them all with a can opener!"

"What!"

He was back on stage in an instant, inspecting the damage while the others clustered around. Nick edged toward the door but made no effort to escape.

"The balls are still inside," the girl said. "Someone just opened them and left them."

Sloan scratched his head. "Now who in hell would want to do that? What for?"

"A joke of some sort."

"Yeah. Only I don't see the humor." He thought about it and finally decided, "Okay, get next week's set of cans out of the safe—we'll have to use them. And put them right out here at stage center where no one can fool with them!" He seemed to have forgotten Nick's absence for those few moments.

"First the fire and now this!" the girl said. "Is somebody sabotaging us?"

"No, no," Cappy Sloan soothed. "Don't you worry, Phyllis. By seven-thirty we'll be on the beam. Now get that other set of cans out here. I've got to go eat with the Governor."

Nick decided things were going along better than he could have hoped for. He wandered outside and dropped the can opener down a convenient sewer, then went across the street to a lunch counter for a bite to eat.

He managed to be back in plenty of time for the 7:30 telecast, picking up his ticket and entering the studio just before seven. There was no sign of Rona Felix anywhere, but he was startled to see Thomas Trotter on stage. The fat man was talking earnestly with Cappy Sloan and inspecting the opened tin cans.

Nick spotted Sloan's assistant, Phyllis, and asked, "Do you know the man who's talking to Mr. Sloan?"

She glanced at Nick and then away, intent on more important matters. "That's the Governor's press secretary, Ramsey Reynolds."

Ramsey Reynolds, not Thomas Trotter.

All right, Nick decided, but that still doesn't tell me anything. Was it the Governor who'd really hired him, through Trotter-Reynolds? And what was the connection with Rona Felix and her scheme to fix the state lottery?

When the show began, he sat watching the people on stage go through their motions. Cappy Sloan came out, cracked a couple of bad jokes, and got right to the business at hand. The slip containing the order of finish for a previously run horse race was drawn with much fanfare—Nick wondered if the slips were all the same too—and the last four digits of the winning number were posted.

7821.

Then the Governor made his entrance, to a lengthy ovation. He was popular in the state, and he fed the popularity by public appearances like this one. He said a few words, then stepped over to the cart and selected one of the 100 aluminum cans. Cappy Sloan led him to an electric can opener where the top was removed and the plastic ball revealed. It was number 67.

The week's winning number, 677821, went up on the board. Nick hoped Rona Felix was holding it. If she wasn't, she'd wasted his $20,000 fee.

Nick was feeling good as he filed out of the studio after the show. He was feeling good right up until the moment when he saw Ramsey Reynolds standing at the door with two burly State Troopers.

"Arrest that man!" Reynolds ordered, pointing at Nick.

They took him to the police station and booked him on a variety of charges relating to tampering with the operation of the state lottery. He used his one phone call to tell Gloria he'd been called away overnight, and then settled down in his cell. It was a new experience for him, and one he hoped would be of short duration.

Late in the evening, close to eleven, Ramsey Reynolds came to his cell. "I tried to tell you that nobody crosses me, Velvet. I paid you not to steal anything today!"

"And I didn't," Nick answered with a smile.

"No? I checked with Cappy Sloan and he pointed you out in the audience. You're the only one who had the opportunity to open those hundred cans."

"I don't deny I opened them."

"Good! The District Attorney is outside and you can admit it to him."

"Seems like a minor crime to involve the D.A. in at eleven o'clock at night."

"The Governor asked him to see to it personally."

The District Attorney was a brisk, balding man obviously displeased at being there. "What is this foolishness, Reynolds?"

Nick grinned at the fat man. "I thought your name was Trotter."

"Shut up!" Then, turning to the District Attorney, he said, "Obviously he opened those cans in an attempt to cheat the lottery."

"I don't see how," the D.A. muttered. "What about it, Velvet? Why did you open those cans?"

"I overheard some men talking about a bomb in one of the cans. It was some sort of plot to kill the Governor. I didn't report it to the police because it seemed farfetched. But I opened the cans myself just to make sure."

"What garbage!" Reynolds said with a sneer. "Do you believe that for a minute, sir?"

"It's as good an explanation as any I've heard," the D.A. snapped. "We can't hold this man unless we can show criminous intent!"

"But I—"

"Step outside with me, Reynolds."

Nick relaxed as they left him alone. He was quite certain he wouldn't be spending much more time in this jail.

Presently the fat man returned, looking enraged. "He's dismissing the case against you for lack of evidence."

"I'm glad to hear that."

"But I'm not dismissing *my* case against you. I'm going to ruin you in this state, Velvet. I'm going to see you never get another job from anyone, and if you do I'm going to have the cops breathing down your neck so close that you'll end up in prison for life!"

"Now wait a minute," Nick protested. "I did exactly what you hired me to do. I stole nothing."

"But you opened those cans—"

"And took nothing from them. Oh, yes, I took *one* thing from them. By opening them I removed the vacuum from each can. I stole a vacuum, Reynolds, and as any dictionary will tell you, a vacuum is a space entirely devoid of matter. A vacuum is nothing at all, and that's what I stole by opening those cans—nothing at all!"

Reynolds mulled this over. "Who paid you?" he asked finally. "It was that Felix woman, wasn't it?"

"How do you know her?" Nick countered.

"I know her boyfriend. He works at the canning plant."

"So you got onto her scheme through him. She said she was going to hire me and you hired me first."

"That's right," Reynolds admitted. "It was for the good of the state. I didn't want anyone cheating on the lottery."

"For the good of the state you paid me fifty thousand dollars? That's hard to swallow. It's a lot more likely you've got your own scheme for collecting that million-dollar prize. You're in it with Rona Felix's friend yourself, only poor Rona was going to get left out in the cold. You heard from him that she was planning to hire me, and you thought that the money you paid me was a good investment to keep me away for three weeks till your stooges could win the million. Right?"

"That's ridiculous!"

"Is it? I wonder what your boss the Governor would think."

Reynolds was silent for a moment. Finally he opened the door and said, "Get out, Velvet. You're free to go. Get out and never let me see you again."

Nick didn't need to be told twice. He paused only long enough to say, "Remember, you still owe me twenty thousand for stealing nothing today." Then he hurried out.

The steel door slammed behind him.

Nick met Rona Felix the following day and collected his fee. All had gone according to plan and she showed him the winning ticket. "Next Thursday I'll be a hundred thousand—or maybe a million—richer!"

"I'm happy for you," Nick said. "Good luck—I'll be watching."

But as it turned out, he wasn't watching on Thursday night and neither was anyone else. Thursday morning's papers carried the story under bold headlines: *Governor Suspends Lottery Pending Inquiry: Press Secretary Reynolds Resigns.*

"Did you see this, Nicky?" Gloria asked, shaking the paper at him. "The District Attorney became suspicious of this Ramsey Reynolds after Thursday night's drawing and started examining the lottery equipment. He discovered the cans the Governor chose from all contained balls with the same number. And now Reynolds has resigned and last week's drawing has been voided! Isn't that amazing?"

Nick thought about Rona Felix, who was destined to miss her big moment on television. And he thought about the total of $70,000 he'd collected for stealing nothing at all. He'd been the big lottery winner without even buying a ticket!

Stanley Ellin

The Day of the Bullet

I believe that in each lifetime there is one day of destiny. It may be a day chosen by the Fates who sit clucking and crooning over a spinning wheel, or, perhaps, by the gods whose mill grinds slow, but grinds exceedingly fine. It may be a day of sunshine or rain, of heat or cold. It is probably a day which none of us is aware of at the time, or can even recall through hindsight.

But for every one of us there is that day. And when it leads to a bad end it's better not to look back and search it out. What you discover may hurt, and it's a futile hurt because nothing can be done about it any longer. Nothing at all.

I realize that there is a certain illogic in believing this, something almost mystical. Certainly it would win the ready disfavor of those modern exorcists and dabblers with crystal balls, those psychologists and sociologists and case workers who—using their own peculiar language to express it—believe that there may be a way of controlling the fantastic conjunction of time, place, and event that we must all meet at some invisible crossroads on the Day. But they are wrong. Like the rest of us they can only be wise after the event.

In this case—and the word "case" is particularly fitting here—the event was the murder of a man I had not seen for thirty-five years. Not since a summer day in 1923, or, to be even more exact, the evening of a summer day in 1923 when as boys we faced each other on a street in Brooklyn, and then went our ways, never to meet again.

We were only twelve years old then, he and I, but I remember the date because the next day my family moved to Manhattan, an earth-shaking event in itself. And with dreadful clarity I remember the scene when we parted, and the last thing said there. I understand it now, and know it was that boy's Day. The Day of the Bullet it might be called—although the bullet itself was not to be fired until thirty-five years later.

I learned about the murder from the front page of the newspaper my wife was reading at the breakfast table. She held the paper upright and partly folded, but the fold could not conceal from me

61

the unappetizing picture on the front page, the photograph of a man slumped behind the wheel of his car, head clotted with blood, eyes staring and mouth gaping in the throes of violent and horrifying death.

The picture meant nothing to me, any more than did its shouting headline—RACKETS BOSS SHOT TO DEATH. All I thought, in fact, was that there were pleasanter objects to stare at over one's coffee and toast.

Then my eye fell on the caption below the picture, and I almost dropped my cup of coffee. *The body of Ignace Kovac,* said the caption, *Brooklyn rackets boss who last night—*

I took the paper from my wife's hand, while she looked at me in astonishment, and studied the picture closely. There was no question about it. I had not seen Ignace Kovac since we were kids together, but I could not mistake him, even in the guise of this dead and bloody hulk. And the most terrible part of it, perhaps, was that next to him, resting against the seat of the car, was a bag of golf clubs. Those golf clubs were all my memory needed to work on.

I was called back to the present by my wife's voice. "Well," she said with good-natured annoyance, "considering that I'm right in the middle of Walter Winchell—"

I returned the paper to her. "I'm sorry. I got a jolt when I saw that picture. I used to know him."

Her eyes lit up with the interest of one who—even at second-hand—finds herself in the presence of the notorious. "You did? When?"

"Oh, when the folks still lived in Brooklyn. We were kids together. He was my best friend."

My wife was an inveterate tease. "Isn't that something. I never knew you hung around with juvenile delinquents when you were a kid."

"He wasn't a juvenile delinquent. Matter of fact—"

"If you aren't the serious one." She smiled at me in kindly dismissal and went back to Winchell, who clearly offered fresher and more exciting tidings than mine. "Anyhow," she said, "I wouldn't let it bother me too much, dear. That was a long time ago."

It was a long time ago. You could play ball in the middle of the street then; few automobiles were to be seen in the far reaches of Brooklyn in 1923. And Bath Beach, where I lived, was one of the farthest reaches. It fronted on Gravesend Bay, with Coney Island to the east a few minutes away by trolley car and Dyker Heights and its golf course to the west a few minutes away by foot. Each was an entity separated from Bath Beach by a wasteland of weed-grown lots which building contractors had not yet discovered.

So, as I said, you could play ball in the streets without fear of traffic. Or you could watch the gas-lighter turning up the street lamps at dusk. Or you could wait around the firehouse on Eighteenth Avenue until, if you were lucky enough, an alarm would send the three big horses there slewing the pump-engine out into the street in a spray of sparks from iron-shod wheels. Or, miracle of miracles, you could stand gaping up at the sky to follow the flight of a biplane proudly racketing along overhead.

Those were the things I did that summer, along with Iggy Kovac who was my best friend, and who lived in the house next door. It was a two-story frame house painted in some sedate color, just as mine was. Most of the houses in Bath Beach were like that, each with a small garden in front and yard in back. The only example of ostentatious architecture on our block was the house on the corner owned by Mr. Rose, a newcomer to the neighborhood. It was huge and stuccoed, almost a mansion, surrounded by an enormous lawn, and with a stuccoed two-car garage at the end of its driveway.

That driveway held a fascination for Iggy and me. On it, now and then, would be parked Mr. Rose's automobile, a grey Packard, and it was the car that drew us like a magnet. It was not only beautiful to look at from the distance, but close up it loomed over us like a locomotive, giving off an aura of thunderous power even as it stood there quietly. And it had *two* running-boards, one mounted over the other to make the climb into the tonneau easier. No one else around had anything like that on his car. In fact, no one we knew had a car anywhere near as wonderful as that Packard.

So we would sneak down the driveway when it was parked there, hoping for a chance to mount those running-boards without being caught. We never managed to do it. It seemed that an endless vigil was being kept over that car, either by Mr. Rose himself or by someone who lived in the rooms over the garage. As soon as we were no more than a few yards down the driveway a window would open in the house or the garage and a hoarse voice would bellow threats at us. Then we would turn tail and race down the driveway and out of sight.

We had not always done that. The first time we had seen the car we had sauntered up to it quite casually, all in the spirit of good neighbors, and had not even understood the nature of the threats. We only stood there and looked up in astonishment at Mr. Rose, until he suddenly left the window and reappeared before us to grab Iggy's arm.

Iggy tried to pull away and couldn't. "Leggo of me!" he said in a high-pitched, frightened voice. "We weren't doing anything to your ole car! Leggo of me, or I'll tell my father on you. Then you'll see what'll happen!"

This did not seem to impress Mr. Rose. He shook Iggy back and forth—not hard to do because Iggy was small and skinny even for his age—while I stood there, rooted to the spot in horror.

There were some cranky people in the neighborhood who would chase us away when we made any noise in front of their houses, but nobody had ever handled either of us or spoken to us the way Mr. Rose was doing. I remember having some vague idea that it was because he was new around here, he didn't know yet how people around here were supposed to act, and when I look back now I think I may have been surprisingly close to the truth. But whatever the exact reasons for the storm he raised, it was enough of a storm to have Iggy blubbering out loud, and to make us approach the Packard warily after that. It was too much of a magnet to resist, but once we were on Mr. Rose's territory we were like a pair of rabbits crossing open ground during the hunting season. And with just about as much luck.

I don't want to give the impression by all this that we were bad kids. For myself, I was acutely aware of the letter of the law, and had early discovered that the best course for anyone who was good-natured, pacific, and slow afoot—all of which I was in extra measure—was to try and stay within bounds. And Iggy's vices were plain high spirits and recklessness. He was like quicksilver and was always on the go and full of mischief.

And smart. Those were the days when at the end of each school week your marks were appraised and you would be reseated according to your class standing—best students in the first row, next best in the second row, and so on. And I think the thing that best explains Iggy was the way his position in class would fluctuate between the first and sixth rows. Most of us never moved more than one row either way at the end of the week; Iggy would suddenly be shoved from the first row to the ignominy of the sixth, and then the Friday after would just as suddenly ascend the heights back to the first row. That was the sure sign that Mr. Kovac had got wind of the bad things and had taken measures.

Not physical measures, either. I once asked Iggy about that, and he said, "Nah, he don't wallop me, but he kind of says don't be so dumb, and well—you know—"

I did know, because I suspect that I shared a good deal of Iggy's feeling for Mr. Kovac, a fervent hero worship. For one thing, most of the fathers in the neighborhood "worked in the city"—to use the Bath Beach phrase—meaning that six days a week they ascended the Eighteenth Avenue station of the B.M.T. and were borne off to desks in Manhattan. Mr. Kovac, on the other hand, was a conductor on the Bath Avenue trolley-car line, a powerful and imposing figure in his official cap and blue uniform with the brass buttons on it. The cars on the Bath Avenue line were without side walls, closely lined with benches from front to back, and were manned by conductors who had to swing along narrow platforms on the outside to collect fares. It was something to see Mr. Kovac in action. The only thing comparable was the man who swung himself around a Coney Island merry-go-round to take your tickets.

And for another thing, most of the fathers—at least when they had reached the age mine had—were not much on athletics, while Mr. Kovac was a terrific baseball player. Every fair Sunday afternoon down at the little park by the bay there was a pick-up ball game where the young fellows of the neighborhood played a regulation nine innings on a marked-off diamond, and Mr. Kovac was always the star. As far as Iggy and I were concerned, he could pitch like Vance and hit like Zack Wheat, and no more than that could be desired. It was something to watch Iggy when his father was at bat. He'd sit chewing his nails right through every windup of the pitcher, and if Mr. Kovac came through with a hit, Iggy would be up and screaming so loud you'd think your head was coming off.

Then after the game was over we'd hustle a case of pop over to the team, and they would sit around on the park benches and talk things over. Iggy was his father's shadow then; he'd be hanging around that close to him, taking it all in and eating it up. I wasn't so very far away myself, but since I couldn't claim possession as Iggy could, I amiably kept at a proper distance. And when I went home those afternoons it seemed to me that my father looked terribly stodgy, sitting there on the porch the way he did, with loose pages of the Sunday paper around him.

When I first learned that I was going to have to leave all this, that my family was going to move from Brooklyn to Manhattan, I was completely dazed. Manhattan was a place where on occasional Saturday afternoons you went, all dressed up in your best suit, to shop with your mother at Wanamakers or Macy's, or, with luck, went to the Hippodrome with your father, or maybe to the Museum of Natural History. It had never struck me as a place where people *lived*.

But as the days went by my feelings changed, became a sort of apprehensive excitement. After all, I was doing something pretty heroic, pushing off into the Unknown this way, and the glamor of it was brought home to me by the way the kids on the block talked to me about it.

However, none of that meant anything the day before we moved. The house looked strange with everything in it packed and crated and bundled together; my mother and father were in a harried state of mind; and the knowledge of impending change—it was the first time in my life I had ever moved from one house to another—now had me scared stiff.

That was the mood I was in when after an early supper I pushed through the opening in the hedge between our back yard and the Kovacs', and sat down on the steps before their kitchen door. Iggy came out and sat down beside me. He could see how I felt, and it must have made him uncomfortable.

"Jeez, don't be such a baby," he said. "It'll be great, living in the city. Look at all the things you'll have to see there."

I told him I didn't want to see anything there.

"All right, then don't," he said. "You want to read something good? I got a new Tarzan, and I got *The Boy Allies at Jutland*. You can have your pick, and I'll take the other one."

This was a more than generous offer, but I said I didn't feel like reading, either.

"Well, we can't just sit here being mopey," Iggy said reasonably. "Let's do something. What do you want to do?"

This was the opening of the ritual where by rejecting various possibilities—it was too late to go swimming, too hot to play ball, too early to go into the house—we would arrive at a choice. We dutifully went through this process of elimination, and it was Iggy as usual who came up with the choice.

"I know," he said. "Let's go over to Dyker Heights and fish for golf balls. It's pretty near the best time now, anyhow."

He was right about that, because the best time to fish for balls that had been driven into the lone water hazard of the course and never recovered by their owners was at sunset when, chances were, the place would be deserted but there would still be enough light to see by. The way we did this kind of fishing was to pull off our sneakers and stockings, buckle our knickerbockers over our knees, then slowly and speculatively wade through the ooze of the pond, trying to feel out sunken golf balls with our bare feet. It was pleasant work, and occasionally profitable, because the next day any ball you found could be sold to a passing golfer for five cents. I don't remember how we came to fix on the price of five cents as a fair one, but there it was. The golfers seemed to be satisfied with it, and we certainly were.

In all our fishing that summer I don't believe we found more than a total of half a dozen balls, but thirty cents was largesse in those days. My share went fast enough for anything that struck my fancy; Iggy, however, had a great dream. What he wanted more than anything else in the world was a golf club, and every cent he could scrape together was deposited in a tin can with a hole punched in its top and its seam bound with bicycle tape.

He would never open the can, but would shake it now and then to estimate its contents. It was his theory that when the can was full to the top it would hold just about enough to pay for the putter he had picked out in the window of Leo's Sporting Goods Store on 86th Street. Two or three times a week he would have me walk with him down to Leo's, so that we could see the putter, and in between he would talk about it at length, and demonstrate the proper grip for holding it, and the way you have to line up a long putt on a rolling green. Iggy Kovac was the first person I knew—and I have known many since—who was really golf crazy. But I think that his case was the most unique, considering that at the time he had never in his life even had his hands on a real club.

So that evening, knowing how he felt about it, I said all right, if he wanted to go fish for golf balls I would go with him. It wasn't much of a walk down Bath Avenue; the only hard part was when we entered the course at its far side where we had to climb over mountains of what was politely called "fill." It made hot and smoky going, then there was a swampy patch, and finally the course itself and the water hazard.

I've never been back there since that day, but not long ago I happened to read an article about the Dyker Heights golf course in some magazine or other. According to the article, it was now the busiest public golf course in the world. Its eighteen well kept greens were packed with players from dawn to dusk, and on weekends you had to get in line at the clubhouse at three or four o'clock in the morning if you wanted a chance to play a round.

Well, each to his own taste, but it wasn't like that when Iggy and I used to fish for golf balls there. For one thing, I don't think it had eighteen holes; I seem to remember it as a nine-hole layout. For another thing, it was usually pretty empty, either because not many people in Brooklyn played golf in those days, or because it was not a very enticing spot at best.

The fact is, it smelled bad. They were reclaiming the swampy land all around it by filling it with refuse, and the smoldering fires in the refuse laid a black pall over the place. No matter when you went there, there was that dirty haze in the air around you, and in a few minutes you'd find your eyes smarting and your nose full of a curious acrid smell.

Not that we minded it, Iggy and I. We accepted it casually as part of the scenery, as much a part as the occasional Mack truck loaded with trash that would rumble along the dirt road to the swamp, its chain-drive chattering and whining as it went. The only thing we did mind sometimes was the heat of the refuse underfoot when we climbed over it. We never dared enter the course from the clubhouse side; the attendant there had once caught us in the pond trying to plunder his preserve, and we knew he had us marked. The back entrance may have been hotter, but it was the more practical way in.

When we reached the pond there was no one else in sight. It was a hot, still evening with a flaming-red sun now dipping toward the horizon, and once we had our sneakers and stockings off—long, black cotton stockings they were—we wasted no time wading into the water. It felt good, too, as did the slick texture of the mud oozing up between my toes when I pressed down. I suspect that I had the spirit of the true fisherman in me then. The pleasure lay in the activity, not in the catch.

Still, the catch made a worthy objective, and the idea was to walk along with slow, probing steps, and to stop whenever you felt anything small and solid underfoot. I had just stopped short with the excited feeling that I had pinned down a golf ball in the muck when I heard the sound of a motor moving along the dirt track nearby. My first thought was that it was one of the dump trucks carrying another load to add to the mountain of fill, but then I knew that it didn't sound like a Mack truck.

I looked around to see what kind of car it was, still keeping my foot planted on my prize, but the row of bunkers between the pond and the road blocked my view. Then the sound of the motor suddenly stopped, and that was all I needed to send me splashing out of the water in a panic. All Iggy needed, too, for that matter. In one second we had grabbed up our shoes and stockings and headed around the corner of the nearest bunker where we would be out of sight. In about five more seconds we had our stockings and shoes on without even bothering to dry our legs, ready to take flight if anyone approached.

The reason we moved so fast was simply that we weren't too clear about our legal right to fish for golf balls. Iggy and I had talked it over a couple of times, and while he vehemently maintained that we had every right to—there were the balls, with nobody but the dopey caretaker doing anything about it—he admitted that the smart thing was not to put the theory to the test, but to work at our trade unobserved. And I am sure that when the car stopped nearby he had the same idea I did: somebody had reported us, and now the long hand of authority was reaching out for us.

So we waited, crouching in breathless silence against the grassy wall of the bunker, until Iggy could not contain himself any longer. He crawled on hands and knees to the corner of the bunker and peered around it toward the road. "Holy smoke, look at that!" he whispered in an awed voice, and waggled his hand at me to come over.

I looked over his shoulder, and with shocked disbelief I saw a grey Packard, a car with double running-boards, one mounted over the other, the only car of its kind I had ever seen. There was no mistaking it, and there was no mistaking Mr. Rose who stood with two men near it, talking to the smaller one of them, and making angry chopping motions of his hand as he talked.

Looking back now, I think that what made the scene such a strange one was its setting. There was the deserted golf course all around us, and the piles of smoldering fill in the distance, everything seeming so raw and uncitylike and made crimson by the setting sun; and there in the middle of it was this sleek car and the three men with straw hats and jackets and neckties, all looking completely out of place.

Even more fascinating was the smell of danger around them, because while I couldn't hear what was being said I could see that Mr. Rose was in the same mood he had been in when he caught Iggy and me in his driveway. The big man next to him said almost nothing, but the little man Mr. Rose was talking to shook his head, tried to answer, and kept backing away slowly, so that Mr. Rose had to follow him. Then suddenly the little man wheeled around and ran right toward the bunker where Iggy and I were hidden.

We ducked back, but he ran past the far side of it, and he was almost past the pond when the big man caught up with him and grabbed him, Mr. Rose running up after them with his hat in his hand. That is when we could have got away without being seen, but we didn't. We crouched there spellbound, watching something we would never have dreamed of seeing—grown-ups having it out right in front of us the way it happens in the movies.

I was, as I have said, twelve years old that summer. I can now mark it as the time I learned that there was a difference between seeing things in the movies and seeing them in real life. Because never in watching the most bruising movie, with Tom Mix or Hoot Gibson or any of my heroes, did I feel what I felt there watching what happened to that little man. And I think that Iggy must have felt it even more acutely than I did, because he was so small and skinny himself, and while he was tough in a fight he was always being outweighed and overpowered. He must have felt that he was right there inside that little man, his arms pinned tight behind his back by the bully who had grabbed him, while Mr. Rose hit him back and forth with an open hand across the face, snarling at him all the while.

"You dirty dog," Mr. Rose said. "Do you know who I am? Do you think I'm one of those lousy small-time bootleggers you double-cross for the fun of it? *This* is who I am!" And with the little man screaming and kicking out at him he started punching away as hard as he could at the belly and face until the screaming and kicking suddenly stopped. Then he jerked his head toward the pond, and his pal heaved the little man right into it headfirst, the straw hat flying off and bobbing up and down in the water a few feet away.

They stood watching until the man in the water managed to get on his hands and knees, blowing out dirty water, shaking his head in a daze, and then without another word they walked off toward the car. I heard its doors slam, and the roar of the motor as it moved off, and then the sound faded away.

All I wanted to do then was get away from there. What I had just seen was too much to comprehend or even believe in; it was like waking up from a nightmare to find it real. Home was where I wanted to be.

I stood up cautiously, but before I could scramble off to home and safety, Iggy clutched the back of my shirt so hard that he almost pulled me down on top of him.

"What're you doing?" he whispered hotly. "Where do you think you're going?"

I pulled myself free. "Are you crazy?" I whispered back. "You expect to hang around here all night? I'm going home, that's where I'm going."

Iggy's face was ashy white, his nostrils flaring. "But that guy's hurt. You just gonna let him stay there?"

"Sure I'm gonna let him stay there. What's it my business?"

"You saw what happened. You think it's right to beat up a guy like that?"

What he said and the way he said it in a tight, choked voice made me wonder if he really had gone crazy just then. I said weakly, "It's none of my business, that's all. Anyhow, I have to go home. My folks'll be sore if I don't get home on time."

Iggy pointed an accusing finger at me. "All right, if that's the way you feel!" he said, and then before I could stop him he turned and dashed out of concealment toward the pond. Whether it was the sense of being left alone in a hostile world, or whether it was some wild streak of loyalty that acted on me, I don't know. But I hesitated only an instant and then ran after him.

He stood at the edge of the pond looking at the man in it who was still on his hands and knees and shaking his head vaguely from side to side. "Hey, mister," Iggy said, and there was none of the assurance in his voice that there had been before, "are you hurt?"

The man looked slowly around at us, and his face was fearful to behold. It was bruised and swollen and glassy-eyed, and his dripping hair hung in long strings down his forehead. It was enough to make Iggy and me back up a step, the way he looked.

With a great effort he pushed himself to his feet and stood there swaying. Then he lurched forward, staring at us blindly, and we hastily backed up a few more steps. He stopped short and suddenly reached down and scooped up a handful of mud from under the water.

"Get out of here!" he cried out like a woman screaming. "Get out of here, you little sneaks!"—and without warning flung the mud at us.

It didn't hit me, but it didn't have to. I let out one yell of panic and ran wildly, my heart thudding, my legs pumping as fast as they could. Iggy was almost at my shoulder—I could hear him gasping as we climbed the smoldering hill of refuse that barred the way to the avenue, slid down the other side in a cloud of dirt and ashes, and raced toward the avenue without looking back. It was only when we reached the first street-light that we stopped and stood there trembling, our mouths wide open, trying to suck in air, our clothes fouled from top to bottom.

But the shock I had undergone was nothing compared to what I felt when Iggy finally got his wind back enough to speak up.

"Did you see that guy?" he said, still struggling for breath. "Did you see what they did to him? Come on, I'm gonna tell the cops."

I couldn't believe my ears. "The cops? What do you want to get mixed up with the cops for? What do you care what they did to him, for Pete's sake?"

"Because they beat him up, didn't they? And the cops can stick them in jail for fifty years if somebody tells them, and I'm a witness. I saw what happened and so did you. So you're a witness, too."

I didn't like it. I certainly had no sympathy for the evil-looking apparition from which I had just fled, and, more than that, I balked at the idea of having anything to do with the police. Not that I had ever had any trouble with them. It was just that, like most other kids I knew, I was nervous in the presence of a police uniform. It left me even more mystified by Iggy than ever. The idea of any kid voluntarily walking up to report something to a policeman was beyond comprehension.

I said bitterly, "All right, so I'm a witness. But why can't the guy that got beat up go and tell the cops about it? Why do we have to go and do it?"

"Because he wouldn't tell anybody about it. Didn't you see the way he was scared of Mr. Rose? You think it's all right for Mr. Rose to go around like that, beating up anybody he wants to, and nobody does anything about it?"

Then I understood. Beneath all this weird talk, this sudden access of nobility, was solid logic, something I could get hold of. It was not the man in the water Iggy was concerned with, it was himself. Mr. Rose had pushed *him* around, and now he had a perfect way of getting even.

I didn't reveal this thought to Iggy, though, because when your best friend has been shoved around and humiliated in front of you, you don't want to remind him of it. But at least it put everything into proper perspective. Somebody hurts you, so you hurt him back, and that's all there is to it.

It also made it much easier to go along with Iggy in his plan. I wasn't really being called on to ally myself with some stupid grown-up who had got into trouble with Mr. Rose; I was being a good pal to Iggy.

All of a sudden, the prospect of walking into the police station and telling my story to somebody seemed highly intriguing. And, the reassuring thought went, far in back of my head, none of this could mean trouble for me later on, because tomorrow I was moving to Manhattan anyhow, wasn't I?

So I was right there, a step behind Iggy, when we walked up between the two green globes which still seemed vaguely menacing to me, and into the police station. There was a tall desk there, like a judge's bench, at which a grey-haired man sat writing, and at its foot was another desk at which sat a very fat uniformed man reading a magazine. He put the magazine down when we approached and looked at us with raised eyebrows.

"Yeah?" he said. "What's the trouble?"

I had been mentally rehearsing a description of what I had seen back there on the golf course, but I never had a chance to speak my piece. Iggy started off with a rush, and there was no way of getting a word in. The fat man listened with a puzzled expression, every now and then pinching his lower lip between his thumb and fore-finger. Then he looked up at the one behind the tall desk and said, "Hey, sergeant, here's a couple of kids say they saw an assault over at Dyker Heights. You want to listen to this?"

The sergeant didn't even look at us, but kept on writing. "Why?" he said. "What's wrong with your ears?"

The fat policeman leaned back in his chair and smiled. "I don't know," he said, "only it seems to me some guy named Rose is mixed up in this."

The sergeant suddenly stopped writing. "What's that?" he said.

"Some guy named Rose," the fat policeman said, and he appeared to be enjoying himself a good deal. "You know anybody with that name who drives a big grey Packard?"

The sergeant motioned with his head for us to come right up to the platform his desk was on. "All right, kid," he said to Iggy, "what's bothering you?"

So Iggy went through it again, and when he was finished the sergeant just sat there looking at him, tapping his pen on the desk. He looked at him so long and kept tapping that pen so steadily—tap, tap, tap—that my skin started to crawl. It didn't surprise me when he finally said to Iggy in a hard voice, "You're a pretty wise kid."

"What do you mean?" Iggy said. "I *saw* it!" He pointed at me. "He saw it, too. He'll tell you!"

I braced myself for the worst and then noted with relief that the sergeant was paying no attention to me. He shook his head at Iggy and said, "I do the telling around here, kid. And I'm telling you you've got an awful big mouth for someone your size. Don't you have more sense than to go around trying to get people into trouble?"

This, I thought, was the time to get away from there, because if I ever needed proof that you don't mix into grown-up business I had it now. But Iggy didn't budge. He was always pretty good at arguing himself out of spots where he was wrong; now that he knew he was right he was getting hot with outraged virtue.

"Don't you believe me?" he demanded. "For Pete's sake, I was right there when it happened! I was this close!"

The sergeant looked like a thundercloud. "All right, you were that close," he said. "Now beat it, kid, and keep that big mouth shut. I got no time to fool around any more. Go on, get out of here."

Iggy was so enraged that not even the big gold badge a foot from his nose could intimidate him now. "I don't care if you don't believe me!" he said. "There's plenty other people'll believe me. Wait'll I tell my father. You'll see!"

I could hear my ears ringing in the silence that followed. The sergeant sat staring at Iggy, and Iggy, a little scared by his own outburst, stared back. He must have had the same idea I did then. Yelling at a cop was probably as bad as hitting one, and we'd both end up in jail for the rest of our lives. Not for a second did I feel any of the righteous indignation Iggy did. As far as I was concerned, he had led me into this trap, and I was going to pay for his lunacy. I guess I hated him then even more than the sergeant did.

It didn't help any when the sergeant finally turned to the fat policeman with the air of a man who had made up his mind.

"Take the car and drive over to Rose's place," he said. "You can explain all this to him, and ask him to come along back with you.

Oh, yes, and get this kid's name and address, and bring his father along, too. Then we'll see."

So I had my first and only experience of sitting on a bench in a police station watching the pendulum of the big clock on the wall swinging back and forth, and recounting all my past sins to myself. It couldn't have been more than a half hour before the fat policeman walked in with Mr. Rose and Iggy's father, but it seemed like a year. And a long, miserable year at that.

The surprising thing was the way Mr. Rose looked. I had half expected them to bring him in fighting and struggling, because while the sergeant may not have believed Iggy's story Mr. Rose would know it was so.

But far from struggling, Mr. Rose looked as if he had dropped in for a friendly visit. He was dressed in a fine summer suit and sporty-looking black-and-white shoes and he was smoking a cigar. He was perfectly calm and pleasant, and, in some strange way, he almost gave the impression that he was in charge there.

It was different with Iggy's father. Mr. Kovac must have been reading the paper out on the porch in his undershirt, because his regular shirt had been stuffed into his pants carelessly and part of it hung out. And from his manner you'd think that he was the one who had done something wrong. He kept swallowing hard, and twisting his neck in his collar, and now and then glancing nervously at Mr. Rose. He didn't look at all impressive as he did at other times.

The sergeant pointed at Iggy. "All right, kid," he said, "now tell everybody here what you told me. Stand up so we can all hear it."

Since Iggy had already told it twice he really had it down pat now, and he told it without a break from start to finish, no one interrupting him. And all the while Mr. Rose stood there listening politely, and Mr. Kovac kept twisting his neck in his collar.

When Iggy was finished the sergeant said, "I'll put it to you straight out, Mr. Rose. Were you near that golf course today?"

Mr. Rose smiled. "I was not," he said.

"Of course not," said the sergeant. "But you can see what we're up against here."

"Sure I can," said Mr. Rose. He went over to Iggy and put a hand on his shoulder. "And you know what?" he said. "I don't even blame the kid for trying this trick. He and I had a little trouble some time back about the way he was always climbing over my car, and I guess he's just trying to get square with me. I'd say he's got a lot of spirit in him. Don't you, sonny?" he asked, squeezing Iggy's shoulder in a friendly way.

I was stunned by the accuracy of this shot, but Iggy reacted like a firecracker going off. He pulled away from Mr. Rose's hand and ran over to his father. "I'm *not* lying!" he said desperately and grabbed Mr. Kovac's shirt, tugging at it. "Honest to God, Pop, we both saw it. Honest to God, Pop!"

Mr. Kovac looked down at him and then looked around at all of us. When his eyes were on Mr. Rose it seemed as if his collar was tighter than ever. Meanwhile, Iggy was pulling at his shirt, yelling that we saw it, we saw it, and he wasn't lying, until Mr. Kovac shook him once, very hard, and that shut him up.

"Iggy," said Mr. Kovac, "I don't want you to go around telling stories about people. Do you hear me?"

Iggy heard him, all right. He stepped back as if he had been walloped across the face, and then stood there looking at Mr. Kovac in a funny way. He didn't say anything, didn't even move when Mr. Rose came up and put a hand on his shoulder again.

"You heard your father, didn't you, kid?" Mr. Rose said.

Iggy still didn't say anything.

"Sure you did," Mr. Rose said. "And you and I understand each other a lot better now, kiddo, so there's no hard feelings. Matter of fact, any time you want to come over to the house you come on over, and I'll bet there's plenty of odd jobs you can do there. I pay good, too, so don't you worry about that." He reached into his pocket and took out a bill. "Here," he said, stuffing it into Iggy's hand, "this'll give you an idea. Now go on out and have yourself some fun."

Iggy looked at the money like a sleepwalker. I was baffled by that. As far as I could see, this was the business, and here was Iggy in a daze, instead of openly rejoicing. It was only when the sergeant spoke to us that he seemed to wake up.

"All right, you kids," the sergeant said, "beat it home now. The rest of us got some things to talk over."

I didn't need a second invitation. I got out of there in a hurry and went down the street fast, with Iggy tagging along behind me not saying a word. It was three blocks down and one block over, and I didn't slow down until I was in front of my house again. I had never appreciated those familiar outlines and the lights in the windows any more than I did at that moment. But I didn't go right in. It suddenly struck me that this was the last time I'd be seeing Iggy, so I waited there awkwardly. I was never very good at saying good-byes.

"That was all right," I said finally. "I mean Mr. Rose giving you that dollar. That's as good as twenty golf balls."

"Yeah?" said Iggy, and he was looking at me in the same funny way he had looked at his father. "I'll bet it's as good as a whole new golf club. Come on down to Leo's with me, and I'll show you."

I wanted to, but I wanted to get inside the house even more. "Ahh, my folks'll be sore if I stay out too late tonight," I said. "Anyhow, you can't buy a club for a dollar. You'll need way more than that."

"You think so?" Iggy said, and then held out his hand and slowly opened it so that I could see what he was holding. It was not a one-dollar bill. It was, to my awe, a five-dollar bill.

That, as my wife said, was a long time ago. Thirty-five years before a photograph was taken of little Ignace Kovac, a man wise in the way of the rackets, slumped in a death agony over the wheel of his big car, a bullet hole in the middle of his forehead, a bag of golf clubs leaning against the seat next to him. Thirty-five years before I understood the meaning of the last things said and done when we faced each other on a street in Brooklyn, and then went off, each in his own direction.

I gaped at the money in Iggy's hand. It was the hoard of Croesus, and its very magnitude alarmed me.

"Hey," I said. "That's five bucks. That's a lot of money! You better give it to your old man, or he'll really jump on you."

Then I saw to my surprise that the hand holding the money was shaking. Iggy was suddenly shuddering all over as if he had just plunged into icy water.

"My old man?" he yelled wildly at me, and his lips drew back, showing his teeth clenched together hard, as if that could stop the shuddering. "You know what I'll do if my old man tries anything? I'll tell Mr. Rose on him, that's what! Then you'll see!"

And wheeled and ran blindly away from me down the street to his destiny.

"Q"

Margery Sharp

The Perfect Model

The Poule d'Argent was one of the best restaurants in London. It never advertised, and was always full. The cooking and service were admirable, the decorations—silvery walls and sea-green hangings—had a peculiar elegance. No cabaret was offered, but in the evenings a discreetly persuasive band matched the small but perfect floor. It was characteristic of the place that there was very little dancing between courses; for one thing, the food was too good to be trifled with; and for another, a rumor had gone round that Raoul did not approve.

If M. Raoul disapproved of you, it was wise to give up, at once, all hope of ever eating at the Poule d'Argent again.

For Raoul was the maître d'hôtel and the genius of the place. Some said he was the proprietor as well, but not even the boldest had ever cared to question him directly. His urbanity was equaled only by his aloofness; his manner, though exquisitely suave, was also commanding; and though urbanity and aloofness, suavity and force may seem qualities hardly compatible with each other, the fact remains that they were all four perfectly apparent, and perfectly harmonized whenever Raoul showed a debutante to her seat.

"He's got a remarkable face," said Rabin the artist to his friend Murdoch the playwright. "I'd like to do a drawing of him. A big thing. Line and wash." And he began making lines with his thumbnail on the sea-green tablecloth.

"Why don't you?" asked Murdoch idly. "He'd probably be only too flattered to sit."

"Not he. To Augustus John, perhaps, but not to a commercial bloke like me." And Rabin grinned cheerfully, for though his art was undoubtedly commercial—otherwise, indeed, he would scarcely have been able to pay for two lunches at the Poule d'Argent—it was also extremely intelligent and often beautiful. He was a caricaturist, finding most of his subjects in the theater; and as a star of revue at that moment swept in, his hand moved instinctively to another patch of cloth.

"This ought to be one of your happy hunting grounds," said Murdoch.

Rabin nodded. That was one reason why he had become an habitué: the Poule d'Argent had a knack of attracting not only beauty, but also character. One saw there city magnates and foreign musicians, publishers, diplomats, surgeons, and K.C.s; and one saw also a sprinkling of countrified old ladies in expensive but dowdy hats. A pair of them—the Misses Frewen, of Fosgate Hall—had drifted in by accident soon after the place was opened; and Raoul had made them so comfortable and so much at home that they had been sending their friends there ever since.

"There's old Williams," said Murdoch.

But Rabin did not turn. He knew old Williams too well, and had never found his face particularly interesting. It was smooth and placid, supported by a stiff white collar, topped by stiff white hair, and but for these two boundary-marks, so to speak, almost completely characterless. Yet Mr. Williams, of Hammer House, Oxfordshire, was in his own way famous; he was a connoisseur of Georgian silver, and, with means to gratify his taste, had made himself a definite niche in the world of London sale-rooms. He had, too, an amiable habit, if he had bought anything in the morning, of bringing it along with him to lunch: porringers, cream-jugs, Mr. Williams carried them away in his hand like a child with a new toy, and as soon as he sat down drew the object from its case or chamois bag, and set it up before him on the table. Then indeed did his mild eyes light up and his face wreathe itself in smiles; he looked about eagerly to see his treasure admired. In this the countrified ladies, when present, never failed to gratify him, and it was said that with several of them he had struck up quite a warm friendship, based on hallmarks. Otherwise he had to rely upon M. Raoul, who—inevitably—appeared to know almost as much about silver as did Mr. Williams himself. The maître d'hôtel was a perfect Admirable Crichton.

Slightly bored by his companion's silence, Murdoch ostentatiously hailed a pageboy and asked to be given a paper. He had already seen all the chief news, and accordingly turned through the sheets reading desultorily here and there in the hope of some item that would catch his interest.

"Nothing but burglaries," he announced at last; he had the irritating habit of reading bits aloud. " 'Daring Jewel Theft Lady Relton's loss . . . Lady Relton's emerald pendant . . .' "

Rabin looked up.

"Silly old goose," he said unsympathetically. "I don't wonder she got it pinched. The thing must be worth thousands, and she wore it here one night on a thin platinum chain about two yards long. I've never seen Raoul look so worried in his life."

"A nasty object to have lost on one's premises," agreed Murdoch.

"It damn nearly was. She was dancing and somehow snapped the chain; got back to her table, too, before she even noticed. Then just as she let out the first shriek, there was Raoul with the thing in his hand. He must have had his eyes on her the whole time. Where was she when she lost it?"

Murdoch consulted the paper again.

"At home. 'Last night, while the occupants of Relton Lodge were at dinner, the safe in Lady Relton's bedroom was rifled and her famous emerald pendant—' "

A voice at his elbow—a voice suave, charming, slightly authoritative—interrupted him.

"Coffee, messieurs?"

"Yes, black," said Rabin, while Murdoch hastily shifted his gaze to another paragraph. He had a feeling that Raoul would probably consider Police Court news out of keeping with the atmosphere of the Poule d'Argent.

"I wonder what he does in his spare time?" mused Rabin aloud.

"He hasn't any."

"He must have. He isn't always here, though I don't think he takes any regular day off. And the relaxations of a fellow like that should be at least interesting."

"He's probably the henpecked husband of a plain wife," said Murdoch, who had written three successful plays on that one theme. It now struck him that the time was perhaps ripe for a fourth, and he lapsed into meditation.

During the days that followed, both men kept an eye open for any further news of the Relton emeralds, but their recovery was nowhere reported and the press seemed to have lost all interest in them. Several other burglaries were reported, however, and Murdoch noticed that as often as not the victim was an habitué of his favorite restaurant. It began to look as though the Poule d'Argent had something unlucky about it; on the other hand, it was obvious that since all its clients were persons of wealth, they in any case formed a class specially likely to be burgled. Then, some time later, Murdoch's new play went into rehearsal, and for the next fortnight he wouldn't have bothered if someone stole the Crown jewels.

"You're driving yourself silly," said Rabin, meeting him one night in the bar of the Café Royal. "Why don't you take a day off and leave them to it?"

The dramatist groaned, and all the more bitterly because he knew that the other spoke sense. He had stuck to rehearsals too closely, watching every gesture, listening to every word till neither words nor gestures had any meaning, and till his brain, when asked for an extra line or a change of dialogue, refused to function. So when Rabin proposed to take him the next day for a run in the country—the artist had a passion for autumn motoring—Murdoch willingly agreed.

"We'll start early and get a good run before dark," Rabin had said, but in the morning Murdoch's leading lady insisted on his presence at her dressmaker's, after which he had naturally to take her out to lunch, and four o'clock found the motorists no farther than the Marble Arch. They were in the thick, moreover, of a fine traffic jam that extended (or so it seemed) as far as eye could reach.

"We're here till Doomsday," grumbled Murdoch. "It's my fault, and I apologize, but honestly I think we'd better chuck it. Let's go along to Christie's instead; there's some rather good silver up this afternoon. Old Williams is sure to be there and I'd like to see him do his stuff."

But Rabin was paying no attention. Indeed, he had his head so far out of the window that it seemed likely he had not even heard. Murdoch sat back to wait: he knew that until an artist had finished looking at whatever it was that caught his eye, there was no use shouting at him; and since he himself was often similarly caught up and absorbed by a fragment of overheard dialogue, or by the mannerism of a passerby, he could sympathize.

"What have you seen now?" he asked patiently as Rabin at last drew in his head.

The answer was more interesting than he had expected.

"Our friend Raoul," said Rabin. "In the next car but one. And incognito."

At once—such was the magnetism of that personality—Murdoch craned over and peered through the traffic. He saw a small, rather shabby two-seater driven by a man in a rather shabby cap.

"It isn't!" he said disgustedly.

"I tell you it is."

Murdoch looked again.

"He'd never drive a car like that. He'd never wear a cap like that. Why, it isn't even very like him."

"If I've drawn his face once," said Rabin, "I've drawn it a dozen times. I know the bones. If he looks different, it's partly because of the clothes and partly because he's stopped being the perfect maître d'hôtel. That's what I've always wanted to see—Raoul off duty."

At that moment the car in front began to move, and as they followed the stream they saw the two-seater slip neatly ahead. The confident efficiency of that driving did more to convince Murdoch than any of Rabin's arguments.

"It may be," he admitted, "but all the same it's a dashed queer thing. I wonder where he's going?"

The artist grinned.

"Our way, it looks like. I've a good mind to trail him."

Murdoch sat up. He had no desire to spend the rest of the afternoon in a wild-goose chase round the London suburbs, and he had little confidence in his friend's discretion. Rabin, despite many admirable and attractive qualities, was undeniably a busybody—positively un-English, in fact, in his readiness to risk a snubbing in order to gratify his curiosity. He was the sort of man who didn't mind making a fool of himself. Murdoch, on the other hand, was the sort of man who did.

"Don't be such an ass," he protested as they followed the two-seater round the Marble Arch and into the Edgware Road. "You've got a bee in your bonnet about the man. I've no doubt he's a perfectly ordinary respectable sort of fellow, and whatever he's up to is no business of ours."

"Ah, but you've never really appreciated him," retorted Rabin. "Whatever else he is, I'll swear he's not ordinary. He's got a terrific personality—such an absolute whopper of a personality that he's made the Poule d'Argent his oyster; and I don't believe even that satisfies him. Once or twice lately I've seen him look a bit bored. Majestically bored. Like Alexander sighing for new worlds to conquer."

"You're mad," said Murdoch comfortably. "Running the Poule d'Argent is a job for any man."

"But he does it too easily," insisted the artist. "With one hand, so to speak. What I want to know is what he does with the other. Something either very exciting, or very big. Perhaps he's a power in the city and a director of the Bank."

M. Raoul's immediate actions, however, hardly supported this last hypothesis. His first stop, which occurred some five minutes later, was outside a small public house behind Paddington Station; the Fox and Goose by name, it was definitely not the sort of place to be frequented by financial magnates. He did not go in, but merely halted long enough to take up a passenger—a small, narrow-faced man whose obviously new suit somehow accentuated his general seediness. He greeted M. Raoul with great deference, but wasted no time in conversation, and at once the car moved off.

"How about that?" asked Rabin triumphantly.

"Odd," admitted Murdoch.

"Very odd indeed; an old lag, by the look of him. Feeling any curiosity yet?"

Murdoch did not answer, but he ceased to protest. He still felt slightly uncomfortable about the business, but that last episode had done much to allay his qualms. It was—well, suspicious; and when people acted suspiciously it was practically the duty of a good citizen to keep an eye on them. He sat passively acquiescent, therefore, while Rabin slowed down in the thinning traffic and dropped well behind the quarry, with the acknowledged aim of escaping observation, and presently showed a more active interest by remarking that for so small and ancient a car the two-seater seemed to possess a very fair turn of speed.

"It does indeed," agreed the artist. "Did you see him accelerate? It's my belief that car goes a good deal faster than you'd expect."

The judgment proved correct; as soon as Edgware was left behind, M. Raoul's car shot suddenly ahead. In the unrestricted areas it was doing a good fifty miles an hour, and though Rabin had no difficulty in keeping up he began to be afraid that a sudden spurt would finally shake him off. The two-seater was in no way conspicuous; except for its surprising speed, it resembled dozens of other cars of the same popular make and once lost would be almost impossible to find again. Little by little, therefore, Rabin crept up till he was no more than twenty yards behind.

"It's getting damned cold," said Murdoch, with a shiver. "I'd like to know where he's making for."

"You'd better pray for a weekend cottage near Tring," replied the artist.

Murdoch sneezed.

"Let's chuck it," he said imploringly. "I'm frozen stiff, and after all it's damned silly. The fellow probably *has* a weekend cottage; he's probably just going down to take a look at it."

But Rabin only grinned.

"With an ex-convict to buttle?" he said. "Not likely. If you want to cry off I'll put you down at the next A.A. box and you can phone to a garage for a car."

Murdoch was too much annoyed to answer, but merely slumped down as far as possible in the seat, dug his chin into the collar of his overcoat, and closed his eyes. He was very tired, and in spite of cold, irritation, and general discomfort presently dropped into a deep sleep.

He was awakened about an hour and a half later by the sudden silence of the engine. Rabin had stopped the car outside a good-sized village inn—not on the lighted stretch of gravel that served as car-park but in the darkness beyond.

"Good idea," said Murdoch, preparing to get out. "Mine's a double whiskey. Where are we?"

Rabin unceremoniously thrust him back.

"You're not going in," he said callously, "and I think we're some-where in Oxfordshire. You wait there. And you needn't worry, be-cause I'm not going in either. I'm just going to see what Raoul has been looking at."

Murdoch looked towards the inn again and saw a tall silhouette move away from one of the windows. The next minute there was the sound of an engine being accelerated and Rabin strolled across the gravel. He was back almost at once.

"Nothing out of the way," he reported, starting the car, "except one big fellow sleepy-drunk."

"And nothing particularly out of the way about that," snapped Murdoch crossly.

"Except—thank heaven no one can go fast in these lanes!—except that he looked like a manservant. Black jacket and all the rest. Gentlemen's gentlemen don't usually get tight at the local. On the other hand, he might have met an old friend, because there were a couple of obvious townees. The one thing certain is that from where Raoul was standing he got a good clear view of the party . . . By gum, look at that!"

The lane had suddenly twisted; immediately ahead, pulled in well to one side, stood an unoccupied two-seater. Rabin drove slowly by and within fifty yards found himself on a main road. It was plain that no one contemplating that route would first have abandoned his car, and Rabin took the hint.

"This is where we get out," he said, backing up the lane again, "and I believe Raoul's chosen the best parking place. Or at any rate the least conspicuous. There was a sort of drive to the right as we passed his car, but anyone using that would be most likely to come from the road. The lane's simply a shortcut to the pub."

With exemplary courtesy, he brought his car to a stop well behind the two-seater, and so close to the hedge that Murdoch had to follow him out across the driving-seat. Rabin reached back into the pocket and there found a torch, which was lucky, since without it they would scarcely have been able to make out the small, dilapidated finger-post that leaned among the bushes at the opening of the drive.

"To Hammer House," read Murdoch. "Good Lord—isn't that old Williams's place?"

Rabin nodded.

"It is. And it's almost a dead cert that Williams is still in town. If our fellow wants to pay a social call, he's showing unusual lack of intelligence."

Then, as they followed the drive, they instinctively stopped talking.

Hammer House, despite its imposing name, was little more than a large cottage, but it presented a lovely example of the black-and-white style. Even through the dusk there was no mistaking its perfect proportions; the deep thatch showed smooth and solid, the white plaster and black beams made a fine conspicuous pattern, and it was evident that Mr. Williams spared no expense in the upkeep of his dwelling.

He's a connoisseur, all right, thought Rabin, with unenvious pleasure, for it was good to see such a place safe in appreciative hands. What a setting, too, for that collection of silver! The house was no doubt as perfect inside as out, and Rabin could imagine the old man pottering through the exquisite rooms in perpetual contemplation of his shining treasures. Lucky they're not fragile, added Rabin mentally. I wonder who looks after him? Then he remembered the manservant at the inn; unintoxicated, he would fit in very well with Mr. Williams and Hammer House, though at the moment patently neglecting his duty—as Raoul, if he knew anything about the household, must have seen.

A fantastic suspicion crossed Rabin's mind: it occurred to him that M. Raoul might indirectly have been paying for the manservant's drinks. Before he had time to reject, or even to consider the idea, however, Murdoch spoke.

"A dashed nice little place," he commented softly.

Rabin took a step forward.

"Let's go round. I want to see the back."

To avoid passing too close to the house, they essayed a narrow sapling-bordered path which appeared to follow the edge of the lawn, but which, after the first few yards, began to wind so unnecessarily and persistently that Rabin had little hesitation in identifying it as a Wilderness Walk on the Victorian model. It corkscrewed through a spinney, struck boldly out to the right, and finally looped round again to be brought to an ignominious end by a small wicket gate. Looking across this, the two men found that they had made a half circuit not only of the house but of the grounds as well; they were standing at the bottom of a rose garden and their devious approach had given them at least this advantage, that they were able to observe unseen, and unsuspected, the remarkable proceedings of M. Raoul.

He was engaged in burglary.

As might have been expected, he engaged in it with the utmost dignity.

There was no vulgar breaking of locks or shinning of waterpipes; a window had indeed by some means been forced, but it was the seedy little confederate who scrambled through. M. Raoul simply waited patiently until the back door was opened to him and then walked quietly in.

Down by the gate, Murdoch, who had unconsciously been holding his breath, let out a long astonished sigh.

"Good Lord! Did you see that?"

"Yes," said Rabin—but in a very different tone. "It was charming."

The dramatist swung round.

"Charming be hanged! We ought to go for the police!"

"You can. You'd better take the car and get back to the pub, or else try for a phone box on that road. I'll stay here. I might be able to stop him getting away. And besides, I want to *see* him."

Murdoch looked at his friend suspiciously. He had an artistic temperament himself—but not to that extent.

"If I come back and find you an accessory," he warned, "there'll be no bailing you out."

Rabin laughed.

"As a proof of my good faith," he said, "let me recommend that you pause by the other car, find a spanner, and take the top off the carburetor . . ."

Rabin's subsequent adventures, from the time Murdoch left him until the extraordinarily prompt arrival of the police, occupied no more than ten minutes, but every moment was packed with interest. As a beginning, he went quietly up through the rose garden and investigated the back door. It was closed, but not locked; Rabin pushed it open, stepped inside, and thrust it to again. Within, all was dark save for a square of light high up at the other end of the passage. Keeping close to the wall, the artist stole towards it. He stumbled once, but without noise, against what felt like a large chest, edged past, and reached a second door. The light came from a small window or peephole cut in it at the height of a man's head and towards this Rabin, with infinite precaution, approached and applied his eye.

Luck was with him. The first thing he saw was a back.

It was the back of M. Raoul. The smaller man, seen in profile, was fully occupied in opening a safe.

Now there occurs sometimes in real life a situation so obviously reminiscent of the stage or the novelet that the spectator cannot take it seriously. If it be tragic, he cannot weep; if threatening, he cannot feel afraid; and so it was now with Rabin. He stood there watching with as calm (though intense) an interest as if he had been seated in an orchestral stall.

He took it all in. He noted the reason for the pierced door: the window was there to give light, since the room into which he was looking had been built in the thickness of the house, with walls, save for one other door, completely blank; and also for ventilation, since there was an arrangement by which the pane of glass could be lifted. The room itself was furnished, with a good deal of taste, as a gentleman's study.

Against this setting the two persons of the drama had a most piquant incongruity. The tall back of M. Raoul—it never occurred to Rabin that he might turn round—was distinguished but shabby; the little man at the safe might have stepped straight out of a thriller. He was so neat, so skillful; he worked with a queer contented smile; his fingers fluttered, his ears as he listened seemed to cock like a terrier's before a rat-hole; and every now and then he glanced up to make sure of his companion's attention. It was almost a pity that he never noticed Rabin, for he would no doubt have found the expression on the artist's face extremely gratifying.

At last the door of the safe swung open: the little man stepped back, his look a curious mingling of pride and contempt—pride in his own skill, contempt for the simplicity of the job; and Rabin very nearly applauded. M. Raoul, however, spared no more than a casually approving nod before he stepped forward and thrust in his hand. What he brought out was no fine piece of silver, but a jewel case.

Rabin waited eagerly. On the stage, on the films, a successful burglar at this point always took a moment off to display his booty—to let the rope of pearls slide through his fingers, to flash the tiara in the best light: M. Raoul did nothing of the sort. He did indeed open the case, but so swiftly and discreetly that the safe-breaker evidently saw nothing and the artist no more than a prismatic flash. Then the case was slipped into his pocket, and it seemed that the show was over.

Never in his life had Rabin's mind or body moved so swiftly as during the next few minutes. The mood of cool spectatorship dropped from him: he, too, had a part in the play, but it necessitated a change of scene. His first and most urgent thought was to get out of the passage before M. Raoul entered it; he had no intention of taking on two men in so small a space. Outside in the darkness there was at least a chance of knocking M. Raoul out with a flying tackle, snatching the case, and getting away to the car; and Rabin was out in the garden again before he remembered that the car had in all probability been taken by Murdoch.

Damn! thought Rabin, running for the shadow of the trees. I'll have to sit on his head till that fool turns up with the police. And if the little fellow gets away, I can't help it.

This hare-brained plan seemed, at that melodramatic moment, perfectly feasible, and Rabin was never disillusioned, since before he could put it into action, and as he plunged through the belt of trees, someone tackled him. Oddly enough, it was exactly the tackle he had himself contemplated—low down, from behind. Rabin pitched forward on his head and took no further interest in the proceedings.

When he came to again he found himself very comfortable except for a heavy weight behind his eyes. He was stretched out on a sofa, and as he lay there on his back he could see, by turning his eyes to the right, a high mantelshelf ranged with some very beautiful silver. To the left, beyond the sofa-back, he was vaguely conscious of two figures, one wearing an ordinary bobby's helmet, the other the flat cap of an inspector.

The police! thought Rabin thankfully. And they've brought me into the house.

He tried to raise himself to see more, but the exceeding heaviness of his head convinced him that it would be better to lie still. At that moment a voice spoke: he had an idea it proceeded from the inspector, but though the tones—deep, official, and authoritative—were just what might have been expected, the words were not.

"You oughtn't to have done it, Mr. Smith," said the voice reproachfully. "One of these days you'll get into trouble—and then where shall we be?"

The invisible Mr. Smith, however, seemed completely unabashed.

"It was the only way, my dear chap. By the time you fellows had got a search warrant, the bird—or rather the booty—would have flown."

"There you are!" returned the inspector, half mollified, half resentful. "*You* can act on suspicion—if you'll take the risk—we can't. Even watching the house was a risk for us. We've got to be very careful. If we so much as hurt a gentleman's feelings there's questions in Parliament. And when it's such a gentleman as *he* seemed—!"

The gentleman addressed as Mr. Smith laughed.

"All so genuine, wasn't it? This place, and the touch about collecting silver. He's a genuine connoisseur, pays in genuine cash, and has got a genuine reputation by it . . . I suppose you know where to lay your hands on him now all right?"

"Naturally we do, sir." The inspector sounded a trifle hurt. "He's at Black's Hotel—and the cheek of it, leaving the stuff down here while he spends the night in London! Audacious, as you might say! But you needn't worry, sir; audacious as he is, you needn't worry at all."

"I won't," promised Mr. Smith. "I shall go straight back to town and give my thoughts exclusively to my dinner."

The weight on Rabin's brain suddenly increased. For a moment he struggled against it, straining his ears. Was that second voice familiar, or wasn't it? It had no trace of foreign accent, as had M. Raoul's; it was crisper, lighter, yet with a certain similarity of inflection. Was it, or wasn't it? Was it, or—

The weight crushed down again, and Rabin wondered no more.

Five minutes later, when he finally recovered his wits, the room was empty save for a large and apologetic sergeant. It was he, apparently, who had been responsible for Rabin's mishap, and he earnestly hoped that the gentleman bore no ill will.

"That's all right," said Rabin, rising rather groggily to his feet. "If I get in the way of you fellows, I must take the consequences."

"Not at all, sir; we always like to encourage public spirit," returned the sergeant kindly. "Do you think you feel well enough for your friend to drive you home?"

"Perfectly," said Rabin. "By the way, what was it all about?"

"Just a little matter of duty, sir. If you're quite sure you're all right—"

"Who was the tall fellow I saw?"

"Tall?" repeated the sergeant vaguely. "Why, that would be the inspector, sir. Inspector Musgrove. And now, sir—"

"I don't mean the inspector," persisted Rabin, "I mean the fellow I saw break in."

With great firmness the sergeant assisted him towards the door.

"That's just what we mustn't tell you, sir. You'll see all about it in the papers—all that's necessary, that is. But we're very grateful to you, sir, and I've no doubt you're wanting to be off."

Rabin went. The leavetaking was marked, on the official side, by great affability, on the artist's by a certain sulkiness. Murdoch, who had brought the car up to the front door, was more resigned.

"It's no good," he said when he had digested Rabin's information without offering any in exchange. "You never get anything out of them. Until a couple of minutes ago they left me sitting outside in the lane."

"Where did you come across them?" asked Rabin, still thirsting for enlightenment.

"As soon as I turned into the main road. They'd just got out of a car. When I said there was a burglary on, they thanked me politely and told me to stay put. So I'll tell you what I did do: I finished this morning's paper."

"You would," groaned the artist. "Why didn't you follow?"

"Because I always believe," explained Murdoch rather primly, "in obeying police instructions. And as it happens, I seem to have discovered something relevant: you remember those two old girls who lunch at the Poule d'Argent? Their name's Frewen, and they live at Fosgate Hall; and Fosgate Hall was burgled last night."

The next day, inevitably, both Murdoch and Rabin lunched at the Poule d'Argent. M. Raoul was there, and in his best form. His handling of an irritable peer was a lesson in tactics, his homage to an aging beauty a masterpiece of discreet flattery. He had more than ever the air of a man on top of his own particular world.

"It wasn't," said Murdoch for the sixth time.

For the sixth time Rabin disagreed.

"It was. I saw more of him than you did."

"But never properly. I'll admit there was a likeness, but that's all."

They had finished their sweet; in another moment M. Raoul, as was his courteous habit, would come up and inquire in person if they desired coffee; and as his tall distinguished figure approached, both men fell silent. Instinctively, they saved all their wits for the purposes of observation.

"Coffee, messieurs?"

Instead of answering, Rabin suddenly leaned across to his friend.

"By the way," he said, inventing rapidly, "a queer thing happend to me this morning. I left my car outside the flat for not more than ten minutes, and when I came back to it some hooligan had taken the top off the carburetor."

In M. Raoul's handsome face not a muscle flickered; for an instant he looked at the artist with genuine, if sardonic, interest. Then his features once more composed themselves into a calm and courteous mask; he stood patient, impassive, the perfect model of a maître d'hôtel.

Ernest Savage

The Man Who Liked Noise

Al Cooper was one of the nicest fellows you'd ever care to meet. Big strapping man with a ready grin and an open hand. Oh, he had his faults and peculiarities, as who doesn't? He'd fall into moods now and again, for instance, and you wouldn't see him for days in a row, and he didn't like cats or dogs, and he had a rare passion for things that went bang—guns, cannons, firecrackers, cherry bombs, anything that made noise. But on the whole you wouldn't want a nicer neighbor. He'd give you the shirt off his back and he fairly doted on his wife, a thing you don't see too often any more.

Al had made a lot of money in his forties (real-estate speculation, stock market) and bought his place on Cherry Hill before he was 50. Now Cherry Hill is one of a kind—23 estates scattered over its crown and slopes, anywhere from one to four acres each, its single road snaking around the hill, with little offshoots here and there and no way out except the way in. Very private, very exclusive. Big trees all over the place—you can hardly see one house from another—and only one vacant lot left. It has been there since Cherry Hill opened 35 years ago (owned by some outfit back east, I've heard) and if it hadn't been smack dab between Cooper's place and the Gillettes' (now that I think about it, and I'm just *now* beginning to think about it, really), I don't suppose the Cherry Hill killings would have happened. Anyway, until last night I wouldn't have wanted to live any place but here. Now I'm not so sure.

I met Al and Martha Cooper the day they moved into the Randall house, across the road and around the bend from mine. He'd bought it for *her* he told me right off, and I got the impression he'd have bought a piece of the moon for her if he could have built a road to it. Said she'd heard about it being for sale after old man Randall died and he didn't even ask the price (which must have been something!)—just bought it for her. That was two and one-half years ago and he's bought her about everything else you can get with money since then—a pool she goes into about twice a year, antique furniture, Paris clothes, foreign sports cars, trips to Europe, you name it.

But Martha wasn't one bit spoiled by it all. A real down-to-earth lady who laughed a lot and did most of her own work around the house and yard, and was the type who would bring over an apple pie every once in a while. I'll miss her something fierce.

That first day I found out more about Cooper than I really wanted to know. He told me how he'd made his money and what he'd done with a lot of it. Showed me his gun collection (both antique and functional) as it came off the truck, even that damn cannon of his. Showed me a big box of fireworks he'd smuggled across the border from Mexico, said he'd throw a neighborhood fireworks party on the Fourth (it was the middle of June when they moved in) and get to meet everybody on the Hill. Said he liked to get to know his neighbors quick, that he valued a good neighbor more than money in the bank. He was one of those men who's all up front and makes you wonder (later) why he lays himself out so quick, what he's hiding. Still, you had to like him.

Bill Peters, the retired actor, came drifting down that day from his place on top of the Hill, and George and Ginny Gillette came over (he was still alive then) with a coffee urn and sandwiches, and it turned into a pickup neighborhood party, the way it happens now and again. We're close-knit up here. We tend to be a little older than the average neighborhood (I'm 62) and we tend to keep tabs on one another a little more than in other places. About the only time a Cherry Hill house trades is when somebody dies or when some youngster has over-reached himself and has to trade back down again.

Yes, we're close and we gather together at the traditional times, like Christmas, or the Fourth, or when one of our kids (or grandkids) marries, or one of us dies. Almost everybody was out for Ginny Gillette's funeral a couple weeks ago and almost everybody will be out for Al and Martha Cooper's, whenever that's held. Although I'm not so sure about that either, now that I think about it. I've got a lot to think about now.

That first summer Cooper still had his boat down at Newport, where I used to keep mine. Said he'd bought it for Martha, but it turned out she had no stomach for the sea, and he figured he'd keep it just that one season. And he did, too. Sometimes a man will use his wife as a foil for things *he* wants, but not Al. He really doted on that woman.

Anyway, the two of us would go down to Newport once in a while on a weekday (weekends were like the Freeway at quitting time) and cruise the harbor (past Duke Wayne's place, for instance) or out in the channel where he had enough sea room to practice with his cracker shells.

A cracker shell (in case you don't know, which I didn't then) is what they use to scare birds off airport runways or out of a cornpatch, or some such thing. They're regular 12-gauge shotgun shells, except they send out a little wad of explosive that goes off with a loud bang about 75 to 100 yards out, and what Al would do is see how close to the water he could put the charge before it went off. He'd go through a couple boxes at a time out there and didn't often miss; but what he really liked (you could tell it from his eyes) was the noise they made. It did something for him, something way down deep inside.

By that time, of course, Al knew that I'd been a trainer of dogs for the motion picture business, and the last trip we took before he sold the boat, we saw the Duke outside in his patio facing the Bay, stripped to the waist and playing cards, and Al began to question me about the picture business and about dogs and about Duke.

He was in a pensive mood that day, that hail-fellow front of his put aside. We'd been out in the channel that afternoon firing cracker shells and he'd taken that damn cannon of his along, the only time I ever saw it fired. It was a pretty little thing, I must admit, about two feet long, its black iron barrel truncheoned down into a beautifully built step-carriage, like an Old Ironsides, and Al lashed it down on the deck-house roof, pointing aft. He'd brought along a box of the one-inch diameter zinc balls and what he did was stick a length of fuse in the hole at the back of the barrel, then pack a scoop of black powder down the muzzle, pack in the wadding and the zinc ball, aim it, light the fuse, and stand back.

I was on the wheel that time and he'd holler "Right rudder" or "Left rudder" from the roof and then "Hold it!" And then I'd hear this big *whoomf!* and look aft to see if he'd hit what he was aiming at, and usually he did. Blow the hell out of it. What he was aiming at was a piece of flotsam out there, and I'm sorry to say there was lots of it around—orange crates, cardboard boxes, deck pillows, junk of all kinds.

But he didn't seem to take his usual pleasure in the game that afternoon, and when we passed the Duke's place back in the Bay and he began asking me questions about my past, it was as though he was trying to find something outside himself to latch onto. Well,

I opened my standard bag of yarns about the good old days, but his mind was still somewhere else, out there at sea, I figured.

Anyway, later, on the way home, with the cannon and 12-gauge in the back of his station wagon (he *always* had a gun nearby, I'd learned by then), he asked me why, if I was such a dog man, I didn't have one as a pet, and I gave him the easy answer, not the hard one. I told him that my wife Nettie (she was still alive then) and I were too old to break in a dog to our fussy ways, it wouldn't be fair to any of us.

I didn't tell him the hard answer, that I'd had 17 years of the best dog I ever saw or ever heard of, Lucky Lady, and there was no way she could be replaced. I didn't tell him because I knew by then he didn't like dogs. He had a deep-down feeling against them, a fear. Besides, I don't tell anyone about Lucky Lady, never have. No way to do it.

Well, life went forward on Cherry Hill, stalked by death as it always is. The Forsters were killed on the Freeway a year and a half ago; Bill Peters died peacefully in his sleep last summer; and last January George Gillette and my Nettie passed away within a week of each other. It happens; you survive and wait your turn. There's nothing else to do.

But Al, I think, was at his best when death struck. He seemed to have a keener sense than anyone else of the new absence in your life, of how big it was, how unfillable. He wasn't pushy about it, but his sympathy—or awareness, maybe—was there to draw on when you needed it. It was a place of unexpected depth in him and it surprised me more than it pleased me. In fact, it didn't please me at all; it was as though he knew something that was unknowable, that shouldn't be known. It made me uneasy.

But I'm carping. Ginny Gillette and Helen Peters and the Forster kids, and even my daughter Marion (when she came down for her mother's funeral) thought the world of Al. Marion said we were all lucky to have him as a neighbor, and I'll leave it at that.

A little after George Gillette died, Ginny got her dog, Leo. He was a Newfoundland, two, maybe three years old, 27 inches at the shoulders, 150 pounds, solid black hair, bright quick eyes, a fast study. Ginny knew, of course, I was the local dog man and asked me what I thought of him and I told her right off—9 on a scale of 10. (Lucky Lady was 10, the only 10 I ever knew.)

Well, that pleased Ginny—confirmed her own feelings about him, she said. Between 'em it was love at first sight, not like a kid with a puppy (with a lot of tail wagging) but like two grown intelligent beings, quiet and solid. There's no devotion like that. It's forever. Ginny (with her bad heart) had expected to die before George and it depressed her that she hadn't. But with Leo there to train and love, she brightened overnight—it was a pleasure to see.

But I didn't even consider getting one for myself. For both reasons, the easy one and the hard. Lucky Lady, in fact, seemed to emerge from the shadows of memory, and during the long silent hours without Nettie, Lucky Lady's eyes seemed to look into mine now and again, with love and patience. Some of them are that way: they live for you and they live in you, and they join you when the time comes. Or you them. I'm more sure of that now than I ever was.

No, instead I took up with Nettie's garden by day and walked the Cherry Hill road by night. Martha Cooper was a brick, as we used to say. She had a way with rhododendrons and other acid-loving plants, and I had none at all. She'd come up of a morning with her green thumb and bag of tricks (and maybe an apple pie) and everything on my acre and a half would be the better for it.

And at night on my walks I'd chat with the neighbors if they were out or if they weren't, with the stars, and sometimes visit with Leo. Ginny Gillette's place sloped away from the road downhill. Standing in front of the vacant treeless site between her place and the Coopers' I could see the full length of her lot, chain-link fenced all the way from the greenhouse below up to the road. Leo's part of the yard (his night station) was between the greenhouse and Ginny's patio, and sometimes I'd go down the slope by the fence and have a word with him. He'd bark once or twice, but it was just by way of greeting and he'd bark again to say goodbye as I trooped back up the hill. He had a big voice.

One night I saw a light on in Cooper's basement workshop and after my visit with Leo I cut across the vacant lot to the side gate in Cooper's fence and Leo's bark followed me all the way. It was so pointed and determined that I turned around and went back and told him to shut up. Well, he tried, but it took him a while. He didn't want me to go to the Coopers' and he made sure I got the message. I had him just about quiet when Ginny came darting out of her patio door to see what the ruckus was about, and of course that tamed him down all the way. The big brute just curled himself around her legs and grinned.

But he didn't like Cooper, that was clear, and there's always a reason for that—a dog reason if not a man reason.

Cooper was making fireworks that evening. It was the middle of June again (last June) and he was getting ready for the Fourth. By then his fireworks parties had become a tradition, honored by about half of the neighborhood, scorned by the rest. I'd always had the feeling that Martha didn't like them at all, not just because fireworks are illegal (which they are), but because Al was almost embarrassingly childlike in the pleasure he took in them. His eyes would rejoice (as I'd seen them do on the boat that first summer) in the big bang and the unfolding fiery plumage in the sky. Martha had never voiced her opinion, but if you thought about it, it was embarrassing. After all, the man was 52 years old.

But he'd been having trouble with supply in recent years (he told me it was illegal even to ship them) and had begun making his own. That's what he was doing that evening when I came over from Ginny's. He had a half dozen fat cardboard cylinders lined up on the workbench, and he was spooning in formulations of powder and other things, a book of instructions propped up in front of him. He was as absorbed as an alchemist in pursuit of gold and I stayed only long enough for him to tell me what these little babies (that's what he called them, babies) were going to do on the Fourth. Light up the whole sky. They were new, he said, something he'd never tried before.

Back inside I peered at Leo's night station through the screen of trees that rings the Cooper property. I could see him, still standing there by the fence, the intensity of his pose apparent even 75 yards away. A hundred fifty pounds of focused power, black as night. He could have gone over that fence if he wanted to, but he didn't know that yet, and I was hoping he never learned. He wasn't barking, just looking. Something up here stirred his deepest fears, and was beginning to stir mine. I went home disturbed and troubled.

Cooper almost blew his hands off on the Fourth. It was one of those big devils he'd built himself—went off almost the instant he lit the fuse and burned the hell out of his hands and forearms. The crowd was stunned. In the midst of gaiety, sudden horror. It was awful. Martha got to him first and then me.

He was just standing there, staring at his hands. I got behind him and put my hands around his waist and told Harry Marsh to phone the hospital and tell them to get ready for a bad burn case. Then Martha and I put him in the car and took him down.

It was enough to make you sick. He sat between us, me at the wheel, the smell of his burnt flesh choking your throat, his forearms stretched rigidly out in front of his chest, his head back, eyes closed, lips writhing in silent pain, his face white as fresh snow. Not a sound came from him.

They were ready for him when we got there and took him in the emergency operating room right away. It was a busy night for them (the Fourth always is, they told me) and we didn't see him again that night. Martha and I were directed to a waiting room and we sat there talking or just sitting silent until they told us finally to go home.

She told me she knew this was going to happen, that he'd hurt himself or kill himself one day with his things that go bang. Then she cried softly, the first tears I'd ever seen her shed, and I went over and got some tissues from the girl and then some coffee from the machine down the hall. But she composed herself quickly and began telling me things about Al's life that he hadn't revealed in that up-front way of his. The important things, I'd guess.

Al was born in Wales, she said, a foundling left at an orphanage door. He never knew his parents, or even who they were. Was adopted and brought to this country as a kid. Lived in Seattle. Earned a law degree when he was 21, but never practiced. Was with the OSS during the war, married her in Washington, did special things for the government during the next ten years, then quit and in the next 10 to 15 years made a fortune. He seemed to have an intuitive feel for the stock market and real-estate speculations. Was generous with his money, gave a lot to orphanages, boys' towns, and summer camps, things for young people, and was truly loved for it. But he was never happy, she said.

She told me all that in a steady calm flow, but her hands were working like rabbits in her lap, the tissues wadded into small damp balls. And then she was silent a long while before she turned to me with tears in her eyes again.

I don't know what it is, she said in a rush, but I'm the only thing that keeps him sane. At first I thought it was his inability to have children, but that's not it. That's not why he gives me so many things, things I don't even want. I thought at first he was trying to make up to me for that lack, but that's not it. I thought that's why he loves so much to shoot guns—to make big bangs, a *macho* thing (you thought that too, didn't you, and I nodded), but that's not it, I don't know what it is. He hardly sleeps at all any more. Before you started walking the road at night, he walked at night, sometimes all night. You didn't know that, did you?

She leaned against me and sighed; she was vastly wearied. I love him, she whispered. He's a tormented man, but so good, so good in so many ways— He's lost, he's somewhere nobody else is, he's alone. Sometimes he looks at me as if—

She never finished that sentence. She sighed again and her head fell heavily against my shoulder and she went to sleep.

Al made a quick, an almost miraculous recovery. I saw him twice during the five days he was in the hospital and one of the doctors told me he'd never seen a burn case recover so fast. At first they thought they'd have to do extensive skin grafting on his wrists and forearms, but it turned out they had to do none at all and it amazed them.

He came home on Saturday, July tenth, and when I saw him the next day he was as up-front cheerful as he'd ever been. He was in his den (where he kept his gun collection and the cannon) enthroned comfortably in his red leather chair, accepting court from a stream of neighbors. He was at his best, but I sat there tuning out the surface charm and trying a little psychic sonar on what was underneath. Martha had told me more than I was comfortable knowing about his past, and last night, Leo had told me more than I was comfortable knowing about his here and now.

The five days Al had been in the hospital, Leo was as relaxed as a boiled sock. But last night he'd been at the fence again, facing Cooper's place, tense and watchful. I'd stood up on the road, out of his sight and scent, and watched him for a half hour. He'd stand at the fence a few minutes at a time, umoving, then dance around with frustration and put his big paws up on the fence as though trying to climb over. Now and again he'd bark, not loud, but low and businesslike. He'd not seen Al come home and Al hadn't appeared outside, but Leo knew he was there and he didn't like it.

And I didn't like it either. I'm not psychic and make no pretense of being so. I'm not like Lucky Lady or Leo, who can draw on atavistic sources long dead in us; but I had the powerful feeling something awful was going to happen (which did) and maybe I could stop it. I'm not going to kill myself that I didn't, but I'm deeply saddened now, and will always wonder.

Al did the expected thing. When his burns had healed enough, he took Martha on a thirteen-week cruise around the world. It was predictable. It is what a rich man does after a death, accident, or operation. It was the expected thing and I'd learned that Al did the expected thing, when he could determine what it was, and then usually overdid it. It was as though he was living some prototype of life, not his, but some model he'd chosen to follow.

I saw them off at San Pedro—champagne in the cabin and flowers all over the suite. It was a happy time and I must say I liked Al then as much as I ever had. You couldn't help it. And I loved Martha. You couldn't help that either, or at least I couldn't. The last thing I saw were her eyes, pleading with me to understand, maybe to forgive. Her eyes hung in my mind (the way Lucky Lady's still do) long after the boat disappeared.

They came back three weeks ago yesterday, laden with loot from every port they'd touched. Al had guns, both antique and new for his collection, boxes of Chinese firecrackers (from Hong Kong), and cases of stuff to give away.

They threw a party the second night they were back and Al distributed the presents (much too expensive; he'd overdone it again) to everybody on the hill. It was awkward, for me anyway (he gave me an embarrassingly expensive porcelain statuette of a dog that looked uncannily like Lucky Lady, and how he did *that*, I'll never know). But most people were pleased, not only with what they got, but to have Al and Martha back again, as if the family were complete once more.

Not me, though. I guess I knew too much, and sensed more than I knew, but couldn't puzzle it out. Leo for instance. The night of the party he went through that routine at the fence again. Now, there's a wide stretch of rock and mesquite-strewn arroyo surrounding Cherry Hill and there are still enough rabbits living there to arouse a dog's business sense; but outside of a little banter with them Leo had been a model citizen during the Coopers' absence.

But that night Leo was tense again. That was one thing, and Martha's eyes were another. Every time they touched mine there was that flashing plea in them, as though—as though what? That's what got me—as though what? The trip had aged her. Her face was deeply lined under the tan she'd acquired on the seven seas.

I walked the road long that night after the party, and the next night and the next. I saw Leo in that strained pose of his at the fence every time I passed and heard his occasional bursts of barking. But I didn't go down. He'd have to work it out himself, he and Al.

It was the fifth night after they returned, a Tuesday, cold, the first frost of the year. After the eleven o'clock news I went for my usual walk and heard Leo's bark the first step I took out of the door. On the road I passed the Coopers' and then the vacant lot and then

Ginny's and then the Marshes', next to Ginny's. I was walking fast, but the sound stopped me dead in my tracks. I hadn't heard it for a long time, but there was no mistaking it, the sharp flat snap of a cracker shell.

I thought, well, Cooper's done it at last. He's laid a shell in Leo's face to scare him into silence. And it worked. I stood there for a full minute and heard nothing else, no bark, no nothing. And no lights flicking on along the road as they would have in summer. People were asleep, their windows closed. I shivered and turned and continued on around the hill to home and bed.

Helen Marsh found Ginny's body the next morning at ten, and came directly to me. We went back down together. Ginny was in the patio on her back, her arms spread out. The patio door was open, the living-room lights on, the TV on. Helen had come over for her usual midmorning coffee break with Ginny, found the front door unlocked, went in when Ginny didn't respond to her ring, and found her.

Now she turned her back and was crying into her hands, grieving. I led her back in the house, sat her down, and spent the next half hour making the necessary phone calls, searching for her son's number in Lincoln, Nebraska. Harry Marsh came home from his studio to be with his wife, but nobody else knew about it until later that afternoon. Nobody else but Al.

They took her body away at noon. Her doctor and a deputy coroner agreed on the cause of death, obviously heart attack, and the thing was done with speed.

I was alone then in the Gillettes' house and went out to the patio and stood where Ginny's body had been and looked up at Cooper's house. I saw no sign of life or movement behind his trees, but didn't expect to. Didn't want to. Then I got down on my hands and knees and crawled around on the patio and the grass next to it and found a half dozen specks of white waxy paper stuff, shreds of the casing around the explosive charge in the cracker shell.

I got up again and looked at Cooper's. Al had stood up there last night and fired off a cracker shell to scare Leo into silence and just as he pulled the trigger Ginny must have come darting out the door in that quick, birdlike way of hers to shut Leo up and the charge had gone off a yard or so in front of her face, stopped the heart, and blown her down on her back. I'd known it could not have been any other way from the moment I saw her body.

But why say anything? What good would it do? The thing was done, Ginny was gone.

And Leo was gone too. Nobody had thought to ask about him all morning, but I'd wondered from the first. I thought maybe he was hiding out behind the greenhouse or in the toolshed, or in the garage; but when I looked for him he wasn't anywhere and I wasn't surprised. He was no faint-heart. He wouldn't hide. He might run, but he wouldn't hide, and what he'd done was run. But there was no trace of him.

I don't know how to describe Al at Ginny's funeral. It wasn't so much that he was in a state of shocked mourning (we were all that), it was that he had a kind of glazed-over, locked-in look. Ginny's son had flown in from Nebraska the night of the day she died and taken full charge of the arrangements. He'd asked me and Al and Harry Marsh and three other neighbor men to act as pall bearers and Al was placed in the middle of the left side of the casket, just ahead of me and I couldn't have taken my eyes off him even if I'd wanted to. He didn't say a word from the beginning to the end, and when he moved it was as if he were an automaton, counting the steps forward, the turns, the stops. I'd never seen him so distant, so self-absorbed.

Of course he knew he'd killed her. He must have seen her run out the door when he fired and fall back when the shell went off. And probably he'd gone down to check. Small wonder his movements were stiff and unnatural, his eyes inward-seeing.

But why had he fired at Leo? Did he want merely to shock him into silence, or kill him, or what? What was between them? What did Leo know about Al that we were too insensitive to know and he too tongueless to tell?

I didn't see Al again until nearly a week after Ginny's funeral. I was out walking and saw him in the arroyo on the far side of the hill, a half mile from home. It was near midnight. I'd been searching the arroyo myself that night, thinking Leo might be down there somewhere mourning. A good dog will do that sometimes: he'll go away and mourn and then return.

Al was almost 50 yards from where I stopped when I saw him. He was crouched in a listening pose, his back to me, the barrel of a gun in his hand glinting in the light of a clear-night moon. He was hunting. I felt a thrill rush up my spine at the sight of him, but after a moment I turned and went away.

He was out the next three nights, and then again last night—for the last time. I could spot him from high points on the road all around the hill. He'd walk a while, then listen, sit on a rock and wait, then walk again. Leo was out there too, but I never saw him and I don't think Al did either. Leo had a different plan. But whatever it was between them (I told myself) it was theirs to resolve, not mine, and I stayed back.

It was after one o'clock last night when I quit the eerie game and started home. On the way past the Coopers' house I saw the dance of a flashlight behind the trees. It was Martha, poking along the edge of their lot nearest Ginny's. She was wearing something white that trailed on the ground behind her and showed luminescently in the light of the moon. I wanted to go and tell her that what she hunted couldn't be found by her, only by Al. But I didn't. I wanted to tell her to come home with me and let Al run the game to its end, but I didn't. I should have interceded three or four times in the course of these events, but I didn't, and that's another thing I'll carry with me for a long time.

I went home, made a drink, and turned on the TV. Halfway through the second late late show I fell asleep, a light twitchy sleep. I didn't know what it was at first that wakened me, but it was something felt as well as heard, a kind of *whoomf* sound that shook the air. A thin predawn light trickled through my windows. I got up, went out, and listened some more from my front yard, and then went down to Cooper's place.

Martha was on her back the way Ginny had been, her arms spread wide. She was by the gate leading to the vacant lot. The gate was open. The flashlight was on the ground a yard from her right hand, and it was dead too. In the thin steely light of that hour I could see the fear still locked in her eyes, or thought I could. I closed them gently. Her mouth was open, her jaw rigid. Maybe she'd screamed, maybe she hadn't. It was hard for me to press her lips closed, but she looked better when I did, more peaceful in the long white dress she was wearing. I whispered goodbye.

Al was seated, comfortable-looking, in his red leather chair in the den. He had pushed it around to face the low cabinet top on which he kept the cannon. He'd nailed the four wooden wheels of the cannon carriage to the wooden top of the cabinet with eight-penny nails. I hadn't heard the sound of hammering.

What I'd heard, and felt, was the sound of the cannon going off. The muzzle was about four feet from his chest and the zinc ball had smashed his heart before it blew itself out the back of the chair and into the wall behind. There was no mistaking the smell of cordite—it was fresh and heavy in the room. A thin gray line of fuse ash snaked across about a foot of the cabinet top and there was a small pile of it on the floor below. He must have cut about a yard of fuse and it must have burned for a half minute while he sat there and waited and watched.

His head had fallen forward on his chest. I raised it and was shocked at how pale and gaunt his face had grown in just a few days. And nights.

I eased his head back down gently.

Then I went back outside to where Martha was and in the rosy golden tints of dawn I laid her arms across her breast. She looked better that way—as though she'd just lain down and died in peace, instead of unthinkable fear.

I said goodbye to her again, went out the open gate and across the vacant lot to Ginny's gate below the greenhouse and up her terraced back yard to the patio where Leo was. At first glance he appeared to be asleep, but I knew he was dead before I touched him. I knew he had to be.

He was a mess, his coat tangled and dirty, and he must have lost 50 pounds. He'd laid himself down exactly where his mistress had died, and it had to be that way too. Dogs work by patterns that men can't read, and when they have a thing to do, the good ones will get it done at any cost.

There hadn't been a mark on Martha. Leo had simply frightened her to death and then come home to die himself. His real enemy was Al and always had been and I have no doubt Leo knew that from the first. And he knew also how best to destroy him—to kill the only thing Al loved, the only thing Al *could* love, Martha, his one tie to life.

I picked Leo up, carried him down to the toolshed, got a shovel, and then went down into the arroyo and buried him. If any of the others had wondered about him, where'd he'd gone, now they'd never know.

Then I went back home and sat in my breakfast room and watched the sun rise above the big hills to the east, and I thought about Al. Most men, when they kill themselves, put a bullet through the head. Very seldom the heart. But Al, to kill himself good and true, had driven a one-inch zinc ball through his heart. Not a wooden stake, but a zinc ball.

It was all he had, and maybe he knew it was the only way to make sure.

Peter Godfrey

Time Out of Mind

From the battery on Signal Hill the midday gun boomed. The dull sound mushroomed out in the still air, shivered, and was gone. The little table clock in the dining room started to strike. In the lounge the old grandfather cleared his throat wheezingly, preparatory to coughing out his deep reverberating chimes.

Miss Brett shook her head regretfully. It was all wrong, of course—the time was really half past three. All the clocks would have to be altered. She sighed and rose.

The minutes crept by. In her room, plump Mrs. Fenwick opened her curtains slightly and gazed at the smartly cut pair of shoes on the sill. She reached out her hand to touch them, and then the temerity of her action froze her muscles. She remained, with her hand stretched out, eyes drinking in the symmetrical music of the shaped and fluted leather, her soul caressed into ecstasy by wave after wave of adoration.

She stood like this a very long time.

Upstairs, old Mrs. Calloran looked at the mark on the wall and made baby noises. She had looked at the same mark and made the same noises all the time Nurse Villiers had washed and dressed and fed her. She was much worse than usual today. The nurse thought something had upset her but, of course, it was no use asking. So she left her cooing to the wall and went out to gather the others together for lunch.

She found Miss Kemp flat on her stomach in the garden, peering fiercely through a rhododendron bush. As Nurse Villiers approached, she sprang up suddenly, put her fingers to her lips, and said, "Hush!" She continued, quite conversationally: "I'm looking for a tall man with a fair mustache. I don't think you've met him, but he's my husband. The Jungle Queen kidnaped him, but I shot her with an arrow this morning, and now he's disappeared again. I must find him soon or else the municipality will prosecute him for the bad drainage."

"Yes, yes," said Nurse Villiers soothingly. "Have you thought of the dining room? He may have gone there for lunch. All the others are going, you know."

Miss Kemp went like a lamb.

Mrs. Perry was peering in through the window of Sister Henshaw's office. When she turned round to look at Nurse Villiers, her eyes were full of tears. "Everyone is against me," she said.

"Oh, come now," said Miss Villiers, "nobody hates you here—we're all your friends. You'll feel much better after lunch."

"You're not telling the truth," said Mrs. Perry. "Oh, it's too cruel. You all lie to me. Even Sister Henshaw lies to me."

"Really?" said Nurse Villiers good-humoredly. "What about?"

"That knitting needle I lost. You know I looked everywhere for it and Sister said she hadn't seen it."

"Yes?"

"Well, look," said Mrs. Perry, pointing through the window. "She's had it all the time."

Nurse Villiers looked.

Until she caught a grip on herself, she felt the blood rushing from her head. Almost automatically she consoled Mrs. Perry, and led her gently to the dining room. She saw all her charges settled and beginning the meal.

Only then she went to the telephone and dialed a number frantically. For endless seconds she heard the t-r-r-ing, t-r-r-ing of the bell on the other phone; then there was a click as the receiver was lifted, and a familiar voice came over the wire.

"Oh, thank God, Doctor," she said. "This is Nurse Villiers here. Can you come over right away? Sister Henshaw is dead. Murdered. Yes, Doctor, murdered, M-U-R—yes. No, it couldn't be anything else. Please come right away, Doctor—please."

She put the receiver back on the rest, not to end the conversation but because even that little action helped to steady her.

The house was in the upper fringes of Oranjezicht, on the slopes of the mountain, and was set in large grounds surrounded by a high paling fence. It was called "The Haven."

The police came in two cars. In the larger were Detective-Sergeants Johnson and Botha, the medical examiner, Dr. McGregor, and a uniformed driver. Inspector Joubert drove from Caledon Square in his own little Austin, and his uncle, Rolf le Roux, came with him. Dr. Patterson, as he had promised over the telephone, was waiting for them outside the wrought-iron gates.

He knew McGregor, and the medical examiner introduced him to the others.

"I want to make a statement," said Patterson, "but before I do, I would first like you to examine the body. There are certain things I should point out on the spot."

The time was then a quarter past two.

They went into the room, and the unseeing left eye of Sister Henshaw stared at them. From the right eye the end of a steel knitting-needle projected.

"The cause of death," said Patterson, "is obvious. But I want you to take particular note of the weapon."

"Any chance of fingerprints?" asked Joubert, but Johnson shook his head.

"Very doubtful," he said. "The surface of the needle is too small. Even if we find anything, it'll be doubtful if it'd be sufficient to make a positive identification."

McGregor was examining the body, testing muscle flexion, peering carefully at the trickle of congealed blood on the right cheek. He met Joubert's inquiring gaze, and shrugged. "Not less than one and not more than four hours ago," he said. "I canna tell more certainly. But there is one thing here that is queer. There is powder on this blood trickle—someone powdered the corpse after death."

"I'm glad you noticed that," said Patterson. "I never looked closely enough myself, but I was going to point out the makeup to you. You see, Inspector, it's completely out of the ordinary. Sister Henshaw never used lipstick or rouge—and you'll note there's plenty of it on her face now." He added: "As far as the time of death is concerned, I think I may be able to narrow it down for you."

"Yes?" said Joubert.

"Not now, Inspector—when I make my statement later. First, there is just one more oddity I would like to point out. Her shoes."

Joubert squinted down at the body. "I see what you mean. She's not wearing any. But why is that particularly queer? After all, she seems to have laid down on the sofa for a rest or a nap, and was probably attacked during her sleep, judging by the absence of signs of a struggle. She probably would remove her shoes before lying down."

"You're missing my point, Inspector. I happen to know she always does take her shoes off when about to lie down—but where has she put them? I've had a fairly good look around, and I can't see them anywhere. To my mind, they've been removed from the room, probably by the murderer."

Joubert said: "That's interesting," and then added, "I think we

should have a thorough search before jumping to conclusions. Johnson—Botha—let's get down to it."

They did. They peered under furniture, opened drawers and cupboards. No shoes.

"It seems you are probably right," said Joubert. "Well, let's go
into the other room and get your statement down."

Rolf le Roux said, "Just a minute, Dirk." He was standing near
the head of the couch, unlit pipe gripped between his white teeth
and projecting beyond his bushy beard, and his soft brown eyes were
peering intently at the body.

Joubert looked at him inquiringly.

Rolf took out his pipe to use as a pointer. "The matter of this
makeup has been raised," he said. "Dr. Patterson has not yet told
us why, and I don't know whether what I have noticed has a bearing
on his explanation. Nevertheless, come and have a look here. You
have already seen that the face was powdered after death. Now I
want you to note that the eyebrows have been carefully penciled
before the powder was put on the face. You can see that because the
powder is over the eyebrow-pencil marks. But the rest of the
makeup—the lipstick, the rouge—is also under the powder. In other
words, each individual cosmetic was put on first, and *then* the face
was powdered."

"And all this means—?"

Rolf shrugged. "I do not know at this stage, Dirk. It is merely that
it might have some significance. Perhaps after we hear the state-
ments—"

They went into the little lounge adjoining, found seats, and made
themselves comfortable. Patterson spoke up clearly and concisely,
like a man used to marshaling his facts. "I had better start with my
personal connection with the affair," he said. "In the first place, 'The
Haven' is a residential clinic for psychotics—in popular terms, a
private lunatic asylum. It was owned by myself with Sister Henshaw
as a full partner, and we have one other trained nurse as an assistant. At 1:15 P.M. today the assistant, Nurse Villiers—yes, I am
sure of the time, I made a note of it—telephoned me at my house
with the news that Sister Henshaw had been murdered. I rushed
straight over here, inspected the situation without touching anything, and telephoned you immediately."

Joubert interrupted: "So it was not you, but Nurse Villiers who
discovered the body?"

"Yes."

"Where is she now?"

"She's in the house, Inspector, busy with her duties. I will relieve her in a few minutes and send her to you. May I go on?"

"Yes."

"What I want to tell you may possibly save you a good deal of unnecessary work. I don't know very much about normal police methods, but I am convinced this is not a rational crime, and any inquiries along normal channels are bound to be fruitless. For instance, if you were to ask me if Sister Henshaw had any enemies, I would have to tell you that I don't think she had a single friend. She was super-efficient, domineering, stubborn, and almost aggressively insulting to everyone she came across. I can speak from personal experience. I recently had an offer for this place which I thought we should accept, but Sister Henshaw refused. She continually kept bringing the offer up, for the sole purpose, apparently, of criticizing me for what she called my gullibility. So you see, I had an accentuation of all her worst traits piled on my head in the last three weeks—and I can speak with authority on the effect she had on the people who disliked her. The reaction was to avoid her at all costs—not to do her physical harm."

"You realize," said Joubert, "that you have just provided us with what might be construed as a possible motive for murder?"

"I am perfectly conscious of that," said Patterson, and smiled. "I am also conscious of the fact that you would find similar motives for every other person who knew her. I have told you my opinion as a psychiatrist that this isn't a rational crime. Yet, although I cannot name the murderer, I know where she is at this moment."

Rolf asked, "She?" and Joubert said, "Where?" at exactly the same time. Patterson answered both.

"Somewhere in this house," he said. "We have five patients here at the moment—all women—and I am morally certain that one of them is guilty of the crime." He sighed a little wearily. "And I am afraid, Inspector, that my science, which should be able to help you at this stage, cannot give me any ideas. At the time of original examination of these patients, I could not discern homicidal tendencies in any of them. If I had, the one concerned would never have been admitted here—we have no facilities for dealing with violent cases. Nor have I noticed anything subsequently which could give us a clue. It may be any of them."

Joubert said, "I see." He paused, and then added: "You said something just now about narrowing down the time factor."

"Yes. You will realize in a clinic like this it is necessary to adhere to a rigid routine in order not to upset the patients. Everything went by the clock. The day started at 6:30, and various well defined duties kept Nurse Henshaw busy until 11:30. At that hour sharp she went into her office to lie down and rest, rising at 1 P.M. for lunch which was served to her in her office. She stayed in the office until I arrived to discuss cases and treatment with her at three o'clock sharp. During the period she was in the office, it was a rigid rule that she should not be disturbed until lunch. Nurse Villiers tells me the body was discovered at approximately 12:50 P.M., which means that the murder must have been committed within the eighty minutes preceding that time."

"And the various things you pointed out to us in connection with the body?"

"They may have significance in terms of the case histories of the various patients, but perhaps I had better deal with them after you have seen the patients themselves. Would you like to come round with me now? They are all in their rooms at this time, waiting for my visit."

Joubert hesitated. "I think perhaps we had better interview Nurse Villiers first. Would you call her for us? I'll send her for you again as soon as we've finished the interview."

Patterson left, and a few minutes later Nurse Villiers came into the room. She took the chair Joubert indicated. In answer to his question, she told of her conversation with Mrs. Perry, and how she looked through the window.

"I understand," said Joubert, "that this was approximately at ten minutes to one?"

"Yes."

"And I suppose it was quite a shock to you to see your employer murdered in so brutal a fashion?"

"Naturally."

"Did you go in and examine the body, to make sure life was fully extinct?"

"It wasn't necessary, Inspector. I know death when I see it. There was no possibility of her being alive."

Joubert said, "I see," and then added almost negligently: "And, of course, you hated her, too."

She sat up very straight. "Naturally I hated her. She wasn't a very likeable person. But I didn't murder her, if that's what you're insinuating. I don't like your tone of voice, Inspector. I don't know how you learned that I'd quarreled frequently with her, but I wasn't the only one. And I don't think that fact in any way justifies your attitude that I am under suspicion."

"No?" said Joubert. "Well, perhaps you can enlighten me in another direction. You say that at ten minutes to one you looked through the window and recognized with a shock that Sister Henshaw had been murdered. How is it, then, that you didn't telephone Dr. Patterson until 1:15?"

She was still tense. "I can see you've had no experience of mental institutions. The first rule we learn is that under no circumstances must patients be upset. I adhered to that rule. I took Mrs. Perry to the dining room, saw all the others were settled and had started to eat lunch, and then I went to telephone. I suppose in a way it was my duty to report the matter immediately—but it was also my duty not to alarm the people I am looking after. If I did wrong, I'm sorry."

"But surely Mrs. Perry had already been upset?"

"No, I don't think so—at least, not in the way you mean. I had the impression that she was preoccupied with the discovery of the missing needle, and didn't realize the significance of its—position."

Joubert nodded to Johnson, who closed his notebook and replaced it in his pocket. They stood up. Nurse Villiers seemed surprised.

"Are you finished with me?" she asked.

"For the moment," said Joubert. "We are going on an inspection of the patients. We would like you to fetch Dr. Patterson, and then come round with us."

McGregor took advantage of the interval to excuse himself. "I'm no' a psychiatrist," he said, "and I've got an autopsy to perform. If you dinna mind, I'll take the car and then send it back to you. When the van arrives, show them where the cadaver is."

He waved farewell not only to them, but also to Dr. Patterson and the nurse, who had just arrived through the other door.

"I'm going to follow my regular round, if you don't mind," said Patterson. "The first is Mrs. Perry, the owner of the weapon that killed Sister Henshaw. The clinical diagnosis of her case is paranoia—an insanity of delusions. She believes she is being persecuted. Like all the others here, she comes from a good family. Her insanity dates from the time her husband left her."

While he talked, he led them along a passage, eventually knocking on a door, which he pushed open without invitation.

Mrs. Perry looked up wild-eyed from the bed on which she was sitting. "Oh, Doctor," she said. "It wasn't my fault. Really it wasn't my fault. I know everyone blames me, but I didn't mean it."

"Didn't mean what, Mrs. Perry?"

"Letting the patient die under the operation, Doctor. It wasn't my fault. The scalpel slipped, that was all."

"We all know it wasn't your fault, Mrs. Perry. I hear you've got good news for me? I hear you found your knitting needle?"

Mrs. Perry became quite animated, but it was the animation of despair. "Oh, no, Doctor, I thought I had, but I hadn't. I know where it is, though. Sister Henshaw has it, and she won't give it up. She hates me. I know she hates me. She had a look in her eye—"

At a signal from Patterson, the police party backed out into the corridor. They heard Mrs. Perry sobbing, and a soothing undertone of words; eventually the doctor and nurse joined them.

"The next," said Patterson, "is Miss Brett. Quite frankly, I don't know how to describe her case. She is perfectly normal, except for one morbid fixation. It appears that when she was a young girl her watch was wrong, and she missed aN important appointment. Ever since then she spends the whole day ascertaining the time, and checking its correctness. You may question her yourself, if you like."

He led them into the room and introduced them to Miss Brett. Joubert saw her eyes travel to his wristwatch and then to the clock over her dressing-table. He felt quite relieved that the two instruments agreed.

"Do you remember what you did this morning, Miss Brett?" he asked her.

"Oh, yes, I didn't waste a minute."

"Did you see Sister Henshaw go into her office?"

"Yes. That was at half past eleven."

"Did you see anyone else go into the office?"

"No. I wasn't there, you see. I went round to check the clocks."

"And did you return a little later?"

"Yes. Just before the noon gun went off. There was something wrong with it today, though. It went off at the wrong time. I had to alter every clock in the house. It threw everything out, too. Lunch was later, everything was later. I wonder why it happened?"

Joubert said, "I'm sure I don't know." But he had quite obviously thrown up the sponge. He added, "Thank you," and "good afternoon," and sidled into retreat.

"I think you do much better than I do," he told Patterson. "I'll leave the others to you." He added: "In any case, little as I got out of her I still have the impression that she's by no means a murderous type."

Patterson looked at Nurse Villiers and smiled. "As a matter of fact, Inspector," he said, "Miss Brett is the only one of all our present patients who has ever given any indication of violence. It was the other afternoon. When we made our rounds, she was out of the room when we arrived—probably checking up the clocks somewhere—and Sister Henshaw tactlessly asked her why she was late. Miss Brett became quite hysterical and would certainly have assaulted Sister Henshaw if Nurse and I hadn't intervened."

He stopped opposite a third door. "I'm afraid we're going to get very little out of this patient, Inspector. She is what is technically termed a foot fetichist—the only real emotional response she gives is to feet or footwear. I'm afraid it's not uncomplicated, either. There are definite symptoms of religious mania."

He turned the handle and walked in.

Mrs. Fenwick—coarse, crude, and fat—knelt at the window, with an expression of ethereal spirituality in her eyes. She was gazing at a pair of shoes on the sill. Her lips were moving, but without sound, and her hands were clasped under her chin. It was obvious that she was talking to the shoes. Just before she rose, Joubert saw with a quiver of shock that she mouthed the word "Amen."

Patterson questioned her, but her answers were vague and meaningless, and she looked not at their eyes but at their feet.

Nurse Villiers suddenly shivered and caught Joubert by the arm. "The shoes on the sill," she said. "Those are Sister Henshaw's! She was wearing them this morning!"

Patterson heard. "Tell me, Mrs. Fenwick," he said sharply, "where did you get those shoes on the window?"

For the first time she seemed to understand. "They came," she said. "It was a miracle. They came with the pain of fire and the flash of steel. Let us pray."

She was down on her knees again, and Patterson shrugged. They moved out of the room.

They went upstairs.

Patterson asked Miss Kemp what she had been doing that morning and she smiled knowingly. "I will tell the Court Martial," she said. "In the meantime, it is a secret. Only you and I know, eh, Nurse?" She would say nothing more.

Outside the door, Nurse Villiers said: "She's very strange today.

I mean more so than usual. I think I know what she was referring to about a secret, though. She told me this morning that she had killed the Jungle Queen with an arrow. Oh, Doctor, do you think—?"

"Why her more than the others?" said Patterson, and turned to Joubert.

"As a matter of fact, Inspector, if I were to suspect one more than any other, on psychological grounds, I would choose Mrs. Calloran, the old lady we are now going to see.

"I think I had better explain. There is an insanity called dementia praecox in which the sufferer gradually becomes sunk into himself to such an extent that he becomes as helpless as a newborn babe. By the time they reach this stage, the patients are perfectly harmless and lose all cognitive power and initiative. Mrs. Calloran has similar symptoms as far as the regression of an infantile state is concerned, but she has stopped regressing at the period equivalent to a child of ten months. However, I have definitely formed the impression that she is not a praecox patient at all. For instance, it is only her emotional responses that have been affected—I am reasonably certain that she can act as purposefully as you or I under certain conditions and circumstances. Remember the makeup on Sister Henshaw's face? Mrs. Calloran once owned a beauty parlor. Against this, of course, is the irrefutable fact that the door of her room is always kept locked."

He turned the key as he spoke, and opened the door.

Mrs. Calloran lay on her back on the bed with a large wax doll gripped in her left hand. She was rolling from side to side and crooning inarticulately. She stopped the movement suddenly, vindictively jabbed her extended forefinger in the doll's eye, and said, "Goo!"

She didn't even look at them.

"It's no good talking to her in this state," said Patterson. "Let's go downstairs and finish our discussion."

In the lounge again, Joubert said: "Naturally I've come to my own conclusions, Doctor, but after all you're the expert. You said you'd attempt to correlate the various factors with the case histories of the various patients. Will you do so now?"

Patterson said, "Yes," and lit a cigarette. "I must stress again that although there are clues pointing in certain directions, they are not conclusive—in fact, they are mutually contradictory and I can make very little sense out of them. I think the easiest thing for me to do is run through the arguments for and against the guilt of each individual patient.

"First, Mrs. Perry. The weapon was a knitting needle which she made a great fuss of losing two weeks ago. She has a persecution mania and often such a mania can become converted into a homicidal one. It is psychologically possible, if she found the needle in Sister Henshaw's possession, that she'd attack her. On the other hand, her attitude that Sister Henshaw is still alive and still has the needle seems to argue against that possibility—and I cannot find grounds, psychiatric or otherwise, which would have led her to remove the shoes or make the face up.

"The same objection holds good in the cases of Miss Brett and Miss Kemp, although we must have suspicion against the former for her violence last week and against the latter for her cryptic remarks to Nurse Villiers. The disappearance of the shoes and their recovery definitely seems to point to Mrs. Fenwick, but I can't imagine her committing such a crime or in such a manner. The most likely psychological type, as I mentioned before, is Mrs. Calloran, and the making-up of the face seems to point in her direction. Even the method of the crime is quite consistent with her mental makeup—did you notice her gesture with the doll?—and it is not impossible that she could have removed the shoes and placed them on Mrs. Fenwick's window. Only, of course, her door was locked."

"Are you quite sure?" asked Joubert, and turned to Nurse Villiers. "Isn't it possible, Nurse, that Mrs. Calloran's door was left unlocked even for a few minutes during the morning?"

She said, very positively: "No. I went into the room half a dozen times during the morning, and each time I both unlocked and locked the door. I came up last about a quarter to twelve, when I changed her clothing and fed her. I distinctly remember locking the door when I left, because I had to put the tray on the floor to do so. I also remember unlocking it when I came in, for the same reason."

Patterson threw up his hands in a gesture. "There you have it, Inspector. That one of them did it I am perfectly sure, but which one I cannot say. I don't even know whether the points I have brought forward in defense are valid or not—they only represent my own opinion. If the various factors had made a consistent pattern, I would have had no hesitation in naming one or the other. As it is—"

"But there is a consistent pattern," said Rolf le Roux, and the others turned to him in surprise. "Yes, Doctor," he went on, "all your reasoning has been completely logical—*except your conclusion.*

The individual clues point to one or the other of your patients; not all the clues point to any one of them. Yet you have fallen into the fallacy of still contending that one of your patients is the guilty party."

"Then what is your interpretation?" said Patterson.

Rolf seemed to sheer off from the subject abruptly. "Before I tell you, there are one or two points I want to be perfectly clear about. First, that the routine of this house is always unchanging?"

"Yes."

"That in accordance with this routine you never arrive until a quarter before three? In other words, at the time the murder was committed you were neither here nor expected here for some time?"

"Quite right."

"So that when Sister Henshaw went to lie down at 11:30, the only person about who had anything to do with the handling of the patients, who knew about the routine, was Nurse Villiers."

"Yes. But what are you getting at?"

"The only explanation of the clues. Yes, I will tell you now. I say those clues were *deliberately laid by the murderer*, and that therefore *the murderer was a person with some knowledge of the mental twists of your patients*. Contrary to your theory, the crime was completely rational and premeditated."

Nurse Villiers said: "You can't—" and then all eyes were turned on her.

"But the clues themselves," said Rolf, "help us a little further in the matter. Remember the makeup on the face and consider that in the light of the fact that the crime was a rational one."

Joubert said: "What do you mean?"

"Remember how I pointed out the powder was *over* the penciled eyebrows. There is a definite indication as to the sex of the murderer. Women use eyebrow pencil after the face has been powdered, not before. No, *the murderer was a man*."

The eyes swung back to Patterson. He stubbed out his cigarette violently and said, "Do you realize the seriousness of your allegation? Do you think your very ingenious theory is sufficient evidence?"

"No," said Rolf, "but that can still be remedied." He turned to Nurse Villiers. "Bring Miss Brett in here."

There was no sound in the room until the nurse returned. Patterson lit another cigarette.

Rolf said to Miss Brett: "You told us before that you saw Sister Henshaw going into her office, and left to check the clocks?"

"Yes."

"What was the time?"

"It was half past eleven."

"You mean it was half past eleven because Sister Henshaw went into her office?"

"Of course. It's always half past eleven when she goes into her office."

"And if the clocks showed a different time, then you would put them right?"

"Naturally."

"You remember when the gun was fired on Signal Hill this morning? You told us that something was wrong with it and you had to alter all the clocks. What was wrong with the gun?"

"Usually when it fires it's twelve o'clock. Today it was half past three."

Rolf leaned forward in his chair. His voice was calm, but his knuckles showed white from the pressure of his fingers round his pipe.

"You mean," he said, "that as the gun fired today, something else happened which always happens at half past three?"

"Of course. What else could I have meant?"

Rolf sat back, relaxed. His voice was very quiet. "Tell me, Miss Brett, how do you know when it's half past three? What happens every day which tells you that it's half past three?"

"Don't you know?" she asked in surprise, and then added as though she was instructing a child: "It is half past three every day when Dr. Patterson comes out of Sister Henshaw's office."

Charlotte Armstrong

The Other Shoe

"Jenny." A hand on my bare arm pulled me away from the group around the piano in the den. "Celia and Blair, in there—" Carmen said. "Look, I'm a pretty easy-going hostess, but Blair is drunk and Celia is screaming at him and it isn't funny any more. Do you think you could stop them?"

"Oh, Carmen, I'm sorry. But Celia pays less than no attention to me."

"She's your sister."

"Stepsister," I corrected.

Carmen's big eyes flashed. "You better do something—for Blair's sake," she added knowingly.

"I'll try," I said.

I went into the living room. It wasn't hard to spot my stepsister, Celia, since she and I were dressed exactly alike. All of us at this party were the remains of a wedding—gay souls who had chased the bride and groom with traditional hilarity and had then wound up at this country house of Carmen's to carry on into the night.

Celia and I still wore our bridesmaid's dresses, pale apricot organdy, and both of us still had on our feet the fantastic straw-colored devices, a few narrow straps tying on some four-inch heels, that were supposed to be shoes.

Those shoes!

In the living room, people were silently listening—in malice or in helpless distaste. Celia was standing in an ugly pose, as if her feet hurt and she didn't care who knew it. Her face, that could look like an angel's, was pinched and sharpened.

"And if you thought," she was saying in a piercing voice, "that you were just going to use my money without any advice from me, you were living in a dream world, genius boy."

"Advish, sure," Blair Meaghan mumbled. There had been a lot of champagne at the wedding and he seemed to have had more than his share of it. "Always glad to lishen to advish. But don't give me orders. Have another drink."

"You take my money, you take my orders," Celia snapped. "And be glad to get both. I'm in on this deal all the way, or I'm out. Understand?"

"You don't unnerstan'," he muttered. "Papers signed. Bishness deal. Ashk anybody." Blair waved his glass. His dark hair wouldn't plaster down—it rose in a crest. I adored him and I hated this ugly scene, but I didn't see what I could do.

"Business!" Celia hooted. "When you came whining to me, I said I'd keep on with the financing. That was for pity's sake. But I'm not *giving* you the money."

Blair's face was pale. "Coursh not. Inveshment."

Celia said, "You do what I say or I take my money *out!* Do you hear, or are you too drunk?"

"Orders, no." Blair shook his head. "Papers don't say—"

"I spit on the papers," shrieked Celia. "You do it or I'm getting out and there won't be any money. If you want to start any lawsuits you can count on me telling how you whined and cried after I threw you over. You'd enjoy that. And you'd lose. Don't think you wouldn't. Last chance." She still thought she might get her way.

But Blair raised his glass. "To the money! Hail and farewell! And I hope it's farewell to you, forever." He drained the liquid down. "I ought to wring your neck," he said, rather quietly. "A public servish."

Nobody else in the room was speaking or moving. Everybody knew that Celia and Blair had been engaged last summer. Everybody knew that Celia had wanted someone else—and hadn't got him. Everybody knew how much her money meant to Blair.

It was her own money—from her dead mother's family. Neither father nor I had any. Celia did as she pleased with what was her own. She had invested it, all properly, in Blair's project, and in what he thought was good faith.

Celia could look like an angel, and be bright and beautiful. It took a while to realize how spoiled, how totally unreliable she was. Blair knew it now, twice over. There she stood, welshing on a business deal in a fit of arrogance, and there he stood, watching his hardwrought plan, his work, his hope, his dream, dying by her hand.

He wasn't in love with Celia any more.

He had thought she was civilized. But she was like a stone.

There was only one thing I could think of doing. I took Blair's arm. "Blair, take me home?" I begged.

"What, Jenny?" He was so angry or so drunk he seemed blind.

"I've got to go home right away," I said urgently. Blair had always been fond of me, and kind.

"Why, what's the matter?" He wasn't seeing me, blind as he was, but at least he recognized my voice. He let me lead him out of that room. I didn't have to turn and look to know the contempt that would be on Celia's face. She, and everyone else in the room, knew very well how deeply I was in love with Blair.

At least I had broken up the nasty scene. Carmen fluttered after us with my stole. Her husband warned me that Blair must not drive a car. So there we were, ten o'clock that night, in Blair's convertible, with me driving and Blair sodden on the seat beside me.

The last sound I heard from that house was Celia's voice: "Let Jenny comfort him. Jenny likes nothing better." I made the car jump away from the sound of her laughter.

Carmen's long low house sits on a hill and the driveway goes to the north and winds down gradually to the highway. We hadn't yet reached the main road when I discovered that I couldn't possibly drive a car in those ridiculous shoes.

I pulled in close to the shrubbery and parked, unbuckled the ankle straps, got the silly things off my feet, and sat massaging my toes.

Blair said in a clear and sober voice, "I'll drive, Jenny. Thanks for getting me out of there. I thought it was better to act drunk," he told me quietly. "Because that is a scene I never want to remember."

His voice made me want to cry. But I am not one to cry or rage or carry on. Celia did too much of that. I said in my normal commonsense voice, "What does it mean if Celia takes the money out?"

"I start at the bottom again," he said. "It's all to do over."

What Blair Meaghan wanted to do is not impossible. It can be done; it has been done. Yet there is really no way to do it. He wanted to produce and direct a motion picture. The "way" to that is so arduous and chancy, such a zigzag among hopes and promises, such a miracle of timing, that nothing can produce an independent motion picture but a powerful dream and the courage to survive a thousand heartbreaks.

I listened to him and I knew he would survive. He wasn't whining. He spoke in a clear tight voice, about loans and percentages and banks and the screenplay and the actors who would not and could not wait—the whole web of tentative and interdependent commitments that had taken him two years to weave, but which had now vanished with Celia's decision.

We forgot to change seats, he in his need to talk and me in my need to listen. Celia was wrong about my liking nothing better than to comfort Blair. There were many things I would have liked better than to listen to the crisp exact details of his ruin.

Half an hour went by. Cars passed on the highway below us. Not many. They couldn't see us, nor we them. No car came down Carmen's drive. Nobody else left the party. There we were, halfway down the hill, forgotten and forgetting, until finally Blair's voice ran down. He looked at his watch.

"Ten thirty-six," he said. "We better get going. Thanks for listening, Jenny. It helped. You always help me."

He did sound eased. He swung me over his lap and took the wheel. We continued downward, turned to the right on the highway, and came opposite the long, little-used flight of wooden stairs that led up the middle of the hill to Carmen's house.

There was something lying out of place there in the margin.

Blair braked. The moon was up and we could see the heap of organdy.

We sprang from the car and there she was. Celia. In the dusty weeds and dead.

No car came by while Blair used his flashlight long enough to make sure she was dead, and to see that she had been strangled.

"We can't help her," he said harshly. His fingers bit my arm. "Get in." I limped on stockinged feet. "Quick!" He lifted me into the car. "Oh, Lord, don't leave a shoe!"

He picked it off the pavement and threw it into my lap. He ran around, jerked the car away from there, and yanked it sharply to the left onto a country road, which was another way back to town—the way we called "going around the mountain."

I couldn't speak. I couldn't think. But when we were into a fold of the hill, he stopped the car. "You don't get it." I could feel him trembling.

"We shouldn't run away," I said.

"What else can we do?" he said grimly. "No, you don't get it. But I do. I said I'd like to wring her neck, remember? In front of a room full of witnesses. Who is going to believe that you and I were talking in the car all this while, and that *somebody else* came and wrung her neck?"

"But I can swear—"

"Who would believe you?" he said sadly. "Ah, Jenny, that's the way it is. Don't you see?"

I saw. That was the way it was. My heart had been on my sleeve for all to see, for him to see, a long, long time. No testimony of mine could help him.

"What good can it do if you and I are both dragged into the limelight and dirtied by the newspapers?" he demanded. "We didn't hurt her. But we'll be the first ones suspected. We are set up for it. Perfectly."

"We'd be cleared," I said feebly, "as soon as they find out—"

"And will suspecting us and dirtying us *help* them find out?" he said angrily. "How could it? Suspecting us will only help the one who did do it. By the time they get through with you and me . . ." He shook his head desperately. "I'm not going to let this happen. You were good to listen. You were doing what was kind. You don't deserve to be dragged into something like this. Just because I had to cry on your shoulder—"

"You didn't cry," I murmured.

But I could see ahead now and if I had been the kind to carry on, I would have cried. I could see myself trying to tell the truth, which would sound so feeble and unbelievable beside the powerful motives both of us had to—hurt Celia, who had hurt us.

I thought of my father, who was old and not well. Celia's death would be rough enough on him. How much worse to have to watch me being suspected of her murder! I felt a pang of terror when I realized that on top of all the rest, I was Celia's heir. And loved the man, as everyone knew, who needed Celia's money so much.

Blair was right. We were set up for it—both of us, together, perfectly.

"Jenny," Blair said, "we are going to have to get out from under."

"I don't see how," I said.

"We've lost—let's see—thirty-nine minutes. If we could account for that time some other way . . ."

"Hurry on to town, you mean?"

"No, we can't make up that much time. And we can't take the chance of speeding. But I've got an idea so crazy . . . Jenny, have you nerve enough to fake an alibi?"

"I guess so."

"I suppose it's wrong—"

"I'm not so sure it would be wrong." My teeth were chattering. "It might be foolish."

"We'll go back if you say so," Blair told me. "I could take it. Don't much care. But I want to get *you* out of this mess. Please let me, Jenny?" he begged. "It will be so damn nasty."

The thing I was thinking now was purely selfish. If we had to go through something "so damn nasty," then never (never, never, never!) could Blair and I be together. "What do you think of those two? Hah!" "Pretty fishy." "What's the answer? He got the money, she got her man. Hah!" I could hear it . . .

The law couldn't *make* us innocent. We would be guilty the moment we got together—or judged guilty by people's tongues. So we would have to stay apart.

I took hold of myself. "If you've got an idea, tell me," I said.

We sat there a few more minutes, while Blair figured it out. That scenic mountain road was not much used at night. We were lucky, and no car came by.

Blair was doing arithmetic. He explained. I understood. We could try.

Finally we went on another mile. High on the bank to our right was a cabin. Blair knew who sometimes lived there. It was a wild and lonely spot, but we could see a light in the windows.

Blair let the car coast silently on the slight downgrade, until we were well beyond that cabin. Then he stopped the car and I got out.

"It had better be you," Blair whispered, "because everyone thought I was drunk, remember? Can you do this, Jenny?"

"Of course," I said. "Wait till I get my shoes."

"Shoes?" He fumbled around on the seat of the car. "Jenny, we can *use* your shoes," he exclaimed. "Take just this one. Hook the heel in your belt. You are supposed to have been walking, but of course you couldn't walk in those things. Look, I'll throw your other shoe out of the car a couple of miles farther on. You watch out for it. That's going to look good. Look like evidence. Now, don't try to rouse anybody for nine or ten minutes. Can you time it? Use the waiting to beat up your stockings. Maybe your dress. Remember, you have walked you don't know how far. But it's taken you nearly an hour. This is how we make up those lost minutes. Use the phone right away. I know this guy, Frederick, is there, this weekend. There's a light. But if by chance he isn't home, you break a window and get in and use that phone."

"I will. I will. I understand."

"It's risky. If I meet anyone in the next few miles, we'll be in the soup, Jenny." He touched my cheek. "So young and fair . . ." I thought he said.

"We are in the soup," I said impatiently. "Let's do it, Blair. Better to try to get out than just stay there."

His fingertips trailed off my face. The car started and softly crept away.

I paced and stamped and kicked the ground with my stockinged feet. I dragged my organdy along some briary stuff. I tore my stole. I fell on my knees to dirty my skirt. These were mad antics, alone in that wild dark silent spot. All the time I was counting off the minutes. Not thinking about Celia. Not thinking about anything but making his plan work.

Finally, I went limping and panting up the rutted way to the cabin. I beat on the door. The man who opened it was stricken dumb.

"Excuse me for disturbing—" I was really breathless. "Our car is stuck up the road. Could I please use your phone?"

"Of course," he said shrilly, as if I had frightened him out of his wits. "Come in. Come in."

He rolled his eyes at me as I limped in, looked about, and spotted his phone. I called my father's house. "Dad? It's Jenny. Blair and I started home around the mountain and the car broke down. I just don't want you to worry. What time is it now?"

"It's eleven-o-four," said my dad in gruff precision. "I thought you were going to stay over to Carmen's."

"No, we started home. But I don't know when we'll get in now. Got to call a garage."

"Was it a crackup, Jenny?" Dad was suspicious.

"No, no. I'm perfectly all right, and so is Blair. Something conked out in the motor, that's all. Don't worry."

"Where is Celia?"

"Oh, she stayed," I said carelessly. (I couldn't tell him she was dead. I wasn't supposed to know it. Ah, but he would know it all too soon!)

I called an all-night garage.

"Lady, that's a long way around the mountain and it's pretty late."

"It's only a little after eleven," I said tartly, and gratefully. I argued with him, emphasizing the time, insisted that I had left a friend marooned in the car. At last he agreed to send somebody. Then I sagged.

"Sit down," my host said cordially, as if he had now assimilated his surprise. "You look tired. My name, by the way, is Lloyd Frederick."

"I'm Jenny Olcutt. I guess I look outlandish. This costume was for a garden wedding, a long time ago today."

"You look very pretty," he said gallantly. "A bit bedraggled. Haven't you any shoes? How far did you have to walk? Better let me pour you a drink."

He was an extraordinarily handsome man. A small-time actor, Blair had said. No one could have been kinder. He brought me the drink. He also brought a big bowl full of warm water and I stripped off my ruined nylons and put my feet, that I had taken care to bruise, into the warm comfort of it.

Frederick watched with amusement as I plucked the shoe from where it was hanging at my belt.

"You can see that these aren't exactly hiking boots," I said, patting my belt. "Oh, me," I sighed. "I've lost my other shoe."

"Shoe!" He raised an eyebrow at the frivolous contraption. "I thought it was some kind of modernistic corsage. How could you even stand up in such a thing?"

"They are pretty much for sitting down," I laughed. "Still, it's possible." I thrust my damp toes into it and fingered the straps. "Like this. Oh, darn, the other one is lost. And they cost a fortune."

"A fortune? For three cents' worth of whatever that is?" He seemed amused. "There's never any traffic on this road at night. No one is going to run over your other shoe. We'll find it."

He was going to take his car out and bring me to Blair. I knew that Blair had had plenty of time to fake a breakdown, so I didn't stall too long with the footbath. I played my role. I thrust aside the heavy knowledge of Celia's death, and the heavy knowledge that I was telling lies and using this kind man for a purpose he couldn't imagine. I even found it possible to be rather gay and to look at him flirtatiously.

We went outside. I was barefoot. I "forgot" my one shoe.

He went behind the cabin and backed his car out from a kind of lean-to. I got in. It was a strange ride. For some reason neither of us spoke of anything but my missing shoe. We were obsessed by it. We went on a mile, two miles. No shoe in the road. We went almost three miles.

Then we saw the flames. I screamed. A car was burning, down there, down at the bottom of the mountain slope off to the left. We got out and ran. A strange man stood at the brink. Then I saw Blair lying on the road.

I knelt beside him in panic. His warm hand clung to mine. I could hear the stranger talking rapidly to Mr. Frederick. "Me and a friend was coming around the mountain in his half-truck. Didn't mean to get on this road. Fact, we was lost. We was looking for a turnaround. So we find this fella, stalled in a fancy car. Well, so we manage to turn the truck and we was going to give him a push, see would that start his motor. By golly, that fancy job went right outa control! He pretty near went over with her. Just made it out as she tipped and went over. Busted his leg, though, or so it looks like. Fella that was with me, *he's* gone back to town in the truck to get an ambulance out here. Better wait on *it*, I'd say. Don't want to move no broken bones. Cheee, look at her burn!"

Only I could hear Blair's whisper. "Jenny, too many shoes. I must have given you *her* shoe."

Celia's shoe!

"They are just alike," I whispered.

"When I found a *pair* of shoes on the car floor . . . didn't know what to do. Couldn't throw one of them out—Jenny, I didn't know which foot! Do you see? Couldn't let you end up with two left shoes. Fatal. Didn't know which one was the 'other' shoe."

"Ssh." I was so close we could have kissed. "Where are my shoes now?"

"In the car. Burning."

"They'll burn fine," I said. "It won't matter. Are you hurt very much?"

"Not so bad," he said, his voice low but calm, almost cheerful. "Doesn't anything shake your nerve?" He caught at my shoulder. "Skip all this, Jenny. You'd better tell the truth. Nobody on earth could ever believe . . . So young and fair."

His voice had become too loud. So I kissed him. Afterward, I whispered, "Too late. We have to stick to the story. Don't you talk at all."

"If you get hurt—" he began, and then he fainted.

I rode into town in the ambulance when it came. All the way I thought about those shoes. Celia's right shoe was in the man's cabin. Both my shoes had burned with Blair's convertible. But I'd said I'd lost one on the road. Well, I would say that it must have been taken away by some animal.

When Blair, still unconscious, had been delivered to the hospital and I was limping wearily through the lobby to call a cab and get home, I ran into the policeman.

"You Miss Jenny Olcutt?" He wore plain clothes, but he was some kind of policeman—I knew it at once. "Had a little trouble?" he asked.

"Well, yes, we did, and I'm—a little bit worn out." I smiled politely.

"I don't know if you've been told." He shifted his weight. "Miss Celia Olcutt. Isn't that your sister?"

"Stepsister," I corrected mechanically.

"She was found dead," he said, abruptly enough to shock me.

It wasn't difficult to look shocked. I was scared.

"I understand there was a quarrel at this party." So he knew about that.

"Yes, that's why Mr. Meaghan and I left early."

"Pretty drunk, was he?"

"Well, I drove. He fell asleep."

"Left that house out there at ten o'clock? Took the mountain road? Why?"

"I don't know why," I said flatly. Blair and I had not discussed any possible reason. But I saw, now, that my very lack of reason was more convincing.

"Car stalled, you say? So you walked about three miles back to this Frederick's place? Why back?"

"Going ahead was farther and steeper," I explained.

"Why didn't your boy friend do the walking?"

"Well, you see, he had been drinking."

"Yeah," the policeman said. It was convincing. "Now you were at Frederick's place by eleven-o-four?"

"Was I?" I frowned.

"That's when you phoned your father. The garage says you phoned them at eleven-o-eight. That right?"

"I guess so," I said, looking bewildered. (But I was not. He was only doing the arithmetic that Blair and I had planned for him to do.)

"Now, Celia Olcutt," he went on, "she left the party at ten-twenty. Must have walked down those long stairs."

"Why?" I burst out. "What for? Was she going to hitchhike on the highway? Or what?" I honestly did not know the answer. My bewilderment was so convincing that I felt a surge of confidence.

"We think she could have had a rendezvous," he said. "She was seen talking on the phone. Or could be she just wandered outside and somebody called to her." He looked sly.

I looked as baffled as I genuinely felt. "*Called* to her?"

"Maybe I better check some figures with you, young lady. Mr. Meaghan's car went a mile down the drive to the bottom of the stairs, then three miles beyond. At maximum speed on that kind of road at night it would have got to the place where it broke down in, say, seven or eight minutes. After that you walked in your stocking feet three miles up and downgrade in the dark. Superhuman if you did it in, say, less than forty-five minutes. So even taking the fastest times, it didn't work out. Celia Olcutt left the house at ten-twenty, and it must have taken her *some* time to get down to the highway and get killed. Let me see—all you and Meaghan had was between, say, ten twenty-five and—"

"What are you talking about?" I said. "Ten twenty-five?"

"I mean if you killed her," he said.

I just stared at him.

"If you did, then you got to tear off four miles on the mountain road and walk back three and get there not long after eleven. It just don't work out."

"You've lost me," I said to him boldly.

"I'm saying that if you really walked back from that breakdown, then you and Blair Meaghan are alibied for the murder of Celia Olcutt."

"I should hope so," I said angrily.

"Now, now," he said in a gentle tone. "I can see you aren't a stupid young lady. You had motives, you know—both of you."

"Did we?" I protested. "Well, how did we get at her? Did we wait around for our victim to 'wander' out?"

"Or you called her out, on the phone," he said soberly. "There's a phone booth in a gas station not too far down the highway."

"But who could have phoned her?" I asked in real perplexity. "Did someone *call* her to the phone? Would *she* answer the phone in Carmen's house?"

He let out a humming sound. I had dented him. "Well, I'll tell you, Miss, I got to go over the ground. And that's my duty. How about coming with me? And talk to this Frederick, too?"

"Now?" I rubbed my eyes.

"I know you're tired. Especially after that long walk." I didn't like the sound of that.

"I might as well," I said. "How could I sleep?"

I went with him. I knew, all the time, that our story hinged on one thing. The body of Celia must have had only one shoe. (Her other shoe was at Frederick's and supposed to be mine.) But no shoes of mine were lying in the road. Our story lacked that bit. And Celia's missing shoe was potentially dangerous—as soon as my policeman saw it.

Yet the one thing that would really give us away would be if the police were to find any traces of my own two shoes in the burning car. Then Blair and I would be proved liars—we would be prime suspects. Celia's shoe would then become evidence against us.

I went with the policeman because I had to know.

I couldn't ask, but I might find out.

I did. We stopped at the point of the accident and looked down at the ruins of Blair's car. A man in uniform came up to us. "Not a thing left," he said. My policeman checked his speedometer and we drove on.

I breathed a little easier.

It was close to dawn, but Lloyd Frederick was up and about. "Couldn't sleep," he said. "Burning automobiles, broken legs, young woman in distress—too much for *me*."

He let us in and offered coffee.

My policeman said, "Reason I got to check up on this car breakdown, there's been a murder. Stepsister of *this* Miss Olcutt got strangled to death last night."

"Not Celia Olcutt!" cried Lloyd Frederick.

"You know the lady?" The policeman and I were both suddenly suspicious.

"Of course. I met her in a business way." He went through a gamut of explanations, which added no light. Then my policeman got down to Celia's murder.

"Tell me what happened around here last night. You hear Mr. Meaghan's car go by, for instance? If so, when?"

"I may have heard it." Frederick cocked his handsome head. "Lord, I don't know. I was reading scripts. Paying no attention. I don't even know when Miss Jenny Olcutt got here." He smiled at me.

"You know this Miss Olcutt, too?"

"Never saw her before tonight, to my sorrow," he said gallantly. His eyes sought mine.

"I'm looking for some kind of tricky time business," said my policeman frankly. "This Meaghan had a real dilly of a fight with the murdered girl. He even said he ought to wring her neck. He had plenty of motive. What I need now is his opportunity."

Frederick looked startled. "But wasn't Miss Jenny with him? You don't think she—"

"Oh, I wonder," my policeman said blithely, "because it's my job to wonder. Now, they tell me that shoes were worn at this wedding. But it's a funny thing." My heart stopped. "Where are this Miss Olcutt's shoes? Maybe their condition could tell me something."

He looked shrewd. Didn't he believe that I had walked three miles? Was there a sign on me, something I didn't know about, to tell him that I hadn't?

"This lady's shoes, if that's what you can call them, won't tell you much," Lloyd Frederick said. "I'll show you." He rummaged on a shelf and turned to us with a pair of shoes in his hands. "See? I finally found your other one," he said to me, flashing his smile. "You must have dropped it just after you started walking to this cabin. You see, officer? She couldn't walk in these. In fact, these are sitting-down shoes, so I am told."

He was being very charming.

"*Those are shoes!*" my policeman said, staring at them incredulously.

"May I put them on?" I said.

So I put them on. I stood up in the silly things. My feet were swollen and the straps cut into them. But, standing there in *two* shoes, I was safe. Blair was safe. Our story was safe; it would hold up. Who could prove it wasn't true?

I could.

"I guess I'm not Cinderella," I sighed. "I'm the stepsister. These are Celia's shoes. See, they're too small for me!"

"But that's impossible!" cried Frederick.

"Celia had *no* shoes on, did she?" I asked my policeman. "No shoes at all. Well, I can tell you how *one* of them got here. You will have to ask Mr. Frederick about the other one."

"What are you trying to say?" cried Frederick. "What do you mean, these are Celia's shoes? They can't be too small for you. They're exactly the same—"

"That's because they are *both* Celia's," I said patiently.

"That's not so! Only the one . . ." Frederick yelled—and when he saw that he had tripped on his own tongue he dove for me. My policeman jumped protectively, before Lloyd Frederick could wring my neck . . .

I said to Blair in the hospital, "She phoned him."

"Celia was bound he'd have a part in my picture," Blair told me. "He's pure ham. I couldn't do that. I suppose she called to tell him that we'd split up."

"He met her at the bottom of the stairs," I went on. "Probably she got into his car to talk. Probably she had her shoes in her hand—she couldn't have walked down all those steps with them on. He was furious that she'd muffed the deal, and she was in that vicious mood. She made him feel like wringing her neck. And he did. Dumped her out. Hurried home. No wonder I scared him! I must have looked like Celia's ghost, in the same dress."

"And then you left her shoe in the cabin—the shoe I'd picked up next to her body."

"Celia's other shoe must have been in his car," I said. "He found it too late. Maybe he found it when he got the car out for me. That was a strange ride. Shoes on our minds. Both of us."

"Why too late, Jenny?"

"If he'd found it *before* I came, he'd have paid more attention."

Blair twisted in the hospital bed. "I don't see why he didn't just destroy the shoe that he knew was Celia's."

"Instead, he helped our story," I said. "Of course, he believed me—he knew who had killed Celia. He just saw a chance to get rid of Celia's shoe."

"I don't get it."

"Well, I did. After we had gone to the hospital, he must have rushed back to the cabin, took her shoe in, and picked up the one he thought was mine, to compare them. They were mates, a right and a left. They were the same size. Don't you see why he had to do what he did? He hadn't paid close attention to me. He'd seen me put my foot into one of those shoes. But he must have shuffled them, got them mixed up, and didn't know which one *I* had brought to the cabin. Don't you see?—he couldn't be sure *which one to destroy*. But *I'd* know which one I'd put my foot in. He didn't."

"So he cleverly produced both."

"We'd watched the road. No shoe of mine there. He thought it was pretty clever."

"It *was* clever," Blair said.

"Yes, I know."

Blair sighed. "Until you took a notion to lie about the size."

"That wasn't hard," I said. "My feet were all puffed up. So I knew he'd think some store could prove that they really were Celia's shoes. It rattled him. He just blew up."

"You ought to be in the motion-picture industry," Blair said. "Anybody who can *think* in the midst of all that trouble and confusion . . ." Then he went on gently. "But he had helped us, Jenny. We were pretty safe."

"No," I said. "Because he was a murderer. Besides, I don't like telling lies." I broke off. "Blair, what are they going to do to us?"

Blair was laughing at me. "You beat all," he teased. "You don't like telling lies and so you told another. Know what I think? You've got the police baffled."

After a while I said, "One thing . . . I'll have Celia's money. So if they don't get around to putting us in jail or anything, do you want a partner?"

Blair sat up as far as he could. "No," he shouted. Then he shouted, "Yes."

"Well, which?" I said.

"I want *you* for a partner all the rest of my life," he said, "as you well know. But not that money!"

"S-sh," I said. "Don't look so wild. There isn't any problem. And we'll make your picture."

Blair said, "I think we will," in a funny voice.

Well, they didn't put us in jail. We'd told a lot of lies. Yet our lies had helped to catch the murderer, so I suppose it was a little confusing to the police.

Anyhow, the real murderer has been caught. No doubt hangs over us now and nothing can keep us apart.

People talk, of course. People say we must be crazy. We are going to make a motion picture, although all we have is the dream. We gave away the money. To a charitable foundation. It buys things for poor needy persons. Especially shoes.

Dennis O'Neil

Report on a Broken Bridge

It wasn't love or money that drove Otis Belding to his very thorough suicide: it was something bigger, lots bigger, and knowing about it is pushing me toward a premature demise, too.

You know, boss, we might have guessed the *why* of his death if we'd bothered to think about who he was, where he came from, and especially what he'd accomplished. I'd already completed my investigation by the time I got round to looking at the movies that kid happened to be taking when Belding made his spectacular exit; but as soon as I saw them I knew my guesses were correct. I sniffed an apocalypse.

You're now reading this night letter and you'll never see the prints I've forwarded to the New York office, so I'll give you a preview. Here's what the kid's camera caught:

Background: the Bridge Research complex. Foreground: a lake, placid, dotted with tiny ripples, deep-blue near the shore and power-blue in the center. In the far distance: the Ozark Mountains. Above: more blue, streaked with wisps of white. And around, everywhere: deep-green—leaves that look heavy enough to use as anchors.

Enter Belding, in a sleek shiny aluminum dinghy, rowing to the middle of the water—rowing despite a hefty outboard perched on the stern. (At this point the kid changed to a telescopic lens.) Belding carefully cuts off the end of a long brown cigar, places the gold cigar clipper and severed tip in the pocket of his shirt, puts fire to the cigar with a gold lighter. Draws, exhales, slowly gazes up, down. Then he cautiously edges to the bow and sits on top of the wooden keg: the boat lists, and he has a few bad moments getting balanced. He does, though, and after another long look at the scenery he reaches down with his cigar and calmly touches a fuse stuck in the keg's lid.

He sits quietly and I'm pretty sure he's smiling. Sits relaxed as a stone, peacefully smoking. There is a hard red flash and the camera shakes violently, and searches randomly, glimpsing a small army of frogs leaping like dervishes, and then focuses on where Belding had been. He isn't, not any more. There is only a widening circle of

133

dirty gray in the powder-blue, and a cloudlet of bluish haze crowning a roiling column.

It reminds me of the climax of an arty foreign flick—the kind that beats you over the head with profound Symbolism and in which the director uses the H-Bomb mushroom the way a comic strip uses exclamation points.

My favorite headline was on page three of the *Daily News,* amid human-interest drivel about our Indian Summer heat wave. You remember: *Boy Wonder Multimillionaire Ends with a Bang.*

Before the ink was dry on that little paradigm of class journalism you had me and my hangover in your office. The air-conditioning was on the blink—again!—and your bald pate was sweat-shiny enough to use as a shaving mirror. You looked like you'd been moldering in a rain forest for a couple of centuries, and coherency was not your strong trait, not that morning. I understood from your sputtering that Otis had done himself in, that the Board had panicked, and that unless we could demonstrate that our late president had shuffled off for reasons unconnected with the affairs of Bridge Enterprises, Inc., our stock certificates would soon be worth something less than bus transfers. I concurred, and hied away to shoot the trouble.

By noon I was aboard an Eastern jet out of Newark, grimly contemplating the early market report in the first edition of the *Post:* Bridge Enterprises was selling at 31½, down 7 in the first two hours of trading. My wallet ached: I own 300 shares myself.

I picked up a St. Louis paper while waiting for my rent-a-car at Lambert Field: at the day's closing we were selling at 29.

I drove southwest wondering why nobody touts the beauty of that part of the country. There's nothing out here so awesome as the Grand Canyon or as numbingly spectacular as the Rockies, but nonetheless the geography is lovely—soft-edged hills and quiet valleys and lush forests. That land, west of St. Louis, is feminine America, loving and open: maybe if I'd ever found a human equivalent I wouldn't be typing this with a Beretta in my lap.

Ugliness begins about five miles north of Belding's birthplace, a town called Feeley that used to be small and isn't now because our company built a lead-refining plant close by. Along came Bridge Enterprises and zapped 75 acres of trees and bulldozed 75 acres of grass and filled a stream with pulped garbage, bringing population and prosperity. Belding's gift to his childhood. Swell gift. The stink is so powerful it must have seeped into the soil; the sky is the color of sooty canvas; the buildings are as shocking as tarantulas on a loveseat. Up there in our air-conditioned, pastel-hued headquarters we just don't realize how gruesome the nitty-gritty is.

Feeley itself can't have changed much. Basically it's one square containing a post office, a bar with liquor store attached, an I.G.A. supermarket, a funeral parlor, and a gas station. Sundry other businesses and a scattering of houses border the square, and more are abuilding. I patronized the liquor store, obtained a fifth of my favorite, and the information that one Hap Elsenmeyer had once been Otis Belding's boyhood buddy. I went to see old buddy Hap, owner of the gas station.

Detective fiction is full of scenes in which the amiable private eye loosens the tonsils of suspicious locals with a dram of the barley. No lie, boss. Elsenmeyer is obviously a man familiar with a bottle. I had to merely hint, to sort of wave the bottle nonchalantly. Old Hap told an adolescent to mind the pumps and we retired to his office.

He produced cracked china mugs with the panache of a carny conjuror producing bunnies, and I poured. The room was pleasantly old-fashioned—even had an overhead fan that sort of sloshed the humidity around—and the pungent smell of petroleum was a relief from the lead fumes outside. We opined on the heat, agreed it sure was fierce for November, and nitter-nattered our way to talking about Otis.

I won't attempt to transcribe Elsenmeyer's dialect in all its drawly splendor. You'll have to be satisfied with the bones of the story he told me.

Otis Belding's real-life Horatio Alger saga began with a hook and a worm. The lad was a pure genius at finding fishing holes. From age six on he had hunches where they'd be biting on any given morning, and the hunches were always dead-center. That was a useful talent for him, giving him a tot of social acceptance and putting food in his belly. Came fishing time his schoolmates forgave him his pa, the town ne're-do-well, and his ma, the town crazy. During the winter Otis starved and was taunted; summers he ate fresh fish and was grudgingly respected. Elsenmeyer once asked Otis how he could be so gol-ding *certain,* and Otis said he didn't know, he just had these *feelings.*

He was, in effect, orphaned at the age of ten. His father expired in a ditch one winter night and the authorities carted his mother off to the county mental hospital, where she died some years later. An aunt did a perfectly rotten job of guardianship. Mostly, Otis lived alone in a shack near the site of the future refinery, getting to school now and again, somehow surviving the cold months. Age eleven, he discovered games and took his first hesitant steps toward the Dow Jones Index and a cask of high-grade blasting powder.

A bunch of the good old boys used to meet in the back room of the tavern evenings for cards. Friendly poker, two-bit limit. Otis took to hanging around, probably to escape the cold of the shack. I'm guessing now, but I think he must have swiped some money from his aunt's purse one day and wangled himself a seat at the table. Played smart, according to Elsenmeyer—real smart. Uncanny smart. Walked away with enough dollars to stand beers for the bunch, root beer for himself. Kept out a stake, though, and sat in the following session, and every session thereafter, and won more than he could have made in a whole summer's field laboring. The boys were mildly amazed but, I gather, tolerant. Otis became a pet topic of Feeley conversation.

A trucker named Batson J. Frink ended Otis's poker career. Frink pushed a tractor-trailer rig for a Kansas City outfit and often joined the game when he was passing through. Nobody much liked Frink, but nobody told him, because he was big and mean. He was also a sore loser. He lost heavily to Otis on July 4, 1951—Elsenmeyer remembers the date exactly—and didn't enjoy it, not one bit.

He waited for Otis outside the bar while Otis was buying drinks, caught the boy, dragged him behind the building, and beat him mercilessly. Elsenmeyer was a witness; he tells it with a connoisseur's glee—how the trucker punched Otis to blood and bruises, broke a rib, kicked out teeth. Finally Frink was too tired to continue. He paused to catch his breath—and heard his death pronouned.

Sitting against the rear wall, Otis looked up through swollen eyelids and said, "You're going to die tonight." Just those five words, spoken with absolute conviction. Frink must have been shaken by them, because he went to his rig and drove off.

I checked with the Highway Patrol. The official report confirms Hap Elsenmeyer's story. Between 9:00 and 9:15 on the night of July 4, 1951, a tractor-trailer driven by Batson J. Frink was rounding a steep curve eight miles south of Feeley. The load in the trailer apparently shifted, causing the rig to topple off the road, down into a gulley, and explode. The cargo of magnesium ingots caught fire. Frink's body was never recovered.

Leaving Feeley, I had my first intimations that our late leader had been a hint spooky. Then I thought, no, it was only a coincidence. Sure.

The data you supplied led me next to East St. Louis. The records there showed that Belding had resided in a boardinghouse near the Obear Nestor bottle factory, which is not any urban gem of a neighborhood, believe you me. A Mrs. McNally was, and is, the landlady. Picture the dark side of the moon and see McNally—a walking crater, this senior citizen, and easily 90 percent malice. The remaining 10 percent praises the memory of Otis Belding.

"A *good* boy," she insisted. "Best boy I ever knew."

To prove the assertion she pointed to a plaster Virgin set on a doily on a shelf in the parlor. "Bought me that with his first big winnings, Otis did," Mrs. McNally crowed. "Ain't it lovely?"

You bet, Mrs. McNally, I agreed. Now about those winnings—

Belding's co-boarder had been a man named Lewis Thalier, a wine jockey and doer of odd jobs at a racetrack, Cahokia Downs. Thalier, it seems, had been a big noise in the Twenties. The usual weepy history: he'd lost everything in the '29 crash, cocooned himself inside the grape, and never really emerged. Until young Otis appeared, that is.

In the beginning Otis developed his gambling talent—studied the horse forms Thalier brought home and had the wino place bets for him. Thalier noticed that the lad won consistently, and he began making duplicate bets. Thalier prospered, as did his youthful mentor. After a particularly spectacular afternoon with the ponies Thalier fueled himself with champagne—no more California port for *this* ex-tycoon—and reminisced, aloud and at length. Dug forth from his trunk a sheaf of gaudy stock certificates, displayed them to Otis, and discoursed regarding the market.

Otis was interested, and how. He exhausted Thalier's lore and the next morning got an armful of books from the public library. He spent days poring over the books and the financial sections of local papers and, when he learned of its existence, *The Wall Street Journal*. Then he bought Thalier a new suit and embarked on his second and penultimate career.

"The other boarders' eyes plain bugged when they see old Lewis and Otis come out on the porch looking like a bandbox," Mrs. McNally croaked warmly. "They go over the bridge downtown and come back with a big envelope. They spread a bunch of papers on the kitchen floor and look at them like they was gold or something. 'We gonna be rich,' Lewis says. Young Otis, he nods his head yes."

Belding stayed at Mrs. McNally's for nine years. Thalier resurrected dormant expertise in food, drink, music, and in the midst of that slum they lived lavishly. Each Wednesday Thalier obediently guided a spanking limousine across the bridge and returned bearing a fresh envelope and the grandest largess that St. Louis could provide—records, clothes, prime steaks, bonded bourbon.

"Boarders was green with envy," Mrs. McNally solemnly assured me.

Let it be noted that Belding's appetites extended beyond his stomach, as is normal, and as the gossip columnists have frequently observed. With whom is not relevant, and anyway, you'll have a chance to leer further on in this narrative.

Belding terminated the slum idyll on his twenty-first birthday. He and Thalier drove across the Eads Bridge for the last time, saw a lawyer, signed papers, and returned to the boardinghouse. At the curb Belding took the wheel, said goodbye to Thalier, and went away without bothering to collect the belongings from his room. Thalier was official owner of $100,000 worth of blue-chip securities; Belding held for himself $600,000 worth of wildly speculative issues.

Thalier's income kept him happily juiced for his remaining half decade: his liver had the privilege of succumbing to only the finest French and Italian vintages.

Our accounting department will confirm that Mrs. McNally still receives a check for $400 every month—more than the old witch deserves.

I won't bore you with my pursuit of the Belding success saga. What you're getting, boss, is pure poetry; if you want prosaic details send another lackey for them. Suffice to say, for a week I relearned what we both vividly know. If you've forgotten any of it, read the clippings from *Time, Fortune, Forbes, The Wall Street Journal*, et al.

Boy Wonder Belding could do no financial wrong: he got rich, richer, damn near richest. Two weeks before the beginning of the great computer boom he bought the software outfit. Two weeks prior to the McDonnel-Douglas merger he bought McDonnel. Two weeks before the Apollo contracts were awarded he bought Texas Instrument. And two weeks before the start of the TV season that made camp as obsolete as button hooks he unloaded that corny television show. The list goes on and on, like a list of Howard Hughes's fondest dreams.

I'm an investigator, an expert snoop, so I snooped, thoroughly and relentlessly; through the pads in Malibu, Newport, and Acapulco; the permanent suite in Las Vegas; the yacht; and I disproved to my complete satisfaction the hoary notion that the wealthy can't be happy. Listen, he was *happy*. Young, healthy, handsome, and able to buy spares of anything—a regular bouncing bundle of sybaritic joy was Otis Belding. Until last September.

In 1966 he formed Bridge Enterprises and unleashed on the world the hokey motto that graces our letterheads: *Building Bridges to the Future*. Otis Belding believed those words, I think. He was cut from a fairly idealistic cloth; he was maybe that rare mass entrepreneur who actually saw himself and his affairs as a force for progress. Sure, he engineered dirty deals, but he was unique in *admitting* them, and he had an excuse. You remember the speech he delivered at the convention of the National Association of Manufacturers—the lines quoted in all the press releases: "I regret having harmed a few relatively innocent parties. I harmed them in order to insure a brighter tomorrow for their children."

Horrible speech. Honest sentiment, though. Bear it in mind while I take you to upstate New York.

I won't give you my impressions of our Hudson River plant: you've already been treated to my description of the Feeley refinery, right? Well, the Hudson facility isn't quite as bad—not quite. A lot of money was spent on landscape cosmetics.

The manager, Tyrone Thomas, gave me the grand tour. He's a proud fellow. He speaks of extracting detergent phosphates from raw chemicals like a frat brother boasting a conquest. I understood maybe one-tenth of his rap. We finished the tour at the wide grass terrace between the plant and the river. Looking out over the Hudson, with the industrial labyrinth at my back, I could almost forget where I was, except that I felt the vibration of drainage pumps through my shoe soles and saw the churning of the water where the pipes empty into it.

"You can see for yourself this is the finest facility of its kind in the world," Thomas was saying. "Per diem gross is forty tons. We hope to up that the coming fiscal period."

"Very impressive," I said. "Was Mr. Belding pleased?"

"Pleased as Punch. Gave me a bonus, promised another."

"No problems?"

"None worth talking about. We had some trouble with the radicals at the beginning, but Mr. Belding handled it all right."

"Radicals?"

Thomas smiled wearily. "Not the card-carrying sort. The dupes. At least, I think they're dupes."

I asked, "Who exactly are they?"

"The crowd from the university. They did a lot of picketing when we first went into operation. Men with the beards and the hair, girls with the signs and the beads—the whole shebang. It got on the TV news shows."

"They have something against phosphates?"

"They have something against progress," Thomas said righteously. "Darn fools. Claimed we were ruining the environment. That's a pile of you-know-what. Look around, judge for yourself. This land was going to waste before Bridge moved in. Nothing here but chipmunks. We pumped millions into the local economy, put five thousand men to work, going to take another two thousand if we get a go-ahead on the new wing. I ask you, is that *ruining?*"

"Did Mr. Belding do anything about the protests?"

"Oh, sure. He met with 'em on four or five separate occasions. He was a heck of a sight more patient than I'd've been in his position. He volunteered to put in the sod we're standing on and the drainage network underground. Cost a bundle, but they weren't satisfied. They said we're killing fish. Imagine. All that fuss over some fish. Heck-fire, I'd've offered to buy 'em a carload of fish to shut 'em up. Finally Mr. Belding promised to finance a research laboratory and that got rid of the pests."

And it got rid of me, too. I left Thomas to his phosphates and tucked myself into a motel for the night. You're getting nowhere, I told myself sternly, and myself agreed. My notebook and tape recorder were jammed with information, true, but I'd discovered no tidbits absent from *Who's Who.*

The only thing I had learned was that Otis Belding never—*never*—made a financial mistake. I'd always assumed he must have committed a blunder or two along the way, even as you and I. He hadn't. Not one blunder. He'd cast his mortal remains to the lake breeze with a perfect financial record, and although his tranquillity had been infinitesimally marred by the Hudson protests, they shouldn't have upset him much, considering that they clued him to the sweetest tax dodge-cum-public relations coup a multimillionaire could wish for. Compared to the Bridge Research Center, Carnegie's libraries were so many sandboxes: the intellectuals applauded, the I.R.S. condoned, and the Silent Majority didn't hear about it, as usual. In short, the Center is another monotonous success.

As I was leaving the motel the next morning, you phoned and told me that the corporate fortunes were improving—we were selling over 30 again—and you said I should stay with the investigation another twenty-four hours, prepare a document to exhibit in the annual stockholders' booklet—show the Bridge Family that their officers *care*—and bring my expense account home. We'd gone through the motions and that was sufficient. You said.

As it happened, I *did* nail the reason for the suicide within a day, but if I hadn't I would have hung with the case regardless. Suddenly you didn't seem so almighty impressive, boss; suddenly your wrath held no terrors for me. Nor the loss of my job, either. Conclusion: subconsciously, I had the answer. Or I was on the edge of an inkling—no, in this context, better call it a premonition.

I had two more people to see. Dr. Harold Seabrook, head of the Research Center, would be in Europe until Thursday, his secretary told me long distance. So that left Miss X—Belding's mistress. I'd known about her, of course, as had you and most of the guys in the executive suite. Otis Belding's bucolic lady was the worst kept secret in the company. As acting chief of security, I'd made it my business to obtain her name and address; more, I'd run a somewhat-more-detailed-routine check on her—wouldn't do to have Belding victimized by an adventuress, I rationalized. I needn't have worried. Sandra Burkholt is nobody's *femme fatale.*

Frankly, I was curious. What manner of woman, I wondered, would cause a man like Belding to abandon his string of pneumatic starlets, theatrical *grandes dames,* and society sweethearts? Because abandon them he did—lopped them off like diseased limbs last summer, about the time he established the Research Center. My field personnel said *la Burkholt* was 32, single, living alone in a small isolated house not far from the Center, and the mother of an illegitimate son. Belding probably met her in November 1968, while she was employed as a typist at the Feeley refinery. It's possible he'd known her earlier, during his miserable childhood.

I arrived at her house at dusk on Wednesday. There was a sports car in the driveway: no other signs of prosperity. On the contrary. A bent rusty tricycle lay on the walk; the grass needed cutting; the house itself needed shingles and paint. Hardly a magnate's love nest.

She answered my knock and led me into the living room. The

inside was a perfect reflection of the exterior: shabby furniture, cracked linoleum floor, peeling wallpaper. And Sandra completed the motif. She isn't homely: there are lingering phantoms of an artful feline girl in her bold glance, in her quick sensuous smile. But she's worn. The red hair is stringy and faded, the skin rough, the figure sagging. Had Belding liked his women pitiable? Was it really love?

Feeling strangely like an archeologist prowling an ancient temple, I followed Sandra to the bedroom they had shared and viewed Belding's artifacts: a medium-priced portable phonograph, a mixed collection of records, and the books and magazines he'd read himself to sleep with. Three sorts of reading matter, divided into separate piles. Books on extra-sensory perception, ranging from inexpensive paperbacks to footnotey tomes to science-fiction novels. Stuff on ecology of approximately the same range, including a complete set of Sierra Club publications and a series of pamphlets from Barry Commoner's group at Washington University. And history books, mostly comprehensive texts. I paged through them, to no avail: Belding had not been an underliner.

We went into the kitchen. I unobtrusively turned on my tape recorder while Sandra concocted lemonade. That's right, boss—lemonade. As remarked, Miss Burkholt is not a *femme fatale*.

"I'll have to ask you to hold down your voice," the tape recorder echoes Sandra as I write. "My boy is sick in the next room there. Generally he's healthy as a horse. Must be one of those viruses."

Me: "I hope he feels better."

Sandra: "Thank you."

Me (hesitantly): "Did you know Mr. Belding well?"

Sandra: " 'Course. Not long, but well as can be. We were lovers."

Me (embarrassed): "Forgive me for asking—but did he buy you gifts? Did he have an arrangement with you?"

Sandra (chuckling, bless her): "You mean was I a kept woman? No, sir. Oh, he bought little presents for the house and for my boy. He bought me a mixmaster once, was I think the biggest thing. He never give me money and I didn't ask for any. Didn't expect any. It was purely a man-woman thing with us. I liked him. I believe he liked me. I'll miss my Otis."

Me: "Did you notice any recent change in his behavior?"

Sandra: "He was always—well, odd. Funny, he could be touching you and somehow not be there at all, like he'd left his body behind.

Oh, yes, there was one present Otis brought on his last visit I forgot about. He said something strange—"

She was interrupted by a thump from behind the wall. We rushed into the boy's cubbyhole. The child was lying in a tangle of quilt beside the bed, breathing in harsh rattling gasps. He was drenched with sweat, his skin wax-white. He wasn't suffering from virus: the kid was dying.

"We'd better get him to a hospital," I said.

Sandra wrapped him in the quilt and carried him to my car. I pegged the speedometer needle at 70 most of the distance to the local clinic. The decrepit general practitioner there diagnosed a ruptured appendix and confessed he had no facilities for treating acute peritonitis. I knew a clinic that did—coincidentally, the best medical setup in that area is at the Bridge refinery in Feeley. I got on the phone, chartered a private plane, and alerted one of those bright young specialists the company boasts of recruiting that Sandra and her son were on the way.

At the airfield I gave her my card and asked her to call the office if she or the boy needed anything. She promised she would.

Not being tired yet, I drove into the Ozark foothills, toward the Center. I surrendered to bizarre reflections—bizarre for me, anyway. Not since I'd been an altar boy waiting scared in the musty closeness of the confessional had I contemplated eternity. Maybe it was the country. If there were ghosts, they lurk in those hills, flash briefly, mockingly in headlight glare, and rattle forebodingly in leaves. Or maybe it was simple shame, an attempt to excuse my lack of professionalism. I hadn't seen Sandra earlier, during the Feeley phase of the inquiry, and that oversight had been wasteful, costly. But if I *had*, then I wouldn't have been there to bully medicos and pilots, and the boy might not have got the attention he needed. I entertained the notion that I served a benevolent destiny. Fate? Predestination? Whose will was my master? Certainly not Belding's.

Bridge Enterprises can be proud of its Research Center. Architecturally it's the best we have: instead of the usual eyesore, the building is dignified—predominantly vertical lines harmonizing with the surrounding pines. I parked in the visitor's lot and admired the flood-lit scene a bit. A guard demanded to know who I was. Then, miraculously transformed by my credentials, he hefted my bag and escorted me to the VIP quarters. Nice digs. Pastel and Danish plastic modern. Home away from . . .

A shaft of sunlight across my face woke me. I put on my most expensive lightweight suit and a white-on-white shirt-tie combo—to impress the scientific yokel with my Manhattan class.

Huh-*uh*. I doubt that Dr. Harold Seabrook *can* be impressed. He's a large chunk of dour impatience—six-six, big-bellied, features drawn as though his jowls were weighted. He doesn't speak: he spews.

We met in the lounge. As we talked he traced tiny precise geometrics on the formica table top in a spilling of iced tea.

"I can give you five minutes," he said brusquely.

I was annoyed. I'm a bigger corporate cheese than Seabrook. "You've got somewhere to go?" I asked.

"I've got to see about saving the human race from itself," he replied, managing not to sound corny. "I won't do it prattling with you."

"Funny," I mused sarcastically. "I read your job description. It said 'ecologist,' not 'messiah.' "

"No difference," he snapped.

Having nary a comeback to that I asked, "What exactly are you doing with the company's money? What's the project?"

He raised a brow. "At the moment? We're seeking a way to reduce the so-called 'greenhouse effect.' "

"You're messing with flowers?"

His tone put me back in knee pants and a dunce cap: I was the Second Grade's biggest dumbo, he the exasperated teacher. He said, "You've noticed the weather? Not enough heat is escaping into space. Pollutants have formed a curtain that traps short-wave radiation near the ground, and the temperature is rising to—"

I interrupted, "I don't need a pee-aitch-dee to tell me it's a hell of a hot November. I'm sure you geniuses will dope out the damnedest refrigerator in twenty years and we'll give you either a gold watch or a Nobel Prize, take your choice."

"Many of my colleagues would agree with you," he said with unexpected gentleness. "I do not, and neither did Otis Belding. He had a theory that a critical point will come in our poisoning of Earth, and when it does the planet will simply stop living—*stop*. All the life-support systems will disintegrate at once, and that will be the end. Finish. No more. We may have a few days, or a few hours, to regret our stupidity."

"That doesn't sound like it makes a lot of sense, Doc."

"I didn't think so either, at first. But I was reasoning conventionally. Then I pursued a line of research that Otis suggested and—"

His voice changed: the gentleness was gone. "You've wasted enough of my time."

He pulled a folded memo sheet from his yellow-stained lab jacket. "Otis said I was to give you this."

My name was scrawled on it, in Belding's handwriting.

"Hold it, Doc," I said. "I never *met* Otis Belding. He didn't even know I exist. You want me to believe he addressed a note to me personally before he died and left it with you? No way."

"Facts are facts," he said, getting up. "Excuse me."

He was gone, that fast, leaving another protest snagged in my throat and a zero limned in cold tea on the table. Vowing to humble him later, I opened the note.

It read:

"There's nothing to be done. It is too late. See model in my office." Signed: Otis Belding.

I obtained the key to his private office from the receptionist, climbed to the top floor, and entered. The room was barren as a Trappist cell—furnishings consisted solely of an army cot and a metal stand on top of which was a scale model of the Eads Bridge. The model was broken. Someone had hit it and broken it in half. It was a bridge that went nowhere.

There was a question yet to be answered. I used a phone in the lobby to call Sandra.

"How's your son?" I asked.

"He's doing nicely. That nice Dr. Benedict said he caught it in time. I want to thank you."

"My pleasure. Sandra, you remember what you were saying? About a present Otis bought?"

"That was the funniest he ever did. It was a gun—a pistol. I still have it, though Lord knows what I'll ever do with a gun. He gave it to me and said, 'If you love your son you'll do him this favor.' I suppose he was joking."

"Could be. 'Bye, Sandra."

I strolled outside and ambled across the sweep of lawn, down to the lake.

No hurry, not any more, for me, for you, for anyone. Because it's obvious why Otis Belding killed himself. He had a genius for prophecy, remember? I figure he had premonitions about the future—premonitions that slowly grew to convictions until, two weeks before an event, they became certainties. Once he became aware of something, he could predict its course. He became aware of ecology, he saw the "critical point" coming; he saw his future—our future—and sought refuge with a simple woman and her son, and failing to find comfort he chose to die.

Exactly thirteen days ago he chose to die.

I know how he felt. Like a man standing on a broken bridge.

I have my gun, and I've always hated being the last one out.

So—goodbye, boss.

Dorothy Salisbury Davis

Spring Fever

Sarah Shepherd watched her husband come down the stairs. He set his suitcase at the front door, checked his watch with the hall clock, and examined beneath his chin in the mirror. There was one spot he sometimes missed in shaving. He stepped back and examined himself full length, frowning a little. He was getting paunchy and not liking it. That critical of himself, how much more critical of her he might be. But he said nothing either in criticism or compliment, and she remembered, uncomfortably, doing all sorts of stunts to attract his eye: coy things—more becoming a girl than a woman of fifty-five. She did not feel her twelve years over Gerald . . . most of the time. Scarcely aware of the movement, she traced the shape of her stomach with her fingertips.

Gerald brought his sample spice kit into the living room and opened it. The aroma would linger for some time after he was gone. "There's enough wood, dear, if it gets cold tonight," he said. "And I wish you wouldn't haul things from the village. That's what delivery trucks are for." He numbered his solicitudes as he did the bottles in the sample case, and with the same noncommittal attention.

As he took the case from the table, she got up and went to the door with him. On the porch he hesitated a moment, flexing his shoulders and breathing deeply. "On a morning like this I almost wish I drove a car."

"You could learn, Gerald. You could reach your accounts in half the time, and —"

"No, dear. I'm quite content with my paper in the bus, and in a town a car's a nuisance." He stooped and brushed her cheek with his lips. "Hello, there!" he called out as he straightened up.

Her eyes followed the direction in which he had called. Their only close neighbor, a vegetable and flower grower, was following a plow behind his horse, his head as high as the horse's was low, the morning wind catching his thatch of grey hair and pointing it like a shock of wheat.

"That old boy has the life," Gerald said. "When I'm his age that's for me."

"He's not so old," she said.

"No, I guess he's not at that," he said. "Well, dear, I must be off. Till tomorrow night, take care of yourself."

His step down the road was almost jaunty. It was strange that he could not abide an automobile. But not having one was rather in the pattern. A car would be a tangible link between his life away and theirs at home. Climbing into it of an evening, she would have a feeling of his travels. The dust would rub off on her. As it was, the most she had of him away was the lingering pungency of a sample spice kit.

When he was out of sight she began her household chores—the breakfast dishes, beds, dusting. She had brought altogether too many things from the city. Her mother had left seventy years' accumulation in the old house, and now it was impossible to lay a book on the table without first moving a figurine, a vase, a piece of delft. Really the place was a clutter of bric-a-brac. Small wonder Gerald had changed toward her. It was not marriage that had changed him—it was this house, and herself settling in it like an old buddha with a bowl of incense in his lap.

A queer thing that this should occur to her only now, she thought. But it was not the first time. She was only now finding a word for it. Nor had Gerald always been this remote. Separating a memory of a particular moment in their early days, she caught his eyes searching hers—not numbering her years, as she might think were he to do it now, but measuring his own worth in her esteem.

She lined up several ornaments that might be put away or, better, sold to a junkman. But from the lineup she drew out pieces of which she had grown especially fond. They had become like children to her, as Gerald made children of the books with which he spent his evenings home. Making a basket of her apron she swept the whole tableful of trinkets into it.

Without a downward glance, she hurried them to the ash-box in the backyard. Shed of them, she felt a good deal lighter, and with the May wind in her face and the sun gentle, like an arm across her shoulders, she felt very nearly capersome. Across the fence the jonquils were in bloom, and the tulips, nodding like fat little boys. Mr. Joyce had unhitched the horse. He saw her then.

"Fine day this morning," he called. He gave the horse a slap on the rump that sent him into the pasture, and came to the fence.

"I'm admiring the flowers," she said.

"Lazy year for them. Two weeks late they are."

"Is that a fact?" Of course it's a fact, she thought. A silly remark, and another after it: "I've never seen them lovelier, though. What comes out next?"

"Snaps, I guess this year. Late roses, too. The iris don't sell much, so I'm letting 'em come or stay as they like."

"That should bring them out."

"Now isn't that the truth? You can coax and tickle all year and not get a bloom for thanks. Turn your back on 'em and they run you down."

Like love, she thought, and caught her tongue. But a splash of color took to her cheeks.

"Say, you're looking nice, Mrs. Shepherd, if you don't mind my saying it."

"Thank you. A touch of spring, I suppose."

"Don't it just send your blood racing? How would you like an armful of these?"

"I'd be very pleased, Mr. Joyce. But I'd like to pay you for them."

"Indeed not. I won't sell half of them—they come in a heap."

She watched his expert hand nip the blooms. He was already tanned, and he stooped and rose with a fine grace. In all the years he had lived next to them he had never been in the house, nor they in his except the day of his wife's funeral. He hadn't grieved much, she commented to Gerald at the time. And little wonder. The woman was pinched and whining, and there wasn't a sunny day she didn't expect a drizzle before nightfall. Now that Sarah thought of it, Joyce looked younger than he did when Mrs. Joyce was still alive.

"There. For goodness' sakes, Mr. Joyce. That's plenty."

"I'd give you the field of them this morning," he said, piling her arms with the flowers.

"I've got half of it now."

"And what a picture you are with them."

"Well, I must hurry them into water," she said. "Thank you."

She hastened toward the house, flying like a young flirt from her first conquest, and aware of the pleased eye following her. The whole morning glowed in the company she kept with the flowers. She snapped off the radio: no tears for Miss Julia today. At noon she heard Mr. Joyce's wagon roll out of the yard as he started to his highway stand. She watched at the window. He looked up and lifted his hat.

At odd moments during the day, she thought of him. He had given her a fine sense of herself and she was grateful. She began to wish that Gerald was returning that night. Take your time, Sarah, she told herself. You don't put away old habits and the years like bric-a-brac. She had softened up, no doubt of it. Not a fat woman, maybe, but plump. Plump. She repeated the word aloud. It had the sound of a potato falling into a tub of water.

But the afternoon sun was warm and the old laziness came over her. Only when Mr. Joyce came home, his voice in a song ahead of him, did she pull herself up. She hurried a chicken out of the refrigerator and then called to him from the porch.

"Mr. Joyce, would you like to have supper with me? Gerald won't be home, and I do hate cooking for just myself."

"Oh, that'd be grand. I've nothing in the house but a shank of ham that a dog wouldn't bark for. What can I bring?"

"Just come along when you're ready."

Sarah, she told herself, setting the table, you're an old bat trying your wings in daylight. A half hour later she glanced out of the window in time to see Mr. Joyce skipping over the fence like a stiff-legged colt. He was dressed in his Sunday suit and brandishing a bottle as he cleared the barbed-wire. Sarah choked down a lump of apprehension. For all that she planned a little fun for herself, she was not up to galloping through the house with an old Don Juan on her heels. Mr. Joyce, however, was a well mannered guest. The bottle was May wine. He drank sparingly and was lavish in his praise of the dinner.

"You've no idea the way I envy you folks, Mrs. Shepherd. Your husband especially. How can he bear the times he spends away?"

He bears it all too well, she thought. "It's his work. He's a salesman. He sells spices."

Mr. Joyce showed a fine set of teeth in his smile—his own teeth, she marveled, tracing her bridgework with the tip of her tongue while he spoke. "Then he's got sugar and spice and everything nice, as they say."

What a one he must have been with the girls, she thought, and to marry a quince as he had. It was done in a hurry, no doubt, and maybe at the end of a big stick.

"It must be very lonesome for you since Mrs. Joyce passed away," she said more lugubriously than she intended. After all, the woman was gone three years.

"No more than when she was with me." His voice matched hers in seriousness. "It's a hard thing to say of the dead, but if she hasn't improved her disposition since, we're all in for a damp eternity." He stuffed the bowl of his pipe. "Do you mind?"

"No, I like the smell of tobacco around the house."

"Does your husband smoke?"

"Yes," she said in some surprise at the question.

"He didn't look the kind to follow a pipe," he said, pulling noisily at his. "No, dear lady," he added when the smoke was shooting from it, "you're blessed in not knowing the plague of a silent house."

It occurred to her then that he was exploring the situation. She would give him small satisfaction. "Yes, I count that among my blessings."

There was a kind of amusement in his eyes. You're as lonesome as me, old girl, they seemed to say, and their frankness bade her to add: "But I do wish Gerald was home more of the time."

"Ah, well, he's at the age when most men look to a last trot around the paddock," he said, squinting at her through the smoke.

"Gerald is only forty-three," she said, losing the words before she knew it.

"There's some take it at forty, and others among us leaping after it from the rocking chair."

The conversation had taken a turn she certainly had not intended, and she found herself threshing around in it. Beating a fire with a feather duster. "There's the moon," she said, charging to the window as though to wave to an old friend.

"Aye," he said, "there's the moon. Are you up to a trot in it?"

"What did you say, Mr. Joyce?"

"I'd better say what I was thinking first. If I hitch Micky to the old rig, would you take a turn with me on the Mill Pond Road?"

She saw his reflection in the window, a smug, daring little grin on his face. In sixteen years of settling she had forgotten her way with men. But it was something you never really forgot. Like riding a bicycle, you picked it up again after a few turns. "I would," she said.

The horse ahead of the rig was a different animal from the one on the plow that morning. Mr. Joyce had no more than thrown the reins over his rump than he took a turn that almost tumbled Sarah into the sun frames. But Mr. Joyce leaped to the seat and pulled Micky up on his hind legs with one hand and Sarah down to her cushion with the other, and they were off in the wake of the moon.

The sun was full in her face when Sarah woke the next morning.

As usual, she looked to see if Gerald were in his bed by way of acclimating herself to the day and its routine. With the first turn of her body she decided that a gallop in a rusty-springed rig was not the way to assert a stay of youth. She lay a few moments thinking about it and then got up to an aching sense of folly. It remained with her through the day, giving way at times to a nostalgia for her bric-a-brac. She had never realized how much of her life was spent in the care of it.

By the time Gerald came home she was almost the person he had left the day before. She had held out against the ornaments, however. Only the flowers decorated the living room. It was not until supper was over and Gerald had settled with his book that he commented.

"Sarah, what happened to the old Chinese philosopher?"

"I put him away. Didn't you notice? I took all the clutter out of here."

He looked about him vacantly as though trying to recall some of it. "So you did. I'll miss that old boy. He gave me something to think about."

"What?"

"Oh, I don't know. Confucius says—that sort of thing."

"He wasn't a philosopher at all," she said, having no notion what he was. "He was a farmer."

"Was he? Well, there's small difference." He opened the book.

"Aren't the flowers nice, Gerald?"

"Beautiful."

"Mr. Joyce gave them to me, fresh out of his garden."

"That's nice."

"Must you read every night, Gerald? I'm here all day with no one to talk to, and when you get home you stick your nose into a book—" When the words were half out, she regretted them. "I didn't tell you, Gerald. I had Mr. Joyce to dinner last night."

"That was very decent of you, dear. The old gentleman must find it lonesome."

"I don't think so. It was a relief to him when his wife died."

Gerald looked up. "Did he say that?"

"Not in so many words, but practically."

"He must be a strange sort. What did she die of?"

"I don't remember. A heart condition, I think."

"Interesting." He returned to his book.

"After dinner he took me for a ride in the horse and buggy. All the way to Cos Corner and back."

"Ha!" was his only comment.

"Gerald, you're getting fat."

He looked up. "I don't think so. I'm about my usual weight. A couple of pounds maybe."

"Then you're carrying it in your stomach. I noticed you've cut the elastic out of your shorts."

"These new fabrics," he said testily.

"They're preshrunken," she said. "It's your stomach. And haven't you noticed how you pull at your collar all the time?"

"I meant to mention that, Sarah. You put too much starch in them."

"I ran out of starch last week and forgot to order it. You can take a size fifteen-and-a-half now."

"Good Lord, Sarah, you're going to tell me next I should wear a horse collar." He let the book slide closed between his thighs. "I get home only three or four nights a week. I'm tired, I wish you wouldn't aggravate me, dear."

She went to his chair and sat on the arm of it. "Did you know that I was beginning to wonder if you'd respond to the poke of a hat-pin?"

He looked directly up at her for the first time in what had seemed like years. His eyes fell away. "I've been working very hard, dear."

"I don't care what you've been doing, Gerald. I'm just glad to find out that you're still human."

He slid his arm around her and tightened it.

"Aren't spring flowers lovely?" she said.

"Yes," he said, "and so is spring."

She leaned across him and took a flower from the vase. She lingered there a moment. He touched his hand to her. "And you're lovely, too." This is simple, she thought, getting upright again. If the rabbit had sat on a thistle, he'd have won the race.

"The three most beautiful things in the world," Gerald said thoughtfully, "a white bird flying, a field of wheat, and a woman's body."

"Is that your own, Gerald?"

"I don't know. I think it is."

"It's been a long time since you wrote any poetry. You did nice things once."

"That's how I got you," he said quietly.

"And I got you with an old house. I remember the day my mother's will was probated. The truth, Gerald—wasn't it then you made up your mind?"

He didn't speak for a moment, and then it was a continuance of some thought of his own, a subtle twist of association. "Do you remember the piece I wrote on the house?"

"I read it the other day. I often read them again."

"Do you, Sarah? And never a mention of it."

It was almost all the reading she did any more. His devotion to books had turned her from them. "Remember how you used to let me read them to you, Gerald? You thought that I was the only one besides yourself who could do them justice."

"I remember."

"Or was that flattery?"

He smiled. "It was courtship, I'm afraid. No one ever thinks anybody else can do his poetry justice. But Sarah, do you know—I'd listen tonight if you'd read some of them. Just for old time's sake."

For old time's sake, she thought, getting the folder from the cabinet and settling opposite him. He was slouched in his chair, pulling at his pipe, his eyes half closed. Long ago this same contemplativeness in him had softened the first shock of the difference in their ages.

"I've always liked this one best—*The Morning of My Days*."

"Well you might," he murmured. "It was written for you."

She read one piece after another, wondering now and then what pictures he was conjuring up of the moment he had written them. He would suck on his pipe at times. The sound was like a baby pulling at an empty bottle. She was reading them well, she thought, giving them a mellow vibrance, an old love's tenderness. Surely there was a moment coming when he would rise from the chair and come to her. Still he sat, his eyes almost closed, the pipe now in hand on the chair's arm. A huskiness crept into her voice, so rarely used to this length any more, and she thought of the nightingale's singing, the thorn against its breast. A slit of pain in her own throat pressed her to greater effort, for the poems were almost done.

She stopped abruptly, a phrase unfinished, at a noise in the room. The pipe had clattered to the floor, Gerald's hand still cupped in its shape, but his chin now on his breast. Laying the folder aside, she went over and picked up the pipe with a rather empty regret, as she would pick up a bird that had fallen dead at her feet.

Gerald's departure in the morning was in the tradition of all their days, even to the kiss upon her cheek and the words, "Till tomorrow evening, dear, take care."

Take care, she thought, going indoors. Take care of what? For what? Heat a boiler of water to cook an egg? She hurried her chores and dressed. When she saw Mr. Joyce hitch the wagon of flowers, she locked the door and waited boldly at the road for him.

"May I have a lift to the highway?" she called out, as he reined up beside her.

"You may have a lift to the world's end, Mrs. Shepherd. Give me your hand." He gave the horse its rein when she was beside him. "I see your old fella's taken himself off again. I daresay it gave him a laugh, our ride in the moonlight."

"It was a giddy business," she said.

"Did you enjoy yourself?"

"I did. But I paid for it afterwards." Her hand went to her back.

"I let out a squeal now and then bending over, myself. But I counted it cheap for the pleasure we had. I'll take you into the village. I've to buy a length of hose anyway. Or do you think you'll be taken for a fool riding in on a wagon?"

"It won't be the first time," she said. "My life's full of foolishness."

"It's a wise fool who laughs at his own folly. We've that in common, you and me. Where'll we take our supper tonight?"

He was sharp as mustard.

"You're welcome to come over," she said.

He nodded. "I'll fetch us a steak, and we'll give Micky his heels again after."

Sarah got off at the post office and stayed in the building until Joyce was out of sight—Joyce and the gapers who had stopped to see her get out of the wagon. Getting in was one thing, getting out another. A bumblebee after a violet. It was time for this trip. She walked to the doctor's office and waited her turn among the villagers.

"I thought I'd come in for a checkup, Dr. Philips," she said at his desk. "And maybe you'd give me a diet."

"A diet?" He took off his glasses and measured her with the naked eye.

"I'm getting a little fat," she said. "They say it's a strain on the heart at my age."

"Your heart could do for a woman of twenty," he said, "but we'll have a listen."

"I'm not worried about my heart, Doctor, you understand. I just feel that I'd like to lose a few pounds."

"Uh-huh," he said. "Open your dress." He got his stethoscope.

Diet, apparently, was the rarest of his prescriptions. Given as a last resort. She should have gone into town for this, not to a country physician who measured a woman by the children she bore. "The woman next door to us died of a heart condition," she said, as though that should explain her visit.

"Who's that?" he asked, putting away the instrument.

"Mrs. Joyce. Some years ago."

"She had a heart to worry about. Living for years on stimulants. Yours is as sound as a bullet. Let's have your arm."

She pushed up her sleeve as he prepared the apparatus for measuring her blood pressure. That, she felt, was rising out of all proportion. She was ashamed of herself before this man, and angry at herself for it, and at him for no reason more than that he was being patient with her. "We're planning insurance," she lied. "I wanted our own doctor's opinion first."

"You'll have no trouble getting it, Mrs. Shepherd. And no need of a diet." He grinned and removed the apparatus. "Go easy on potatoes and bread, and on the sweets. You'll outlive your husband by twenty years. How is he, by the way?"

"Fine. Just fine, Doctor, thank you."

What a nice show you're making of yourself these days, Sarah, she thought, outdoors again. Well, come in or go out, old girl, and slam the door behind you.

Micky took to his heels that night. He had had a day of ease, and new shoes were stinging his hooves by nightfall. The skipping of Joyce with each snap of the harness teased him, the giggling from the rig adding a prickle. After the wagon, the rig was no more than a fly on his tail. He took the full reins when they slapped on his flanks and charged out from the laughter behind him. It rose to a shriek the faster he galloped and tickled his ears like something alive that slithered from them down his neck and his belly and into his loins. Faster and faster he plunged, the sparks from his shoes like ocean spray. He fought a jerk of the reins, the saw of the bit in his mouth a fierce pleasure. He took turns at his own fancy and only in sight of his own yard again did he yield in the fight, choking on the spume that lathered his tongue.

"By the holy, the night a horse beats me, I'll lie down in my grave," Joyce cried. "Get up now, you buzzard. You're not turning in till you go to the highway and back. Are you all right, Sarah?"

Am I all right, she thought. When in years had she known a wild ecstasy like this? From the first leap of the horse she had burst the girdle of fear and shame. If the wheels had spun out from beneath them, she would have rolled into the ditch contented.

"I've never been better," she said.

He leaned close to her to see her, for the moon had just risen. The wind had stung the tears to her eyes, but they were laughing. "By the Horn Spoon," he said, "you liked it!" He let the horse have his own way into the drive after all. He jumped down from the rig and held his hand up to her. "What a beautiful thing to be hanging in the back of the closet all these years."

"If that's a compliment," she said, "it's got a nasty bite."

"Aye. But it's my way of saying you're a beautiful woman."

"Will you come over for a cup of coffee?"

"I will. I'll put up the horse and be over."

The kettle had just come to the boil when he arrived.

"Maybe you'd rather have tea, Mr. Joyce?"

"Coffee or tea, so long as it's not water. And I'd like you to call me Frank. They christened me Francis but I got free of it early."

"And you know mine, I noticed," she said.

"It slipped out in the excitement. There isn't a woman I know who wouldn't of collapsed in a ride like that."

"It was wonderful." She poured the water into the coffee pot.

"There's nothing like getting behind a horse," he said, "unless it's getting astride him. I wouldn't trade Micky for a Mack truck."

"I used to ride when I was younger," she said.

"How did you pick up the man you got, if you don't mind my asking?"

And you the old woman, she thought; where did you get her? "I worked for a publishing house and he brought in some poetry."

"Ah, that's it." He nodded. "And he thought with a place like this he could pour it out like water from a spout."

"Gerald and I were in love," she said, irked that he should define so bluntly her own thoughts on the matter.

"Don't I remember it? In them days you didn't pull the blinds. It used to put me in a fine state."

"Do you take cream in your coffee? I've forgotten."

"Aye, thank you, and plenty of sugar."

"You haven't missed much," she said.

"There's things you see through a window you'd miss sitting down in the living room. I'll wager you've wondered about the old lady and me?"

"A little. She wasn't so old, was she, Mr. Joyce?" Frank, she thought. Too frank.

"That one was old in her crib. But she came with a greenhouse. I worked for her father."

Sarah poured the coffee. "You're a cold-blooded old rogue," she said.

He grinned. "No. Cool-headed I am, and warm-blooded. When I was young, I made out it was the likes of poetry. She sang like a bird on a convent wall. But when I caged her she turned into an old crow."

"That's a terrible thing to say, Mr. Joyce."

The humor left his face for an instant. "It's a terribler thing to live with. It'd put a man off his nut. You don't have a bit of cake in the house, Sarah, to go with this?"

"How about muffins and jam?"

"That'll go fine." He smiled again. "Where does your old fella spend the night in his travels?"

"In the hotel in whatever town he happens to be in."

"That's a lonesome sort of life for a married man," he said.

She pulled a chair to the cupboard and climbed up to get a jar of preserves. He made no move to help her although she still could not reach the jar. She looked down at him. "You could give me a hand."

"Try it again. You almost had it that time." He grinned, almost gleeful at her discomfort.

She bounced down in one step. "Get it yourself if you want it. I'm satisfied with a cup of coffee."

He pounded his fist on the table, getting up. "You're right, Sarah. Never fetch a man anything he can fetch himself. Which bottle is it?"

"The strawberry."

He hopped up and down, nimble as a goat. "But then maybe he doesn't travel alone?"

"What?"

"I was suggesting your man might have an outside interest. Salesmen have the great temptation, you know."

"That's rather impertinent, Mr. Joyce."

"You're right, Sarah, it is. My tongue's been home so long it doesn't know how to behave in company. This is a fine cup of coffee."

She sipped hers without speaking. It was time she faced that question, she thought. She had been hedging around it for a long time, and last night with Gerald should have forced it upon her.

"And if he does have an outside interest," she said, lifting her chin, "what of it?"

"Ah, Sarah, you're a wise woman, and worth waiting the acquaintance of. You like me a little now, don't you?"

"A little."

"Well," he said, getting up, "I'll take that to keep me warm for the night."

And what have I got to keep me warm, she thought. "Thank you for the ride, Frank. It was thrilling."

"Was it?" he said, coming near her. He lifted her chin with his forefinger. "We've many a night like this ahead, Sarah, if you say the word." And then when she left her chin on his finger, he bent down and kissed her, taking himself to the door after it with a skip and a jump. He paused there and looked back at her. "Will I stay or go?"

"You'd better go," she choked out, wanting to be angry but finding no anger in herself at all.

All the next day Sarah tried to anchor herself from her peculiar flights of fancy. She had no feeling for the man, she told herself. It was a fine state a woman reached when a kiss from a stranger could do that to her. "It was the ride made you giddy," she said aloud. "You were thinking of Gerald. You were thinking of—the Lord knows what." She worked upstairs until she heard the wagon go by. She would get some perspective when Gerald came home. It seemed as though he'd been gone a long time.

The day was close and damp, and the flies clung to the screens. There was a dull stillness in the atmosphere. By late afternoon the clouds rolled heavier, mulling about one another like dough in a pan. While she was peeling potatoes for supper, Frank drove in. He unhitched the horse but left him in the harness, and set about immediately building frames along the rows of flowers. He was expecting a storm. She looked at the clock. It was almost time for Gerald.

She went out on the front porch and watched for the bus. There was a haze in the sweep of land between her and the highway, and the traffic through it seemed to float thickly, slowly. The bus glided toward the intersection and past it without stopping. She felt a sudden anger. Her whole day had been strung up to this peak. Since he had not called, it meant merely that he had missed the bus. The next one was in two hours. She crossed the yard to the fence. You're starting up again, Sarah, she warned herself, and took no heed of the warning.

Frank looked up from his work. "You'd better fasten the house," he said. "There's a fine blow coming."

"Frank, if you're in a hurry, I'll give you something to eat."

"That'd be a great kindness. I may have to go back to the stand at a gallop."

He was at the kitchen table, shoveling in the food without a word, when the heavy sky lightened. He went to the window. "By the glory, it may blow over." He looked around at her. "Your old boy missed the bus, did he?"

"He must have."

Frank looked out again. "I do like a good blow. Even if it impoverished me, there's nothing in the world like a storm."

An automobile horn sounded on the road. It occurred to Sarah that on a couple of occasions Gerald had received a ride from the city. The car passed, but watching its dust she was left with a feeling of suspended urgency. Joyce was chatting now. He had tilted back in the chair and for the first time since she had known him, he was rambling on about weather, vegetables, and the price of eggs. She found it more disconcerting than his bursts of intimate comment, and she hung from one sentence to the next waiting for the end of it. Finally she passed in back of his chair and touched her fingers briefly to his neck.

"You need a haircut, Frank."

He sat bolt upright. "I never notice it till I have to scratch. Could I have a drop more coffee?"

She filled his cup, aware of his eyes on her. "Last night was something I'll never forget—that ride," she said.

"And something else last night, do you remember that?"

"Yes."

"Would you give me another now to match it if I was to ask?"

"No."

"What if I took it without asking?"

"I don't think I'd like it, Frank."

He pushed away from the table, slopping the coffee into the saucer. "Then what are you tempting me for?"

"You've a funny notion of temptation," she flared up, knowing the anger was against herself.

Joyce spread his dirt-grimed fingers on the table. "Sarah, do you know what you want?"

The tears were gathering. She fought them back. "Yes, I know what I want!" she cried.

Joyce shook his head. "He's got you by the heart, hasn't he, Sarah?"

"My heart's my own!" She flung her head up.

Joyce slapped his hand on the table. "Ho! Look at the spark of the woman! That'd scorch a man if there was a stick in him for kindling." He moistened his lips and in spite of herself Sarah took a step backwards. "I'll not chase you, Sarah. Never fear that. My chasing days are over. I'll neither chase nor run, but I'll stand my ground for what's coming to me." He jerked his head toward the window. "That was only a lull in the wind. There's a big blow coming now for certain."

She watched the first drops of rain splash on the glass. "Gerald's going to get drenched in it."

"Maybe it'll drown him," Joyce said, grinning from the door. "Thanks for the supper."

Let it come on hail, thunder, and lightning. Blow the roof from the house and tumble the chimney. I'd go out from it then and never turn back. When an old man can laugh at your trying to cuckold a husband, and the husband asking it, begging it, shame on you. She went through the house, clamping the locks on the windows. More pleasure putting the broom through them.

An early darkness folded into the storm, and the walls of rain bleared the highway lights. There was an ugly yellow tinge to the water from the dust swirled into it. The wind sluiced down the chimney, spitting bits of soot on the living-room floor. She spread newspapers to catch it. A sudden blow, it would soon be spent. She went to the hall clock. The bus was due in ten minutes. What matter? A quick supper, a good book, and a long sleep. The wily old imp was right. A prophet needing a haircut.

The lights flickered off for a moment, then on again. Let them go out, Sarah. What's left for you, you can see by candlelight. She went to the basement and brought up the kerosene lamp and then got a flashlight from the pantry. As she returned to the living room, a fresh gust of wind sent the newspapers out of the grate like scud. The lights flickered again. A sound drew her to the hall. She thought the wind might be muffling the ring of the telephone. When she got there, the clock was striking. The bus was now twenty minutes late. There was something about the look of the phone that convinced her the line was dead. It was unnerving to find it in order. Imagination, she murmured. Everything was going perverse to her expectations.

And then, annoyed with herself, she grew angry with Gerald again. This was insult. Insult on top of indifference.

She followed a thumping noise upstairs. It was on the outside of the house. She turned off the light and pressed her face against the window. A giant maple tree was rocking and churning, one branch thudding against the house. There was not even a blur of light from the highway now. Blacked out. While she watched, a pinpoint of light shaped before her. It grew larger, weaving a little. A flashlight, she thought, and wondered if Gerald had one. Then she recognized the motion: a lantern on a wagon. Frank was returning.

When she touched the light switch there was no response. Groping her way to the hall she saw that all the lights were out now. Step by step she made her way downstairs. A dankness had washed in through the chimney, stale and sickening. She lit the lamp and carried it to the kitchen. From the window there, she saw Frank's lantern bobbing as he led the horse into the barn. She could not see man or horse, only the fading of the light until it disappeared inside. When it reappeared she lifted her kerosene lamp, a greeting to him. This time he came around the fence. She held the door against the wind.

"I've no time now, Sarah, I've work to do!" he shouted. "He didn't come, did he?"

"No!"

"Is the phone working?"

She nodded that it was and waved him close to her. "Did the bus come through?"

"It's come and gone. Close the door or you'll have the house in a shambles!" He waved his lantern and was gone.

She put the pot roast she had prepared for Gerald in the refrigerator and set the perishables close to the freezing unit. She wound the clock and put away the dishes. Anything to keep busy. She washed the kitchen floor that had been washed only the day before. The lantern across the way swung on a hook at the barn, sometimes moving toward the ground and back as Joyce examined the frames he was reinforcing.

Finally she returned to the living room. She sat for a long time in Gerald's chair, watching the pattern of smoke in the lamp-chimney. Not even a dog or cat to keep her company. Not even a laughing piece of delft to look out at her from the mantelpiece; only the cold-eyed forebearers, whom she could not remember, staring down at her from the gilt frames, their eyes fixed upon her, the last and the least of them, who would leave after her—nothing.

It was not to be endured. She lunged out of the chair. In the hall she climbed to the first landing where she could see Joyce's yard. He was through work now, the lantern hanging from the porch although the house was darkened. It was the only light anywhere, and swayed in the wind like a will-o'-the-wisp.

She bounded down the stairs and caught up her raincoat. Taking the flashlight she went out into the storm. She made her way around the fence, sometimes leaning into the wind, sometimes resting against it. Joyce met her in his driveway. He had been waiting, she thought, testing his nerves against her own, expecting her. Without a word, he caught her hand and led her to his back steps and into the house. "I've an oil lamp," he said then. "Hold your light there till I fix it."

She watched his wet face in the half light. His mouth was lined with malicious humor, and his eyes as he squinted at the first flame of the wick were fierce, as fierce as the storm, and as strange to her. When the light flared up, she followed its reaches over the dirty wall, the faded calendar, the gaping cupboards, the electric cord hanging from a naked bulb over the sink to the back door. There were dishes stacked on the table where they no doubt stood from one meal to the next. The curtains were stiff with dirt, three years of it. Only then did she take a full glimpse of the folly that had brought her here.

"I just ran over for a minute, Frank—"

"A minute or the night, sit there, Sarah, and let me get out of these clothes."

She took the chair he motioned her into, and watched him fling his coat into the corner. Nor could she take her eyes from him as he sat down and removed his boots and socks. Each motion fascinated her separately, fascinated and revolted her. He wiped between his toes with the socks. He went barefoot toward the front of the house. In the doorway he paused, becoming a giant in the weird light.

"Put us up a pot of coffee, dear woman. The makings are there on the stove."

"I must go home. Gerald—"

"To hell with Gerald," he interrupted. "He's snug for the night, wherever he is. Maybe he won't come back to you at all. It's happened before, you know, men vanishing from women they don't know the worth of."

Alone, she sat stiff and erect at the table. He was just talking, poisoning her mind against Gerald. How should she get out of here? Run like a frightened doe and never face him again? No, Sarah. Stay for the bitter coffee. Scald the giddiness out of you once and for all. But on top of the resolve came the wish that Gerald might somehow appear at the door and take her home. Dear, gentle Gerald.

She got up and went to the sink to draw the water for coffee. A row of medicine bottles stood on the window-sill, crusted with dust. Household remedies. She leaned close and examined a faded label: "Mrs. Joyce—Take immediately upon need."

She turned from the window. A rocker stood in the corner of the room. In the old days the sick woman had sat in it on the back porch, rocking, and speaking to no one. The stale sickness of her was still about the house, Sarah thought. What did she know of people like this?

He was threshing around upstairs like a penned bull. His muddy boots lay where he had taken them off, a pool of water gathering about them. Again she looked at the window-sill. No May wine there. Suddenly she remembered Dr. Philips's words: "Lived on stimulants for years." She could almost see the sour woman, even to her gasping for breath . . . "Take immediately."

Fix the coffee, Sarah. What kind of teasing is this? Teasing the dead from her grave before you. Teasing. Something in the thought disturbed her further—an association: Joyce watching her reach for the preserves last night, grinning at her. "Try it again, Sarah. You almost had it that time." And he could still hear him asking, "Which bottle?" Not which jar, but which bottle.

She grabbed the kettle and filled it. Stop it, Sarah. It's the storm, the waiting, too much waiting—your time of life. She drew herself up against his coming, hearing his quick steps on the stairs.

"Will you give us a bit of iodine there from the window, Sarah? I've scratched myself on those blamed frames."

She selected the bottle carefully with her eyes, so that her trembling hand might not betray her.

"Dab it on here," he said, holding a white cuff away from his wrist.

The palm of his hand was moist as she bent over it and she could smell the earth and the horse from it. Familiar. Everything about him had become familiar, too familiar. She felt his breath on her neck, and the hissing sound of it was the only sound in the room. She smeared the iodine on the cut and pulled away. His lips tightened across his teeth in a grin.

"A kiss would make a tickle of the pain," he said.

Sarah thrust the iodine bottle from her and grabbed the flashlight. "I'm going home."

His jaw sagged as he stared at her. "Then what did you come for?"

"Because I was lonesome. I was foolish—" Fear choked off her voice. A little trickle of saliva dribbled from the corner of his mouth.

"No! You came to torture me!"

She forced one foot toward the door and the other after it. His voice rose in laughter as she lumbered away from him. "Good Lord, Sarah. Where's the magnificent woman who rode to the winds with me last night?"

She lunged into the electric cord in her retreat, searing her cheek on it. Joyce caught it and wrenched it from the wall, its splayed end springing along the floor like a whip. "And me thinking the greatest kindness would be if he never came home!"

The doorknob slipped in her sweaty hand. She dried it frantically. He's crazy, she thought. Mad crazy.

"You're a lump, Sarah," he shouted. "And Mr. Joyce is a joker. A joker and a dunce. He always was and he will be till the day they hang him!"

The door yielded and she plunged down the steps and into the yard. In her wild haste she hurled herself against the rig and spun away from it as though it were something alive. She sucked in her breath to keep from screaming. She tore her coat on the fence hurtling past it, leaving a swatch of it on the wire. Take a deep breath, she told herself as she stumbled up the steps. Don't faint. Don't fall. The door swung from her grasp, the wind clamoring through the house. She forced it closed, the glass plate tingling, and bolted it. She thrust the flashlight on the table and caught up the phone. She clicked it wildly.

Finally it was the operator who broke through. "I have a call for you from Mr. Gerald Shepherd. Will you hold on, please?"

Sarah could hear only her own sobbing breath in the hollow of the mouthpiece. She tried to settle her mind by pinning her eyes on the stairway. But the spokes of the staircase seemed to be shivering dizzily in the circle of light, like the plucked strings of a harp. Even the sound of them was vibrant in her head, whirring over the rasp of her breath. Then came the pounding footfalls and Joyce's fists on the door. Vainly she signaled the operator. And somewhere in the tumult of her mind she grasped at the thought that if she unlocked the door, Joyce would come in and sit down. They might even light the fire. There was plenty of wood in the basement. But she could not speak. And it was too late.

Joyce's fist crashed through the glass and drew the bolt. With the door's opening the wind whipped her coat over her head; with its closing, her coat fell limp, its little pressure about her knees seeming to buckle them.

"I'm sorry," came the operator's voice, "the call was canceled ten minutes ago."

She let the phone clatter onto the table and waited, her back still to the door. Ten minutes was not very long ago, she reasoned in sudden desolate calmness. She measured each of Joyce's footfalls toward her, knowing they marked all of time that was left to her. And somehow, she felt, she wanted very little more of it.

For only an instant she saw the loop he had made of the electric cord, and the white cuffs over the strong, gnarled hands. She closed her eyes and lifted her head high, expecting that in that way the end would come more quickly.

H. R. F. Keating

A Hell of a Story

They snatched the Oil Sheik's kid, exactly as planned, at 11:06 precisely. There were no difficulties. The girl they'd got for the job distracted the boy's bodyguard for just long enough. The boy himself reacted to the little flying helicopter on a string just as they'd calculated he would. But then a kid of eight, and an Arab from the sticks first time in London, that part couldn't have gone wrong. Worth every penny of all it had cost, that toy.

Everything else had gone like clockwork too. No traffic holdups when they were moving away from the Park. No trouble in the changeover of cars. No one about in the mews to see it, and not a bit of fuss out of the lad. Quiet, big-eyed, doing what he was told, scared to death most likely.

So inside half an hour he was safely in the room they'd prepared for him in the old house waiting for demolition up over Kilburn way. No one had spotted them taking him in. He hadn't had time to see enough of the outside of the place to remember it again when they'd got the cash and let him go. And Old Pete was there minding him. Dead right for the job.

Forty years in and out of the nick had soured Old Pete to such a point that anybody who met him accidentally began at once to think how they could get away. No one would come poking their nose into the Kilburn place when there was sixteen stone of Old Pete there, fat but hard, never much of a one for shaving, always a bit of a smell to him. The kid was in as safe hands as could be while they conducted the negotiations.

They put in the first call to the rented Mayfair house at six o'clock that evening when they calculated the Sheik would have had just about enough time to have unpleasant thoughts and be ready quietly to agree to dodge the police and pay up. "The kid's safe," they said. "He'll be having his supper now. He's being well looked after."

It was true. Old Pete was just going into the room with the boy's supper, baked beans and a cup of tea, prepared on the picnic stove they'd put into the place. The boy looked at the extraordinary food—extraordinary to him—without seeming to be much put out by it. Old Pete even grunted a question at him, which he hadn't meant to. Only the kid's calm was a bit unexpected. It threw Old Pete a little. "All right, are you?" he grunted.

The boy looked at him, his large dark eyes clear and unwavering. "Will you mind being in Hell?" he asked.

Old Pete, lumbering toward the door with its dangling padlock, stopped dead in his tracks and turned round.

"English," he said dazedly. "English. You speak English."

"Of course I do," the boy replied. "I always speak English with the Adviser. Talking with me is all he has to do, now my father has the oil and doesn't need advice any more."

Old Pete, crafty enough in his way but not one for confronting new situations easily, stood blinking, trying to fit this into the framework of his knowledge. And there was something else. Something at the back of his mind that had to be dealt with too. And it was that, surprisingly, that pushed itself forward first.

"'Ere," he said suddenly, "what d'you mean 'Hell'?"

"Will you mind being in Hell forever?" the boy asked.

"What d'you mean, me being in Hell?"

"Well, you will have to go there. Kidnaping is a sin. If you commit sins you go to Hell."

The simple, fundamental philosophy of the desert fell like drops of untarnished water from his lips.

Old Pete, motor-tire tummied, dirt-engrimed, looked at the kid for a long while without speaking a word. Then at last the machinery of his mind ground out his answer.

"Look, lad," he said, "that's all gone out. They finished with all that. Word may've not got round to where you come from, but they found out all that's wrong. Just tales. You know, what ain't so."

He stood, bending forward a little, examining the slight form of the boy in his neat, expensive Western shirt and shorts.

"Yes," he said, ramming it home, "you take my word for it, lad. That's all past-times stuff now. Gone and forgotten."

He made his way out, an evil-smelling forty-ton tank, and carefully refitted the padlock to the little secure room.

But the next morning, when the Sheik was still holding out and the rest of them were considering what would be the easiest way of putting the pressure on a bit, the boy proved not to have absorbed the latest developments in Western thought at all. When Old Pete brought him his breakfast, the kid accepted the big bowl of corn flakes eagerly enough, but in his conversation he was making no concessions to modernity.

"You will go to Hell, you know," he said, picking up from where they had left off. "You have to—you've done wrong."

"But I told yer," said Old Pete. "They changed all that."

"You can't," the boy said, with all the calm certainty of someone pointing out an accidental breach in the rules of a game. "If you do something wrong, you have to be punished for it. Isn't that so?"

"Well, I don't know about that," said Pete. "I mean, the cops don't always catch you. Not if you're sharp. They're not going to catch us for this lot, that's for sure. Those boys has it worked out a right treat."

"Yes," said the Sheik's son, "but that's just the reason."

"Just the reason?"

"Yes, if you do not get caught and punished here, you must be punished when you are dead. When you cross the Bridge of Al Sirat, which is only as wide as the breadth of a hair, the weight of your sin makes you fall. Into Hell."

His large brown eyes looked steadily into Pete's battered face. "It's forever, of course," the boy added.

Old Pete left the room in too much of a hurry to collect last night's dirty baked-beans plate.

He did not come back at lunchtime as he had meant to do. But at about six that evening—when the Sheik, after talk of making life hard for the boy, had just caved in and promised to deliver the cash—Old Pete once more removed the heavy padlock on the door and entered with another plate of steaming baked beans. The boy said nothing but seized eagerly on the beans. Old Pete turned to the door. But then he stopped, and began to gather up the two previous lots of dirty crockery. The boy ate steadily. Pete picked up the plates and put them down again. At last he broke out.

"Forever?" he said.

"Of course," the boy answered, knowing at once what they were talking about. "If you go to Paradise forever if you've been good, then you must go to Hell forever if you've been bad."

"Yeah," said Pete. And after a little he added, "Stands to reason, I suppose."

He put the now emptied second baked-beans plate on top of the others.

"I'm not meant to tell yer," he said, "but you'll be going back 'ome soon. Yer old man's coming up with the dibbins."

"It won't make any difference," the boy said, again answering an unspoken question.

Pete blundered out of the room, snapping the big padlock closed with a ferocious click. And entirely forgetting the dirty crockery.

But he was back within twenty minutes.

"Look," he said. "If I'd forgotten to lock the door when I brought you your nosh just now, you could've sneaked out and nobody the wiser."

"No," said the boy. "You must *take* me home, all the way. Otherwise it wouldn't count."

Sweat broke out under the dirt of Pete's broad, fat-bulged face. "I can't do that. They'd catch me. Catch me for sure."

At the steps leading up to the door of the big corner house in Mayfair the boy turned to his companion.

"All right," he said. "I will ring myself. You can go now."

Pete swung away and lumbered off round the corner, fast as if he was a tanker lorry out of control on an ice-slippery hill. But his legs were too jellylike to support him for long, and once safely round the corner out of sight, he just had to stop and lean against the tall iron railing and let the waves of trembling flow over him.

For two whole minutes he did nothing but lean there, shaking. Then he began to relieve his feelings in dredging up from a well stored memory every foul word he had ever heard. He only came to a halt, after some ten minutes, in order to draw breath.

When he did so the cool, clear, horribly familiar voice of the boy spoke from the open window over his head.

"I'm afraid with all that you will have to go to Hell after all," the boy said.

W. R. Burnett

Traveling Light

Johnny ate slowly, relishing the good hot coffee and the combination sandwich. He had intended getting a plain ham sandwich, as he wanted to conserve his money, but the smell of cooking had been too much for him.

The counterman leaned on his elbow and stared past Johnny at the broad macadam highway in the glare of the Arizona winter sun. To the counterman Johnny was just another weary hitchhiker. Hordes of them passed every day; some of them headed for California, some of them headed East. Only one thing about Johnny interested him; he was wearing an old football sweater, and the numeral 7 could still be made out on the faded fabric across his shoulders, though the number itself had been ripped off long ago. The counterman turned from the road to stare languidly at Johnny.

"Come a long way?"

"Only from Ohio." Johnny grinned feebly.

The counterman whistled. "Football sweater you're wearing, ain't it?"

"Yeah. Freshman team at Ohio State."

"Make the varsity?"

"Yeah. I played my sophomore year. Halfback. But my old man ran out of dough."

"Hitting for Southern Cal?"

"Yeah," Johnny answered. "Los Angeles."

"Everybody is."

There was a loud shriek of tires and a big, expensive-looking sedan turned suddenly from the highway and stopped at the filling station with a jerk. Two men got out. One was big and broad-shouldered and redheaded; the other was small and frail-looking with a narrow face and black hair.

"Fill 'er up, Cap," called the big man. "We chow. Back in a minute."

"Boy," said the counterman, "that car's been places. Look at the dust on it."

The men came in and sat down at the counter. Their well cut clothes were covered with dust. Their eyes were bloodshot and they both looked haggard and done in, the small one especially.

"Hey, pal," said the big one, "we want two club sandwiches and a couple o' coffees. And make it fast, will you?"

The counterman went to make the sandwiches. The little man stared at Johnny for a moment, then he leaned forward and whispered something to the redhead, who turned, stared briefly, then said: "Hiya, kid. Hoofing?"

"Yeah."

"How'd you like to drive a couple guys to El Portal?"

"That's right on my way."

"Okay," said the big man. "Eats, if any, and transportation; maybe a little dough if you give us service. We're in a hurry."

"I'll do my best."

Red smiled. "Buddy, you'll have to push that hack to hit the road like we want to hit it."

"Yeah," said the little man, "my wife's sick over in El Portal. We got a telegram saying they thought maybe she might kick off, so I want to get there and get there quick."

"I'm sorry," said Johnny. "I'm not afraid to open a car up."

"Good," said the big man. "Let's get acquainted. Call me Red—that's practically the only name I got. My skinny friend here is George. What's your name?"

"Johnny."

"Okay, Johnny. As soon as we chow we start."

The counterman came with their sandwiches. They wolfed them down, then gulped down their coffee. The counterman watched them with raised eyebrows—never in his life had he seen anybody eat so fast. They got up. Red threw a dollar on the counter.

"Okay?" he asked.

"You got some change coming."

"Keep it. Go out to a good restaurant and get your lunch."

The two men walked so fast Johnny could hardly keep up with them.

Red paid for the gasoline, then he and George got into the back seat. Johnny jumped in and started the motor with a roar. This was a real hack; he hadn't driven one like it since his freshman year in college when the real-estate business was good and his dad was in the big money.

The counterman was standing in the door of the barbecue joint when Johnny drove past.

"Luck, eh?" he called.

"You tell it," said Johnny . . .

In a few moments Johnny had left the little Arizona town and the barbecue joint far behind. In the rearview mirror he could see Red and George leaning back against the cushions, their hats over their eyes, their legs stretched out. Those two birds were certainly worn out, all right; they were already half asleep.

Once Red sat up suddenly and, leaning forward, looked at the dashboard.

"Atta stuff, buddy," he said. "George was right about you. He said you looked like you wasn't scared of no blowout. Don't worry. These tires are good. Keep moving."

Johnny nodded and Red lay back. They passed through some Mexican villages and Johnny slowed down. At several places they saw Indian hogans with fat squaws sitting in front of them. There were no towns in this desolate region: only a handful of Mexicans and Indians lost in this gigantic flat valley, hemmed in by gigantic lavender mountains.

For some reason, traffic was very light on this national highway and when Johnny saw a car running slowly ahead of him he slackened his pace a little, then gradually slowed down almost to a stop. George didn't miss a beat in his snoring, but Red sat up at once. "Keep moving," he said harshly.

But Johnny pointed. A girl hitchhiker in brown slacks and a green sweater was struggling with two men who were trying to pull her into their car. A third man was inching the car along, keeping up with them as the girl pushed her way forward, trying to get away.

"She's doing all right," said Red. "A little ride will do her good. Keep moving."

"No," said Johnny, jamming on the brakes. "I won't keep moving." He turned and looked straight into Red's chill gray eyes. He saw Red clench his fists and saw the huge muscles rippling under his coat sleeves, but he wasn't intimidated. That girl needed help and she was going to get it.

"Okay," said Red wearily, turning away. Then he grinned and said: "It's your party, Johnny, old sock. Let's see you go to work."

Johnny jumped out of the car and ran toward the struggling girl. The men let loose of her when they saw Johnny coming and one of them drew back his fist. "Stay out of this, partner, if you know what's good for you," said one of them. "This is my gal and she's trying to beat it."

Johnny hesitated. The men looked tough. The girl didn't. Quite the contrary, she reminded him of some of the girls he had gone to school with back in Ohio. "What about it, sister?" he demanded.

"I never saw these men before."

"It's a lie."

"Okay," said Johnny. "You guys leave this girl alone. Beat it."

"Sez you!" said the man in the car.

The two men who had been struggling with the girl jumped Johnny. One of them hit him behind the ear and turned him half around; the other kicked him hard three times. Then one of them hit him on the jaw and he went down. But he was boiling now and came up fighting. The third man jumped from the car and got into the fight. Johnny had never seen so many fists before in his life, but finally he landed a good solid blow and one of the men moved out of the fight, holding his stomach. Johnny went down again. Dazed, he sat looking up at the blazing blue sky. Much to his surprise, Red, with a broad grin on his freckled face, moved into his line of vision.

"You ain't doing so good, Johnny," he said. Then he turned to the two men who were waiting for Johnny to get up: "Now, now, you boys are getting too rough. Mustn't play rough." Then he threw back his head and laughed.

The men looked at each other uneasily. This redheaded guy was big as an ox and looked plenty tough.

"You, baby," said Red, turning to the girl, "give us the lowdown quick. Family affair?"

"I never saw these men before."

"Wouldn't like to go bye-bye with 'em?"

"Of course not."

"No use, boys. Get in your kiddie car and shove off."

"Sez you," one of the men said feebly.

Suddenly Red reached out and, taking the men by their coat collars, jammed their faces together. They both staggered back, dazed. "Sez me."

The man who had been hit in the stomach was already sitting at the wheel; the other two climbed in beside him groggily. The car moved off.

Johnny was still a little dazed; he stood rubbing his jaw. The girl came over to him and put her hand on his arm. "Thanks. I'm glad you came along."

"Don't mention it."

Red looked on, smiling sardonically, then he said, "Sister, we're going as far as El Portal and we're going fast. Hop in, we ain't got all night."

"Well, I—" She looked at Johnny for a long time, then she said, "All right."

When they got back to the car, Johnny held the door open for her.

"Wouldn't like to ride back here with old Red, would you?" Red demanded.

The girl said nothing. She didn't know just what to say. She climbed in with Johnny.

Johnny drove in silence for a long time. In a few minutes he picked up the car with the three men in it and went past them blowing the horn. The girl glanced at the speedometer. It read seventy-six.

"Do you have to drive that fast?" she demanded.

"Yes," said Johnny. "The little one's wife is very sick. He's afraid she'll die. She's in El Portal."

"The little one?" She turned to look. "That's a funny way to—aren't these men friends of yours?"

"No. I'm hitchhiking to sunny Cal. I'm just the chauffeur. They drove all night and are worn out."

She turned again and Red grinned at her. "I didn't thank you," she said. "Thanks."

"Just routine," said Red. "I always go around fighting over dames. Or else they're fighting over me. You know how it is. Like to come back here?"

"Nix," said George. "Let the kid alone."

"Can't I have any fun?"

"You just had your fun. Beating up guys is your fun." George groaned and lay back. "I'm tired! Only clucks use their fists. You always was a cluck, Red."

Red yawned and, lying back, put his hat over his eyes.

There was a long silence. The monotonous, burned country rushed past. Suddenly the girl leaned forward and began to cry.

"Excuse me," she said, "but I've had about all I can stand. I hitched from Texas. It's my first time. I never had any idea things would be so bad."

Johnny patted her on the shoulder. She tried to stifle her sobs. Red leaned forward. "Johnny," he cried, "let the girl alone. Where was you brung up? Look at the state you got her in."

Johnny turned slightly.

"Listen, I—"

Red burst out laughing, delighted, then he leaned back and put his hat over his face again.

Johnny shook his head. To the girl, who was calmer now, he said, "Going far?"

"El Portal."

"That's where we're going."

"I know. I could hardly believe my ears."

"Live there?"

"Yes. My boy friend lives there, too. He's a lawyer, trying to get a start."

"It's tough now for anybody to get a start."

"We were going to get married but we had a row. I wanted to go to work. He wasn't making enough for us to get married on. Oh, we had a beautiful row, and I ran away."

Johnny turned to look at her.

"Yeah? You wanted to go to work and he wouldn't let you? I'd like to see that guy."

"He wins. I give up," said the girl, smiling slightly. "But I'll never let him know what a time I've had."

Turning, Johnny glanced out of the corner of his eye at the girl. She was mighty pretty with her wavy light-brown hair, her blue eyes, and her clear-cut, refined face. He began to envy the lawyer.

They were nearing the California line now and were getting into a true desert region. Great drifts of sand rose on either side of them. They went for miles at a time without seeing any vegetation. It was early afternoon and the sun was beating down with almost summer intensity.

George was sleeping peacefully, but Red had had a good rest, he said, although he had seemed to sleep but little, and was sitting up with his legs crossed, smoking a cigarette and whistling.

From time to time the girl looked out across the dazzling wasteland, which stretched unbroken to the enormous lavender mountains to the north. Finally she shuddered.

"What an idiot I was to think I could hike through this place. It's awful."

"Pretty bad," said Johnny, nodding.

"It gives me the creeps. There ought to be a law."

"Too many laws now," said Red, leaning forward. "You never know when you're going to break one. Eh, baby?"

"My name's Edna," said the girl. "I don't like to be called 'baby.' "

"Don't you, baby? That's tough, baby. I always call my babies baby."

The girl turned and looked straight into Red's eyes. "Why don't you be nice?"

Red lowered his head and made his shoulders shake. "George," he said, punching his companion, "she's appealing to my better nature. Now that touches me. Say, Johnny, what're we making?"

"A little over sixty."

"Slow down till this copper goes past."

Johnny saw a motorcycle cop coming toward them from the opposite direction. He slowed the car gradually. Glancing into the rearview mirror, he saw that George was sitting up, alert now. Red's face was hard and menacing. The cop looked at them sharply as they passed him.

"He's turning," said Red. "Outrun him, Johnny."

"They sting you here for speeding," said Johnny.

"You're feeling so good, Red," George sneered. "Take the wheel."

"No time," said Red, leaning forward. "Outrun him, kid. You heard me. Fifty bucks if you outrun him."

"That's different."

Johnny pushed the accelerator to the floorboard and the car shot away, roaring over the black macadam.

The girl touched his arm.

"Do you think—"

"Right now for fifty bucks I'd climb a tree in this hack."

"Now you're talking," said Red. "Give her the gun, boy."

Mile after mile the cop trailed them. There'd be a dip in the road and they'd lose him, but when they got on the flat again, there he'd be. The strain was beginning to tell on Johnny. Little pains began to run up and down his back. His accelerator foot was numb and he could feel the heat of the engine through his shoe.

"Curve!" cried Red. "He's gaining a little. We may lose him here."

Just as Red spoke, the cop's motorcycle began to wobble—he had either blown a tire or had hit a stone in the road. The motorcycle slewed round, then rolled end over end, throwing the cop in a long arc over into the mesquite.

"Yow!" yelled Red. "A nose dive! Nice work, Johnny!"

"But, good heavens—" the girl began. Johnny nudged her with his elbow. He knew they were in a spot. Red and George were real bad ones; he was sure of it now.

"Keep her moving," said Red. "We shook that rat off but he might get up."

Johnny glanced at the girl. He could see she was very nervous. He laughed to cover up and said the first thing that came into his head: "That boy friend of yours expecting you?"

The girl started.

"No. It's a surprise. He thinks I'm still in Dallas."

"Oh, just a little surprise. Well, we'll soon be in. I wish you luck."

"Thanks. Are you going to stay in El Portal a while?"

"Maybe I'll stay the night. I've got to get on to Los Angeles."

"Good luck to you, too."

"Thanks."

They were close to El Portal now. The girl saw the familiar ragged line of hills to the north and smiled. They had left the desert and the lavender mountains behind.

George said: "All right, Red. You take the wheel—we're getting in close."

Johnny slowed down as they passed through a little village on the outskirts. Red started over the seat and Johnny, still holding the wheel and keeping his foot on the accelerator, moved over out of his way. The girl made room for them.

Just as Red took the wheel, they heard the roar of motors. Turning, Johnny saw a couple of squad cars skidding into the main highway from a side road.

"It's a trap!" yelled George. "Give her the gun, Red!"

The girl screamed. George was knocking the glass out of the back window with the butt of an automatic. Gasping, Johnny pushed the girl into a kneeling position on the floor.

"Stay there, honey," he cried, "we're in for it!"

They were getting into the suburbs. Cars swerved to the side of the road as the huge sedan bore down on them at eighty miles an hour. Red had his jaw set and the accelerator to the floorboard. With a slight twist of the wheel he miraculously avoided car after car. Behind them the sirens were going full blast.

George pulled up the back seat and took out a submachine gun, then, kneeling, he poked it through the back window.

"Where does this next road go, baby?" yelled Red, reaching down and slapping the girl.

She looked up. "I—"

"You're a great help. If we don't get off this main highway we'll be right in the center of town."

The girl looked over the car door.

"Turn right, next road," she said. "It's a straight shoot to San Diego."

"Atta girl."

Scarcely slacking speed, Red whipped the car around in a wide turn. The tires shrieked wildly and the car careened and skidded, but righted itself. George was thrown violently to the floor. "Call your shots, you lug!" he cried, getting up groggily.

Looking back, Johnny saw one of the squad cars go over as it tried to make the turn, saw a man thrown clear and into a field at the side of the road. But the second car came on. George began to fire out the back window with the machine gun.

"Guy shooting with a rifle," he said calmly.

A bullet whined past them, then another. Suddenly they heard a loud metallic ping and then there was a terrific explosion.

"Good night," said George. "Church is out."

The man with the long-range rifle had hit their rear tire. The car turned half around, careened wildly, then jumped the road and rolled over into the field.

When Johnny came to, they were carrying him into the county jail on a stretcher. Looking up, he saw Red, handcuffed, walking beside him. Red grinned. "Nice party, eh?"

Johnny saw the stern faces of the deputy sheriffs. An old man with a tobacco-stained mustache was staring down at him.

"Okay, sonny?" he asked, smiling.

"I guess so. Where's the girl?"

"They just took her in. What she's doing with you, I don't know. She used to be a mighty nice girl. I knew her father."

Johnny sat up.

"Listen here—"

"Never mind, son," said the sheriff. "It'll all come out later."

Red and Johnny had been put into the first cell in the corridor and, pressing their faces against the bars, they could see what was going on in the sheriff's office at the front of the jail. George was in the cell next to them. Beyond George was the tank, where some drunks were shouting and laughing. The girl had been put into a cell at the far end of the L-shaped cell block and they couldn't see her.

The sheriff's office was jammed all afternoon. Lawyers, deputies, city officials of all kinds, newspapermen, and photographers milled about. There was so much noise that George got up from time to time and yelled to them to be quiet, he was trying to rest.

The cell block was not partitioned off from the sheriff's office but was a continuation, with a low railing dividing it from the front hallway. All afternoon men crowded to the railing to stare in at the famous bank robbers—Red Hammond and George (Gloomy) Cooke.

Johnny sat on his bunk, staring at the floor. "Red," he said, "why don't they let the girl and me go? You told them all about us."

"Fat chance," said Red. "They're all scared. Two to one you both stand trial. 'Course I'll testify for you. So will George—and he can make any prosecuting attorney look like a deuce. He's smart, that guy. You'll get off, don't worry. But you may stand trial."

"I'm surprised the girl's boy friend hasn't turned up."

"How'd you like it, if she was your girl, not knowing all the facts?" Johnny said nothing.

Red turned from the bars and came over to the bunk.

"What's up?" asked Johnny.

"Nothing. I thought it was the chief of police again. It's just one of the process servers. Didn't you get a bang out of that chief of police? Boy, we got friends in this place. All the big shots want us to come and stay with them. The chief sure would've liked to get us in his new escape-proof jail. Boy, didn't the old whittler swell up, though? We was his prisoners. Hot-cha!"

"Pipe down, Red," called George.

"Okay." Red sat down and lit a cigarette.

"That sheriff's all right," said Johnny. "He doesn't treat you like you were dirt, like all the others."

"No, he's friendly," said Red with a laugh; then he added: "God bless his dear old heart of gold."

Johnny said nothing.

"I told you to pipe down. That mouth of yours will get you in trouble someday," called George.

Red jumped up.

"Look here—" he said.

A matron was coming down the corridor with the girl. Johnny ran to the front of the cell. He saw a tall, thin, light-haired young man standing at the railing, waiting for the girl.

"Her boy friend," said Johnny.

"I lose," said Red.

The girl turned and smiled wanly at Johnny. Then she went up to the young man. His face was stern. He began shouting at her. She started back, bewildered, then lowered her head. Johnny and Red strained their ears, trying to hear. From time to time they caught a phrase: "You weren't satisfied to stay here . . . all the way to Texas . . . mixed up with gangsters . . . what will everybody say? How do I know you were hitchhiking . . . getting in with three strange men . . . I'd have sent you the money . . . No, I can't help you now . . . You asked for it, now you've got it . . . disgracing all my people."

Red laughed and shouted: "What a baboon you turned out to be! Say, that gal's on the square."

"Some of your friends, I see," said the young man, then he turned and went out.

The girl followed the matron back along the corridor.

"Stiff upper lip," Johnny called after her.

"You got yourself a girl," said Red. "Right on the good old bounce. See? She's right in your lap."

Johnny sat down on the bunk. He felt better now, much better. After a while, without realizing it, he began to whistle.

After they had eaten and the turnkey had taken the tin plates away, the sheriff came down the corridor and stopped before the first cell.

"How you doing, boys?" he asked, smiling at them. He had his coat off, as it was a hot evening, and they saw that he had a big revolver in a shoulder holster in addition to the automatic on his hip.

"Two-gun man, eh, sheriff?" said Red, grinning.

"Used to be," the sheriff replied. "I can remember the days of the gun-fanners. Well, boys, sleep tight. Food okay? We aim to please."

They saw him go into the front part of the jail, where his office was, and sit down at his desk. Near him a clerk was working at a typewriter, painfully typing a letter with one finger. A new turnkey came on duty and sat for a while on the sheriff's desk, talking to him, then disappeared.

George had been looking out the window of his cell ever since he had eaten.

"What's up?" Red demanded.

"Squad car cruising this district. Sort of making regular rounds. The chief of police's not taking any chances, I guess. Time is it?"

Red pressed his face against the bars and stared out into the front office. "Ten after six."

Johnny watched them. They seemed excited. He was almost certain they were up to something; what, he couldn't imagine. Of course, Red had boasted that they had friends in El Portal, but Johnny thought he might be joking. After all, "friends," if any, don't storm jails. But why had they been in such a hurry to get to El Portal? Were they running away from something or toward it? Johnny watched, while Red walked back and forth slowly.

"How many left now?" George asked suddenly.

"Three," said Red, "but the clerk don't count and I can't see the turnkey."

There was a long silence, then Red gave a jump and whispered: "Okay, George."

Pressing his face against the bars, Johnny saw three well dressed men walk quickly into the jail. The sheriff, who had been reading a newspaper, jumped up. But the men were already holding guns on him. A dapper little man in a tight blue suit seemed to be the leader.

"Well, Buffalo Bill," he said, "stick up your paws. Reach for the ceiling."

The sheriff stood with his mouth open, his hands shaking.

"Where are you, boys?" yelled one of the men.

"Right back here," yelled Red. "Get the turnkey." In his excitement Red began to rattle the cell door. He had forgotten all about Johnny, who still had his face pressed to the bars.

"Where is he?"

"Look around for him. He can't be far."

The man in the blue suit shouted at the sheriff: "Where's the turnkey?"

"Don't know."

"Remember quick."

Johnny held his breath.

"I won't tell you."

"Look for him, look for him," cried Red.

The man in the blue suit hit the sheriff over the head with the barrel of his revolver, and when the sheriff didn't fall he hit him again.

Johnny gritted his teeth.

Staggering, the sheriff went for his gun. A man in a brown suit jumped forward suddenly and hit the sheriff in the mouth with his fist. The sheriff fell back into his chair. In spite of his bravado, you could see he was a very old man—his hat had fallen off and his sparse gray hair was standing up all over his head. The man in the brown suit disarmed him, then leaned forward and hit him again with his fist."Talk, you old goat!"

But the man in the blue suit shouted, "There's the turnkey!"

Johnny heard the turnkey cry out.

Then he saw two of the men pulling him up the corridor. The clerk had fainted and had fallen forward across his desk, upsetting an inkwell. Johnny saw the ink dripping to the floor.

The turnkey, pale as death, goaded by the visitors, who were nervous now, fumblingly unlocked the door of Red's cell, then George's. Red leaped out into the corridor. The man in the blue suit handed Red an automatic, then turned and hit the turnkey over the head with the barrel of his revolver. The turnkey fell limp. George grabbed a Thompson gun from one of the men and they all started down the corridor. The man in the blue suit turned.

"What about this monkey?" he demanded, jerking his thumb at Johnny.

"Don't pay no attention to him," cried Red, "he's a softie. Let's get going."

Johnny stood at the door of the cell, not knowing what to do. He was trembling with excitement and rage. Those dirty, lowdown brutes, treating a nice old guy like that. It was just ignorance and viciousness, absolutely unnecessary—they could have managed the jailbreak much better with a little less violence.

The man in the brown suit amused himself by slapping the sheriff's face several times very hard. Johnny saw the old man recoil. His nose began to bleed. Johnny lost his head. Rushing down the corridor, he tackled George from behind, and when they fell he grabbed George's machine gun and got to his knees. George was knocked out by the fall onto the cement floor and lay groaning.

"Beat it," yelled the man in the blue suit. "Ain't that a siren I hear?"

Red glanced at George, then he fired twice at Johnny, two snap shots that went wide. The machine gun cut loose in Johnny's hands. Scared half to death, and amazed by the violent recoil of the gun, Johnny tried to stop it. He was firing high, spattering lead all over the walls and ceiling of the jail. The men ran out, shouting. Red

turned and fired again, missing, then he ran out. The gun slipped
from Johnny's grasp and kicked him in the stomach, knocking him
over—then it subsided.

He heard the screaming of sirens and the roar of a powerful motor
on the getaway, then he got groggily to his feet and walked over to
the sheriff. "Are you all right?" he asked.

"Well," said the sheriff, trying to smile, "I wouldn't go as far as
to say that, but I'm still here."

The judge leaned forward and looked at Johnny and the girl, who
were a little nervous and kept glancing at each other. The judge was
a young man with the face of a humorist.

"Case dismissed," he said, then he shook his finger at them. "Now
I could say let this be a lesson to you. But I know it won't. Nothing
is ever a lesson to anybody, and if that sounds like philosophy, make
the most of it. It was a mighty nice thing you did, standing up for
old Jim Hughes, but why couldn't you have used a revolver? It's
going to cost us five hundred dollars to fix up that jail and we may
take it out of your share of the reward."

A bailiff turned to the sheriff and winked, then they both burst
out laughing.

"Order in the court," said the judge. "Another thing, if Jim Hughes
was a Democrat I'd like him better, but I guess he just got started
wrong. As I said before, case dismissed."

"Thanks, your Honor," said Johnny, grinning.

The sheriff got between Johnny and the girl and put his arms
around them. "Don't suppose you want to go over and see your friends
in the new city jail, eh?" He laughed, then he groaned and rubbed
his jaw. "That one fellow surely had a hard hand. Must have done
some honest work before he started using a gun. You kids come and
have lunch with me and the missus. She wants to meet you. How
about it?"

"Well," said Johnny, "I've got to see a fellow first."

"What fellow?" asked the girl.

"Why," said Johnny, "that boy friend of yours. I feel like I'm
responsible for getting you in this jam, so I thought I'd—"

"Ask him to take me back?"

"Well, I thought—"

The sheriff stood looking at them, smiling slightly.

"What an idiot you are!" said the girl, then she turned to the
sheriff. "Yes, we'll come for lunch."

Gwendoline Butler

The Sisterhood

I was serving the first coffee of the day when the two women came in. It's a hot day, so I'm slow, but I'm a hard worker and I'm getting on with it. That's the picture I see looking back. I could do with help but conditions are bad just now and I don't get help. Frankly, I'm glad to have a job, and I need one. When my husband died (his Feed and Grain business failed the year President Grover Cleveland came into office) he left me penniless.

So I do what I can. I can make coffee and tea and serve it neatly, polish china and cutlery, and give the right change. Also I'm honest; I don't steal from my employers. My employer is the Railroad, an impersonal one but we get along well enough. It don't overpay me and I don't fill my basket with its coffee and sugar, and that's about it. We don't owe each other a thing. At first, I wondered if there'd be any talk about me serving tea and coffee, but no, no one said anything.

The two women came in so early I knew that there'd been another delay on the line. I don't think our railroad will ever pay for itself while we have these little incidents so often. This time it was only the engine caught fire and no one hurt. These two women were the forerunners; I could hear other angry voices behind.

"It's only a little delay," one of them was saying. "We shall get there in the end. Only Father is cross; we need not be." She was a nice-looking young woman, plainly dressed in poplin, but not poor. I know the sort—no show but plenty of money tucked away in the family money-bags. Who controls the purse strings, though?

"And he's the one that counts," said the other one. So this answered my question: in this family it was the father who held the money. This woman was younger than the other one—not a girl, but a woman approaching her prime. She looked as though she feared this prime would come and go unnoticed. I recognized that keen searching look.

They had got on to the subject of marriage by the time I served their coffee, which showed how their minds were running.

"Marriages are made in heaven," the older one was saying. I suppose I've served thousands of cups of coffee and overheard thousands of conversations; but I've never heard anyone say that.

"Marriages are made with money, Emma," snapped the younger one. *Snap.* Her jaws went like little traps. Well, she was right enough there. "Father has the money and Abby will make the marriage."

"Do you think she will, Elizabeth?"

"Yes."

Father and Abby put in their appearance then. He had been held up by a quarrel with the engineer. Abby asked for iced tea and Father for water. He'd have an extra glass with it, please. I kept my eyes on him to see what he did with the two glasses. Father and Abby didn't sit at the same table as the two girls but a little way off. There wouldn't have been room for them, with Abby the size she was. She was wearing a fine silk dress, though.

"My, I'm hot." That was her size, of course. The dress was red-silk, too, which didn't cool her off any. "Do you have any cologne, girls?"

Elizabeth silently handed over a small flask of cologne for Abby to dab her face, and Father took some too and held the bottle while she fanned herself. This seemed to be his manner of doing his courting and Abby nodded and chuckled, and this was her way of doing hers. I never did get to see what he did with his two glasses. Perhaps he had some medicine to take, but he looked a fine healthy man that would live forever. He drank his water, though, then gave the cologne back to Elizabeth and put his hand down on the table near to Abby's.

So Abby sat there cooling off, insofar as she was able, and Father sat there warming up. Every so often he looked at the door as if he might get up and leave soon. It's true there were a few train noises every once in a while, but I knew better. There are only three trains a day through here. The 9:10 in the morning running west, which was now broken down. Then the midday train running east. Then the 5:00 P.M. train running west again. I knew they wouldn't be moving for a spell.

Then the girls started talking again in low voices.

"I don't think she looks at all nice," the older one said and I knew what they were talking about. They were talking about the only other customer.

She'd been there all the time. She hadn't come off the train. No, she'd been there waiting. She was wearing a watered silk dress and a satin-edged bonnet. She made Abby look cheap. I'd served her the first coffee of the day and she was still sitting there sipping it. She was going someplace, no doubt, but I didn't know where and she was giving me no sign—I'm good at reading even very little signs. I'd say she'd come a long way. Was going a long way too.

"Not nice? What does that mean?" asked the younger one.

"Don't flash at me. I know what I mean. She looks worldly. Experienced."

"She looks interesting." Elizabeth was dabbing at her own face with cologne. "Clever. If that's what worldly means." The cologne was putting a shine on her nose. She had a plump face with full cheeks which might lengthen into a long hatchet face later. Now she was a bouncing young woman with the nearest to good looks she'd ever have.

The smell of cologne has done nothing for me since my husband died. Funny, I can smell coffee and feel fine. Cologne, and I'm sick straight away. I used cologne for him a lot in his last days. It was an easy death. I was there and I can tell you: it was an easy death, but he didn't want to go.

To take my mind off my nausea I moved closer to the girls.

"I'd like to get to know the world better," said Elizabeth.

"Perhaps we could go to Europe."

"With Father? With Abby? Does Abby look like a traveler?" No, Abby did not.

I'll tell you how I could get their conversation although they were talking low. I'm something of a lip reader. I taught myself; it's one of my tricks. They were talking soft but I could read them. Abby was talking away too but I couldn't read her. She had her head down. I guess Abby could lip-read too.

The other lady (unknown I was going to say, but of course they were all unknown to me) looked towards them. Just a glance. No more. But I'll bet her eyes and her observation were good. She was the sort that took everything in and wrapped it away in brown paper for future use. Funny way of looking she had—just glancing up under heavy lids and deep lashes. A pretty face really. Or had been. It was lined now, and she used rouge, too.

I just glanced at my own in the mirror. Ah, there was a *look* there. It seemed to me this look was growing and growing—the only live thing about me.

"She looks interesting, but she doesn't look honest. Not straight," said Elizabeth, as if she'd made a discovery.

"Not straight! The way you talk. Like a man."

Elizabeth seemed flattered as if she'd received a compliment and

I can tell she's one of the simple ones who hasn't grasped that she *is* a man. That's why she'll never get a husband. Not because Abby has Father and Father has the money and money makes a marriage, but because she's a man and another man will notice it.

"More coffee, please," sings out the lady. It was a strange little voice, soft yet mighty penetrating and with an accent I couldn't place.

"She's an English lady," whispers Emma.

"Scottish," says the lady, in that gentle lilting voice of hers. She smiled. No one else did.

It was an encounter all right, I could see that, a real moment in life. I haven't traveled much, so I don't know where she came from; but it was a strange place, I'll say that.

"May I join you ladies?" She was carrying her coffee over to their table. "We must pass the time somehow, must we not?" She sat down close to Elizabeth. "It would be coarse and common to make a fuss. Still, it is tedious waiting."

"No," answered Emma.

"Yes," said her sister.

So that was the effect she had on them—not that they'd ever spoken with one voice, I reckon. Take care, I wanted to warn them: she knows something you don't know and if you don't watch out you'll know it too.

There was plenty of noise going on outside. Not the noise of a train which was what they were hoping for, but the noise of something, and I could see Abby and Father looking curious. They'd soon be out there to investigate. I knew what it was. It was a funeral. We have noisy funerals in this little spot. Well, we have had lately. And there have been so many of them. Why, we die off like flies round here.

Abby was heaving herself up and out of the room and Father was hurrying after her, as if his blood was hot, whereas you could tell by the cut of his suit it was cold. It was going to be a marriage all right, the sort I knew about. A kind of exclusive club with only two members.

A suitor of my own came in as they went out, brushing against them with an apology. At least, I suppose he was a suitor. He's always in here talking to me. He sells insurance. I don't imagine he thought he would sell me any. My buying days are over. I bought some for my Willy; that's enough for one family; I won't be buying any for myself.

"I heard the noise," I said, nodding outside. I gave him his coffee.

"Yeah, terrible sad thing. Maisie Gray."

"I heard she was going."

He drank his coffee.

"Bad time?" I said.

"Worse than most."

"I heard."

We stood in silence for a minute. Our tribute, you might say, to the dead.

"So it wasn't an easy end? Funny thing. I'd have sworn Maisie was a woman as'd have an easy end. She seemed made for it somehow."

"Oh, they've all been bad lately. It's something in the season, I think." He sounded depressed. He kept in with the doctors and the undertakers in the way of business, so he always knew about the ends we made.

"Who was making all the noise out there?"

"Oh, Maisie's sister. Crying to beat the band. You heard? It was the *way* Maisie died," he burst out. "Little by little. One day it was a foot, the next day a finger. No telling what next. Then at last it was over her like wildfire."

"What was it supposed to be?"

"Some infection. That's the way they've been lately."

My Will had an easy death, but he didn't want to go, and for that you couldn't blame him. He knew what would be waiting for him. His brother whom he'd cheated, his mother he'd neglected, and his sister he'd help kill. He was leaving me this side, but I doubt that was much comfort to him.

"Was she insured?"

"No. She didn't carry insurance. There wasn't no one who benefited by her death. No one." He shook his head. "Bad business."

He went on drinking his coffee. Watching the three women at their table I saw Emma get up. I guessed the Scotch woman had sent her out. She knew how to say, "Do this," and it was done. She had a pretty elegant way of holding her lips when she spoke. I quite admired her. Elizabeth was just a good plain ordinary speaker. You wouldn't have picked her out from any crowd for the beauty of her diction. I could read both their lips fine.

"So kind of your sister to do that little errand for me. I feel the need for some cologne like you."

"She was glad to go."

"Yes." She sounded doubtful, forming her lips in a little cooing shape. "I think she doesn't like me."

"Emma doesn't consider whether she likes you or not, she doesn't know you." Only a fool would expect flattery from Elizabeth.

"Oh, you Yankee ladies are so smart. You put us poor European creatures to shame." She could live with her lies and even love them. Perhaps this was what she was going to teach the other one.

"Who is that woman?" It was my suitor speaking. I had forgotten him there drinking his coffee.

"I think she's a teacher."

"Where does she teach?"

I shrugged. It was my idea she was teaching right now. But I'd reminded him of something.

"Why do you do this work?" He pointed to my hands, red and stained. "You taught school once. You could teach it again."

"No," I said. "No school."

"She doesn't look like a teacher to me. No. I'll tell you what she does look like—" He frowned.

I could see them both in the mirror behind me, still talking away.

"Why, she looks like you," he finished, in a surprised voice.

"Yes." I'd noticed it myself. "Perhaps we're related."

"What? Not by blood."

"By blood."

"I don't understand you."

"Hush. Listen."

The two women were deep in conversation. I've never seen what that meant before. Now I saw it meant that they were talking at all levels. They were talking with their eyes, with their bodies, and with their silences. And some of the most important things get said that way.

"As soon as I saw you I knew you were someone I must talk to," the Scotch woman was saying.

"Do you feel that way often?" I cannot describe the peculiar note the speaker put into that question. Off-hand, skeptical, and yet profoundly interested in the answer. The one thing that perhaps she didn't want to show was what came across strongest.

"It comes. I can often tell when it will happen. I get a warning."

"So you were getting warnings while Emma and I sat here?"

"Before." She smiled. "Before. I don't say that's why I came here."

"You can't say that's why you came here. I didn't know I was coming here myself. We were going straight through but the engine broke down."

"As if that mattered." She still smiled. "But I don't say so. Notice, I *don't* say so."

They sat looking at each other.

"I am on my way to help a sister. An American girl married to an English businessman. In Liverpool. Cotton, I believe. She is in great trouble and I am going to help her. She has been rather careless, poor girl."

"She's an American girl and she is your sister? But you are not American."

"No, I was Glasgow-born. A Miss Smith before my marriage."

"And she's your sister?" Elizabeth was getting lost. I wasn't though. I was beginning to see my way. I've always been quick on the uptake.

Looking out of the window I could see Abby and Father pacing up and down; they were not talking. No sign of Emma. The funeral had become quiet. They were doing the burying, I suppose.

There's no noise louder nor stronger than the thud of earth against the box.

"I call her my sister," answered the Scotch woman.

"And what does she call you?"

"Oh, we've never met. No, I am on my way now to our first meeting. Even this may not be easy to do. No, it will not be easy to meet her, but I shall try. I know my duty."

"Well, I know *my* sister," declared Elizabeth. "I meet her face to face every day. That's what I call being a sister."

"You have many sisters that you don't know. I must teach you about them." See, I said she was a teacher.

"I know all I want to know about my family."

"Have you noticed," said the other, "that although this is a very hot day there is no sun? This is a sunless town."

This I had noticed. We all do. It can get quite trying in high summer. The deaths are always worse then.

"I don't want any more members added to my family," said Elizabeth, in a pointed kind of way.

"You mean the lady who went out with your Father? That makes you bitter?"

"I don't trust her. We should have our rights."

"Rights?"

"Money," said Elizabeth sullenly. Emma pushed open the door.

"I'm sorry I was so long," she panted. "It was impossible to find a shop open in the town for your cologne. On the way back I came across a large crowd in the town square and I had difficulty in getting through. I don't know what they were doing. Every so often a man would say something. But he didn't speak very loud."

We don't speak very loud in our town. You can't call our voices soft, but we don't raise 'em much. Except at funerals.

"Every so often someone would call out a name and then they would all be silent again. I wonder what they were doing?"

They must be starting the election for mayor. And that means Tom Edwards must be going downhill fast. He's younger than most. The average life expectancy in this town is 45, and we age quick. Tom's still a young man but he looks old. It's a shame he should go. He made a good mayor. He has a growth, I've heard. Back of his throat. Certain he didn't speak well these last years.

But a lot of us have trouble this way. We intermarry a good deal. There are only three or four big family groups, kin we call them, and we're all related. Tom's mother married her cousin. Some people said *his* father was also his brother, but I don't know about that. You hear these stories every so often round here, but I don't know that any one of them has ever been proven.

No one said anything to Emma standing there and in a minute she muttered something about getting some air and went out again. I doubt if they noticed her go.

"You must learn to defend yourself," the old one was saying. I couldn't hear even the breath of these words, I could only read them on her face. "Money is important. Yes, and you should have yours. A woman may get justice, but she must usually get it for herself."

"How can she?"

"A man won't give it to her, that is certain. Oh, he can be persuaded into it, but it has to be contrived. In the end one relies on oneself."

"I always do."

"Yes, you have made a good beginning, but it is not enough. Are you a woman of education? Anything of a scientist? A doctor perhaps?"

"No."

"A pity." She sounded regretful. "There would be so much scope for a sister who was also a doctor. Well, then you must exercise a good deal. Keep in good health. Develop your muscles."

"Why?"

"It may come in useful." She leaned over and felt the girl's arm. "Yes, I thought you looked strong," she said with approval. "Suitable bouffant sleeves will mask a lady's arm muscles. I should not advise you to make a show of them. Always think of a practical point like that. It may be the saving of you. Some sisters have wasted time on theory that would be better spent in attending to the practical details."

"And my legs too?" said Elizabeth, withdrawing her arm.

"Oh, I can't foretell the future. I can't tell you what your need may be. Perhaps at some future date I might advise a lady to cultivate strong legs, but I can't say. It may be that you will invent some ingenious little plan of your own that needs strong legs. I leave it to you. And in any case a strong mind and good manners are your best protection. Many a lady owes her life to her manners."

Oh, how I had needed someone like her in my life. She gave good advice. She said words I wanted to hear. I moved away unsteadily to sit down. My right leg always troubles me worse in hot weather.

"How lame she is, poor thing," said the young one. Much she cared.

"I'm afraid she has been badly used at one time."

"She may have been born like that."

"No. You can see by her face. She has not the expression of someone who has been used to it since birth. She has had to learn how to bear it."

"She's listening."

"Nonsense. She cannot possibly hear." So then I saw that my lady from Glasgow had this limitation: she only believed what she wanted to believe. I suppose this was what made her strong. Because she was strong. I'm strong myself and I could measure hers.

"If I might suggest," she was going on. "You might pay a little more attention to your dress."

"Ladies where I come from don't bother much with their dress."

"Ladies everywhere bother with their dress," the Scotch woman corrected. "A well trimmed bodice or a becoming hat can make a good deal of difference at your time of crisis."

"My time of crisis?"

"You will have one, my dear," she said softly.

"Ah." It was a long, long breath. I felt it more than heard it.

"And when that time comes you must accept your crisis. Be proud. Wear it like a crown."

"We don't have queens in this country. And I don't aim to be a martyr."

"Oh, on no account. They are our least successful members."

"Is this a sort of club?"

"Yes, but it's more important than that. More sacred."

"Do I take an oath or something?"

"You have already taken it."

"What?" Elizabeth recoiled.

"Yes. You took it . . . Now, let me see." She looked thoughtful. "You must have taken it a few minutes after our conversation began. When you said: 'I know all I want to know about my family.'"

And it's true, she had taken it then. From then on there was no looking back for her.

"Now you are one of us. My sister," and the Scotch woman stretched out a fleshy hand.

"So, it's a sisterhood," said Elizabeth, just beginning to take in what she had joined.

"Yes." There was a radiant smile. "Oh, we are a great band stretching out hands down the centuries. Mary Stuart was one of us, Madame Brinvilliers was certainly another."

And what about the nameless ones, I wanted to shout out, the ones who didn't get their names in history books?

"I remember my own initiation," the old one was going on. "I was walking in the country near Glasgow. The old crone frightened me with what she said. But I never forgot it." She looked amused. "Still, do you know, I believe I must have resolved then that when my time came it should all be neatly and tidily managed and nothing sordid like that old woman. Pah, I could smell the blood on her."

Elizabeth took a sniff of her cologne, for which I didn't blame her. My suitor woke up. I'd forgotten him dozing over his coffee.

"It's all in the womb," he said as he came awake. He's the only man I know that would say "womb" right out. I think he drinks.

"What is?"

"Wickedness." That's another word he can say outright.

"You'd better go off home."

"Thanks. I will."

He shuffled out. He'd be back tomorrow.

She was still talking about death when I turned back.

"Of course you must not take me literally when I say I smelled blood. What I smelled was probably something quite different. Dirt, I dare say."

"I don't think blood does smell."

"Not to you. No. You are one of the lucky ones. But it does to some people. Blood will never smell to you, or stick to you, or in any way worry you. You should be glad."

"I am."

"It was because I was tender of the sight of blood that I was obliged to find a different weapon. Come, Louis, my love, I said, drink this chocolate, you will be better for it."

"And was he?"

"We must all be the better for casting off this world and its troubles, must we not? In the end."

She was willing to tell more.

"Mine was an affair of the heart, you understand? I truly and tenderly loved my poor Louis. But then he was poor, and showed no signs of trying to better himself." She sighed. "Poor creature, he tried so hard to cling to me. In the end I had to be brave for both of us. But I was too innocent to live then, my dear, and the result was there was a great deal of nasty talk, quite ill informed, and my trial had to be moved to Edinburgh."

"Oh, so there *was* a trial?"

"One cannot hope to escape all unpleasantness," she said placidly.

"And the result was?"

"The verdict was 'Not Proven.' "

"And that means?"

"It means you go free."

"Is that all?"

"My dear, allow me to say that in the circumstances it is very nearly everything."

Elizabeth became quiet. She hadn't quite accepted the reality of all this, but it was coming. I knew her kind—slow to take anything in, but very tenacious. Hadn't I taught girls like her? I knew their ways. Obstinate, yes, and ruthless, too. Stupid sometimes; you could talk to them forever and ever and get nowhere. Then *snap*, they took something in and it was theirs for life. She was like that.

"And never forget," the old one was saying. "You are a gentlewoman, and in that is your protection. Who will believe a gentlewoman could be violent? Go naked if you must to commit your deed. No one will believe it."

Elizabeth covered her ears with her hands. The other pulled them away.

"You heard me? You listened? You will never forget. Remember, we are sisters."

She was talking quite loudly now, not caring if I heard, but then she was a gentlewoman see, and I was just a stone in the wall to her.

I wanted to call out, "I'm here. I'm listening. You are talking to the converted. Can't you see we look alike? I have done my deed, I am one of you, I am your sister. I gave my husband arsenic in his coffee. And I did it all on my own."

Perhaps I ought to have been proud of my independence.

The train was going to come in soon, the one running east. Already I could hear a noise in the distance. The woman from Glasgow got up, gathered her possessions together, and slowly moved towards the door. We watched her go.

The train came in and still we stood, silent.

Then Emma put her head in at the door.

"Come on, we are going back home. Papa has canceled the trip. We are going back on this train."

Her sister still stood there. Emma became impatient.

"Come on, Elizabeth. Come *on*, Miss Lizzie Borden."

Thomas Walsh

Girl in Danger

John Kelly and Cornelius Holleran, who had drawn the second name on the list—Henesie, Gowns—left headquarters about half past six that night after the usual briefing by Inspector Donnelly, and got over to the Henesie apartment on Central Park West some twenty or twenty-five minutes later.

What they found at Henesie's number appeared to be quite an apartment house, a rich-looking sidewalk awning, not one but two uniformed doormen, and a magnificent cream and gold lobby. For a moment—but only for a moment—they stopped on the pavement and eyed that lobby with the customary trade air of alert and rather menacing contempt; then, not looking at each other, they marched in stolidly and inquired at the desk for Miss Henesie.

She was not home. Soon, however, the house manager was produced from somewhere, and Cornelius Holleran flashed the badge on him, and after that they were all wafted up elegantly and smoothly to the eighteenth floor.

They found quite a place there, too. A round foyer done in a cool ivory shade, and beyond it, down two steps, a breathtakingly long living room with a couple of oversized windows looking out directly across the park.

Kelly, face to face with that, paused momentarily at the top of the foyer steps. Cornelius Holleran, with a brusque and rasping "Okay, Jack," edged the house manager unceremoniously into the hall and then slammed the door on him. At the far end of the room was a terrace doorway through which Kelly was able to make out a narrow plot of grass bordered by dwarf shrubbery, two stone urns, one white metal table, and two chromium and leather reclining chairs. In the living room itself he saw flowers pleasantly arranged, some swirls and angles of odd but comfortable-looking furniture wrought of waxed pale wood and cool-looking gray upholstery, and a fireplace of fine black marble glittering coldly under the most enormous circular mirror Kelly had ever seen.

He inspected the layout for a moment or two, not overly impressed, but impressed, before going down into it. Cornelius Holleran, a bulky man with a seamed dark face and iron-gray hair, followed him—and, still without speaking, the two of them walked through to a small, immaculate dining room, a kitchen, and a back door that led out to the service elevator. After that, they crossed the living room again and found Miss Henesie's bedroom.

A closet in there was filled with shelves of hatboxes and shoes, and a long overwhelming row of coats and dresses and tailored suits, all apparently feminine, all apparently Henesie's. Cornelius Holleran pawed curiously through those things and came up with a pale-blue nightdress about as substantial as spun moonlight.

"Mama," he said, with his first expression of interest. "Look at this. Them French, hey, Kelly?"

"Oh, boy!" Kelly said, but without any particular enthusiasm. He glanced around, sniffed a perfume bottle absently, lighted another cigarette, and went back to the living room. Cornelius Holleran followed him leisurely. "Everything high-class, hey?" he wanted to know.

When Kelly didn't answer him, he scowled, grunted something inaudible, and began to move around and touch things with an inquisitive forefinger. Time passed. At a quarter after eight, when the room was beginning to fill with dim shadows, the door in back of them opened and closed. Kelly got up quickly and saw a yellow dress gleaming at him from the top of the foyer steps, a yellow straw hat balanced tentatively over it.

"Hello, there," the yellow dress said brightly.

Kelly answered with an impassive nod. Cornelius Holleran flashed the badge again and announced in his extraordinary bass voice who they were.

"I know," the yellow dress said.

An electric button snapped and three or four lamps came on in various parts of the room; then Henesie came down the steps, smiling at Cornelius Holleran, and dropped the yellow straw hat, a pair of gloves, and a dull-black leather bag on the coffee table. "I heard about you downstairs. You've got poor Mr. Andrews terribly worried."

A tall girl with very black hair and very white teeth and very clear skin, she gave Kelly a quick but not unfriendly look and the same sort of smile Cornelius Holleran had received.

All the time that they'd been waiting here, Kelly had pictured this Henesie to himself as a small shrewd female, ageless but chic, with a birdlike and rather petulant French face. Now, surprised but not at all intimidated, he cleared his throat and informed her that there wasn't anything to worry about. Did she remember a woman named Mrs. Allen who had been her maid here about a month ago?

"Of course." She ran one hand up through the black hair, shaking it out gracefully. "I've only been able to get a girl in for two days a week since she left me. Why?"

"Sit down, lady," Cornelius Holleran said, closing the wallet over his badge. "He's Kelly. I'm Holleran. Inspector Donnelly sent us over here to see you."

"Oh." She sat down slowly. "Inspector who? I'm not quite sure that I—"

"Acting innocent, hey?" Cornelius Holleran demanded affably. He appeared to have taken an enormous fancy to her at once. "Okay, Kelly, I guess we get out the blackjacks and the rubber hose."

Ignoring that remark, Kelly began to explain the necessary details about the woman who called herself Mrs. Allen or Mrs. Smith or Mrs. Anything-at-all. What she did, or what Inspector Donnelly had come to believe she did, was to hire herself out to single girls, in apartments like this, for a week or so at a time; in a week Mrs. Allen's trained eye could decide whether or not her boss was worth bothering about, and if she were—if jewelry, cash, negotiable bonds or anything else valuable was apparent—Mrs. Allen walked out on her the first payday with a spare key that she'd had made for the back door.

She never came back. But two or three weeks later her husband did. He had the spare key then, and he knew what to look for; furthermore, he was usually cautious enough to pick a weekend when the tenant didn't answer her phone, and the chances seemed good that she was off somewhere in the country. The thing had worked out very nicely for the past three or four months. And then, the weekend before last—

"Yes?" Henesie said, when Kelly paused. She had altogether exceptional dark-blue eyes, and so long as he went on speaking she never seemed to think of moving them away from him. Now, however, they widened after a moment, moved quickly to Cornelius Holleran, and back again to Kelly. "Oh! That girl who was found murdered in her apartment over on East Eighty-first Street, you mean? Mrs. Allen worked for *her?*"

Kelly replied with a grim contraction of the lips that he guessed perhaps she had. Inspector Donnelly had been put onto the case and it was discovered that all the girls who had had their apartments ransacked had at one time employed a woman who looked like this

Mrs. Allen. Meanwhile, through the employment agencies, the department had located three more places where this Mrs. Allen had worked, but which hadn't been touched yet.

This was one, Kelly added curtly. That's why they were here. From now on, at each of the three apartments, Inspector Donnelly wanted two men on hand from seven o'clock in the evening until seven o'clock the next morning. He was sorry, Kelly said, if their staying here would inconvenience her, but he and Cornelius Holleran had to be around this apartment all night and every night, till Mr. Allen came out of his rathole again.

She had watched him so far with a fascinated but slightly disconcerting regard; now she said very quickly, "Oh, my goodness! Stay here? With *me?*"

"That's the general idea," Kelly said stolidly.

She jumped up at once. "But that's impossible," she said.

Cornelius Holleran became a little aggrieved. "What's the matter?" he said. "We been house guests before, lady. Suppose you look at it this way. What do you think you'll have to worry about with me and Kelly around here?"

"I don't know," she said, obviously rattled. "I'm just—oh, upset, I suppose. Give me a minute to think it over, will you?"

She sat down again and chewed her lower lip for more than the minute she had asked for; once she darted another quick and appraising look at Kelly, who betrayed no consciousness of it. At last she clasped her hands in her lap and gave them a small smile.

"A good many people are going to think it a likely story," she said. "However—" she swallowed bravely "—if you think you can put up with me and a few little idiosyncrasies— Don't look so—so professional, gentlemen. May I have your hats?"

As an assignment, of course, it had its points. Even on the most breathless nights of a memorable August they all managed to be very comfortable out on Henesie's terrace, drinking beer or iced tea and watching the lights on Fifth Avenue. Henesie seemed to be a pretty swell girl, Kelly thought quietly. Not much like Rosemary; prettier—a lot prettier—and much more of a homebody. Some evenings she worked over fashion books and had Cornelius Holleran model rolls of material for her. Cornelius Holleran didn't mind at all. He told Kelly that here was certainly a sweetheart; and if he was ten years younger, if he didn't have two kids and the old battleax out in Queens, if he had Kelly's lean looks and—

Kelly made no answer to those elaborate suggestions until the Friday of their first week on Central Park West when Cornelius Holleran, irritated by this complete lack of response, asked sourly whether Kelly knew what was wrong with him.

Every night now, Cornelius Holleran said, he had a chance to get himself in solid with a nice girl who had money, looks, and brains. And what did he do? Moped around; muttered a word or two every other hour. And why? Just because a cheap, double-crossing little floozie like that Rosemary over in Brooklyn Heights—

Kelly spun savagely around. It was seven o'clock at night and they were just walking into the elegant downstairs lobby. "Watch your mouth," Kelly said, very white around his own.

The elevator came then—fortunately perhaps. They rode up in it without speaking. On the eighteenth floor, Henesie, wearing a neat black-and-white outfit and a ridiculous frilled apron, opened the door for them.

"Hi," she said briskly. "How's Cornelius?" She smiled at Kelly, who nodded back at her with very little expression. "Company tonight," she added. "Lots of fun and frolic, Cornelius. You wouldn't want to help me with some sandwiches?"

"Who wouldn't?" Cornelius Holleran said. They went out together, chatting amiably, to the kitchen, while Kelly sat himself down in the living room with a copy of the evening paper. He didn't read it; his insides were still cold and upset, and his head—his eggshell head—felt tighter than usual around the temples.

After a while he reached up and touched the plate the doctors had put into the back of his skull after he was shot in a holdup two years ago—touched it carefully and delicately. Even then it felt as if he were reaching inside and putting a finger on the exact center of his brain.

Presently Henesie came in again from the kitchen, Cornelius Holleran trailing her with a sandwich in one hand and a bottle of beer in the other. She seemed very vivacious.

"Sedate John Kelly," she said, as if he amused her secretly. "Very aloof tonight. Is he always this quiet, Cornelius, or do parties frighten him?"

She had a lot of things that Rosemary had never had. An unaffected cheerfulness—a kind of inward brightness, Kelly thought. She didn't look at you the way Rosemary had; and that cool, easy friendliness in her voice—Kelly smiled painfully.

"This party might," he said. "What's it for? To show off the apes?"

He had meant it humorously, but in these last six months he had
lost the knack of humor, and it didn't come out as he had intended.
Henesie flushed up from the throat. There was a brief silence. Then
Cornelius Holleran put his beer and sandwich down carefully on the
coffee table and came over and stopped flatfooted in front of Kelly.

"Well," he said, in his extraordinary bass voice. "You been askin'
for it a pretty good while, fella. You been goin' around shootin' off
your mouth and actin' smart with people till I got all I can hold of
it. On your feet, Kelly. Up before I—"

"Cornelius," Henesie said. She was breathless. "Please, Cornelius.
It doesn't matter, really."

"What doesn't matter?" Cornelius Holleran demanded, scowling
at her. "You think he's goin' to talk that way to a girl like you just
because some bimbo he used to know—"

The doorbell rang. Henesie, now rather white around the mouth,
took his arm and moved him over toward the foyer. "Please, Cornelius," she said again, fervently. "It's the company. Remember?"

The company—two girls and three men—did not seem to be aware
of any strain. They were all young and pleasant and quite at home,
and Cornelius Holleran got on famously with them. Kelly did not.
He sat off in a corner, smiling when it seemed called for, but not
saying very much. At ten, when Cornelius Holleran began to tell
them how the Hauptmann case had been handled by the East 104th
Street station, he got up and moved out to the terrace.

It was pleasant there, remote from the voices inside and the park
lights below. There were a few clouds in a great, calm sky and a
good many small, dim-silver stars in the tremendous open gulfs
between the clouds. The life of the party, Kelly thought. Crazy Kelly,
always good for a laugh. Quite a card, the boys down in Centre
Street used to think—

Someone came out after him—he knew even before he turned who
it was. She carried a tray of sandwiches with her and she was as
casual as though nothing at all had happened.

"The chicken's on white," she said. "Take a couple, why don't you?
Cornelius must have made three dozen."

"If you had any handy," Kelly said huskily, "I'd take a couple of
pounds of rat paste after the crack I pulled in there."

"St-st-st," Henesie said. "On a night like this?" She put the tray
on the table and looked it over critically. Then she said, "I'm sorry
you're not enjoying yourself."

Kelly told her that was all right. A headache between his eyes—

"What headache?" she said. "And I don't know that it's all right at all." She picked an olive out of a dish and ate it. "You're not fooling anyone, Kelly. Suppose a girl did run out on you? You'll get over it if you want to. Most people do."

Kelly put his elbows on the stone rail in front of him and looked down eighteen stories into the park.

"I guess you can," he said stolidly enough, but with a peculiar dryness in his throat. "You know very much about it?"

"No. Not very much." She took another olive. "I suppose that means I'm being very smart and superior again."

"Maybe," Kelly said, overcoming the dryness, "it just means that Cornelius gets a lot of ideas and that they're not all strictly logical."

"Oh," she said. She leaned on the rail too. "So it's more than a girl. You know, I had an idea that it was."

Kelly gave her the one-sided, second-rate grin that was about all he could manage these days.

"What was?"

"What's worrying you," she said. "What you're afraid of."

"So I'm afraid," Kelly said, and laughed pretty loudly. He wanted the laugh to make his statement ridiculous. He wasn't sure whether or not it succeeded in doing that.

"I had a fantastic idea at first," Henesie said. "I thought you were afraid of *me*. Were you? Up home in Boston they spell the name with three e's and two n's and two s's and a y. Hennessey—Catherine Hennessey. Does that make you feel more comfortable?"

"Not a whole lot," Kelly said tightly. "I'll bet you loved the French twist I've been giving it."

"The Henesie, you mean? That's because my partner's a girl named Margaret Sievier. We put the first part of the Hennessey in front of the first part of the Sievier because nothing very elegant came out the other way. Henesie's got just the right professional touch, don't you think?"

"It always seemed to fit you," Kelly said.

That must have been a remark she liked, because she glanced around at him with amused and lovely blue-black eyes. It would have been a lot different being out here with her six months or a year ago. Then, Kelly told himself heavily, he would have known just what to say and just how to act with a girl like this. But then, also, he wouldn't have had the memory of Rosemary screaming thinly at him from an infinite distance. Had he ever thought that a girl—a normal girl—would marry him? Had he ever imagined that anyone who knew what the doctors had done to him and who understood what, any day and any hour, was liable to happen to him—

Henesie asked quietly, "What's the matter with you? You look like a ghost."

He gave her the stiff grin again; he didn't have to think up anything to say to her because in a moment the fellow in the good-looking gabardine suit walked through the doorway and said in an inquiring and rather petulant voice, "Kitty?"

She touched Kelly's arm. "Come on inside," she said.

He muttered something, but after she stopped in the doorway, looked back at him, and went off, he didn't go in; he was glad enough just then to be alone.

Every night for the next ten days Kelly and Cornelius Holleran showed up about seven in the evening, sat around with Henesie for three or four hours, then waited and watched until the sun came up blazing over Fifth Avenue for the Mr. Allen who never appeared. When she was with them, Kelly was always reserved; when she wasn't with them, he spent a lot of time thinking about her—the soft, quick voice she had, the way she looked at him, the straight, cool, graceful way she carried herself. He couldn't have forgotten her even if he had wanted to, because Cornelius Holleran wouldn't let him.

When she had gone off along the passage to bed, Cornelius Holleran would glare at him with narrowed, surly eyes. This, Cornelius Holleran would say, was something he couldn't understand—not if he lived to be a hundred. The first thing was that she was screwy enough to like Kelly—anyone with half an eye could see that. The second thing was that Kelly hardly ever so much as smiled at her. Was he going to brood about the babe over in Brooklyn Heights all his life? Would he never wake up and see that a sweetheart like Henesie—

After he started on that line, Kelly would get up and move around, out to the kitchen or to the foyer, anyplace where he wouldn't have to listen. They were a long ten days. Then on the second Saturday of their assignment, Henesie asked the two of them to come up early for supper. It was a good supper, served on the terrace, and she looked very slim and charming in a white frock with short, square-cut sleeves and a broad, shiny black belt. Afterward, when she was fixing some more iced tea in the kitchen, Cornelius Holleran nudged Kelly significantly in the ribs.

"All diked out tonight," he said, in the proper conspiratorial whisper. "All diked out every night now. Whenever we come up here it's a new dress and the hair all done up and everything just so. Why do you keep on bein' a dope, stupid? You ought to know who that's for. Not for me."

Henesie came out to them through the darkened living room, raising her brows when Cornelius Holleran stopped guiltily.

"Secrets?" she asked. "Now that's not fair, Cornelius. Not from me."

He gave her a big wink. "Professional secrets," he said. "They're all right, ain't they?"

Later, against all regulations, he got up and announced off-handedly that he was going out for a cigar and a walk around the block.

Kelly said nothing to that coy suggestion. Henesie frowned slightly and then twisted herself around in the chair to stare after him. "He's up to something," she said.

"He always is," Kelly said, elaborately casual. He knew that she understood what Cornelius Holleran had meant, but he also thought he could pass it off lightly, that everything could be settled once and for all if only he forced it out into the open. That was the biggest mistake he made. "Just now he's convinced I ought to get married," he said. "Every night after you go to bed he starts to sell me on the idea."

"Oh," Henesie said, before pausing momentarily. "Who's the lucky girl?"

"Who do you think?" Kelly said, not looking at her because she was the kind who never took her eyes away first. "You got quite a fan in Cornelius. He doesn't see that you're the kind of girl who could pick her spots. I wouldn't be one of them. Why should I?"

"I don't know," Henesie said. "But—well, if it comes to that, why shouldn't you?"

Kelly just moved his shoulders. The sky was all pale-blue and light had begun to gleam in small, scattered clusters on Fifth Avenue.

"One thing he did tell me," she added thoughtfully, "was that you are a very proud and reticent individual. And that if a girl made a bit more money than you did—"

Kelly tightened his jaws. "Cornelius has a pretty big mouth."

"Hasn't he," she said warmly, as if she were in wholehearted agreement. "I'm sure the money wouldn't bother anyone these days. Why should it? I also heard how different you used to be before—before Rosemary. Always merry and bright then, Cornelius said."

"The life of the party," Kelly said, beginning to have some unexpected difficulty with his breathing. "You heard the name they had for me—Crazy Kelly? Now it means something a lot different. Now it means Crazy Kelly with the hole in his head."

"So that's it," Henesie murmured softly. "Cornelius told me about that. But I can't see that it means anything."

Kelly flipping a pebble off into space, said that the Army had seen what it meant, even if they had claimed they were turning him down for an old football knee. Rosemary had seen what it meant, too—probably everyone had seen it before Kelly did himself. He had been unconscious for five weeks after it happened. Then they brought up a brain surgeon from Baltimore and everything seemed to work out fine.

"Seemed to?" Henesie said, watching him even while she lighted a cigarette. "Hasn't it?"

He moved his head. The flesh under his eyes was dark. "Sure," he said, one side of his mouth curled up bitterly. "A hundred percent. Okay, Kelly—you're sound as a dollar, they said in the hospital. Go home now and forget about the plate we put in if it's worrying you. Go home and marry the girl you got and raise yourself half a dozen little cops."

"Only," Henesie said, in a conventional tone, "Rosemary wasn't having any of that. And you thought— Tell me something, Kelly. Tell me exactly what happened between you and Rosemary."

He leaned forward over the stone rail. For a moment it appeared that he wasn't going to answer her. Then he said huskily, "It didn't happen right away—not until I found out about some old friends she was seeing on the side and argued with her about it. She was all right at first and then when I began to ask her about a weekend when she was supposed to be visiting her mother, she began to scream things at me."

"What kind of things?"

"Enough," Kelly said, his cheeks pasty, "so that I understood how the doctors were kidding me. I'll go on all right with this cracked-eggshell head until I trip on a sidewalk or some drunk crowns me with a beer bottle. When that happens, nobody from Baltimore is going to straighten me out again. You know what they'll do then, don't you? They'll put me off in a nice quiet room with barred windows and a lot of fellows in white coats waiting around. Everything set—the old straitjacket right out if you try to get tough about it."

"Well," Henesie said, taking a long angry breath, "if that isn't the most asinine and ridiculous— Rosemary started it, of course. She wanted to hurt you, and she did. Just because—"

The telephone rang inside, suddenly and shrilly. She gave a small, annoyed exclamation and got up to answer it. At the same moment Kelly, who had never been so glad to hear anything in his life, put his arm out and stopped her.

"This might be our Mr. Allen," he said thickly. "He'd call first, and then again in a couple of minutes just to make sure. If you don't answer, he'll come around to look the apartment over from the street to see whether you have any lights on up here. Then—"

He wet his lips. He had just thought that if it were Mr. Allen, he himself wouldn't be coming back here tomorrow night, or ever again. And it was dark up here, and Henesie was practically in his arms because of the way he had stopped her. "You know what's funny?" he whispered in a painful, almost breathless voice. "The way Cornelius used to argue about you. As if, the first night you came down those steps— Here's something I want you to know. I've forgotten Rosemary. But if I forget you—"

"You won't forget me," Henesie said, very calm and determined about it. "I won't give you the chance. Hold still, Kelly."

He held still. He was numb, but he could feel his heart beating. What followed then was not practiced, like Brooklyn Heights—she didn't even know how to hold her head. Kelly kissed her somewhere, her cheek, the side of her mouth.

"Wait a minute," Kelly whispered. "This isn't—"

The phone rang again, on and on, and when it stopped Henesie pushed away from him.

"You better *not* forget me," she said breathlessly. "Now I'll find Cornelius. You'll need help."

"All right," Kelly said. He knew who had kissed him—Henesie had kissed him. "Look," he said, as lightheaded as if he wasn't breathing air at the moment, but pure oxygen. "I tell you what to do, baby. You get the boys from the East 104th Street station up here. They're the cream."

"Oh, you fool!" Henesie said. She ran across to the foyer door and out without closing it. A second or so later she put her head back in and said in a fierce, shaky voice, "You be careful."

"Who?" Kelly said, making a fist at her. Everything was just right;

everything was exactly as it should have been; but of course, the lightheadedness endured only until he floated himself out to the kitchen door. Then he remembered suddenly and flatly that he was still Kelly with the eggshell head. Nothing had changed that; nothing could change it.

He wet his lips again. He'd remember this evening, he thought—remember it as long as he remembered anything. But—the elevator went up outside; he thought he heard it stop about two floors above, and he rubbed his right palm carefully against his shirt and got out the service revolver. Then he waited again, not so long this time. Somebody came down the stairs very quietly, put a key in the lock, started in. Somebody reached one hand around for the light button just as Kelly got the gun up and inches deep into this guy's armpit with one smooth, unhurried movement.

"Easy does it," Kelly said, pretty well satisfied with himself. "Keep the hands where I can see them. Don't—"

It was timed just right—every detail perfect. The only thing he had not anticipated was that there would be two of them. The one out in the hall betrayed himself by a quick scuffle of feet and a smothered exclamation, then jumped away toward the stairs. Kelly, ducking around quickly, fired twice at him and saw him fall, but the guy still inside the kitchen—the one who couldn't get out because Kelly was in his way—smashed Kelly in the side of the jaw and then got both hands on his gun wrist.

They wobbled around Henesie's nice kitchen table. They bumped into the sink, and Kelly lost his gun. After that, they fell with Kelly underneath. Then the man was standing over him with a kitchen chair raised high above his head, and Cornelius Holleran was bellowing out in the living room, and something smashed down at Kelly but did not stop him from getting up. He caught the man halfway to the kitchen door, swung him around, and dropped him with a beautiful right hook into Henesie's Chinese-red kitchen cabinet. A dish fell on his head, exactly as it would have done in one of those two-reel slapstick movies. Then Cornelius Holleran had him, and Kelly was past them both, out onto the landing. The man he had shot at was still out cold.

Later, when the men from the precinct had come and gone, Henesie said something about getting a nice cold cloth for that bump on Kelly's head.

"What bump?" Kelly said, putting up one hand carelessly. "He never touched me. He swung once, but—"

It felt very big, though; it felt enormous. Over in the mirror Kelly stared at it, from two or three angles, for half a minute. Then he turned. His throat had closed up almost completely.

"What did that?" he croaked.

Henesie curled her forefinger at him several times in a come-after-me gesture. She didn't say anything at all. In the kitchen—they had done a lot of damage out there in thirty or forty seconds, Kelly thought absently—she pointed without a word at a solid-looking white chair that had one of its cross legs snapped off cleanly in the middle. Kelly stared at it, then he touched it. Hard wood, he thought.

"Practically unbreakable," Henesie said, as if she'd read his mind. "He'd have killed anyone with sense. So what do you think about that eggshell head of yours now?"

"I don't know," Kelly said. He did, of course. Henesie did, too.

They went out to the terrace and watched Cornelius Holleran and the men from the precinct and the two casualties disperse themselves in a couple of squad cars. Just before he got in the car, Cornelius Holleran looked up in their direction and gave them one of those grandiose, winning prizefight gestures—hands clasped above his head. Henesie gave it back.

"That was for luck," Kelly said, altogether unnecessarily. "You figure you'll be needing some?"

"Well," Henesie said, and pondered over it for a moment or two, "I don't know why I should. Not now. Not unless you're going to go back to Brooklyn Heights and forget me."

"I'll forget you," Kelly said. But it was a threat, not a promise. There was a wonderful full moon coming up over Fifth Avenue, and he knew when he looked at it, if he knew anything at all, that he had never been so far from Brooklyn Heights in his life.

Florence V. Mayberry

No Tomorrows

Hold my hand, Jimmy. Tight. So I'll know you're still here. Don't leave me, even if I ask you to. The way I did before.

Where is this room? It's strange, I don't remember this room. When did we come here? I must have fallen asleep as we came. Where are we, Jimmy? See, over there, that woman in white, she looks like a nurse. Is she a nurse? Jimmy, come close, I want to whisper: are we in a hospital, are we dying? Hank and you and I, are we dying . . .

Listen! That's my name. Someone is saying my name, over and over, soft and muffled—Laurel, Laurel.

Come closer, Jimmy. Yes, like that, your cheek on my hand, close. All those years we were apart—we have to make up for those lost years. It wasn't your fault, I know that, it was mine. But Hank needed me so much. Jimmy, I want to explain how it was, everything about it so you'll understand what happened. No, don't cover my lips with your hand, I have to explain. Everything.

Remember that first night we met? At my engagement party? Mine and Hank's. Such a lovely, lovely night and I was so happy, laughing, singing along with the dance music. Hank didn't act happy, he was in one of his lonely moods. That's what it seemed to me then. It was only later I learned it was Hank himself, not moods, just himself. A built-in brooding for what he once had, or thought he had, and didn't have any more.

Today never belonged to Hank. No tomorrows either. Only yesterdays. For a while I believed Hank truly wanted the lost people, places, and moments he yearned about. I tried to help him find them after we were married. But he never could. They didn't stay yesterday when he found them, they became today. And he never wanted today.

That night of the engagement party you were playing the piano with the college combo, remember? I hadn't met you before and that was odd because you were a big man on campus and Hank's fraternity brother besides. But I hadn't. Your face had such a smiling look, like a light in it somehow, and I felt I had to tell you how great your piano-playing was, how really great. I dragged Hank over to tell you so, Hank saying why bother, he could tell you any time. But I had to tell you myself. So Hank introduced us. The next number, you asked the trumpet player to carry the lead in your place and you danced with me.

Hank had been remote and brooding ever since I had promised to marry him. Not eager to see me, the way he was when we were only dating. But that night as you whirled me into a second dance—you know?—Hank became lonely for me all over again. He followed us around the floor on the sidelines, then grabbed me as soon as the music stopped.

I remember how pleased I was to have two tall good-looking men eager to dance with me. But whatever was aroused in Hank didn't last long. Only a few days later, with the wedding scheduled for the end of the term when Hank was graduated from the U, he started mooning over a wonderful girl he used to know in some long-lost hometown. He had a lot of long-lost hometowns with long-lost people in them. He had been moved around a lot as a child—his dad had a big construction company and moved with his jobs, taking Hank and Hank's mother along with him. Maybe that was the start of Hank's loneliness, who knows?

I took off my engagement ring and told Hank to go find that girl. So he became lonely for me all over again. He said it would break his heart if I wouldn't marry him, that he desperately needed my help, couldn't handle his moods alone; he even cried. So what could I do? Put his ring back on. To me, he was like a big lost child I could help to find himself—a lover and child all in one.

Besides—maybe you've forgotten, but I was a third-year major then in psychology—Hank fascinated me. My very own case history to practice on.

Strange trio, weren't we? Musician, athlete—the only time Hank seemed really happy was with a baseball in his hand—and a dabbler in how minds work. Because that's what we became just before Hank and I were married, a trio. Hank did the brooding, while you and I did the talking and laughing.

Jimmy, someone is crying. I hear someone crying—sad crying. They cried the night of our wedding too. But not sad. Happy crying, like weddings always have. Everything was so pretty, pink and white, the bridesmaids, flowers. A tall wedding cake with a bride and groom on top. All my sorority sisters and Hank's fraternity brothers there. My mother and Hank's father. My mother was still too angry at my father to have him come, because of their divorce. And Hank's mother was dead.

Everything so pretty. I was pretty too, everyone said so. But then, brides are always pretty.

After the bride danced with her groom, I danced with you. You put your face close to mine and whispered, "Be happy, little Laurel." I whispered back, "I'll try to make it forever."

Later Hank and I, with everyone following, walked down the pathway from the sorority house to the maple-lined street, the leaves of the trees whispering secret promises. When we reached Hank's new car, a wedding present from his father, I turned to tell everyone goodbye. And there you were, so close I bumped into you. "Sweet Laurel," you said. And you kissed me. It was all right for you to kiss me, everyone kissed the bride.

But you should have done it before. On my wedding night it was too late.

Hank tried to laugh, but his voice had a sharp edge, "Hey, knock it off, Jim. Remember, I'm the groom."

Your face raised. I stepped quickly into the car and waved goodbye. Who can see a hand tremble when it's waving?

It wasn't long before Hank was lonely again—only a few weeks after the wedding. Not lonely for me. I can't remember who it was, doesn't matter now. Then, yes, it did. I found Hank crying, sitting on our living-room floor, his face buried in the pillows of our sofa. I thought something dreadful had happened—a phone call or telegram I didn't know about, something wrong with his father.

I knelt beside him and put my arms around him. He jerked away, wouldn't talk. Finally he said our marriage was a mistake, that he couldn't forget whoever it was he was lonely for. I never knew her, and later I wondered if even Hank did, or if he was lonely for someone he dreamed up.

Oh, well, we came through that crisis. At first I said I would leave, and got out my suitcases. Then he begged me to stay. You see, he always wanted whatever he was losing. As for me, I hated divorce. I always hated my parents' divorce.

That scene, or something like it, was repeated many times before I saw you again. After the wedding you dropped out of our lives except for the occasional postcard. You were busy, I know that, struggling to break into bigtime music. And maybe you just didn't want to see us for a while.

Hank and I were still at the university, both of us carrying classes.

Hank was working on a M.A.—he thought he might become a coach. Not working very hard though. He didn't need money. His mother had left him a trust fund and his father was always sending us gifts, mostly money.

It was two years after the wedding when you came back to our university town—for the class reunion, yours and Hank's. You arrived on its final night, the night of the formal dance. I happened to be looking at the ballroom entrance and suddenly there you were, scanning the dancers as though searching for someone. The orchestra leader recognized you, called on the crowd to give you a big hand, and insisted you lead the next number. That wasn't just because you used to lead the campus combo. By that time you'd been on network TV, playing piano with a name band, and had a song out that disc jockeys were playing.

Halfway through the number you saw me sitting on the sidelines waiting for Hank. You handed the baton over to the leader, came straight to me, took my shoulders, and smiled. Close to, I was shocked to see how strained and thin you were, with dark circles under your eyes. I suppose getting a foothold in the music game hadn't been easy. Or perhaps—oh, well, whatever it was. You said, "Laurel, this is what I've been looking forward to." You kept holding me, looking at me.

Finally you dropped your hands and asked, "Where's old Hank?"

"Around," I said. My voice sounded squeaky, tight. "Somewhere around." And added, "He'll want to see you."

I knew he wouldn't. Hank had stopped being lonely for people. Except for himself. Sounds queer, but it was true. Just lonely for himself, as though he had lost whatever he was and was going around empty. It hadn't been easy getting him to that reunion dance. He didn't want to see people.

"Let's dance," you said. "Bring back old times." You took me in your arms and we glided around the floor. I tried to say something, anything, but the first word caught in my throat. "Hush," you whispered. "Dreams don't need sound."

We drifted off the dance floor onto the veranda, into the fragrant softness of the Indiana spring night. You took my hand and we walked across the lawn, onto the path under the big maple trees.

At last you said, "Maybe you've guessed. That I fell in love with you that first night we met. Told myself, that's the girl I have to marry. Only I didn't. But the way I felt then has never changed.

Apparently I'm a dumb kind of guy who falls in love once. Just once. Dumb because I realize I can't have you. But I wanted you to know."

We walked along without speaking, the soft scuffing of our shoes on the path the only sound. Then, as though a signal had been given, we turned to each other and I put my arms around your neck and held up my face to be kissed.

You said, "Let's find Hank. Tell him. Now."

I gave you my hand again and we turned back across the lawn, back to the veranda, moving fast in rhythm with the hard-rock beat that the orchestra was pounding out, *hurry, hurry, hurry* . . . Jimmy, don't take your hand away, please! Keep holding it tight just as you did that night.

Hank wasn't on the dance floor. Not in the lounge. Not in the hall, or the upstairs lounge. We searched so long I had too much time to think, to worry that Hank might get lonely for me all over again.

We finally found him in the upstairs men's room, sick—he was drinking too much by then. We had to clean him up before we could help him down the back stairs, staggering between us, out through the kitchen and the back door. Outside in the fresh air Hank reared straight and yanked free. "Wha' you tryin' do, you'n this good-for-nothin' li'l—"

You slapped him on the mouth, flat, as dispassionately as an adult might slap a foul-mouthed adolescent. Which, I suppose, Hank really was. He began to cry.

"All right, Hank, I'm sorry," you said. "But keep your mouth shut and keep walking. You need to sleep this off."

"Good ol' Jim, missed you, boy, missed you." He leaned on you, blubbering, and we stumbled to our car. When we reached our house you half carried Hank inside, stretched him across his bed. I put a coverlet over him and we left him.

Back in the living room we faced each other, not touching, just looking at each other. I said, "I can't leave him."

I didn't explain why. That Hank was like a child. That what does one do with children? Well, you look after them. Good or bad. You don't tear them to bits with a divorce. As my parents had done with me.

"Are you sure, Laurel?"

I nodded.

"I'm not," you said. "Let me tell him. When he's sober. If tonight is a sample, this kind of life is misery, for him as well as you. And beyond that, you belong to me, Laurel, because I know now you feel the same about us as I do."

I began to cry, shaking my head back and forth. You took me in your arms and said, "Okay, don't cry, don't cry. But I'm waiting for you. Because sometime, somehow, you'll be mine."

The next day you left.

You waited three years to come back—so long that I began to think you had forgotten or had found out I wasn't the only one for you. That was the hard part, to fear you had changed your mind, because by then I was ready to go with you.

During those three years I pretended Hank really was my child, that I must take care of him no matter what. That helped. A mother can be angry at a child, but not in the same way as a woman can be angry at a man. When Hank was drunk and struck me—well, when a little child strikes his mother, the mother catches his hand, tells him that was naughty. She doesn't run away, leave him. When a child has a tantrum because a toy is lost or broken, the mother doesn't say goodbye forever. It wasn't easy to humor Hank out of his moods, to pet him, to cater to him. He was the only child I had. Straighten up, Hank, I would tell him, you're acting like a baby, get a job. It isn't good for a man not to work. You used to be an athlete, try to get on the coaching staff at the U. You'll be happier with a job.

But he never really tried. He had plenty of money, so why bother, he said. A big slob of a 180-pound kid who needed constant care.

Jimmy, when you finally came back I was worn out, sick to death of baby-sitting a grown man. Those three years had seemed like thirty and I knew I couldn't endure even another month. Not even another day. I had to leave now.

Was it yesterday or today when you came back? I can't seem to remember. But I remember what you said. That I must leave now with you. And I kept saying *yes, yes, yes* over and over, that I loved you and was afraid you were never coming to take me away.

Neither of us heard Hank come in. Suddenly he was there between us, screaming, lunging with his fists. I ran between you, tried to hold his arms, tried to tell him we couldn't go on like a mother and child. He kept yelling, hitting at us. I suppose he wasn't to blame after what he heard us say, but he was so violent—ranting, crying, threatening.

The angry sounds beat against my ears. My head became a massive throbbing ache and I ran from the living room, down the hall, to escape. But the sounds followed, pound, pound, like hammer blows.

That's why I thought of it, Jimmy. I'm sure that's why I thought of it—the noise hammered at me, wouldn't stop. So I went looking for it. The hammer. I found it in the kitchen, beneath the sink.

I hid it behind my back and returned to the living room. I raised it. Hank grabbed my arm but I twisted free, spun out of reach. My head floated away, separated from me, became free of what my body did. Everything blurred, Hank, you, everything. But an arm reached through the blur and I swung the hammer. The hammer struck and I seemed to be falling, falling . . .

What happened next, Jimmy? I can't remember, why can't I remember? Jimmy, I'm afraid. Look, I'm shivering. Did something terrible happen, did I . . .

Jimmy, help me remember! I felt the hammer hit him! Is Hank dead? Tell me, Jimmy, did I kill him, did I kill him?

"Oh, God, now she's screaming," whispered the nurse to a second nurse who had joined her. "She's yakkety-yakked to that poor guy ever since she regained consciousness, and now she's screaming. No, we can't give her a hypo, not with concussion."

"Why did they bring her here? There's no psycho ward in this hospital," said the other nurse.

"County hospital's full up, no private rooms available. And there's no hospital in our dinky jail."

"Jail? You mean, she's in custody?"

"Why do you think that cop's at the door? Didn't you see him when you came in?"

"Sure, that's why I ducked in here, to find out why. What did she do? She doesn't look the type to *do* anything, I mean anything criminal."

"Yeah, sure, she's real refined. Just murdered a guy, that's all. Bashed in his head with a hammer. Hit him so hard she fell and struck her head on something hard. I heard about it when I was down in reception to help bring her up."

"Who's the man with her?"

"Husband," said the first nurse. "He's the Hank she's asking did she kill him. Saw him sign her in. Henry Summerfield, husband. But she's flipped. She thinks she's talking to the other one, the man downstairs in the morgue."

Michael Gilbert

The Unstoppable Man

We were talking about violence. "Some people," I said, "are afraid of people and some people are afraid of things."

Chief Inspector Hazlerigg gave this remark more consideration than it seemed to merit and then said: "Illustration, please."

"Well, some people are afraid of employers and some of razors."

"I don't think that sort of fear is a constant," said Hazlerigg. "It changes as you grow older, you know—or get more experienced. I haven't much occasion for bodily violence in my present job." (He was one of the chief inspectors on the cab rank at Scotland Yard.) "When I was a young constable, the customers I chiefly disliked were drunken women. Nowadays—well, perhaps I should look at it the other way round. Perhaps I could describe the sort of man *I* should hate to have after *me*."

In the pause that followed, I tried hard to visualize what precise mixture of thug and entrepreneur would terrify the red-faced, grey-eyed, bulky, equitable man sitting beside me.

"He'd be English," said Hazlerigg at last, "Anglo-Saxon anyway, getting on for middle-age and a first-class businessman. He would have had some former experience of lethal weapons—as an infantry soldier, perhaps, in one of the World Wars. But definitely an amateur—an amateur in violence. He would believe passionately in the justice of what he was doing—but without ever allowing the fanatic to rule the businessman.

"Now that's a type I should hate to have after me! He's unstoppable."

"Is that a portrait from life?" I said.

"Yes," said Hazlerigg slowly. "Yes, it's a portrait from life. It all happened a good time ago—in the early Thirties, when I was a junior inspector. Even now, you'll have to be very careful about names, you know, because if the real truth came out— However, judge for yourself."

Inspector Hazlerigg first met Mr. Collet (*the* Collets, the shipping people—this one was the third of the dynasty) in his managing director's mahogany-lined office. Hazlerigg was there by appoint-

217

ment. He had arrived at the building in a plain van and had been introduced via the goods entrance, but once inside he had been treated with every consideration.

Even during the few minutes which had elapsed before he could be brought face to face with Mr. Collet, Hazlerigg had managed to collect a few impressions. Small things, from the way the commissionaire and the messenger spoke about him, and more still from the way his secretary spoke *to* him: that they liked him and liked working for him; that they knew something was wrong and were sorry.

They didn't, of course, know exactly what the trouble was. Hazlerigg did.

Kidnaping—the extorting of money by kidnaping—is a filthy thing. Fortunately, it does not seem to come very easily to the English criminal. But there was a little wave of it that year.

Mr. Collet had an only child, a boy of nine. On the afternoon of the previous day he had been out with his aunt, Mr. Collet's sister, in the park. A car had overtaken them on an empty stretch. A man had got out, pitched the boy into the back of the car, and driven off. As simple as that.

"So far as we know," said Hazlerigg, "there's just the one crowd. I'll be quite frank. We know very little about them. But there have been four cases already, and the features have been too much alike for coincidence."

"Such as—?" said Mr. Collet. His voice and his hands, Hazlerigg noticed, were under control. He couldn't see the eyes. Mr. Collet was wearing heavy sunglasses.

"Well—they don't ask for too much to start with, that's one thing. The first demand has always been quite modest. The idea being that a man will be more likely to go on paying once he has started."

"Right so far," said Mr. Collet. "They asked for only five thousand pounds. They could have had it this morning—if I'd thought it would do any good."

"Then there's also their method of collecting. It's disarming. They employ known crooks. I don't know what they pay them—just enough to make it worth their while to take the risk. These crooks are strictly carriers only. We could arrest them at the moment they contact you without getting any nearer to the real organizers."

"The Piccadilly side of Green Park, at two o'clock tomorrow," said Mr. Collet. "I got the rendezvous quite openly over the telephone. Could they be followed?"

"That's where the organization really starts," said Hazlerigg. "Every move after that is worked out—and when you come to think about it, the cards are very heavily stacked in their favor. All they've got to do is to hand the money on. There are a hundred ways of doing it. They might pass it over in a crowd in an Underground train or a bus in the rush hour, or they might be picked up by car and driven somewhere fast, or they might hand it over in a cinema. They might get rid of the money the same day, or they might wait a week."

"Yes," said Mr. Collet, "a little organization and that part shouldn't be too difficult. Any other peculiarities about this crowd?"

He said this as a businessman might inquire about a firm with whom he was going to trade.

Hazlerigg hesitated. What he was going to say had to be said sometime. It might as well be said now.

"Yes, sir," he said. "There's this to consider. However much the victim pays, however often he pays, however promptly he pays, he doesn't get the child back. You've given us the best chance so far by coming to us immediately."

Mr. Collet said nothing.

"You know Roger Barstow—he lost his little girl. Zilla was her name. He paid nine times—more than a hundred thousand pounds—until he had no more left and said so. Next morning they found Zilla in the swill bin at the back of his house."

There was another silence. Hazlerigg saw the whites of the knucklebones start up for a moment on one of Mr. Collet's thin brown hands. At last he got to his feet and said: "Thank you, Inspector. I have your contact number. I'll get hold of you as soon as I—as soon as anything happens."

As he walked to the door, he took off his glasses for the first time and Hazlerigg saw in his eyes that he had got his ally. It had been a risk, but it had come off.

Mr. Collet was going to fight.

When the door had closed behind the chief inspector, Mr. Collet thought for a few moments and then rang the bell and asked for Mr. Stevens.

Mr. Stevens, who was a month or two short of fifteen, was the head of the Collet messenger service and a perfectly natural organizer. He spent a good deal of his time organizing the messenger boys of the firm into a sort of trade union, and he had already engineered two beautifully timed strikes, the second of which had called for Mr. Collet's personal intervention.

It says a good deal for both parties that when Mr. Collet sent for him and asked for his help, young Stevens listened carefully to what he had to say and promised him the fullest assistance of himself and his organization.

"No film stuff," said Mr. Collet. "These men are real crooks. They're dangerous. And they're wide awake. They expect to be followed. We're going to do this on business lines."

That was Wednesday. At four o'clock on Thursday afternoon, Inspector Hazlerigg again visited Archangel Street, taking the same precautions. Mr. Collet was at his desk. "You've got something for me." It was more a statement than a question.

"Before I answer that," said Mr. Collet, "I want something from you. I want your promise that you won't act on my information without my permission."

Hazlerigg said: "All right. I can't promise not to go on with such steps as I'm already taking. But I promise not to use your information until you say so. What do you know?"

"I know the names of most of the men concerned," said Mr. Collet. "I know where my son is—I know where these people are hiding."

When Hazlerigg had recovered his breath, he said: "Perhaps you'll explain."

"I thought a good deal," said Mr. Collet, "about what you told me—about the sort of people we were dealing with. Particularly about the men who would make contact with me and carry back the money. It was obvious that they weren't afraid of violence. They weren't even, basically, afraid of being arrested. That was part of the risk. They certainly weren't open to any sort of persuasion. If they observed the routine, which had no doubt been carefully laid down for them, they would take the money from me and get it back to their employers, without giving us any chance of following them. Their position seemed to be pretty well impregnable. In the circumstances it seemed—do you play bridge, Inspector?"

"Badly," said Hazlerigg. "But I'm very fond of it."

"Then you understand the Vienna Coup."

"In theory—though I could never work it. It's a sort of squeeze. You start by playing away one of your winning aces, isn't that it?"

"Exactly," said Mr. Collet. "You give—or appear to give—your opponents an unexpected gift. And like all unexpected gifts, it throws them off balance and upsets their defense. I decided to do the same.

To be precise, I gave them five thousand pounds *more* than they asked for. I met these men—there were two of them, as I told you—by appointment in Green Park. I simply opened my briefcase and put a brown paper packet into their hands. They opened it quickly, and as they were doing so I said: 'Ten thousand pounds in one-pound notes—that's right, isn't it?' I could almost see it hit them. To give them time to cover up, I said: 'When do I see my boy?' The elder of the two men said: 'You'll be seeing him soon. We'll ring you tomorrow.' Then they pushed off. I could see them starting to argue."

Mr. Collet paused. Inspector Hazlerigg, who was still trying to work out the angles, said nothing.

"The way I figured it out," said Mr. Collet, "they'd have all their plans made for handing on five thousand pounds to their employers. So I gave them ten thousand. That meant five thousand for themselves if they kept quiet about it, and played it right. But I'd put all the notes in one packet, you see. They had to be divided out. Then they had to split the extra five thousand between themselves—they were both in on it. Above all, they had to get somewhere safe and quiet and talk it out. You see what that meant. Their original plan—the careful one laid down for them by the bosses—had to be scrapped.

"They had to make another plan, and make it rather quickly. It would be something simple. They'd either go to one of their own houses or a safe friend's house—and it would probably be somewhere with a telephone because they'd have to invent some sort of story for the bosses to explain why they'd abandoned the original plan. That last bit was only surmise, but it was a fair business risk."

"Yes," said Hazlerigg. "I see. You still had to follow them, though."

"Not me," said Mr. Collet. "It was the boys who did that. The streets round the park were full of them. They're a sort of car-watching club—you see them anywhere in the streets of London if you look. They collect car numbers. Boy of mine called Stevens ran it. He's a born organizer. I went straight back to the office. Fifteen minutes later I got a call. Just an address, near King's Cross.

"I passed it on to a friend of mine—he's quite a senior official, so I won't give you his name. Inside five minutes he had the line from that house tapped. He was just in time to collect the outgoing call. That was that. It was to a house in Essex. Here's the address." He pushed a slip of paper across. "That's the name."

"Just like that," said Hazlerigg. "Simple. Scotland Yard have been trying to do it for six months."

"I had more at stake than you."

"Yes," said Hazlerigg. "What happens now?"

"Now," said Mr. Collet, "we sit back and wait."

Continuing the story, Hazlerigg said to me: "I think that was one of the bravest and coolest things I ever saw a man do. He was quite right, of course. The people we were dealing with moved by instinct—that sort of deadly instinct which those people get who sleep with one finger on the trigger.

"When their messengers reported the change of plan—I don't know what sort of story they put up—their bristles must have been on end. These people can smell when something's wrong. They're so used to doublecrossing other people that they get a sort of second sight about it themselves. If we'd rushed them then, we should never have got the boy alive. So we waited. We had a man watch the house—it was a big, rather lonely house between Pitsea and Rayleigh on the north of the Thames."

And, meanwhile, Mr. Collet sat in his mahogany-lined office and transacted the business of his firm. On the fourth morning he got a letter, in a painstaking schoolboy script.

> *Dear Father,*
>
> *I am to write this to you. You are to pay five thousand pounds more. They will telephone you how to pay. I am quite well. It is quite a nice house. It is quite a nice room. The sun wakes me in the early morning.*
>
> > *Love from David.*
>
> *P.S. Please be quick.*

Mr. Andrews, senior partner in the firm of Andrews and Mackay, house agents of Pitsea, summed up his visitor at one glance—which took in the silk tie, the pigskin briefcase, and the hood of the chauffeur-driven Daimler standing outside the office—and said in his most deferential voice: "Certainly, Mr.—er—Robinson. Anything we can do to help you. It's not everybody's idea of a house, but if you're looking for something quiet and secluded—"

"I understand that it's occupied at the moment," said Mr. Robinson.

"Temporarily," agreed Mr. Andrews. "But you could have possession. The owner let it on short notice to a syndicate of men who are interested in a new color process. They needed the big grounds—the quiet, you understand, and the freedom from interruption. The only difficulty which occurs to me is that you will not be able to inspect the house today. By the terms of our arrangement, we have to give at least forty-eight hours' notice."

Mr. Robinson thought for a moment and then said: "Have you such a thing as a plan of the house?"

"Why certainly," said Mr. Andrews. "We had a very careful survey made when the house was put up for sale. Here you are—on two floors only, you see."

"Only one bedroom," said Mr. Robinson, "looks due east?"

"Why, yes." Mr. Andrews was hardened to the vagaries of clients.

"The sun wakes me in the early morning," said Mr. Robinson softly.

"I beg your pardon?"

"Nothing," said Mr. Robinson. "Nothing. Thinking aloud. A bad habit. Would it be asking too much if I borrowed these plans for a day?"

"Why, of course," said Mr. Andrews. "Keep them for as long as you like."

Four o'clock of a perfect summer afternoon. It was so silent that the clack of a scythe blade on a stone sounded clear across the valley where the big grey house dozed in the sun.

As the double chime of the half hour sounded from Rayleigh Church, a figure appeared on the dusty road. It was a man, in postman's uniform, wheeling a bicycle.

The woman in the lodge answered the bell and unlocked one of the big gates, without comment. Then she returned to her back room, picked up the house telephone, and said: "All right. It's only the postman."

It was a mistake which might have cost her very dearly.

As Mr. Collet wheeled his borrowed machine slowly up the long drive, he was thinking about the bulky sack which rested on the saddle and balanced there with difficulty. He knew that some very sharp eyes would be watching his approach. It couldn't be helped, though. He had been able to see no better method of getting this particular apparatus up to the house.

He propped his bicycle against the pillar of the front door, lifted the sack down—keeping the mouth of it gathered in his left hand—and rang the bell. So far, so good.

The door was opened by a man in corduroys and a tweed jacket.

He might have been a gardener or a gamekeeper. Mr. Collet, looking at his eyes, knew better.

"Don't shout," he said. The gun in his hand was an argument.

For a moment the man stared. Then he jumped to one side and started to open his mouth.

Even for an indifferent shot, three yards is not a long range. The big bullet lifted the man back onto his heels like a punch under the heart and crumpled him onto the floor.

In the deep silence which followed the roar of the gun, Mr. Collet raced for the stairs. The heavy sack was against him, but he made good time.

At the top, he turned left with the sureness of a man who knows his mind and made for the room at the end of the corridor.

He saw that it was padlocked.

He put the muzzle of his gun as near to the padlock as he dared and pulled the trigger.

The jump of the gun threw the bullet up into the door jamb, missing the padlock altogether. He took a lower aim and tried again. Once, twice, again. The padlock buckled.

Mr. Collet kicked the door open and went in.

The boy was half sitting, half kneeling in one corner. Mr. Collet grinned at him with a good deal more confidence than he felt and said: "Stand out of the way, son. The curtain's going up for the last act."

As he spoke, he was piling together mattresses, bedclothes, a rug, and a couple of small chairs into a barricade. When he had done this, he opened the sack, pulled out the curious-looking instrument from inside it, laid it beside his homemade parapet, and started working on it.

"Get into that far corner, son," said Mr. Collet. "And you might keep an eye on the window, just in case it occurs to the gentry to run a ladder up. Keep your head down, though. Here they come."

Joe Keller had tortured children and had killed for pleasure as well as for profit, but he was not physically a coward.

As he watched his henchman twitching on the hall floor, with the indifference of a man who has seen many men die, he was already working out his plan of attack.

"Take a long ladder," he said to one man, "and run it up to the window. Not the bedroom window—be your age. Put it against the landing window, this end. You can see the bedroom door from there, can't you? If it's shut, wait. If it's open, start shooting into the room—aim high. We'll go in together along the floor."

"He'll pick us off as we come."

"Not if Hoppy keeps him pinned down," said Keller. "Besides, I reckon he doesn't know much about guns. It took him four shots to knock off that lock, didn't it? Any more arguments?"

Half a mile away, at points round the lip of the valley, four police cars had started up their engines at the sound of the first shot.

Hazlerigg was lying full length on the roof of one of them, a pair of long binoculars in his hands.

The Essex Superintendent looked up at him.

"I made that five shots," he said. "Do we start?"

"No, sir," said Hazlerigg. "You remember the signal we arranged."

"Do you think he can do his stuff?" The Superintendent sounded worried.

"He hasn't done badly so far," said Hazlerigg shortly, and silence settled down once more.

It was the driver of their car who saw it first, and gave a shout. From one of the first-floor windows of the house, unmistakable and ominous, a cloud of black and sooty smoke rolled upward.

The four cars started forward as one.

In that long upstairs passage, things had gone according to plan—at first.

Covered by a fusillade from the window, Joe Keller and his two assistants had inched their way forward on elbows and knees, their guns ahead of them.

At the end of the passage stood the door, open and inviting. The outer end of Mr. Collet's barricade came into sight as they advanced, but it was offset from the doorway, and Mr. Collet himself was still invisible.

Five yards to go.

Then, as the three men bunched for the final jump, it came out to meet them.

A great red-and-yellow river of flame, overmantled with black smoke, burning and hissing and dripping with oil. As they turned to fly, it caught them.

"There was nothing very much for us to do when we did get there," said Inspector Hazlerigg. "We had to get Mr. Collet and the boy out of the window—the passage floor was red-hot. We caught one man in the garden. His nerve was gone—he seemed glad to give himself up.

"As for the other three—an infantry flame-thrower is not a discriminating sort of weapon, particularly at close quarters. There was just about enough left of them—well, say just about enough of the three of them to fill the swill bin where they found little Zilla Barstow. No, never tangle with a wholehearted amateur."

Alice Scanlan Reach

Father Crumlish
Remembers His Poe

It was the unshakable conviction of Father Francis Xavier Crumlish that, if St. Peter ever opened the pearly gates and ushered him inside, he would be permitted to spend hours on end doing what he was doing now—relaxing his arthritis-plagued joints under a cozy down-filled comforter, reading from the collected works of Edgar Allan Poe, one of his favorite authors, while he kept one ear cocked toward his turned-low bedside radio in case Willie Mays should be doing something grand for the Giants. He'd been enjoying himself thusly for all of half an hour when the telephone bell on his night table shattered the rectory's quiet.

"St. Brigid's," the pastor said as he brought the receiver to his ear.

"It's Tom, Father."

Usually the familiar voice of Lieutenant Thomas Patrick "Big Tom" Madigan of Lake City's police force brought a pleased smile to Father Crumlish's lined face—and for a very good reason; if it hadn't been for his determined intervention some years ago, handsome young Madigan might now be the lawbreaker he started out to be instead of the law enforcer he had become. But on occasions like the present, when the policeman called at such a late hour, the old priest's features shadowed with anxiety. Instinctively he knew that one of his lambs, faithful or stray, was in distress.

"What is it, Tom?"

"Eddie Ring's been shot—bad—and he's asking for you. I could send a car—"

"Give me five minutes, lad," Father broke in, and hung up the phone.

Big Tom was standing at the emergency entrance to Mercy Hospital when the police car drew up and deposited the priest.

"How did it happen, Tom?" Father asked as Madigan steered him down a corridor.

"Ring pulled a gun on Larry Korman in his liquor store. When Larry handed over the cash, Eddie dashed for the door. But before he made it, Korman grabbed his own gun and plugged him."

"God help us!"

"That's not all," Madigan said, grim-faced. "Ring's given us a signed statement confessing to the murder of Honey Garden."

After more than forty years in the priesthood there was little that could shake St. Brigid's snowy-haired pastor. However, Madigan's news left him speechless for a moment.

"But you've already jailed Honey's husband for that!" he finally managed.

"We arrested the wrong man," Big Tom said. "Ring's confession clears Dave Garden, and the sooner he's released, the better I'm going to feel about it." He paused in front of a door. "Eddie's in here, Father, and he's not going to last much longer."

Nodding, Father Crumlish straightened his stooped shoulders and entered the room where Eddie Ring, age thirty-three, oft-convicted petty thief and now a confessed murderer, lay on his deathbed. Ring's eyes were feverishly bright in his bloodless face and when he saw the priest seated by his side, his voice was ragged with urgency as he spoke.

"Father, I told the cops it was me who killed that woman. Not her husband—the guy they're holding. I didn't want to conk out knowing he was going to have to pay for what I did. But now I gotta confess—confess—" He broke off to gasp breath.

"God's listening, Eddie," Father said.

"The Gardens live over that joint of theirs down on Canal Street—The Garden Spot. Last night I broke in, figuring they'd both be busy with the bar trade below. I nabbed two rings and a watch in the bedroom and then started going through the drawers in a desk in the living room. Just as I found a gun and picked it up, I heard her voice right behind me." Ring's pallor deepened as again he fought for breath.

"Easy, lad," Father murmured.

"I turned around. She saw her gun in my hand, but that didn't stop her. She came at me like a wildcat. We mixed it up, pretty rough—she fell—and then I got out fast." The dying man's eyes closed and for a moment Father thought he'd lost consciousness. But he opened his eyes again and went on.

"I heard on the midnight news that she'd been found beaten to death and I know—" again his voice faltered "—I know I did it. And then this morning, when I heard about her husband, I chickened out. Figured that if I could just get my hands on some quick cash I could skip town—" The pastor leaned closer in order to hear Ring's words. "I still had her gun—and that liquor store seemed like a sure thing—a real sure thing—" Abruptly his body sagged. Father Crumlish pressed the buzzer to summon aid. Then he knelt and prayed—and stayed—until the end.

Big Tom drove him back to the rectory. "I know you can't tell me anything Ring said to you, Father." (The policeman was referring to the Seal of Confession, whereby Father was bound by his vows never to divulge any information revealed to him during confession.) "But there are a few things I can tell you." He was silent as he expertly maneuvered the car around a corner and brought it to a halt at the curb in front of the rectory.

"The gun he was carrying for the Korman holdup was registered in Honey Garden's name," Madigan went on. "It's in the lab now, and we expect the report will show that Ring used it to crack her skull. That's what she died of, you know, a fractured skull. We searched his room and found two rings and a watch just where he said we would. So all that, plus his signed confession, means the case is closed." Big Tom couldn't conceal his expression of relief.

Father Crumlish had sat lost in thought and it was another several moments before he spoke. "Have you any idea what time it was when the poor woman was killed, Tom?"

"Sometime between eight and ten according to the M.E. Why, Father?"

"I'm not sure, mind you," Father said slowly, "but I've a vague notion that I caught a glimpse of Eddie during Devotions last night."

"Maybe he dropped in to try to ease his conscience," Madigan remarked dryly.

It wouldn't be the first time Eddie had done just that, the priest thought to himself. "Well, the poor fellow's made his peace with the Lord now," he said as he got out of the car. "Thanks for the lift, lad."

The following morning as Father Crumlish drained his breakfast cup of tea, Emma Catt, a grave-faced, gray-haired woman who had served as St. Brigid's cook-housekeeper for more than twenty-two years, plowed into the room, laid a stack of small white cards beside his saucer, and left.

Father eyed the stack with considerable apprehension. For the past two weeks he had been obliged to call his parishioners' attention to St. Brigid's hopelessly erratic furnace which he'd been warned would not last another winter. Since his people had trouble enough

contributing to the regular collection baskets, the pastor knew they
would be hard-pressed for any extra cash. Therefore he had suggested that they sign pledge cards, payable within a year, for whatever amount they felt they could spare.

So far the results had been disappointing, to say the least. Most
of the pledges were for one or two dollars, or five at the most. And
Father had the feeling that this latest batch—the results of his
appeal made just before Devotions the night before last—would be
for similar small amounts.

Now, as he picked up the cards and began to thumb through them,
he saw that his apprehension was justified. Then suddenly his face
brightened. A pledge for twenty-five dollars! Now who—? He glanced
at the signature and his mouth fell open. It was signed by Eddie
Ring.

So he'd been right, the priest told himself as he got up from the
breakfast table and walked down the hall to his small shabby office.
He *had* seen Eddie in church the night of Honey Garden's murder.
But when? At what time exactly? Big Tom had said it was likely
that the woman had died between eight and ten o'clock.

It had been exactly 7:45 P.M., Father recalled, just before he'd
started Devotions, that he'd walked over to the altar railing, faced
the congregation, and made his appeal. He'd told them that the
pledge cards would be available, after Devotions, at a table set up
in the rear of the church and presided over by Peter Burns, treasurer
of the Holy Name Society. Then he'd gone about the Lord's work.

Eddie must have been in church at 7:45 P.M. and heard the appeal,
Father now reasoned. And it had been at least ten o'clock before the
last of the parishioners who had lined up around Peter Burns had
departed. So if Eddie had been one of the first in line, he'd have had
time to rob and beat Honey Garden. But if he'd been near the end
of the line—

Father picked up the phone on his desk and dialed. "Peter," he
said when Burns came on the wire, "I was wondering if you saw
Eddie Ring the other night when he signed a pledge card."

"Sure, I saw him, Father."

"Do you remember what time it was when he signed? I mean was
he among the first or—?"

"Gee, Father, there were a lot of people—I don't know if he was
at the beginning, the middle, or the tail end of the line."

After expressing his thanks, the pastor hung up the phone. Then
he sat for a long time fingering Eddie Ring's pledge card, a look of

indecision on his face. Should he call Big Tom? he wondered. And if he did, what would he tell him? That he had some doubt in his mind that Eddie was a murderer? That he had a hunch that maybe—just maybe—Eddie had confessed to a crime he only thought he'd committed? That, despite all the evidence to the contrary, the dead man might have been innocent?

Finally Father Crumlish stood up. He'd decided that he didn't have enough information to call Madigan. But maybe if he made a few inquiries himself . . .

The flock that St. Brigid's pastor shepherded was a motley and bedraggled one. His parish, sprawling along Lake City's decaying waterfront section, was perpetually shrouded with grain dust from the mills, and soot and smoke that belched from the steel plant's open hearths. His people were plagued by degrading poverty—and worse. Because of their unsavory environment, immorality, violence, and crime flourished. But the best of them and most of the worst had something in common: they feared God—and Father Crumlish.

The Garden Spot was a neon-rimmed tavern located midway on Canal Street, a garish strip of land which the priest thought of as "Satan's Alley." His archenemy, the Fiend, was so firmly entrenched there that Father, in his more pessimistic moments, despaired of ever dislodging him. Every time it was necessary for the pastor to visit the street, he experienced mixed feelings of compassion, frustration, and rage as he passed by the low-slung, dilapidated buildings which, he knew, harbored nearly every kind of avarice and evil known to mankind.

He was experiencing just such feelings now, in the late afternoon dusk, as he parked his car in front of The Garden Spot. Although most of his parishioners were under the impression that the place was owned by Dave Garden, Father Crumlish knew that it had been the sole property of Dave's murdered wife, Honey, a hardheaded ex-burlesque queen who had invested her life savings in the highly profitable establishment.

Getting out of his car, the priest noticed a side entrance to the building and assumed it led to The Garden's second-floor living quarters. But seeing a dim light inside the tavern, he decided to try his luck there first. He opened the door and stepped into the interior.

"Hold it, bud," a handsome blond giant of a man called out from behind the bar. "Not open yet."

"It's Father Crumlish."

"Oh! Sorry, Father," the man apologized. "C'mon in." Walking to the door, he closed it behind the pastor, took a key out of his pocket, and locked it.

Wordlessly Father Crumlish seated himself at an inconspicuous corner table and tried to place the large man's face, remember his name—and then he did. He was Stan Dulski, a bartender who had the reputation of never turning down a minor who had a little extra cash to pay for hard liquor. There was something else about the fellow that the priest had heard, some rumor. But for the moment it eluded him.

"How long have you been tending bar here, Stan?" Father asked.

"About a year, Father," Dulski said. He looked questioningly at the priest. "You want to see Dave?"

"Is he anywhere around?"

"Upstairs." Stan pointed a thumb toward the ceiling. "Poor guy's been sleeping since the cops sprung him early this morning. But I can wake him—"

"No, no," Father said hastily. "I'll just sit here, if you don't mind, and take my chances that he'll come down."

"Well, uh—" Dulski seemed to be disconcerted for a moment. "Then how about a beer while you're waiting, Father?"

Under normal circumstances the pastor would have declined. But the circumstances weren't normal. "A wee one would do no harm," he said, "Providing you join me." In a moment Stan brought two beers and sat down at the table.

"It was a terrible thing, what happened here," Father said, shaking his head. "I read in the paper that it was you who found the poor woman's body."

"Yeah!" Dulski poured beer into the two glasses. "It sure shook me up, Father."

"I can well imagine," the priest replied in a sympathetic tone. "Particularly with the police asking a lot of questions—"

The bartender's pale-blue eyes turned cloudy. "I only told them the truth, Father," he said. "But it wouldn't surprise me none if Dave figures I'm the guy who fingered him to the cops."

Father Crumlish gazed at him with a look of astonishment. "Now what could you have told the police that would ever give Dave that notion?"

Stan hesitated a moment, then leaned across the table. "You understand, Father, I like Dave personally. He's a great guy and I wouldn't say anything on purpose to get him into trouble. Like I said, when the cops started shooting questions at me, all I did was tell the truth."

"You did the right thing," the pastor said, nodding.

"Everybody knew that Honey and Dave weren't getting along too good," Dulski continued. "When he had too many drinks he'd get mean, slap her around. Not out front here, of course." He waved a hand toward the rear of the room. "Out back—in the kitchen. And that's what he did the afternoon of the murder."

"And she stood for it?"

"Until about five-thirty. Then she got sore at him and went upstairs—to their apartment. Dave hotfooted it up right after her and—wow!" Stan rolled his eyes. "Everybody in the joint could hear the fireworks."

"Then what?"

"Dave came back down here in about five minutes and said she'd locked herself in the john. And then he said—" He paused and gulped from his glass.

Father gave him a questioning look.

"—that when he got his hands on her he was going to kill her."

"He said that, did he?" The priest mused for a moment. "So everybody could hear?"

"Well, no," Stan said. "Just me."

"You two must be good friends," Father observed mildly.

"Sure! That's why, when he made that crack about croaking her, I tried to calm him down, get him to lay off the booze. Other times he'd listen to me. But not this time."

"So he went upstairs after her again, did he?"

"Not right away, Father. He sat here brooding until about eight. Then he went up, but he was back in about ten minutes and said that Honey still wouldn't see him. She'd locked herself in the john again." A frown creased Stan's handsome features. "My telling the cops that is what got them really steamed up, I guess."

"I see what you mean," the pastor said. "You must have heard about the medical report."

"Yeah! That Honey died sometime between eight and ten. So it sure looked like Dave was the last person to see her alive, didn't it?" He leaned back in his chair and sighed. "But of course he wasn't. It was Ring—the guy who confessed."

Father Crumlish made no comment as he stared thoughtfully at his still-full glass. "By the way," he finally said, "how did it happen that you found her body?"

Dulski sighed again. "When it got to be a little after ten and there was still no sign of her, I thought I'd take a run upstairs to see if I could get her to cool off. I started to knock on the door, but it was open an inch or so. I walked in and—" he gave the priest a bleak look "—and there she was."

"Now that Dave's in the clear," Father remarked after a few minutes, "I'd not worry that he'll hold you responsible for his arrest because of what you told the police."

"Maybe."

"It strikes me that you have a lot more to worry about, just working in this place."

"What do you mean, Father?"

"Surely it's crossed your mind that with all the liquor here, let alone that tempting cash register, you yourself could be held up, beaten, and robbed—or worse."

"Nah, Father. Not a chance."

"No? Ah! I suppose you keep some kind of weapon handy," Father said as if the thought had suddenly occurred to him. "Something to defend yourself with in an emergency."

Dulski chuckled. "Sure do. The best, in my racket. A length of iron pipe."

"Do you now!" The pastor was visibly impressed. "Would you let me take a look at the thing?"

"Funny you should ask," Stan replied, frowning. "I always kept it on the shelf under the bar. I started to show it to the cops when they asked the same question you just did—but it was gone."

"Disappeared?"

"Yep—into thin air, like."

"Now that's a strange thing," Father said. He would have continued to press the point but there was a sudden insistent knocking at the locked entrance door. Dulski got up, unlocked it, and admitted a dark-haired, dark-eyed woman in her late twenties. The priest recognized her as Ida Leone—and in the same instant he remembered the rumor about Stan Dulski that had eluded him earlier.

"Who are you locking out—the cops?" Ida asked sarcastically as she walked into the room. "Don't worry. Dave's free, and so are you—" She broke off abruptly and Father guessed that Dulski had flashed her a warning glance.

"How are you, Ida?" Father inquired as she swung around and caught sight of him. "Have you a minute to sit down?"

"Well—ah—sure, Father," Ida replied—rather reluctantly, the

priest thought. He wondered if that had anything to do with what he had just remembered. And he decided to find out.

"Stan," he said, turning to the bartender, "do you suppose that I could have a word or two with Ida—in private?"

"Uh—yeah. Why not?" Stan said, but he appeared to be distinctly unhappy about the situation as he disappeared into the kitchen. Ida seated herself opposite the pastor, fumbled in her purse, finally found a cigarette, and lit it. Watching her, Father noticed that there were dark shadows under her eyes, as if she'd endured too many sleepless nights, and that her mouth was set in sullen, tense lines. Under his scrutiny her pale face flushed.

"I—I suppose you think it's funny, Father, me working here after what happened," she said.

"Do you now?" Father replied tentatively, not sure he understood her meaning.

"I mean about Stan and me breaking up after going steady for nearly two years."

"I knew about that," the pastor acknowledged. There'd been a bit more to it than that, he'd heard—that Stan had thrown Ida over for another woman.

"I've got nobody to blame but myself," Ida said bitterly. "When Honey hired me as a waitress over a year ago, I thought I'd be doing myself and Stan a big favor if I could get him a job here too." She snorted. "Big joke on me."

"Joke?" Father asked. "How do you mean, lass?"

"Stan took one look at Honey and the money she was raking in here and figured he had it made." Ida puffed on her cigarette for a moment. "Would you believe it, Father," she said earnestly, "that Honey was so hooked on Stan she was going to divorce Dave?"

"Was she indeed?"

"That's what she had him thinking, anyway. And he sure acted as if he owned her—and this place too. That's why he went upstairs that night to talk to her—" Ida's voice came to a halt and she turned her head.

Father Crumlish looked at her speculatively. "You mean to say that Stan saw Honey the night she was killed? Before he found her body?"

Ida busied herself snuffing out her cigarette and lighting another.

Father had a sudden inspiration. "Maybe you saw him—when you yourself paid a call on Honey."

Ida's eyes flashed. "I had a right to know what was going on, didn't I?"

"And what time did you say this was?"

"I didn't—" she began, then shrugged. "I don't know exactly—around seven, seven-thirty, I guess."

"Tell me," Father said, "why were you so set on seeing Honey?"

"Because I was fed up with all the hanky-panky going on around here—and I told her so." Ida's voice shook as she blurted out the words.

Was she lying? Father wondered. Out of spite against Stan and Honey—and maybe, from the sour, angry look of her, against the whole world?

"I don't imagine you had a very warm welcome," the priest said lightly.

"Welcome—hah! She slammed the door in my face. But not before I saw that somebody had given her what was going to be a beautiful shiner."

Ida sniffed with what Father thought was almost an air of satisfaction. Hell hath no fury—he started to form the thought when a loud thud from the floor above interrupted him. He gave Ida an inquiring glance. "Would you say that maybe Dave's up and about?"

"I'd say so. You want to see him, Father?"

"I do." He stood up.

She pointed to a door next to the far end of the bar. "Through there and up the stairs."

Moments later, a trifle breathless from the climb, the pastor stood outside a spectacularly painted red-and-gold door. It was typical of the dead woman, Father knew. Big-boned, hard-eyed Honey Garden, whose given name had originally been Harriet, had always betrayed, by her deportment and dress, her almost fanatical fancy for fiery reds and brassy golds. Like all vain, self-centered women, she made every effort to attract attention to herself and invariably she succeeded. Even in the way in which she had died, Father Crumlish thought as he pressed the doorbell.

"Who's there?" a hoarse voice called from behind the door.

"Father Crumlish."

It was a second or two before the door swung open, revealing a potbellied man whose original good looks had receded faster than the hairline of his bald head.

"C'mon in, Father," Dave Garden said as he clutched his coffee-stained bathrobe around him. "Make yourself at home while I get into a shirt and pants."

"Take your time, Dave," Father said as he walked into the living room. "I'm in no hurry." As a matter of fact, he was glad to be left alone so that he could take a closer, and almost incredulous, look at his surroundings. Never in his life had he seen anything comparable. As if the red-and-gold motif and furnishings of the room weren't dazzling enough, Honey had covered virtually every square inch of wall space with some likeness of herself.

Father Crumlish gazed on row after row of charcoal sketches, pen-and-ink drawings, portraits in oils—all of Honey, and all highly flattering. What a pretty price she must have paid the artists to make her appear so attractively slim and youthful, the pastor thought as he paused to look at a palette-knife portrait over the fireplace, a bronze bust on the bookcase, and a copper plaque with her profile in bas-relief. What a pretty price indeed! His thoughts were interrupted by the reappearance of Dave Garden.

"Honey was really something, wasn't she, Father?" Dave said, shaking his head mournfully. "Poor kid. When I think of that—that guy Ring, beating her up—" His voice trailed away as he slumped into a chair, clenching his fists.

"You've had a bad time, Dave," Father said. "It was hard enough about Honey. But then you had the added ordeal of the police arresting you."

"How do you like that, Father? The cops trying to pin my wife's murder on me!"

"I suppose they thought you had a reason."

"Reason! What reason would *I* have?" He made a gesture.

"After they heard that you'd been drinking all afternoon and bickering—"

" 'Heard' is right," Garden said angrily as he straightened up in his chair. "What they heard was a lot of insinuations from that pretty-faced bartender. The first thing I do when I get squared away around here is toss him out on his—"

"Well now," the pastor said in a reasonable tone of voice, "wasn't it his duty to tell the police that, to the best of his knowledge, you were the last person to see Honey alive?"

Garden sat thoughtfully for a moment before, grudgingly, nodding in agreement. "I suppose you're right, Father. It was no secret that Honey and I were having an—ah—argument all afternoon. Or that she really got sore at me, around five-thirty, and came up here."

"What provoked the argument?"

Garden shrugged. "I'd been drinking, and I guess I said some things in anger that I—" He chewed his lower lip and stared gloomily at the floor.

Father eyed him quizzically, wondering if a man who could be driven so easily to speak in anger might also be driven in anger to act.

"I came up after her," Dave continued. "Thought maybe we could patch things up. But she wasn't having any of it. She locked herself in the bathroom and—and that's the last time I saw her alive."

The priest looked puzzled. "But I had an idea you came up here again—about eight o'clock, wasn't it?"

Dave nodded. "But the minute she heard me come in she ducked back into the bathroom and locked the door. I begged her to come out—told her I was sorry—" He buried his dissipated face in his hands.

Father Crumlish gave him a long searching look before he stood up. He walked to the door and then turned. "You'll not be vindictive now, will you, Dave?" he asked.

Garden hesitated, then sighed heavily. "Right now all I want to do is just forget—everything."

"I don't blame you," Father said. He gave one last wondering look around the room laden with the flattering likeness of Honey Garden. "I don't blame you at all."

It was past eleven before Father Crumlish managed to tuck himself under his cozy comforter, turn his bedside radio on low, and pick up the volume containing the story of Edgar Allan Poe that he had been in the midst of reading last night. But he found it difficult to concentrate; his mind persisted in wandering.

What he had seen and heard this day had heightened his uneasy feeling that Eddie Ring was innocent of the crime to which he had confessed. And Father was reasonably certain that one of the three he had talked to—Stan, Ida, or Dave—had been lying. But which one? And how could he prove it? He sighed and shook his head in frustration.

Well, he told himself, resolutely turning his attention back to the Poe story, there was nothing more to be done about it tonight, in any event . . .

A few minutes later, the pastor suddenly sat straight up in bed and let the volume slip from his fingers. "Glory be to God!" he exclaimed, his brain working so busily that he failed to hear the sportscaster on the radio raucously proclaiming that Willie Mays had just clouted a monstrous long home run to win the game for the Giants in the bottom of the tenth.

Satisfied that he now had the answer, Father Crumlish picked up the phone and dialed Big Tom Madigan's number.

Close to noon the following morning Madigan rang the doorbell of St. Brigid's rectory and was admitted by Emma Catt. He joined the pastor in the living room, sank into a chair, and ran a hand wearily through his crisp, curly brown hair.

"You were right, Father," he said. "We picked up that bronze bust of Honey from the bookcase in the Gardens' living room. It had been wiped clean—no prints, hair, anything like that; still our lab boys were able to detect traces of blood, which matched Honey's type. When we confronted Dave with that, he broke down and confessed he killed her—"

"May God have mercy on him," Father murmured.

"That was the second time he went up there—around eight. Eddie Ring had already been and gone. Dave accused her of planning to sell The Garden Spot and team up with Stan Dulski. She admitted it, taunted him, and he became so enraged that he picked up the bust and cracked her skull."

"Poor Eddie," Father said. "An awful thing it was, his dying in the belief he'd murdered the woman."

"But it's easy to see why he thought so. After all, he'd hit her hard, knocked her flat, given her some nasty bruises—including a black eye. So when he heard the news bulletin—that she was dead—he naturally jumped to the conclusion that he was responsible. He had no way of knowing that the blow that really killed her was struck with the bust." Madigan took time out to light a cigarette.

"Her own likeness, lad," Father said.

"Yeah." The policeman smiled wryly. "Ironic, isn't it? But then, this whole case has been kind of wild. First of all—" he leaned forward in his chair, ticking off the points on his fingers "—we arrest a man for murder in what we think is an airtight case. Then—boom! Another man confesses to the crime, so we release the first suspect. And who does it turn out *really* did it?"

"What was the word you used, lad?" Father said with a trace of a smile. "Wild?" As Madigan nodded, the priest's face grew serious again. "There are a few things still troubling me, Tom."

"What, Father?"

"Why do you suppose that Honey didn't call the police after Eddie attacked and robbed her?"

Big Tom smiled knowingly. "When you run a joint like hers you don't invite the cops to come nosing around."

"I suppose not," the pastor agreed. "But then tell me, when you arrested Dave the first time, what kind of weapon did you think he'd used to kill her with?"

"We weren't sure. Never occurred to us it could be the bronze bust—that seemed to us to be—" he shrugged "—just like another piece of furniture. We had a hunch it might have been that missing length of iron pipe that Stan kept behind the bar."

Father sat thoughtfully for a moment. "What do you think happened to it?" he asked.

Madigan chuckled. "Ida Leone admitted this morning that she hid it, hoping we'd suspect Dulski. You know what they say about a woman scorned, don't you, Father?"

The priest looked grim. "I do indeed. And I mean to have a word with that lass. I've a notion that, with the good Lord's help, she'll mend her ways." He gave Madigan a sharp glance. "It would do no harm if you kept an eye on Stan Dulski, too, Tom."

"Anything you say." Madigan grinned. "Now would you mind telling *me* something, Father?"

"What's that, Tom?"

"Why were you so sure Eddie Ring was innocent?"

"If I'd been really sure, if I'd had any proof, I'd have come to you with it—surely you know that. But all I had was a hunch, after I remembered seeing poor Eddie in church during Devotions that night, and then coming across the pledge card he'd signed. I couldn't bear the thought that he'd gone to meet his Maker with that terrible deed on his conscience, if he didn't really do it."

Big Tom Madigan's warm brown eyes were warmer than usual as he gazed at his pastor. "One more question, Father," he said. "How did you know the fatal weapon was that bust of Honey Garden?"

It was Father Crumlish's turn to chuckle with amusement. "Well now—in a way, you might say that I was tipped off."

"No kidding? Who tipped you?"

"An old friend of mine—by the name of Edgar Allan Poe."

The detective looked at him blankly for a moment. "You're not talking about the famous author?"

The priest nodded. "The very same," he said. "Tell me, lad, did you ever read a story of his called *The Purloined Letter?*"

"I've heard of it, but—" Madigan reflected for a moment, then shook his head. "I don't recall ever reading it."

"You should, Tom, you should." Father wagged a gently admonishing finger at him. "Because it teaches a lesson every policeman ought to keep in mind."

"What's that, Father?"

"Just this, lad: if you want to hide something, the best place for it is right out in plain sight, where people see it all the time—where they *expect* to see it."

Ursula Curtiss

The Marked Man

Outside, in the cold rush of the night air, the left side of Walter's face felt iridescent with pain. The just-inflicted scratches seemed to seethe and simmer like neon tubing and at an occasional pair of oncoming headlights, he'd swing his head sharply out of the glare, as if he were summoning a laggardly dog in the shadows. His heart hammered as though he'd been running, which was the one thing he should not do.

The service station where the girl attendant lay unconscious on the floor—the girl who had astonishingly revealed herself as such only when her billed cap flew off with the suddenness of her jump at him—was now six or seven blocks behind him, and there was still no sound of a siren, no racing, revolving ambulance light. But the expectation of them was like an aimed gun, because although Walter had already disposed of the cheap dark mail-order wig, he was literally a marked man. For the first time in his life he needed a safe place to hide for a few days, and to find that he had to locate a telephone booth, and fast.

Gulping for air even at his only brisk walking pace, he arrived at a telephone booth at the entrance to a closed and spectrally lit shopping plaza. He ruffled through the L's in the chained directory, was seized with panic when he appeared not to have a single coin, finally dredged up a quarter, dropped it in, and dialed. A kind of desperate confidence had carried him this far, but the moment of panic had undermined it and let in a thought that he had kept at bay since he'd fled from the service station: *What if Dex was out of town? Or had moved?*

His face flamed while he waited; he hoped viciously that the girl on the concrete floor was dead. Then an elderly female voice quavered a hello into his ear and he asked for Dex.

The voice hesitated. "He's—busy right now. Could I have him call you back—say, tomorrow?"

A party? No, but something was going on—he heard a low mutter of background sounds. "I'm just passing through. Tell him it's Walt," said Walter firmly, and a moment later the familiar voice was saying warily, unwelcomingly, "Hi, Walt."

A measure of Walter's usual cockiness came back, even in the middle of this crisis. Good old Dex, met at the reformatory in the southern part of the state, where Walter had been sent for aggravated assault and Dex for theft during one of his many flights from a broken home. Dex was twenty-four now, the older by a year, but like most essentially gentle people he was vulnerable. He was also married, with a baby, and assistant manager of his father-in-law's small but thriving grocery store. It had been very clear to Walter, who took care to keep in touch with anyone potentially useful, that neither Dex's prim little wife nor his hatchet-faced father-in-law knew of his reformatory past.

Now, tersely and without details, Walter told the other man that he was in a jam and needed a place to stay—garage, woodshed, anywhere—for a couple of days. Dex replied with the caution of someone with a listener beside him that he wished he could put Walter up but the fact was that his wife's mother had passed away the day before and Walter could see that, uh . . .

"Say, that's an idea. Your wife has lived in this town all her life. She'd probably know of some empty house for sale or something, wouldn't she, if you asked her? I mean if you told her it was for an old friend?"

For a dangerous interval of silence Walter was afraid he had gone too far with the implied threat. Then Dex said in a driven voice, "There's one place that might—where are you now?"

While he waited for the car, Walter tidied up the telephone booth, a process he had automatically begun while talking to Dex. Brought up by an elderly aunt as clean and joyless as bleach, further stampeded by the harsh institutional years, he had an active unease—almost a fear—of dirt and disorder. Although he himself was hardly aware of it, public places like washrooms and park benches and telephone booths were always the cleaner for Walter's passing. By the time Dex's car arrived, two cigarette butts, three matches, two gum wrappers, and a paper cup had been amalgamated into a small neat ball and thrown outside into a litter basket.

After a single instantly averted glance at the bloody marks on Walter's face, Dex confined himself to essentials. The house he had in mind would be empty for a week because the owners had gone deer hunting; he knew this because the woman, a Mrs. Patterson, had been in the store yesterday buying supplies and he had heard her talking to the checkout girl. He didn't think there was a dog. He had brought a flashlight. Beyond that, Walter was on his own.

As he finished these stony announcements a siren commenced to shriek miles away to the south, the urgent sound carrying on the cold dry air. Dex kept his eyes unflickeringly on the road ahead, his only and instinctive reaction a sudden pressure on the gas pedal. Rejection came from him almost as visibly as the simmers of heat from above the radiator, but he said nothing until he pulled in without warning under cottonwoods.

"Far as I go," he said then. "Second house on the right. For God's sake watch it."

"Don't worry," Walter told him, confident because of the distance between him and the siren. "You've got nothing to do with this, right? Somebody else overheard the woman and the checkout girl. So long, Dex."

"Goodbye," said Dex tightly, and drove away.

It was a very good house for the purpose, twenty-five yards back from the road with at least that much separation from its neighbors on both sides, and cupped in trees. If the neighbors had dogs they were the sleepy overfed kind: the only sound Walter could hear as he advanced cautiously on the grass was a faint twiggy rustle of wind high above him.

He melted to the rear of the house, his now-adjusted vision able to pick out details other than the black shine of panes. The back door was sturdily resistant; the windows appeared to be the kind that louvered out. Walter traveled along the wall and presently found another door opening on what felt like flagstones. The lock here gave with only a minimum of attention from his knife and he was inside in total darkness and utter silence.

A faint trace of perfume on the air, a fluffiness underfoot: although both were alien to Walter, he knew that this must be a bedroom. After moments of testing with all his senses—not that he believed Dex daring enough for treachery—he aimed the flashlight cautiously between shielding fingers, snapped it instantly off again, stood frozen with the image of the rumpled double bed still seared on his vision. The illusion of a suspicious householder risen to investigate the rooms within was fleetingly so strong that Walter's hand shot behind him for the doorknob.

But nothing happened; the darkness and silence remained tranquil. After a guarded moment he tiptoed through the open doorway that the brief spurt of light had showed him, found himself in a hall, and listened again. Then, because alarm had made his face blaze as though the girl's nails had just bitten into it, he fumbled his way to a bathroom, ran the cold water boldly, and held his dripping palms to it.

He had committed several robberies before this one, and in fact served a short jail term; but until tonight he had never used more than the threat of violence. He had never had to: his victims had the impression—false, as it happened—that he was completely irresponsible, and heedless as to the consequences of his actions.

As a result, he was suddenly so exhausted that he did not even count the bills wadded deep in his jacket pocket under his gloves. He lay down on the unmade bed, faintly shocking to his neat nature even through his fatigue, and was asleep almost at once.

In the morning Walter took an appraising look around the bedroom and discovered that the untidy Pattersons were well off—not that it mattered to him, as his object was to leave this place without a trace as soon as his scratches were healed enough to be disguised with makeup. He also learned that the money the girl had defended so wildly and stupidly amounted to eighty-one dollars.

—The girl who (the bedroom clock-radio informed him through the open doorway while he shaved and washed his damaged cheek with care) is still unconscious and in critical condition in a local hospital. Her head injuries indicate that she was flung with considerable violence against the corner of a metal filing cabinet. The robbery, which occurred at some time between 10:30 and 10:50 P.M. appears thus far to have gone unwitnessed. Police are continuing their inquiries in the area—

Walter turned the radio off. The fact that Dex had undoubtedly been listening to the news did not worry him in the least; if anything, the fact of the girl's condition would make the other man all the more sweatingly anxious that his own part in this never came out.

And when—and if—the girl recovered consciousness she could only describe her assailant as having dark hair and brows. Walter's hair was fair, and without the burnt-match coloring his eyebrows were almost invisible. When the scratches had healed he would be able to saunter down to the bus station, retrieve his shabby suitcase from the locker there, use his already-bought ticket to Denver, and be on his way—free as air. Cheered, Walter set out for the first time to explore his temporary domain.

Three minutes later he almost called Dex at the grocery store;

only the realization that it might be dangerous for anyone to find this number busy stopped him. Because something very strange had happened in this house.

If it had been another kind of house, Walter would have said jeeringly to himself that they had had some party the night before. But in that case you would expect to see liquor bottles about—and something told him that people who lived in houses like this did not give parties like that.

There were two bedrooms, apparently occupied by children, besides the one by which he had entered, and another smaller bath; a long deep kitchen, a dining room with three railed steps down into a big living room; and opening off that, a den.

Everywhere there were costly looking mirrors and rugs and pictures—and everywhere, drawers were not quite closed on their brimming contents and cabinets hung slightly open. In one child's room a sharp scuffle had evidently taken place, knocking the sliding closet doors off their runners and dragging the bedclothes half onto the floor.

Stunned, frightened, careful to stay out of range of the windows that faced the road, Walter checked the front-door lock and then the one in the rear. Both were firmly set. Then how—?

An echo of his own soothing words to Dex came back: "Somebody else overheard the woman and the checkout girl." Somebody had, and had got in somehow, and the thing right now was to make sure that they didn't return. His back prickling whenever he had to turn it on an open doorway, Walter explored deeper and found, in a utility room off the kitchen, a wall ladder which led up into a little room apparently used by a child at some time. There was a canvas cot, a vase of long-dead flowers, a faded cloth doll. And a door, now stirring gently in the morning air, that gave on the long flat roof and the accommodating branches of a cottonwood tree.

Kids, thought Walter with a great rush of relief as he fastened the hook-and-eye that secured the door. Seeing the Patterson family depart in a laden car or camper, deciding that the coast was clear for some casual mischief or vandalism: you read about such things in the newspapers almost daily. That explained the strange disorder below, and also the apparent lack of theft—Walter had counted two television sets, at least three radios, and a typewriter in the bedroom.

The active threat that the house had seemed to contain was now gone. Descending to the kitchen, Walter investigated the refrigerator and found the remnants that a woman might decide were too little to take on a camping trip and too much to throw away: half a loaf of bread, a half stick of butter, four eggs, a partly used jar of strawberry jam. No milk. Walter drank his instant coffee black, scrambled two eggs, and put jam on a slice of bread.

He cleaned up carefully after himself, not touching the litter he found on the long cream-colored formica counters; the earlier intruders, possibly known to the Pattersons, might admit to the soup—there was a pot with withering dregs—and the generous strewings of orange peel. Distasteful though it was, Walter had to leave the disorder alone.

And he would certainly not allow his nerves to be ruffled by the untidiness everywhere else.

But it was a long day. The graveled crescent driveway crunched noisily three times—twice with cars turning around, once with a panel truck disgorging a boy who trundled around to the rear of the house with a sack of whatever they put in water-softeners. Walter held himself flinchingly still against a wall, expecting a knock at the back door; but there was a distant thump and bang and the boy returned to the truck and drove away.

According to the three o'clock news the girl in the service station, Emma Bothwell, had not regained consciousness and was in surgery. A hospital spokesman said there was evidence she had marked her assailant.

Angry at that all over again, Walter went and inspected his scratches, three and a trailing fourth. They had dried and darkened a little, which he took to be a healthy sign, and there was no spreading redness. He then roamed the house at a safe distance from the windows, and grimly did not restore to its rack a man's tie flung over one of the sapphire-upholstered dining-room chairs, did not snatch the weird collection of rubber bands out of the silver tray on the table, or brush off what looked like a wanton sprinkle of sugar on the table top.

At a quarter of five, because he would not be able to move about freely after dark, he opened a can of chili and ate it cold. At five o'clock the telephone rang for the first time.

The sound was terrifying in this refuge, carrying as it did a suggestion that someone was testing the emptiness of this house—or that Dex was warning him of imminent capture. But Dex would know that Walter couldn't lift the receiver. Dex would come himself.

If he had time to.

What if the Pattersons had cut their hunting trip short for some reason and had just stopped at Dex's grocery store for things like milk and butter and eggs? What if this were Dex with a helpless message?—"They're on their way home."

Walter had actually taken a step toward the telephone when it cut itself off in midscream. Some friend of the Pattersons who didn't know they were away, he told himself—telephones must be ringing constantly in empty houses—but he put on his jacket and stood tensely in the now-dark dining room, gazing through the half-drawn curtains at occasional passing headlights.

At the end of a long half hour he considered himself safe from this particular threat, but the deep uneasiness stayed with him and carried over into his sleep.

It was a cold windy night, and the trees around the house creaked with a sound like keys being inserted into locks. The faraway howl of a dog became a woman's advancing voice and brought Walter sitting up with his heart pounding. At some black hour later he came fully awake again with a thought that must have been hovering around the edges of his mind all day.

There was, he was almost sure, something called immunity—some means by which police protected informers. Walter's sole guarantee of Dex's continuing silence was the other man's fear at being an accessory; but mightn't the police shut their eyes to that in return for Walter, in view of all the fuss being kicked up about the girl? Dex wasn't very bright—anyone with brains would have told his wife about the reformatory at the outset, so as to remove that hold; but it might still occur to him that he could lead the police to Walter at almost no risk to himself. He might even emerge looking like a hero, reformatory or not.

By midmorning of his second day in it, Walter had developed a personal hatred for the Patterson house. He had told himself that he would not let the general dishevelment get on his nerves, but in his restless wandering he yanked the door of the child's room shut; that was one place he didn't have to look at. A genuine rage at the marauders rose up in him, accompanied by a woolly feeling that he was missing some very important point.

Twice before noon he was startled by crunching tires in the drive, but although the cars passed close to the front windows they went by at undiminished speed. This seemed to be a natural turning-around spot, and Walter added it to his list of grievances against the house.

After his lunch—at least the pantry was well stocked—he made the ritual inspection of his scratches and experimented with some liquid makeup he found on a bathroom shelf. The scratches stared through, and the trouble was that they did not look like an encounter with a cat or some barbed wire; they looked exactly like what they were. Walter added another layer of makeup and thought that by tomorrow night . . .

The one o'clock news, which he watched on the television set in the curtained bedroom, jarred him to total attention, because the girl in the hospital was holding a news conference. With a thin prominent-jawed face surmounted by bandages, she looked more like a boy than ever. Blurred backs kept getting in the way as she spoke—eerily, for this was the first time Walter had heard her voice.

"I think he was about twenty-one or twenty-two. He had dark hair. He had on a dark jacket—I don't remember what color his pants were. Yes, he was wearing gloves, darkish gloves I think," she said to some off-camera question, "and when he told me to give him the money he took one glove off, I don't know why. I jumped at him, because I knew my uncle kept a gun in the desk—that was behind him—and I thought—"

Walter had stopped listening. He was staring at the television screen in a paralysis of horror. Once again, in a sick dream that sent the blood to his face and made the scratches flame, he felt the tiny menacing prick in the palm of his right glove as he opened the office door—was it a tumbleweed thorn? In the same awful slow motion he watched the girl's submissiveness at the cash register, although he hadn't known she was a girl then, and saw himself remove the glove with its threatening little stab so that he could more securely take the bills she was about to hand him.

But no matter how hard he tried, he did not see himself put on the glove after that lightning attack. Instead, he felt the dry slither of the money he had fumbled out with his bare and shaking hand.

What had he done then? Closed the cash drawer? Touched anything else? Out of that tiny interval of unexpected violence and pain and everything gone wrong, it was impossible for him to remember.

As though he could silence the girl forever, Walter leaped to the television set and snapped it off. His hands had begun to tremble, and he locked them tightly together and walked calmingly up and down. *This* was the blurry issue he hadn't quite grasped earlier, this was what had to be faced. Would the Pattersons, returning to their untidy house, accept it for the mischief it was—or, having picked up a newspaper or listened to a car radio, assume at once that a fugitive had been in hiding there, and send for the police?

Walter's fingerprints were a matter of record, and there was hardly a place in the house where he hadn't left them. The robbery would be secondary to the police by now; they would be haring after him for aggravated assault, at the least.

Wait. All this presumed that the Pattersons found their home in this shocking condition. What if they *didn't* find it in a shocking condition? Walter certainly couldn't leave it exactly as they left it, but first impressions would probably be clouded by the commotion of a return with children. By the time Mrs. Patterson's eye fell on something odd in the arrangement of her ashtrays or frying pans, Walter's fingerprints would have been smeared and overlaid and polished out of existence.

With a vast relief he began to clean up the house.

It was a staggering job, but his spirits began to lift as he got the surface disorder—the straggling tie, a ball of string, the bunched rubber bands, an empty flowerpot—out of the living and dining rooms and into what he hoped were appropriate places. With a little forcing he coaxed drawers and cabinets to close everywhere. When he had swept the floors, the rugs seemed to have a visible overlay of tiny confetti-like debris and he had to get out the vacuum cleaner.

The cleared tops of tables showed strange little sticky places which required sponging, and only the extreme urgency of his situation made Walter tackle the worse of the two children's rooms. His ingrained vision here was of taut tight mitred sheets and blankets, with toys and games, if any, tucked out of sight. It did not include spilled popcorn, an empty Coca-Cola can stuck jauntily in an open bureau drawer, or a yawning closet which looked as though it had been stirred by an eggbeater.

It was almost dark when Walter finished, but the dining-room table gleamed, the living-room couches were unsullied, the floor shone.

The house would certainly not have passed the antiseptic eye of Walter's aunt or the grim glare of the matrons in the reformatory, but nobody entering it would cry out in shock. Exhausted but pleased, his nerves quieted by the new orderliness, Walter consumed a can of the Pattersons' soup and went to bed.

In the morning he heard, but was not alarmed by, one more turning-around car that crunched, paused, and crunched away again . . .

Anne Merrick had swung her little car briskly into her sister's driveway. The hunting trip, irresistible to the Pattersons, would be followed in less than a week by a visit from the senior Pattersons, a gentle and elderly couple from New Jersey who had never been allowed to see the house in its normal state. There were things to be done before even the stoutest-hearted cleaning woman could be brought in. Anne had volunteered.

The Pattersons lived in a manner uniquely their own, only partly explained by the fact that Betsy was a free-lance writer. They had tree surgeons to minister to their trees and sent their Orientals off to be cleaned at the proper intervals; occasionally, after some un-heralded visitor had happened in on a scene of chaos, they laid down stern rules for their three young children: no eating in the living room, keep your bedroom tidy, hang up your clothes.

For perhaps forty-eight hours both the children and the parents observed these strictures, and then fell back into their cheerful dis-orderly habits. Once every six months, for a week at a time, Betsy Patterson and a cleaning woman attacked the bulging closets and brimming drawers, and then the tranquil process of deterioration began all over again.

Anne, remembering the condition of the house three mornings ago when she had helped Betsy and Rob and the children get packed and away, thought now that a fast hour ought to do it. She wasn't aiming at actual cleanliness, after all, but only at the impression that rational people lived here. Bare surfaces were marvelously de-ceptive. If she made a lightning sweep through the living room and the—

—dining room, with the curtains at its low window half drawn to reveal the shining black-walnut table and the immaculate sapphire chairs. Anne's hand stopped sharply before taking out the ignition key.

Three days ago the dining-room table had worn a heavy sprinkle of salt—Adam, the youngest of the children, could never pass a salt-cellar without upending it—but now the table gleamed. So did the silver tray, innocent of the rubber bands dumped into it at the last minute because Betsy had said firmly she would not travel in a vehicle containing children *and* rubber bands. And what had become of Rob's discarded tie, which Anne remembered clearly because the burgundy and gray stripes had looked so decorative against the sapphire chairs?

For a sickening second it was almost as though the Pattersons themselves had been wiped and polished away. Anne's impulse was to race out of the driveway; instead, because it seemed imperative for some reason, she forced herself to leave at the same speed at which she had entered. Two minutes later, at a telephone in the next house, she explained matters to a bewildered voice at the Sheriff's office.

"*Not* ransacked, you say," repeated the deputy uncomprehendingly; without knowing it, he was much in Walter's position. "Then what seems to be the trouble?"

"The trouble is that my sister's house *always* looks ransacked, and now it *doesn't* and there has to be something very wrong," said Anne, unfairly impatient. "There's been someone in there, don't you see? I wish to heaven you'd hurry. They might still be there—"

Walter was feeling almost tranquil as he applied a second coat of liquid makeup to his nearly healed cheek; the order around him, after the antic condition of the house, was like balm. Even when he heard a brisk sound from the region of the front door, a sound of entry, his heart gave a horrible knock but he did not panic.

A friend or relative with a key? The Pattersons themselves, returning earlier than planned? No matter; his foresight and drudgery of the night before had insured against an immediate alarm, and he had a choice of two rear doors.

He used the door in the bedroom, closed it soundlessly behind him, backed over flagstones into the chest of a man as careful and quiet as he. But this one—how could it *be,* after all his labor?—this one had a badge and a hand at his holstered hip.

Melville Davisson Post

The Forgotten Witness

It was a courtroom in which the leisurely customs of the South persisted. The jurors were at ease, as in a sort of club. They were known to one another. The officers of the court, the attorneys, the judge, the prisoner, and the audience filling the seats behind the railing were likewise known to them.

The courtroom had been scrubbed, and through the long windows, open to the air of the summer morning, came the fresh odor of the distant fields.

The criminal trial about to open was of considerable local interest, as evidenced by the alert bearing of the officials and by the respectful silence of the spectators.

The clerk, a man with the classic face of a Greek poet, and who wore a little yellow rosebud on the lapel of his coat, was the most conspicuous person. But he had neither the spirit nor the vocation of his Hellenic cast. One distinction, however, he maintained—he was the prophetic oracle of this court.

He forecast its decisions.

And when he was sober, as he was on this summer morning, his pronouncements were shrewd and accurate. He knew what the judge would do; what the jury usually would do. He knew legal shifts and subterfuges, the stock defenses, the methods and strategy of every attorney at this bar, and he could forecast the development of that strategy when the case was called.

One factor alone disturbed him: he could never be certain of his estimates of Colonel Braxton. He had known this lawyer always, observed him day after day, but for all that the man remained an enigma to him. And he had come to qualify his forecasts with: "If Colonel Braxton is not of counsel for the defense!"

He was looking at the man now, and wondering what substantial defense he could set up for the notorious crook that he represented; some form of alibi or the obscurities of reasonable doubt. But to what end? The jury knew the prisoner's record, the judge knew it—no legal smokescreen could obscure it.

The clerk waited with a keen interest for the case to open.

And, as always when the curtain rose on the legal drama, he

selected Colonel Braxton for the point of interest. The prosecuting attorney had made his statement of the case for the State, after the legal custom obtaining in this court. He had fully explained the charge against the prisoner and the nature of the evidence which he expected to introduce.

It was a clear, accurate statement and shrewdly put.

The facts were certain, and the deductions from circumstances were irresistible.

The sheriff had been robbed, and some ten thousand dollars of the county's money taken. It was the custom in that day for the sheriff to collect the taxes and to travel into the magisterial districts for that purpose. He lived some miles from this little city that was the county seat. He had returned home in the evening with the money he had collected. His wife was absent on a visit and he was alone in the house.

He had not yet retired and was reading a newspaper in his sitting-room when he heard a knocking on the door. When he opened it, he had been confronted by a man with a colored handkerchief tied around the lower part of his face, who, at the point of a pistol, compelled him to hand over the money, and then forced him into a closet. The spring lock of the door had snapped, leaving him imprisoned in the darkness.

He had shouted at the top of his lungs, but, as his house was some distance from the highway and there was no other residence near it, he was not heard.

In the morning a farm hand returning to the premises heard the sheriff call, and breaking the lock on the closet found the exhausted man collapsed on the floor.

The prisoner was at once taken into custody. He had been seen near the sheriff's residence on this evening, and was known to have returned to his saloon in the city about midnight.

The prisoner had been positively identified by the sheriff.

The house had been examined by the chief of police, but so many people had entered that nothing could be determined, although the approaches to the house, and even the rug on the floor of the room, had been carefully inspected for footprints.

Colonel Braxton had been among those present at this official inspection.

The whole courtroom waited to hear upon what defense the counsel for the prisoner depended.

The attorney for the defense rose slowly.

He was a big man, with a heavy, putty-colored face, expressionless as a mask, except when he wished to contort it with a stamp of vigor. His black hair was brushed sleek, an immaculate white handkerchief, tucked into his collar, covered the white bosom of his shirt to protect it from the ash of the cigar that was always present, even in the courtroom. The color of the heavy face and its placidity, together with the somnolent air of the man and his drawling voice, gave weight to the common impression that he was a drug addict.

"Your Honor," he said, "and gentlemen of the jury, I shall have no evidence to introduce in behalf of the prisoner. If he is cleared here, he must be cleared on the testimony of the witnesses for the State."

The whole courtroom was astonished.

This was an abandonment of the defense.

A plea of guilty, putting the prisoner on the mercy of the court, would have been better. Someone sitting near the clerk whispered this conclusion. But the clerk did not reply. He sat fingering his classic chin. What did this appalling frankness mean? And he leaned forward to catch any concluding words that the attorney might utter.

But there was no further word.

Colonel Braxton put out his hand like one who, with an effort, thrusts the inevitable aside, then sat down.

Of all persons in the courtroom, the prisoner seemed the most astonished. He remained for a moment looking in amazement at the big, placid body of Colonel Braxton who, with half closed eyes, sat chewing the end of his inevitable cigar. Then he leaned forward and began to whisper. What he said could not be heard, but his manner indicated an elaborate protest. The man was alarmed and urgent. But his insistence had no visible effect.

Colonel Braxton's drawl silenced him.

"Now, now, Charlie," he said, "don't hire a dog to bark for you and then go to barking yourself."

Everybody laughed.

This eccentric lawyer was to the audience like an actor in a play, the central figure of these legal dramas. His mannerisms and his queer digressions packed the courtroom. And his peculiarities were suffered by the judge out of long custom.

But there was a sense of disappointment among the spectators in the crowded room. They had assembled to witness a bitter legal struggle—the determined assault of the prosecution and a dogged, desperate resistance—and here was unconditional surrender.

Only the old clerk was in doubt.

But even to his rich experience this looked like the strategy of despair. How could this attorney hope to clear the prisoner on the State's evidence?

He would be convicted on it.

All the requisites necessary to a conviction would be established: the proof of the robbery, the identification of the prisoner, and his presence near the sheriff's house on the night of the robbery.

Where were the colonel's usual defenses: the alibi, the mysterious stranger? Could he mean to exclude the State's evidence?

That was clearly impossible.

Such a motion lay only when there was no evidence tending to indicate the guilt of the accused.

The conduct of a criminal trial in this jurisdiction followed the form of the early trials in Virginia. This procedure lent itself to the possibility of a long preliminary skirmish before the general engagement opened. It began usually with an attack on the procedure of the grand jury returning the indictment; technical objections to the indictment itself.

Following this rich field of contest, there was the struggle in the courtroom over the selection of a jury. There was the peremptory right to strike a certain number from the panel, and to question every man drawn on what is called a *voir dire* examination. And back of this there were the many and various devices for obtaining a continuance of the case from term to term, until public indignation at the offense had subsided, and the witnesses for the State wandered—or were spirited—away.

In this broad borderland Colonel Braxton was a skilled duelist.

Shrewd, farsighted, and accomplished, it was his custom to attack, like the great generals of antiquity, at the dawn. He did not wait to be assailed. He assailed the State, and continued to attack it to the end.

The prosecuting attorney found himself on the defensive.

Instead of the prisoner, he found himself and his procedure on trial. In desperate cases Colonel Braxton tried everybody but the prisoner. In the notorious Barker case he even tried the judge, assembling all the instances in which the Supreme Court of the State had reversed him for erroneous rulings.

And, in the modern vernacular, he got their goat.

The jury, eminently human, came unconsciously to favor the virile, decisive side. And so, here in this desperate case, it was a greater wonder that Colonel Braxton evaded this whole field of strategy; gave the prosecuting attorney his head; and, to the casual observer, abandoned hope for his client.

Even the judge was surprised.

The old clerk, very carefully dressed as for a social function, balanced doubtfully between two conclusions: was this a mere form of pleading guilty, or had Colonel Braxton discovered at the last moment some element of guilt that had wrecked his defense beyond all hope of patching it together?

The prosecuting attorney had his way.

He put on his witnesses and proved his case. After the usual custom, he called the police first, as though to give his case a foundation in law and order, then incidental witnesses, leaving the county sheriff for the last.

And to all this Colonel Braxton made no objection.

He did not cross-examine.

He dismissed each witness with a courteous wave of the hand or some comment agreeable to his testimony in the case, coupled with a pleasantry.

"Thank you, Scally," he drawled, as the chief of police was turned over to him, "you are right—you are quite right. Charlie was out at the sheriff's house that night, and he did come into town about twelve o'clock. Of course, Charlie says that the sheriff told him confidentially that if he came out to see him that night, he would arrange some way to give him time on his taxes. He hadn't any money to pay them just then."

The prosecuting attorney objected.

"If you want the prisoner's explanation to go before the jury, you will have to have him sworn."

Colonel Braxton waved his hand in affable assent.

"Alfred," he said, addressing the prosecuting attorney, as in a confidential aside, "do you think the jury would believe Charlie any quicker just because he was sworn?"

Again the ripple of laughter ran over the courtroom. And the prisoner sought the ear of his counsel with some whispered protest. Was one's lawyer to impeach one's veracity before the world?

There is a theory in the law that circumstantial evidence, when properly coupled up, is the most conclusive of all forms of evidence. The early English judges commented on it with a stock dictum. Men may lie, but circumstances cannot! Bias, prejudice, fear, the hope of gain, a friend to save, an enemy to convict may influence the testimony of many a witness. But a fact stands for itself.

These silent witnesses, as criminal lawyers have dramatically named them, are beyond the influence of the human will.

And out of such testimony the State built up its case.

The prisoner had been seen loitering near the sheriff's residence on the night of the robbery. He had been seen on the highway to this house, and he had been seen and recognized returning to the city near midnight.

His criminal record and his need of money established the motive.

He would know the local custom of the sheriff, to go out to the magisterial districts to collect the taxes, and thus, familiar with that official custom, he would know that a considerable sum of money would be in the possession of the sheriff at this time. Also, it was common knowledge in the neighborhood that the sheriff's wife was absent on a distant visit, and that, therefore, he would be alone in the house.

All these indisputable evidences clearly showed that the robbery was the work of someone in the community.

The prisoner was the man the shoe fitted.

And seeing that he was unopposed, the prosecuting attorney pushed his advantage beyond his legal right. Each criminal charge should stand on its own bottom. But he got before the jury, by the incidental answers of the police, by hint and by innuendo, all the petty offenses with which the prisoner had been charged; enumerating them as one catalogues the important events in a life.

Against the whole force of this assault Colonel Braxton made only a drawling comment.

"Alfred," he said, "you can't make one black elephant out of two hundred black crow-birds!"

But the prosecuting attorney knew what he was about. When all these loose threads were gathered up, they would make the knot he wished. Colonel Braxton's wit would not save his client.

Sheriff Henderson was a well known figure in the community.

He was a little, slight man with pale-blue eyes set in a shrewd face—a man of scattering enterprises, not all of them successful; too many irons in the fire was the homely comment. But his election to the office of sheriff had seemed to strengthen his credit. It was a lucrative office under the system then obtaining in the state, and a careful official usually retired from it with a modest fortune.

But the present incumbent was not an official of accurate business methods, and if he were required now to make good the loss of this robbery he would be on the way to a bankrupt court. In fact, he was already on the way. The gains that he would receive from his office were to be sequestered by his creditors. He, individually, would come out at the end of his term with nothing. There was a rumor that he would remove to a distant state at the end of his term; that he had purchased a farm there, and that the reason he was alone on the night of the robbery was that his wife had gone to inspect this purchase.

It was hoped by his creditors and bondsmen that this trial might in some manner point the way to a recovery of the money.

The robber had unquestionably concealed it. But where, and in what manner?

The prisoner had been shadowed from the very day. His house, and the saloon that he ran in the environs of the city, had been carefully searched. It was the plan of the prosecution to convict the prisoner with a quick trial and, under the pressure of a long penal sentence, force him to disclose the place in which the money was hidden.

And it was to this end that the State directed its energies.

When the prosecuting attorney turned the sheriff over to Colonel Braxton for cross-examination, the thing was done. The details of the robbery had been accurately and succinctly recited and verified. The sheriff said he had shouted in the closed closet, and it was clearly evident that, as his residence was remote from any other, this shouting could not have been heard. The handkerchief which the robber had worn about the lower part of his face had slipped down while he was forcing the sheriff into the closet and he had seen the man plainly.

It was the prisoner at the bar.

The State closed with that decisive identification.

Unless Colonel Braxton could break down this destructive fact, his client was doomed. Everybody realized it; and the whole court-room waited, curious to see in what manner he would undertake to negative this disastrous incident.

But he made no allusion to it.

He sat for a few moments, apparently irresolute, as though undetermined whether he would interrogate the witness or permit him to stand aside. Finally he seemed to come to a conclusion. But when he spoke there was no vigor in his voice.

"Mr. Henderson," he said, "in a position of panic, don't you think all men are apt to act unconsciously on simple impulses?"

The witness replied promptly, as with a frank unconcern.

"Yes, Colonel," he said, "I think that's true."

"And we may assume," the attorney continued, "that every normal man will act about like every other normal man?"

"I suppose in a panic we would all act about alike."

"Panic," Colonel Braxton went on, "seems to bring out, unconsciously, primitive acts of self-preservation. We can see it easily demonstrated by the acts of a child in panic . . . What does a child do, Mr. Henderson, when we lock him up in a dark closet?"

"He makes a noise," replied the witness, "and tries to get out."

"And how does he make a noise and how does he try to get out?"

"He shouts and he kicks on the door."

"Precisely," said the attorney, "for these are primitive impulses of self-preservation, common to all. Don't you think a man would do the same?"

"I think he would," replied the witness; "it would be the natural thing to do."

Colonel Braxton passed his hand over his placid, inexpressive face.

"Now, Mr. Henderson," he drawled, "isn't this precisely what you did when you were locked in the dark closet?"

"I guess it is, Colonel."

The attorney moved his fingers on the table as though he brushed something away.

"I'm afraid we can't guess here, Mr. Henderson. What is the fact about it?"

"Well, Colonel," replied the witness, "that's the fact about it."

The counsel for the prisoner paused. He seemed disconcerted. He passed his hand again over his face, as in some reflection.

"Of course," he added, "in your case it was no use trying to get out, as the closet was securely locked and the door was made of heavy planks. And it was no use making a noise or shouting, as there was no other residence near you. Persons passing on the distant highway could not possibly have heard the most powerful voice shouting in that locked closet in that closed-up house . . . Mr. Henderson," the colonel continued, "do you think an Infinite Intelligence conducts the affairs of the universe?"

The witness, with everyone else, was amazed.

"Why, yes, Colonel," he replied, "I suppose He does."

"It's a pretty big job, don't you think?"

The witness smiled: "I'd call it a tremendously big job."

"Do you think a man could take the place of this Infinite Intelligence, and do it?"

The witness continued to smile: "I don't think any man would be fool enough to try, Colonel."

The big attorney made a sudden explosive sound.

"But they *do* try . . . that's what fills me with wonder . . . they *do* try!"

Then he turned aside, as though diverted to something irrelevant.

"You travel out to the magisterial districts on a horse, don't you?"

"Yes," replied the witness; "the roads are usually bad."

"And you meet with all sorts of weather?"

"Yes—I'm out in nearly every kind of weather."

"And you must dress for that sort of rough travel?"

The witness made an apologetic gesture. He looked down at his heavy clothing and his thick shoes.

"Yes, Colonel," he replied, with a little laugh, "that's the reason I go dressed as I am today. Town clothes and dude shoes wouldn't stand what I go through on the Virginia roads."

Colonel Braxton nodded his head, as one without interest.

"Ah, yes," he said, "I was just wondering how you were dressed on the night of the robbery."

The witness replied at once:

"Why, just like I'm dressed now."

Colonel Braxton made a slight gesture, as of one dismissing a triviality. "Ah! yes," he repeated, "precisely as you are dressed now."

Then he dropped back into his former manner, like one meditating aloud on some profound aspect of human conduct.

"At the little points where events touch the great conduct of human affairs, men undertake to substitute their feeble intelligence for the infinite intelligence of the Ruler of Events. They undertake to set that will aside, and to rearrange the moving of events as they wish them to appear. They are fools enough!—that's a good way to put it, Mr. Henderson—they are fools enough! Now, why do you use that term, Mr. Henderson, that term 'fool enough'?"

"Because no man could do it, Colonel."

"Ah!" It was the big booming expletive again. "That's precisely the point. No man can do it!"

He shot a sharp glance at the witness, then dropped into a leisurely drawl.

"The great writers on evidence, Mr. Starkey and Mr. Greenlief, were of the opinion that no human intelligence was able to construct a false consistency of events that could be substituted for the true consistency of events that it undertook to replace. It was an impossible endeavor, for the reason that one would have to know accurately all the varied events that preceded and all the varied events that followed in order to substitute false events that would fit. Now, only an Infinite Intelligence could know all that has happened and all that will happen in the future. No man could know it; therefore, no man can do this. But they are fools enough to try . . . Mr. Henderson, I thank you for the word."

The whole courtroom smiled.

Colonel Braxton continued, as in a friendly monologue to an auditor that pleased him:

"I have a feeling that every event that happens is in some manner connected with every other event that happens; that they are all intricately enmeshed together. You can't tear the threads out and tie in others. The broken ends will show. The knots will show. And so, Mr. Henderson, as you so admirably put it, no man ought to be fool enough to try. He will do too much or he will do too little. He will forget something, or he will overlook something that will show his facts to be fictitious."

The prosecuting attorney interrupted:

"What's all this got to do with the case, Colonel?"

The big attorney paused and considered his opponent for a moment, as though he had only now become aware of his presence.

"Well, Alfred," he said, "it isn't altogether a didactic lecture. It's preliminary to the calling of a witness."

The prosecuting attorney smiled, as with an air of victory. "So you are changing horses in the stream, Colonel; I thought you were not going to make a defense."

"Alfred," replied the lawyer, regarding the attorney as with a new and intriguing interest, "where did you get that extraordinary idea?"

"I got it from your opening statement to the jury." The man was pricked by the irony in his opponent's voice and manner. "You said that you would introduce no evidence on behalf of the prisoner . . . If the prisoner was cleared, he would have to be cleared on the testimony of the witnesses for the State—isn't that what you said?"

"That," replied Colonel Braxton gently, "is precisely what I said."

This veiled sarcastic handling got the prosecuting attorney into a bit of temper.

"Then I'd stick to it, and not call a witness for the prisoner."

"I am not going to call a witness for the prisoner," replied Colonel Braxton, "I am going to call one of the State's witnesses."

"What one of the State's witnesses?"

"One you forgot," replied Colonel Braxton.

He beckoned to a big youth sitting on a step below the judge's bench, and sent him out of the courtroom.

The judge, observing the act, addressed him:

"Do you want a subpoena for the witness, Colonel?"

Colonel Braxton looked up at him.

"Your Honor," he said, "this witness will testify without the compelling authority of a writ of subpoena."

The interest in the courtroom quickened. The clerk of the court fingered the rosebud in his coat and reflected on this inexplicable defense. What witness was it that Colonel Braxton was about to call? What witness had the prosecution forgotten? The whole extent of the State's case was known to him.

The sheriff remained in the witness chair. He had not been directed to stand aside. The attorney for the prisoner seemed for a moment in reflection, as though considering whether he had any further query to put. He moved the articles aimlessly on the table before him, pushing them about with his fingers.

Finally, when he addressed the witness, it was with the stock query common in all criminal trials; the stereotyped questions with which the witness in such a case is usually dismissed. Colonel Braxton seemed to have no particular concern about these concluding questions. Did he add them to cover the interval while he waited for the forgotten witness to appear?

"Mr. Henderson," he said, "every part of your testimony is quite as true as every other part, isn't it?"

The witness replied at once, with no equivocation. "It is," he said. "Every statement that I have made is precisely the truth."

Colonel Braxton looked vaguely about the courtroom.

"You shouted in the closet and kicked on the door—it's all the truth?"

The witness assumed an air of indignation at this repeated query.

"Yes, it's the truth," he said, "it's all the truth. Why do you ask the same question over? I—"

But he was interrupted.

While his mouth opened on the unfinished sentence, a strange thing occurred. The swinging doors to the courtroom opened and the big youth and another entered, bearing a long white object between them. They came in slowly and in silence, as though they bore the wraith of a dead man on a cooling-board.

The two men came on with their burden, down the central aisle, and placed it upright against the wall before the jury and the amazed sheriff.

The judge, astonished, put the query that was in every mouth: "What is this?"

And Colonel Braxton, standing before the sheriff, big, dominant, as though he barred the way against him to some expected exit, answered.

"That, Your Honor," he said, "is the forgotten witness!"

Then, as everybody in the courtroom came to realize what this white, silent thing, standing against the wall, was, he returned to his chair; to his relaxed manner; to his listless interest in events.

"It's the door," he drawled, "to the closet in which the sheriff was locked by the robber . . . It's the door the sheriff kicked with his heavy shoes in his efforts to escape . . . You will notice that *there isn't the faintest scratch of a mark on the white paint!*"

He paused.

The great, obvious fact stood out incontrovertibly to the eye.

Then his voice continued:

"You see, Your Honor, Mr. Henderson went a bit too far in fabricating his events. If he had been content to stop with the assertion that he shouted in the closet, we could not have refuted him. But when he said that he also kicked the door, he overreached himself, for, behold the door, with its painted surface unmarked, appears in this circuit court to prove the man a liar!

"And now," he added, "if Your Honor will send for the stolen money, I think that the prisoner can be dismissed."

"The stolen money!" echoed the judge. "You know where it is?"

"I have a theory," the listless voice went on. "When the police lifted the rug in the sitting-room of the sheriff's house to examine it for footprints, I noticed that a board in the floor was not nailed down . . . It might be under that board. Don't you think so, Mr. Henderson?"

On the sheriff's white, guilt-stricken face was written the answer.

Ellery Queen

Cold Money

The Hotel Chancellor in midtown New York is not likely to forget the two visits of Mr. Philly Mullane. The first time Mullane registered at the Chancellor, under the name of Winston F. Parker, an alert house detective spotted him and, under the personal direction of Inspector Richard Queen, Philly was carried out of Room 913, struggling and in bracelets, to be tried, convicted, and sentenced to ten years for a Manhattan payroll robbery. The second time—ten years later—he was carried out neither struggling nor manacled, inasmuch as he was dead.

The case really began on a blacktop county road east of Route 7 in the Berkshire foothills, when Mullane sapped his pal Mikie the Waiter over the left ear and tossed him out of their getaway car, thereby increasing the split from thirds to halves. Mullane was an even better mathematician than that. Five miles farther north, he administered the same treatment to Pittsburgh Patience, which left him sole proprietor of their $62,000 haul. Mikie and Patience were picked up by Connecticut state police; the Waiter was speechless with rage, which could not be said of Patience, a lady of inspired vocabulary. Three weeks later Philly Mullane was smoked out of the Chancellor room where he had been sulking. The payroll was absent—in those three weeks the $62,000 had vanished. He had not blown the money in, for the checkback showed that he had made for the New York hotel immediately on ditching his confederates.

Question: Where had Mullane stashed the loot?

Everyone wanted to know. In the case of Pittsburgh Patience and Mikie the Waiter, their thirst for information had to go unsatisfied; they drew ten-year sentences, too. As for the police, for all their success in locating the stolen banknotes, they might as well have gone up the river with Mullane and his ex-associates.

They tried everything on Mullane, including a planted cellmate. But Mullane wasn't talking, even in his sleep.

The closest they came was in the sixth year of Philly's stretch. In July of that year, in the exercise yard, Philly let out a yell that he had been stabbed, and he collapsed. The weapon which had stabbed him was the greatest killer of all, and when he regained consciousness in the infirmary the prison doctor named it for him. It was his heart.

"My pumper?" Mullane said incredulously. "Me?" And then he looked scared, and he said in a weak voice, "I want to see the Warden."

The Warden came at once; he was a kindly man who wished his rough flock well, but he had been waiting for this moment for over five years. "Yes, Mullane?" the Warden said.

"About that sixty-two grand," whispered Philly.

"Yes, Mullane?" the Warden said.

"I never been a boy scout, God knows—"

"Yes, He does," said the Warden.

"That's what I mean, Warden. I mean, I figure I can't take it with me, and maybe I can cut down on that book He's keeping on me upstairs. I guess I better tell you where I stashed that dough. The doc tells me I'm going to die—"

But the prison doctor was young and full of Truth and other ideals, and he interrupted indignantly, "I said *eventually*. Not now, Mullane! You may not get another attack for years."

"Oh?" said Philly in a remarkably strong voice. "Then what am I worried about?" And he grinned at the Warden and turned his face to the wall.

The Warden could have kicked both of them.

So everybody settled back to more waiting.

What they were waiting for was Mullane's release. They had plenty of time—the law, Patience, the Waiter, and Mullane most of all. Having behaved themselves as guests of the state, Patience and Mikie got out in something over seven years, and they went their respective ways. Mullane's silence stuck him for the limit.

The day he was released the Warden said to him, "Mullane, you'll never get away with that money. And even if you should, nobody ever gets anything out of money that doesn't belong to him."

"I figure I've earned it, Warden," said Philly Mullane with a crooked smile. "At that, it only comes to a measly sixty-two hundred a year."

"What about your heart?"

"Ah, that doc was from hunger."

Of course, they put a twenty-four hour tail on him. And they lost him. Two headquarters detectives were demoted because of it. When he was found ten days later he had been dead about fifteen minutes.

A long memory and a smart bit of skull work on the part of one of the Hotel Chancellor's house dicks, Blauvelt, were responsible for the quick discovery of the body. Blauvelt had been on a two-week vacation. When he returned to duty, the hotel staff was yakking about a guest named Worth who had checked in nine days before and had not left his room since. The only ones who had seen him were the room service people—he had all his meals served in his rooms—the chambermaid, and a few bellboys. They reported that he kept his door not only locked day and night, but on the chain. The room was 913, and a desk clerk recalled that Worth had insisted on that room and no other.

"I only came on the job this morning, so I haven't been able to get a look at him," Blauvelt said over the phone to police headquarters, "but from what they tell me, except for a change in the color of his hair and a couple inches in height, which could be elevators, he answers the description. Inspector, if this Worth ain't Philly Mullane hiding out I'll get me a job in the Sanitation Department."

"Nice going, Blauvelt. We'll be right over." Inspector Queen hung up and said admiringly, "Same hotel, same room. You've got to hand it to him—" But then he stopped.

"Exactly," said Ellery, who had been listening on the extension. He remembered the case as one of his father's pet bogies. "It's too smart. Unless that's where he hid the money in the first place."

"But Ellery, that room at the Chancellor was searched when we grabbed Mullane off ten years ago!"

"Not the super deluxe type search I recommend in such cases," mourned Ellery. "Remember how cleverly Mullane led you to believe he'd buried the money during his getaway? He had you digging up half the cornfields in Connecticut! Dad, it's been in that room at the Chancellor all this time."

So they went up to the Chancellor with Sergeant Velie and a couple of precinct men and Blauvelt unlocked the door of 913 with his passkey. The door was off the chain, the reason for which became immediately clear when they saw that Mullane had been murdered.

The precinct men went scurrying, and Sergeant Velie got busy on the phone.

Mullane was in a chair at the writing desk in a corner of the bedroom, his face and arms on the desk. He had been cracked on the back of the head with some heavy object which a quick examination told them was not there. From the contusion, the Inspector guessed it had been a hammer.

"But this wound doesn't look as if the blow was hard enough to have caused death," frowned Ellery.

"Mullane's ticker went bad in prison," said his father. "Bad heart, hard blow—curtains."

Ellery looked around. The room had not yet been made up for the day and it was in some disorder. He began to amble, mumbling to himself. "Wouldn't have hidden it in a piece of furniture—they're moved around in hotels all the time... In *nothing* removable... Walls and ceiling tinted plaster—would mean replastering, duplicating the tint... too risky..." He got down on all fours and began crawling about.

The Inspector was at the desk. "Blauvelt. Help me sit him up."

The body was still warm and the house detective had to hold on to keep it from collapsing. Mullane's dressing-gown sleeves and collar were a mess of wet blue ink. He had been writing a note of some kind and in falling forward had upset the ink bottle.

The Inspector looked around for a towel, but there was none in the bedroom.

"Velie, get some used towels from the bathroom. Maybe we can sop up enough of this wet ink to make out what Mullane was writing!"

"No used towels in here," called the Sergeant from the bathroom.

"Then get clean ones, you dimwit!"

Velie came out with some unused towels, and Inspector Queen went to work on the note. He worked for five minutes, delicately. But all he could show for it were three shaky words: *Money hidden in* ... The rest was blotted beyond recall.

"Why would he write where the dough was stashed?" wondered Blauvelt, continuing to embrace Mullane.

"Because after he got up this morning," snapped the Inspector, "he must have felt a heart attack coming on. When he got his attack in prison, he almost spilled to the Warden. This time it probably scared him so much he sat right down and wrote the hiding place of the money. Then he slumped forward, unconscious or dying. Killer got in—maybe thought he was dozing—finished him off, read the note before the ink soaked all the way in—"

"And found the loot," said Ellery from under the bed. "It's gone, Dad."

So Blauvelt let Mullane go and they all got down on their faces and saw the neat hole in the floor, under the rug, with an artistically fitted removable board, where the payroll had lain for ten years. The hole was empty.

When they got to their feet, Ellery was no longer with them. He was stooping over what was left of Mullane.

"Ellery, what are you *doing?*" exclaimed Inspector Queen.

Even Sergeant Velie looked repelled. Ellery was running his palm over the dead man's cheeks with tenderness.

"Nice," he said.

"Nice!"

"Nice smooth shave he took this morning. You can still see traces of talcum powder."

Blauvelt's mouth was open.

"You want to learn something, Blauvelt?" said Sergeant Velie with a nudge that doubled the house detective up. "Now it gives a great big deduction."

"Certainly does," grinned Ellery. "It gives the killer of Philly Mullane."

The Sergeant opened his mouth.

"Shut up, Velie," said Inspector Queen. "Well?"

"Because if Mullane shaved this morning," asked Ellery, "where did he do it, Sergeant?"

"Okay, I bite," said Velie. "Where?"

"Where every man shaves, Sergeant—in the bathroom. Ever shave in the bathroom without using a towel?"

"All right, Ellery, so Mullane used a towel," said the Inspector impatiently. "So what?"

"So where is it? When you asked Velie to get one from the bathroom to sop up the ink, Dad, he said *there were no used towels in there.* And there are no towels at all in the bedroom here. What did Velie bring you from the bathroom? Some *unused* towels. In other words, after Mullane shaved this morning, *someone took the dirty towels away and replaced them with clean ones.* And this is a hotel, and Mullane, who always kept the door on the chain, had obviously let someone in . . ."

"The chambermaid!"

"Has to be. Mullane let the chambermaid in this morning, as usual, she got to work in the bathroom—and she never did get to the bedroom, as you can see. Why? It can only be because while she was cleaning up in the bathroom Mullane got his heart attack!

"It was the chambermaid who struck Mullane on the back of the head with the hammer she'd brought in with her—waiting for a chance to use it, as she's probably waited every morning for the last nine days.

"It was the chambermaid who read Mullane's message and scooped the money out of the hole in the floor."

"But to have come in with a hammer—she must have planned this, she must have known who he was!"

"Right, Dad. So I think you'll find, when you catch up with her, that the homicidal chambermaid is your old friend, Pittsburgh Patience, with a few alterations in her appearance. Patience suspected all along where Mullane had hidden the money, and as soon as she was out of stir three years ago she got herself a job on the Chancellor housekeeping staff . . . and waited for her old pal to show up!"

Barry Perowne

Knowing What I Know Now

A porter gave me a hand to lift the trunk into the luggage van. It was an ordinary brown trunk, fibre with wooden battens, like a million others. It was heavy.

"Blimey, what you got in here?" said the porter. "A body?"

I managed a laugh of sorts, and I hoped it sounded all right to him. It had a queer ring in my own ears. But he didn't seem to notice anything.

The trunk bore a label with the name *Frank Venhold,* an address, and the direction *Passenger to London.* Name and address were both fake, and *Passenger to Hell* would have been a truer direction. I had no intention of going all the way to London with that trunk. I never wanted to see it again.

I tipped the porter and—the luggage van being placed about the middle of the train—walked along the platform toward the rear. The doors of the coaches stood open. There were the usual goodbye groups talking at the doors, the usual station smells, the usual hollow, reverberant station noises. All was as usual, yet all seemed to me subtly different. I felt as though I were walking along the bed of a chasm, with strange echoes beating back at me from soaring rock walls that inclined toward each other. But when, instinctively, I glanced up, there were only spiderwork girders supporting the station roof of dingy glass spattered with rain.

I turned the collar of my trenchcoat higher, jerked my hatbrim lower over my eyes. I kept a sharp watch on the station entrances. I felt cold to the marrow. My teeth wanted to chatter; my jaws ached from the tension of keeping them clamped. I was poised for a sudden pouring in at any second of burly figures in policeman's blue. I stood outside the door of a coach, my hands clenched hard, deep in my pockets. The station clock looked like a white, enigmatic moon. Its hands seemed painted on it, fixed in an eternal immobility, which it seemed to impose over the whole station. So that, as I looked at the clock face, the people around me, glimpsed out of the corners of my eyes, seemed arrested in mid-stride, held motionless, struck still as headstones. Until the slight, visible jerk of the minute hand broke

271

the spell, loosed the bustle around me, a hiss of released steam, the hollow slam of a door.

Along the platform a guard came walking, whistle between his teeth, holding a green flag furled in one hand, consulting a watch he held in the other. I turned and stepped into the corridor of the train. The compartment before me held three middle-aged women and a small boy with his head in a comic book. I sat down in a corner seat on the corridor side, facing forward, my back to the luggage van with the trunk in it. A jerk and a clanking ran through the train from coach to coach, like a scale played on a cracked xylophone, and the platform sights began to slide away. The dirty glass roof went from overhead, letting in the grey, watery daylight of late afternoon. The train gathered speed and I felt the trunk following me.

I had to force myself to sit there, staring from the window. The gloomy suburbs of the midland town died among green, flat meadows, swollen brown brooks with humped bridges, and lines of leaning willow trees.

We were on our way, the trunk and I. So far, so good. I needed a cigarette badly, but I was afraid to take my hands out of my pockets; I knew they'd shake, and I was afraid the women or the kid would notice.

Then I heard compartment doors being slid open, one after another, all along the coach, and coming closer. It sounded to me as though somebody was being looked for, and I held my breath, strained my ears, trying to hear what was going on above the metallic *tat-tat-tat-too, tat-tat-tat-too* of the train. Suddenly a white-jacketed steward appeared in the corridor. He slid back the door of the compartment, put in his head.

"First dinner now being served," he said. "Take your places for dinner, please."

His call went on along the train, and I breathed again. Two of the women got up and left the compartment, turning to the right along the corridor. I had to have that cigarette. The kid was looking at me unwinkingly over the top of his comic. Kids sense things. I got up, stepped into the corridor, slid the door shut, lighted a cigarette. Twilight mist had quenched meadows and willows. The lights had come on. People squeezed past me along the corridor, going to dinner. It occurred to me that they must have to pass through the luggage van to get to the dining-car. If so, I might have a look at the trunk, just make sure it was all right so far. I didn't want anything to happen prematurely.

People had stopped squeezing past me, but I waited till the steward had returned, on his way to the dining-car, then I turned and followed him. Three coaches along, I came to the luggage van. I stopped at the edge of the slightly rocking steel footplate connecting the coaches. I peered into the van, but it was dimly lighted and I couldn't spot the trunk right off. I looked back along the corridor. No one was in sight. I stepped into the luggage van. Nobody here, either—just a smell of kippers from a stack of flat wooden crates, and some bicycles, a folding perambulator, an invalid chair, and four trunks. Two of them were exactly alike, and a moment of panic pumped the blood into my head, because I wasn't sure which was mine.

I had to stoop and glance at the label on the nearer one. The label read *G. N. Trevelyan, Passenger to London,* no address given. My trunk was right alongside. They were identical; they were like thousands and thousands of the same make. A thought came to me.

My plan had been to leave the train at Oxford, the first stop, and let the trunk labeled *Frank Venhold* go on to London, be put in the Unclaimed Luggage Office. Only, something had been nagging at the back of my mind—the thought that the porter who had helped me get the trunk into the van might be a luggage porter who traveled with the train, and he might see me leaving it at Oxford, might chase after me, shouting, "Your trunk, sir!"

Now, as I looked at this trunk labeled *G. N. Trevelyan,* I had a better idea. That label was corrugated; the gum on it must have been dry; it looked as if it might peel off easily. I tried it, and it came right off in my hand. A piston thumped in my chest. I glanced around quickly. On a small counter in a corner of the van were various pink and yellow forms, a hurricane lantern with red glass, a stack of labels, and a gluepot with a filthy brush sticking out of it.

I tell you, the thing was set up for me. *Knowing what I know now, I ask myself by what, by whom? By God? By the Devil? By Fate? By mere Chance? What is the riddle of human life? Why are we here?*

It took me thirty seconds to stick the Trevelyan label over the Venhold label, and to write a new Venhold label and stick it on the Trevelyan trunk. Then I walked back along the corridor. I hadn't really had much hope before. Now, I had hope. I was exultant. I didn't want to go back to the compartment where that wretched kid with the knowing eyes was. I looked into the other compartments I passed, but the nearest I found to an empty was one with just a girl in it. Her eyes were closed. Apparently she was asleep. I slid the door back quietly, sat down in the corner seat farthest from her. I was facing the front of the train. *Tat-tat-tat-too, tat-tat-tat-too.* I could feel the two trunks sliding along behind me through the night. But I felt better, easier. I put my hat on the rack. I undid the belt of my trenchcoat. I could see faintly in the window the reflection of my face against the mist and dark outside. It was a stranger's face to me—the pale, sharpish face of a man of thirty-five, with black hair brushed back with the sheen of enamel from a high, sloping forehead.

I dropped my cigarette, trod on it, and was taking another from my packet when I felt the girl watching me. I met her eyes. They were grey, but looked dark, the pupils were so large. There was something queer about those eyes, though she was an attractive girl, with amber hair done in this short, modern way with a kind of fringe or bang, or whatever they call it. She looked pale, hunched there in her corner, her hands in the pockets of a loose, light, hip-length jacket with a high collar turned up like a frame for her head. She had neat ankles and low-heeled grey-suède walking-shoes, rather pretty.

I offered her a cigarette. She hesitated, her pupils contracting oddly, making her eyes look light and shallow. Then she leaned forward, took a cigarette from the packet I held out, and I noticed her hands, rather square, with long but strong fingers—imaginative hands—the nails only faintly coral-tinted. I held my lighter for her.

"Thanks," she said, and her eyes came close, looking at me, as she leaned forward to dip her cigarette in the flame.

That continual dilating and contracting of the pupils of the eyes—I had read somewhere that it is called the "hippus" and is supposed to be a sign of nervous and emotional instability. As though in confirmation of my thought, I saw her draw her shoulders together in an odd little movement, as though a kind of shudder had gone through her. I didn't like it.

"What's the matter with you?" I said. "Cold?"

"It's all right." She leaned back in her seat. "Just a goose walked over my grave."

I didn't like her saying that, either. I felt those two trunks pouring along like hounds on my heels through the mist and darkness. I didn't answer her. But she went on watching me with those witch's eyes.

"How do *you* account for that goose-over-your-grave feeling?" she said suddenly. "What's *your* theory about it?"

"I've got none," I said. "I'm not a psychiatrist."

"What are you?" she said.

I didn't like her talk. I felt those trunks sliding up closer to my back.

To shut her up—she sounded like one of these intellectual girls to me—I said, "Me? I'm a medievalist."

I couldn't tell whether she believed it, but again I saw that queer contraction and dilation of her pupils.

"Perhaps they knew more than the psychiatrists do," she said, "more of the—the essential truth, the things of—the things of the spirit—the *mysterious* things."

"Are you a student of—the mysterious things?" I said sardonically.

"I'm a student," she said, "an art student. I've just won a scholarship in London. That's where I'm going now."

An art student, I thought. Maybe that accounted both for the good hands and for the emotional instability hinted at by the curious, quite beautiful eyes. She interested me in spite of the trunks that slid along at my back.

She had a slight accent, and I said, "You aren't English, are you?"

"I gew up in Canada," she said, and again I saw that odd tightening of her shoulders, as though to a fleeting chill. "I remember once—"

She stopped. She drew deeply on her cigarette, watching the smoke drift up to the cluster of lightbulbs under the bell-glass. On the rack above her head were a small, soft, green hat and a little overnight bag, faintly vibrant to the monotonous *tat-tat-tat-too* rhythm of the wheels.

"I was thinking, as you came in," she said, "of something that happened to me once in Canada. I was thinking of it because it happened so far away—thousands of miles away—and so long ago. I was thinking of it because I have this scholarship, because I'm going to London, because my real life is just beginning—because," she said, with a flash of vehemence, "I can't forget it, and I wish to heaven I could! But it's always there, following me—waiting." She looked at me with those lovely, disquieting eyes. "Have you ever had that feeling?" she said. "Surely everyone must have had it—in some form. The feeling that something is waiting for you, something—oh, unimaginable, terrible, whether physical or psychical I don't know, but something inevitable, not to be eluded or escaped, just waiting for you, coldly and very patiently—in an appointed place?"

"Certainly, everyone's had the feeling," I said. I could feel my brow coldly damp. "You're talking of Death, a date we all have—only, we don't harp on it."

"My father called it by a different name," she said. "He called it Failure. But that isn't the answer, either. It's—" She frowned for a moment at her cigarette, then looked at me again. "It was in Canada," she said. "My father and I were living in a fair-sized town, in a rather old house, a red-brick Victorian house, on the outskirts. My father was a widower. He had a poorly paid office job, but he owned the house—on mortgage—and he rented off the upper floors as apartments. We lived below, in a kind of semi-basement. He always referred to it as 'the garden apartment.' Poor darling, I loved him dearly, but I have to admit he was—ineffectual, unlucky—oh, I don't know. Only I used to wonder, even as a kid, why nothing ever seemed to go right for him—for us. *Little* things! You know? He tried so hard. But if he bought new furniture, for instance, it would seem to get shabby and gloomy quicker than other people's furniture. He would dig and dig in the garden, but where the neighbors' gardens were neat, with lawns and flowers, nothing ever flourished in ours but weeds. Horrible green weeds! Bad luck seemed to follow us. It seemed as though there never could be any escape from it. It was like a quagmire. I used to feel it was something to do with the house, that great, hideous barn of a house. I began to think there never could be any hope for us as long as we stayed there. I *hated* Number 15 George Street."

I wished she would stop. I didn't like this story. The train beat out its monotonous rhythm; the things on the rack vibrated. Our faces were reflected faintly in the windows against the mist and the night. I wished she would stop.

"One rainy afternoon when I was about ten years old," she said, "I walked home from school alone. That afternoon the teacher had been showing us some pictures of desert country, cactus country, dry and wide spaces full of clean, varied colors. Going home, walking home alone with my books, I was wearing rubbers, and a rubber raincoat with a hood. You know how wet rubber feels. Rain, rain, rain! I loathed it. I loathed the puddled lawns, the dripping trees, the dun sky. I loathed all wet, green, slimy things."

She dropped her cigarette, put her neat suède shoe on it. I was trying not to listen. The trunks were following me.

"I always got home before my father," she said. "There was a woman who came in to clean the place for us, leave the kitchen stove burning, everything ready for father and I to cook dinner for ourselves. I had my own key." She was biting her lower lip; her strange, shallow, changing eyes looked through me. "I didn't want to go into the house that afternoon, I hated it so much. I didn't want to set foot in it. I don't know how I made myself walk up the path and unlock that hateful old green-painted front door. It opened into a passage with coats hanging on a row of hooks to the right. On the left was the door of our living room, beyond that the door of father's bedroom. Farther on, stone steps—four stone steps—led down to a kind of flagstoned lobby, off which, on the right, opened a door to a side street. On the left, the wall of the lobby was glass-paned, like a conservatory, with a door opening into the muddy garden. Across the lobby was the kitchen."

Her breathing was quick and shallow; I could scarcely hear her voice.

"I went down the four steps into the lobby," she said, her strange eyes seeing it. "The lobby was full of grey daylight filtering through the filthy panes. I could hear the rain spattering against them. I kicked off my rubbers, as I always did, and hung up my rubber coat on a shelf, meant for flowerpots, which ran the length of the panes. I looked at the water dripping from my coat, making a pool, trickling across the flagstones. I looked out through the panes at tall sunflowers and rank stinging-nettles. The sunflowers were over, their heads hanging heavy and brown and sodden, rocking a little in the rain. The nettles were high and green, like a forest. There never were such nettles anywhere else. Their veined, hairy leaves were pressing up against the glass. They were as tall as I was. I hated to look at them. I turned to go into the kitchen."

She bit at her lips. They were pale pink where her teeth had scraped the lipstick from them. Her pupils were greatly dilated.

"The kitchen door stood open," she said. "It opened inward, to the right. The kitchen was dark except for the red glow of the coal fire through the bars of the old-fashioned stove. There was an old wicker armchair standing obliquely facing the stove, and in the chair—on the worn cushion that always had a wad of old newspapers crammed under it—was our cat. Its forepaws were folded under its chest. I could see the firelight reflected in its eyes. It seemed to be waiting.

"There was an old alarm clock, with a loud, tinny tick, on the shelf over the stove. I could hear the clock going tick-tick-tick, loudly and questioningly. And I couldn't move. My mouth was dry. I wanted desperately to back away, turn, run. I couldn't move. Only, I felt as though something were drawing me *forward*. But I didn't move at all. I knew that in there, in the shadows behind the open door, there was—something. I don't know. It had no shape. Only, cold came from it. It was waiting. And the clock ticked, the cat watched in the firelight, the rain spattered at the windows, the nettles pressed against the panes, the sunflowers rocked their dead, sodden heads. I don't know—I don't know—"

Suddenly she pressed her hands to her face. She cried as though her heart would break. Never had I seen or imagined such grief. The tragedy of the ages, of the unknown soul of Man and the dim beginnings of life in the swamps of the tree-ferns, was in that brief paroxysm.

"Here," I said roughly, after a minute.

She groped blindly for the handkerchief I held out to her. She wiped her eyes. She blew her nose. I could hear the shudder in her breathing. I looked toward the window, saw the ghost of my own face floating there. I thought of the trunks. I knew, now, that I shouldn't get away. I knew there was no escape for me. Anywhere. I knew they'd get me. I don't know how I knew, but I knew.

The girl spoke.

"When I came to myself," she said, "I was out in the street, in the rain, running; and had run full tilt into a man. I felt his arms go round me, and heard my father's voice, 'Why, Gina, Gina, what's this? What's the matter?' I couldn't tell him, not then. I could only say that I'd never go back into that house—never."

She was silent for a moment.

"He never made me go back," she said. "We went to a hotel for the night. I tried to tell him what had happened. He sat on the edge of my bed, listening. Did I say he was a small man? A small man, with kind eyes. He looked so tragic, so beaten, as he listened. 'Failure,' I heard him murmur—'Failure was there.' I've thought about that so much since. He spoke as though of some projection of himself, of some—some abstraction made carnate, waiting in the house. It was almost as though—as though he spoke of some *hump,* not on his own back, but which he feared he had prepared for mine. For me, whom he loved."

She shook her head. "But that isn't the answer. I've thought so much. I've dreamed those dreadful seconds, that eternity, so many times, since—the nettles, the sunflowers, the rain, the pool dark on the flagstones, the open door, the fire red between the bars, the watching cat with the shine in its eyes—all the room, waiting for me, unchanged, and the thing waiting in the room, and the clock ticking loudly. My father died within the year. He had relations in England—in the Midlands here—and they sent for me. And I was glad as the miles became hundreds, the hundreds became thousands, between me and the waiting room. *But I know it's still there.*"

She looked at me as though asking my opinion, my help; but I had nothing to say to her. The train broke its rhythm, began to clatter over switchpoints. She glanced at my handkerchief, balled in her hand. Then she made a movement—somehow ineffectual, as her father's movements might have been, I imagined—as though to reach down her small grip from the rack, probably to take out a clean handkerchief. I rose and lifted the grip down for her.

I tell you, knowing what I know now—yet, what do I know, or any of us?— I tell you, this whole thing was set up for us. By what design of God or the Devil or Destiny or mere Chance had I chosen this girl's compartment?

As I lifted down the grip for her, I saw for the first time the label on it: *G. N. Trevelyan, Passenger to London.*

The train was slowing. Platform lights slid by, flickering, outside the misted windows. An amplified voice was intoning: *"Oxford—Oxford.* The train now arriving at Platform Four is the train to Paddington."

I muttered, "I'll be back."

But as I stepped out into the corridor, slid shut the door after me, I had no intention of going back. Oxford was where I had planned to leave the train. Yet as it pulled up with a jerk and that cracked xylophone-scale clangor, the girl was in my mind, and the trunks.

It crossed my mind that, though there was not one single Commandment that I had not broken in my futile life, all might yet be forgiven me, at the unknown end of all things, if only I changed those labels back.

I would have done it, too. I would have done it. *But I tell you, this thing was set up.* For when I rubbed the mist from the window and stooped to peer out, the dimly lighted platform was swarming with police.

I knew who they were after, and I forgot the girl. I panicked. I hurried along the corridor to the end of the coach, where there was a door on the tracks side. The door was locked. I let down the window.

There were only two policemen on the opposite platform. Chancing them, I put one foot through the open window, pulled the other foot after it, leaped from the step to the tracks. Under the loom of the train, I walked briskly toward the front, stepping from tie to tie, hoping that, if seen, I might be taken for the man with the hammer who checks on the wheels and couplings. I reached the locomotive, hissing a white cloud of steam from its belly, and glaring red from its cab, when a shout told me I'd been spotted.

I ran for it. I kept to the tracks, leaping from tie to tie. I came to an iron bridge. I knew it was the bridge over the canal. I knew Oxford; I was educated here; I might have made a different life for myself—if I'd been a different man. I'd had chances. If I'd taken them, I might never have known this hour of flight—this insane moment of clawing like an ape over the iron rim of the bridge, hanging by my hands, feeling new tar sticky under my fingers, smelling its strong, aseptic smell close to my nose. I dropped, landing on all fours on a cindered towpath.

I turned and ran.

I was a good distance away, standing—breathing hard, trying to think—between two gasometers of the Gasworks, in its galvanized iron enclosure, when I heard the train whistling. Through the mist and darkness, I saw the smokestack belching a red, pulsing glare with short, quick respirations. I heard the grind of the wheels. I saw the long line of lighted windows go by.

I knew I ought to have changed back those labels.

I kept thinking about them, about the train, about Gina Trevelyan, about what was in the luggage van. I thought Gina somehow an appealing name. I thought about her strange eyes, her good hands, the look of vulnerability about her. She seemed, alone in that compartment with the wheels going *tat-tat-tat-too,* on and on toward London, terribly solitary and defenseless to me. I thought of her as a little girl with braids, wearing rubbers, and a rubber raincoat with a hood—all sleek with rain—coming home alone from school to that great, grim, red-brick house thousands of miles away in Canada. I felt terribly sorry for her. I wanted to sit down, here in the dark, and weep for her.

Somehow, the strength had gone out from me. Guilt about those labels—not about anything I'd done before that—robbed me of the will to fight on, to live.

Knowing what I know now, I can be in two places at once. I can be me on the run and I can be Gina in the train. Take me first . . .

I found I had been walking and walking as I thought about her, and I had come to the grey stone hump of Folly Bridge. The bridge lights glimmered down on the river and on the college barges.

I went on up the lighted slope of St. Aldate's. There was nobody about—just here and there an undergraduate riding a bicycle with his gown wound about his neck like a muffler. Coming on up toward Tom Tower and Carfax, I thought of St. Ebbe's. I thought perhaps I might have a chance in that maze of ancient, squalid alleys. I took to the alleys behind Pembroke College. My mind was with Gina in the train. My own plight had become unreal to me. I knew I ought to have changed back those labels. I was afraid. I had never been so afraid. I was a fugitive in dark and misty alleys, and I was afraid of the dark.

Perhaps I wanted to be caught rather than be alone in the dark. Anyway, I saw lights and figures and heard trumpets. I went with the figures into a plain, varnished hall, glaringly lighted with naked gas-mantels. It was a Salvation Army chapel. I stood at the back of the hall, behind the rows of plain wooden chairs. The people were singing *Onward, Christian Soldiers*. I wanted to sing with them, but I couldn't. I kept thinking of Gina, and the two trunks, and I was so sorry for her that the tears began to stream down my cheeks.

I felt a hand on my shoulder.

"All right, Caird," a voice said, "better come quietly."

I saw the faces of the congregation turn toward me, in the hard, white glare. I saw the women's faces framed in their bonnets, and the work-worn faces of the men. There was understanding in their eyes, and compassion. They were good, kind people.

I was started on my way to London, handcuffed, under escort, by the next train up. Gina's would not yet have reached Paddington. I realized that these policemen knew nothing about the trunk originally marked *Frank Venhold*, but now marked *G. N. Trevelyan*. I wanted to tell them about the trunk in case something could be done to warn her. But since they didn't know about the trunk, there might yet be some hope for me, and I couldn't bring myself to speak the words that would hang me.

Instead I asked, "What time is it?"

They told me. I knew her train must be pulling into Paddington . . .

Knowing what I know now—the questions that I've asked and that have been answered for me—I can be with Gina. I can follow her as if she led me by the hand . . .

As her train drew into the great, dingy, echoing London terminus, Gina drew on her small, soft, green hat. Her little overnight bag lay on the seat beside her. She wondered what had happened to the man in the trenchcoat, the man who had not returned.

She got hold of a porter at Paddington.

"I've a trunk in the luggage van," she said. "The name's Trevelyan."

"Taking a taxi, Miss?" said the porter. "All right, you go and get a place in the taxi line an' I'll bring your trunk."

He brought it, wheeling it on a trolley.

"Strike me, Miss," he said, as he uptilted the trunk into the small luggage-compartment beside the taxi-driver, "what you got in here? The gold reserve?"

"All my worldly belongings," said Gina. "It's my books that weigh so heavy. I'm sorry about that."

"S'all right," said the porter, strapping the trunk, upended, into place.

"Where to, Miss?" said the taxi-driver.

Gina told him to cruise. She wanted to find a moderate-priced hotel.

She gazed from the window as the taxi left the station. The night was very misty; every light had its nimbus; muffled forms passed to and fro before the shop windows. The driver, an elbow resting on the trunk beside him, slowed down before hotel after hotel, looking round at her inquiringly.

"No," she said, shaking her head.

Either they looked too dear or too dirty. But as they passed along a narrow, quiet little street—the only shop in it a small teashop with a steamy window dimly shining through the mist—she caught a glimpse of the word VACANCIES on a sign on some iron railings. She leaned forward quickly to tap on the glass behind the driver's head.

Gina got out, asked the driver to wait. She ran up the steps and rang the bell. After a minute, the door was opened and an untidy, thin woman stood outlined against the dim light of a passage.

"I'm looking for lodgings," said Gina. "I wonder if you have a bed-sitting-room among your vacancies?"

The woman stood aside. "Come in. You can see what I've got."

She preceded Gina up four narrow flights of worn-carpeted stairs to a room which was an attic but fairly large and tolerably clean.

"It has a skylight," said Gina. "That's rather an advantage, because I paint. What is the rent, please?"

They arranged terms. Gina paid a week in advance, and they went downstairs.

"I've got a trunk in the taxi," said Gina. "It's rather heavy—"

The woman turned and called down some stairs, "Arthur!"

A youngish but fat and balding man in his braces and slippers came up the stairs, grinning at Gina inanely. He and the taxi-driver lifted the trunk in, dumped it down in the passage. Gina paid the driver and thanked him, and he went away. The landlady shut the front door, turned and looked at the trunk.

"Arthur'll never get that up all them stairs," she said. "You'd better keep it down in our passage and take up what you want bit by bit."

"I'll do that," said Gina.

"My name's Mrs. Coe," said the woman. "Will you be wanting anything further? Me an' Arthur goes across to the local about now."

"There's nothing I need now, thank you," said Gina.

"Then good night to you."

"Good night, Mrs. Coe."

Gina went up to her room, and, soon after, heard the front door slam . . .

Knowing what I know now, I realize that, at about this time, I was stepping into the neat, closed, dark-blue van—the Black Maria—which had been sent to meet the train . . .

The interior of the Black Maria was brightly lighted. The two policemen sat with their arms folded, watching me, but I was unaware of them. I kept thinking of Gina and the trunk, and what might have become of her on her first night alone in the great, grim city of London.

I kept thinking of the story she had told me—of that and of her sudden, hopeless paroxysm of tears. I kept thinking of my wet handkerchief balled in her hand, and of when she was a little girl with amber braids, walking home alone from school in rubbers and a rubber raincoat with a hood, carrying her strapped books, on a rainy late afternoon in an unknown town in faraway Canada. And on this ride from Paddington across London I couldn't see from my box of a Black Maria, I understood what had happened to me, and why all the strength seemed sucked out of me into those strange eyes of hers. I knew why I kept thinking, "If only we could have met before . . ."

For the first time in my life, I knew I was in love—and had been in love from the moment I had seen her cry. The realization brought me a new fund of resolve. I knew now what I had to do.

The Black Maria pulled up in New Scotland Yard. I was taken to a room glaring with light high up in that grim, turreted building overlooking the Embankment. There was a lean, tight-lipped, grey-haired man sitting beside the desk.

I stood there before the desk, handcuffed to the policeman, and said, "I'm going to confess. I'm doing it for the sake of somebody else. Before I begin, put out a call for a taxi-driver—she'd certainly take a taxi—who picked up a girl in a small green hat and a hip-length checked jacket with a high collar. She got off the earlier train at Paddington."

The man at the desk looked at me steadily. I knew my face was working.

"Any other details, Caird?"

I heard a voice speaking that seemed not to be mine. It sounded like a voice ringing far off in a chasm of green crystal cliffs.

"Yes," said the voice. "Her name's G. N. Trevelyan and she had a large brown trunk in the luggage van."

"There's something in the trunk for her to fear, Caird?" said the man at the desk.

"Yes," I said, "something in the trunk."

I saw the man at the desk reach for the telephone, and I heard a spatter of rain at the window looking out on the Thames.

I tell you, this whole thing was designed. It was prepared for us. Knowing what I know now, I say that every step— Even the rain. Take this rain that came . . .

Gina must have been sitting on the bed in her room. She was sitting on the bed, looking round at her first room in London. An uninspiring room, but she imagined it with her canvases hung on the walls, with a studio easel in it, with shelves put up for all her art books. With its skylight, she could make it look something like a studio.

She realized that she was hungry. She hadn't dined on the train. Halfway up this street, she remembered, she had noticed a teashop. It might still be open. She jumped up. Leaving her hat and grip on the bed, she descended the narrow, dimly lighted stairs. She didn't touch the banisters; she didn't like old houses, didn't like the feel of them.

The house was dead quiet.

She slammed the door behind her. The mist-touch was laid on her brow and lips and hair. She walked fast.

The teashop, still open, was an arty-crafty little place. She was served coffee and poached eggs by a faded gentlewoman. Gina ate hungrily. She was lighting a cigarette when the gentlewoman apologetically presented the bill.

"We're just closing, madam. I'm sorry."

Gina paid the bill. She opened the door. It had suddenly begun to rain. She hesitated. Her jacket was very light. The teashop was midway up the street; the lodging-house was near the end, the last house but one, on the left. The rain seemed to have settled in. She couldn't stand in this doorway all night. She thrust her hands into the pockets of her jacket, ducked her head, and walked as fast as she could.

The lights were shining much more clearly now . . .

This was when the police call went out for a taxi-driver who had driven from Paddington, to a place unknown, with a girl in a green hat, with a large brown trunk. In that glaring room in Scotland Yard, I was making a statement, a confession of murder, which was to put the rope round my neck. But as the rain beat across the Thames and ran wet on the window, it was of Gina that I was thinking. . . .

She was drenched when she hurried up the steps, put her key in the lock of the door. She went in, closed the door behind her. She pushed a hand up into her wet hair, gave it a little quick shake. The light in the narrow passage burned dimly. There was a row of hooks on the right wall, with coats hanging on them. She looked down at herself ruefully. She was soaked to the skin. She had no change of clothes in her overnight bag, up in her room.

She glanced round for the trunk, now, but it was gone; Arthur must have shifted it below. She moved to the head of the short flight of stairs leading to the landlady's quarters.

She called, "Mrs. Coe?"—and listened. "Mrs. Coe?" she called again.

All was still in the house. There was only the sound of the rain.

She could see her trunk, down there in the flagstoned passage. The trunk stood half in light, half in shadow—a very ordinary trunk, hundreds of thousands like it. She took from her pocket the two cheap little keys tied together with a bit of string. She started down the stairs.

The stairs were of stone. There were four of them. Four stairs? She hesitated, looking at the trunk, a pace or two from her. Out of the shadows came the ticking of a clock.

I was thinking of a little girl in rubbers and a rubber coat with a hood, coming home from school through the rain to the enigma of a dark house and a waiting room. But that was in Canada, thousands of miles away . . .

Louder and louder ticked the clock from the darkness, and she could hear the rain spattering on glass somewhere to her left. There was creeping over her a feeling she had known before—in a single memory and many dreams. A feeling of something waiting for her. It had no shape. Only cold came from it. She fought against the feeling. She looked down at the trunk. Rain or something had trickled from it to form a small, dark pool, dimly visible on the flagstones.

In sudden haste, she forced herself to stoop, unlock the trunk.

She threw back the lid, and the cold was released. Wave after wave of cold passed over her. She stared down, backing away, a hand at her mouth. She was backing into the darkness. She wheeled round, as though to run—and there before her, through a door standing half open, she saw the red glow of a fire between the bars of a kitchen stove. She saw an old wicker chair obliquely facing the stove, and in the chair a cat with its forepaws tucked under its chest, the firelight glinting in its intent eyes. The unseen clock was ticking loudly, questioningly. The rain spattered on glass to her left, and she knew that the wet, hairy leaves of stinging-nettles were there, pressed to the glass, and that the huge, dead, sodden heads of tall sunflowers rocked and nodded in the rain.

All was in waiting . . .

When the call came in, I was signing my statement. I sat with the pen in my hand, listening to the grey-haired, grim man at the desk speaking into the telephone . . .

He finished giving instructions. He was about to hang up when I stopped him. "Wait!"

He glanced at me.

I asked certain questions. He relayed them into the telephone. He repeated the answers to me. I sat with my head in my hands, thinking of Gina, with her strange eyes. Thinking how different things might have been for us— *But I tell you this whole thing was set up for us* . . .

The man at the desk said, "All right, Caird—now, what was the point of those questions you asked? The kitchen, the fire, the cat, the chair, the clock, the garden, the sunflowers, the nettles—these are common to most neglected houses anywhere in England."

Not only in England, I thought.

I didn't say it. I looked at the keen, rational man, there at his desk, lighting his pipe. What was the good of talking to him of God or the Devil or Destiny or even mere Chance? He only knew the Law—and facts.

But the address was a fact—the address I had heard him mention on the telephone—that was a fact. What made her go, with that trunk, to that house where she saw the sign saying VACANCIES in the mist?

"Gina, my poor darling—"

Yet, if I hadn't changed the labels on the trunks—

I don't know. Would it have made any difference? I don't know anything. Did *I* kill her? Or what? She knows, now, the address of the house in the London mist. It was Number 15 George Street.